RISE OF THE VICIOUS PRINCESS

RISE OF THE VICIOUS PRINCESS

C. J. REDWINE

BALZER + BRAY
An Imprint of HarperCollins*Publishers*

Balzer + Bray is an imprint of HarperCollins Publishers.

Rise of the Vicious Princess
Copyright © 2022 by C. J. Redwine
Map illustration © 2022 by Sveta Dorosheva
All rights reserved. Printed in the United States of America.
No part of this book may be used or reproduced in any manner whatsoever without written
permission except in the case of brief quotations embodied in critical articles and reviews.
For information address HarperCollins Children's Books, a division of
HarperCollins Publishers, 195 Broadway, New York, NY 10007.
www.epicreads.com

Library of Congress Control Number: 2021953555
ISBN 978-0-06-290893-3

Typography by Jessie Gang
22 23 24 25 26 PC/LSCH 10 9 8 7 6 5 4 3 2 1

First Edition

For Kristin Daly Rens,
whose faith in me never wavered

RISE OF THE VICIOUS PRINCESS

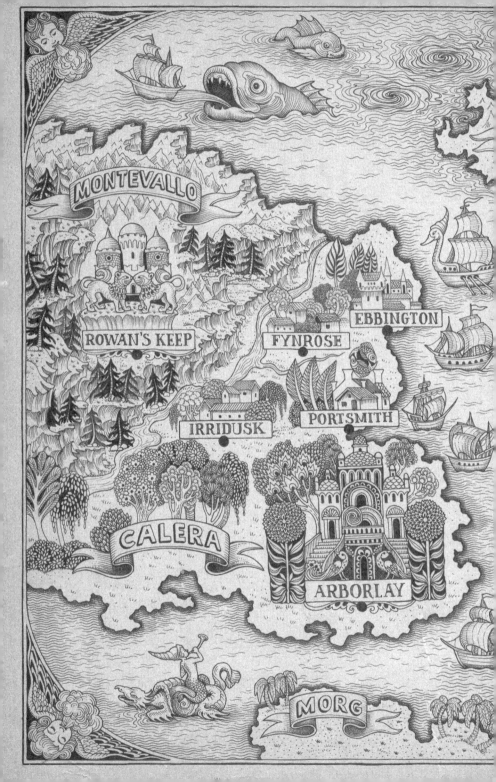

ONE

AFTER TONIGHT, THE new hairstyle of Charis Willowthorn would be the only acceptable updo for a debutante to wear to a ball. The dress of shimmering red silk that hugged her hips and then floated away from her legs as if she were a bird taking flight would be copied in a slew of rainbow hues. It would be hung from dressmakers' mannequins and priced so that only the wealthiest of Calera's nobility could possibly hope to emulate their fashionable princess. Once again, she'd be the topic of conversation at every decadent brunch and afternoon tea.

Half the members of noble society, envious of her position, would be quietly scheming for ways to ingratiate themselves with her. Half, furious with the way the war was being managed, would be whispering ideas for how to get the royal family to either agree with their plans or get out of the way. And all of them would be so busy talking about how Charis looked, how she held herself, and what she said that none of them would notice she'd spent the entire ambassadors' ball playing a deadly political game with the fate of her entire kingdom as the prize.

A game she couldn't afford to lose. Not if she was going to keep Mother happy, shore up Calera's alliances with kingdoms whose trade they desperately needed, and find a path toward peace with Montevallo, the kingdom at their back who'd been wreaking havoc with the northern territories for years.

"If you could hold still just another moment, Your Highness." Milla bit her lip as she concentrated on maneuvering Charis's thick brown curls through the glittering wire frame that was anchored to Charis's head with hairpins. The princess's handmaiden, a delicate girl of nearly fourteen with pale red hair and freckles dotting her nose, stood on her tiptoes to secure the final curl in the elaborate jewel-flecked tower of hair rising from Charis's scalp.

"Sorry, Milla." Charis forced herself to sit quietly while her hand-maiden tugged at the mesh, pushing jewels into place and humming under her breath as she worked.

Milla's wide grin peeked out from behind the tower of hair. "It's not dignified for a princess to apologize to a handmaiden."

Charis rolled her eyes. "Duly noted."

Satisfied with Charis's hair, Milla stepped back, her critical eye sweeping over the lines of Charis's dress as she stood. "Will you be wearing any of the gifts from the noble families at tonight's festivities?"

Charis didn't even glance at the small collection of items that had been left at her guards' station during the day. To wear one would show favor to that family, and on a night that was supposed to be about honoring the newest ambassadors from Verace and Rullenvor, that would be a discourtesy Charis could ill afford. "Not tonight."

Milla circled her once, as though inspecting to be sure she hadn't missed a single flaw. "Every eye in the ballroom will be on you, Your Highness."

Charis's stomach clenched, but she made herself smile as if the weight of the kingdom weren't resting on her shoulders. "You've done a brilliant job as always. Now, be sure to get some dinner before heading to the ladies' parlor. I won't need a touch-up until at least the second hour. After that, you can go to bed."

Milla's eyes widened. "You won't want to sleep on that hair, Your Highness. I'll be waiting up."

"You can be very stubborn."

"My mama has told me the very same, only she doesn't make it sound like a compliment."

Charis laughed, her stomach easing for a moment. And then she lifted her chin and faced the door. Once she stepped outside her private chambers, the game would begin, and Charis had to play her role to perfection.

A pair of guards were waiting for her as she exited her chambers. Elsbet, a guard Charis was moderately fond of, immediately bowed and then stepped to the opposite side of the corridor to flank the princess's left side. Reuben, Charis's head guard and the one she was sure reported directly to her mother, took up his position on her right. He was built like a starving alley dog, his hard brown eyes following her every move as if challenging her to show any hint of weakness he could reveal to the queen.

They moved through the corridor toward the grand staircase that would take Charis down three flights of stairs and into the main hall, just shy of the palace ballroom. Her heels tapped delicately against the gleaming wood floors, and she shivered a little as the sea breeze crept in through the windows that lined the hallway.

Summer was losing its grip on Calera, and a chill was seeping into the air as the sun dipped below the horizon. Another season was passing with the war no closer to ending. Every week brought reports of new casualties, new ground gained by the fierce soldiers from the mountains at Calera's back, and her kingdom was struggling to replenish its armies and retake the territories that were now occupied by the enemy.

There had to be a path toward peace with King Alaric Penbyrn of Montevallo, and Charis was determined to find it.

But those thoughts could be saved for a time when she wasn't fifteen minutes late to the ball being held in honor of two new ambassadors. Mother was hardly going to forgive her tardiness, and Charis had no intention of letting the queen know she was late because Milla had struggled with the new hairstyle the handmaiden had designed.

"Your Highness!" Darold bowed as Charis descended the staircase and approached the side entrance to the ballroom. Her secretary's voice was its usual calm near-monotone, but there was a slight edge to it that sounded like relief. His blond hair looked somewhat rumpled, and he'd buttoned his considerable girth into a dress coat that strained to hold him. "Her Majesty the Queen will be glad to know you've arrived."

Ah, that explained the relief, then. Mother would have held Darold personally responsible for her daughter's tardiness.

"I apologize for distressing you, Darold."

The shadow of relief in Darold's voice was slipping toward worry. "The ambassadors have already arrived. The queen . . ."

The queen would be furious that the crown princess hadn't been in the ballroom to greet the newest diplomatic officials. A single misstep could sever the ties that Calera desperately needed if they were to turn the tide of the war and reclaim their northern territories.

"Fill me in on what I need to know." Charis began moving toward the ballroom door.

Darold shuffled the small stack of papers he held and hurried to keep up. "First, you are to join your mother on the dais and greet the ambassadors. The Veracian diplomat receives the first greeting as they have been our ally longer than Rullenvor. You will then officially open the ball with this speech." He handed her a thin piece of paper with his neat handwriting filling half the page.

"Any particular areas of concern I should address with each ambassador individually?"

"Verace is having trouble with packs of wild giants coming down from their mountains."

"Again?"

"Apparently once giants know there's a readily available food source for the taking, it's impossible to keep them at bay unless you destroy the entire pack."

"They have giants. We have bloodthirsty Montevallians. It seems nothing good ever comes down off a mountain." They moved closer to the ballroom's entrance.

"Indeed." Darold pulled another paper from his stack. "Rullenvor is engaged in a trade dispute with Solvang, though all reports indicate the two kingdoms are solving the issues through diplomatic channels. Also, there are rumors of unrest in the northern seas, though it's unclear if that's related to a sea kingdom or to the basilisk cave or some other threat in the uncharted waters up north. At any rate, if the rumors are true, that may be of concern to both ambassadors."

"I hardly think the basilisks will have left their cave to travel the seas." Charis patted her tower of hair, pressing an errant ruby back into place.

"There is the matter of the trade ship from Rullenvor that went down at sea before it could reach us. Several physicians have expressed concern over shortages in medical supplies as a result, so perhaps the ambassador could be encouraged to support the hasty launching of a new shipment."

"Without letting him know how very badly we need the supplies." Charis nodded. It was a delicate balance, walking the line between stating what her kingdom needed and keeping Calera from appearing weak and ripe for a trade renegotiation that would put them at a serious disadvantage.

Darold examined the paper he held as they came to a stop before the gilt-edged doors. "You are to give your first dance to Lord Ferris Everly."

Charis barely controlled her grimace.

"The queen was very clear that even though you confer the honor of first dance to him, you may not discuss possible marriage with your fourth cousin at this juncture."

"I'll try to restrain myself."

"Very well, Your Highness. There are several council members who will be in attendance. The queen wishes you to divide your dances equally between the faction that supports the war and the faction that supports annexing the north to Montevallo."

"And may I have any dances with partners of my choice?" Her tone gave nothing away, but still Darold cleared his throat, whether in sympathy or in censure Charis wasn't sure. She kept her expression as smooth as the marble floor beneath her feet. She'd rather face her angry mother than have her secretary see the longing that sometimes ached during quiet moments when she allowed herself to imagine being an ordinary seventeen-year-old girl exchanging laughing glances and soft touches with a boy who wanted nothing from her but what she wanted to give.

Not that such a boy existed. Yet. Still, if all of Charis's dances were filled with political maneuvering and carefully controlled conversations designed to open pocketbooks or silence dissent, she would never have the chance to see what it was like to just be a girl dancing with a boy because they both wanted to.

Darold cleared his throat again, and Charis's attention snapped back to him. "There will be a ten-minute intermission from dancing at the top of every hour, and the queen has given you permission to spend that with whomever you choose as long as . . ."

"As long as I don't linger too long with members of one faction or the other," Charis finished for him.

"Just so." Darold nodded to the footman who stood ready at the door. The man pulled the doors open, and a cacophony of laughter and conversation spilled out, brushing against Charis's skin like an unwanted caress.

"Is my father in attendance?" She kept the hope out of her voice, though it dug painfully into her chest all the same.

"His Royal Highness wasn't well enough to leave his chambers tonight."

The hope withered beneath a sharp pang of grief.

Father hadn't been well enough to leave his chambers more days than not for months now. Before that thought could burrow in, Charis shoved it into the corner of her heart and imagined she wore a skin of ice. A thick, impenetrable shield that nothing could breach. When she was sure every trace of herself had been buried beneath a sheen of cold composure, she let her mouth curve into a perfect smile and stepped forward.

"Her Royal Highness, Princess Charis Willowthorn," the footman announced as Charis swept into the ballroom.

TWO

IVORY WALLS GLEAMED beneath the glow of silver chandeliers whose candles matched the blue of the sea on a clear summer's day. A long table against the back wall was draped in matching blue linens and held an assortment of light snacks and beverages, and a cadre of servants in blue and silver circled the room carrying trays of refreshments as well. The windows on the eastern wall that faced the sea were open, and the faint chill of an early autumn breeze tangled with the sheer ivory drapes and ruffled sheets of music belonging to the orchestra that surrounded the bottom of the dais.

Guests in satin and silk were scattered throughout the room, but Charis barely looked at them as they bowed and murmured, "Your Highness." She only had eyes for her mother.

Queen Letha stood on the dais, resplendent in silk the color of purple twilit skies. Gloves covered her hands and arms past her elbows, and jewels sparkled at her wrists, throat, and earlobes. Candlelight glittered against the silvery strands in the queen's dark hair and gleamed in her cold blue eyes. She locked gazes with Charis, and though her expression remained unchanged, Charis's heart thudded.

Keeping her chin high, Charis reached the dais and gracefully climbed the steps, ignoring the footman who offered a supporting hand. There must be no sign of weakness. No chink in her armor. Not just in front of the queen, but in front of the crowd of assembled nobles and dignitaries.

"Your Majesty," Charis said, her voice crisp and clear though the pounding of her heart was a hammer against her temple. She bowed her head briefly, a sign of respect for the one person in the kingdom who outranked her.

"Charis, how lovely you look." Mother's voice was as crisp as her daughter's, and she extended her hands for Charis to take. Pulling Charis close, she leaned in as though to kiss her daughter's cheeks. When her mouth was beside the princess's ear, she whispered, "We will discuss this breach in courtesy tomorrow."

Mother moved to her other cheek. "There are wolves in the room, daughter. Remember what you must be."

What you must be.

Charis met Mother's icy smile with one of her own. She knew this lesson well. It had been drilled into her from her earliest memory.

Be smarter. Strike harder. Never falter, never waver, never break.

Every interaction was a chess move, and only the most ruthless person on the board survived to win the game.

Charis had been born to win the game.

Stepping past the queen, she offered her hand to the ambassador from Verace, a slight woman with olive skin, striking features, and bold eyebrows. "Ambassador Gemanotti, welcome to Arborlay, the jewel of Calera. We are pleased to continue our kingdoms' friendship through you."

"Your capital city is beautiful, Your Highness, and the generosity of your family lives up to its reputation." The woman's voice was firm, her eye contact steady. She took the princess's fingertips in her own and bowed.

Charis then turned to the ambassador from Rullenvor, a man with a smattering of dark freckles on his pale beige skin and close-cut red hair that was turning silver at the temples. Extending her hand, she said, "Ambassador Shyrn, we welcome you to Arborlay and look forward to continuing our kingdoms' goodwill toward each other."

He bowed and pressed a kiss to the back of her hand. Straightening, he said in a deep, gravelly voice, "Your Highness, Rullenvor is most keen to further our kingdoms' mutual interests."

"We will set aside time to discuss those interests and our friendship soon," the queen said, including both ambassadors in her smile. "Now the princess will open the ball with a speech in your honor."

Charis bowed to her mother, turned to the center of the dais, and assessed the crowd with a measured look. Nobility in brilliant gowns or elegant dress coats were scattered around the room. The mix of skin tones and hair colors was a testament to Calera's long history of healthy trade relationships and generous immigration policies with the other sea kingdoms. In fact, many of Calera's families could trace their heritage back to both ancient Caleran families and ancestors across the water. When Charis had met the gazes of many of the onlookers, holding them silent in anticipation, she finally looked at the speech Darold had given her and began to speak.

Two hours later, as the bell to signal the second intermission sounded, Charis stepped back from yet another dance partner—she'd lost count of how many times she'd twirled around the ballroom floor, dispensing smiles and tiny political barbs designed to open pocketbooks for the war effort or silence the gathering opposition to the conflict, and by extension, to the royal family. Her cheeks ached, her feet throbbed, and she'd willingly give away her best tiara for an hour of absolute silence.

Her eyes sought Mother's and held—a quick, unspoken communication that Charis was doing her job and would have details to report in the morning. Queen Letha's lips curved slightly, and then she stepped away from the dais and toward the ladies' parlor. Charis's partner bowed, and she pivoted toward the windows before another could take the man's place and use up her precious ten minutes of intermission with conversation.

"Your Highness!" a woman's strident voice called from behind Charis, but she kept moving forward. A drink. That's all she wanted. Just one drink and a few minutes in front of the open windows so she could collect herself and be ready to face the room once more.

Snatching a fluted glass from a waiter's tray, Charis made for the windows where the blue light from the two sister moons spilled over the ledge like liquid sapphire. The music at her back fell silent as the orchestra set down their instruments and reached for a drink instead, and Charis ignored yet another call of "Your Highness."

Reaching the windows, she turned her flushed face into the breeze and took a long sip of the sparkling plumberry cocktail she held. The curtain closest to her fluttered, and behind it she caught a glimpse of a tall boy with sleek black hair, golden skin, and wide brown eyes.

"What are you doing, Holland?" Charis asked, bemused as he made a shushing motion.

"Shh, you'll give me away." In absolute disregard for the colorful silk finery the rest of the nobility wore, her first cousin was in his usual long black duster—he claimed it counted as ballroom finery because black was always in fashion—a plain white shirt without a cravat, and a sword strapped to his hip in a utilitarian leather sheath that looked like it had already been to war and back. Twice.

"Are you hiding?"

"I was avoiding Nalani." He craned his neck to look past Charis and groaned. "Not that it did me any good, because here she comes."

Charis laughed. "Afraid of your twin?"

"This is your fault. You summoned her just by being near me."

"There you are!" Nalani Farragin said brightly as she came up to Charis and slipped an arm through the crook of her elbow. Her black hair was twisted into a chignon adorned with festive green ribbons that matched her dress, and sea emeralds glittered in her ears. Candlelight gleamed in her narrow dark eyes and shone against her high cheekbones. Both she and Holland looked so much like their father, whose grandparents were originally from the kingdom of Solvang, that their mother, Queen Letha's half sister, often said if she hadn't given birth to them herself, she might wonder if the twins were truly hers.

"What a night. I've had to fend off pompous old Lord Comferoy's advances at least three times, I was unsuccessful at getting stingy Lady Shawling to donate to my idea for a refugee rehabilitation center, and don't even get me started on the pain of listening to sweet Lady Delaire try to flirt with my brother." She paused long enough to give Charis a look from head to toe. "Love the dress, but seers preserve us, what have you done to your hair?"

Charis patted the jewel-flecked tower atop her head. "Don't you like it?"

"It looks like you shoved a beehive in there and spackled it in place with— Is that Holland hiding behind the curtain?" Nalani's tone sharpened.

Holland sighed.

"What are you doing over here?" Nalani twitched the curtain aside to reveal her twin.

"I don't want to dance." Holland sounded grumpy, but then he usually did.

"And why should you?" Charis grinned as Nalani shot her cousin a look that clearly begged the princess not to encourage him. The knot of tension around her chest eased for the first time since she'd entered the ballroom. She took another sip of plumberry cocktail and wisely stayed out of the ensuing fray.

"Because it's a *ball* and therefore requires *dancing*. Plus, I really need Delaire's support for my plan to unionize the docks. She has good relationships with all kinds of rich merchants who might be made to see the value in it." Nalani elbowed her brother. "You know Mama told you to be polite tonight."

His brows rose. "I was polite."

"You shook Delaire's hand off your arm and snapped at her."

"Only because she wouldn't accept my first three refusals." He met Nalani's eyes and raised his hands in mock surrender. "Which were polite. Excruciatingly so."

Charis laughed. "I shudder to think of your version of excruciatingly polite."

Holland sniffed. "I simply told her the truth. I have no interest in parading around in front of everyone, no interest in touching someone I don't care for, and certainly no interest in the invitation to brunch that her mother would surely send my way after she saw us dancing."

Nalani's expression could have shattered glass. "Holland Farragin, please tell me you didn't actually say all that to Delaire."

"Of course I did. It was the truth."

Nalani sighed and turned to Charis. "He's a lost cause, and he's lucky we love him. Now, did I see you dancing with Lord Pellinsworth?" Her voice lowered. "I've heard a rumor he's been saying some very nasty things about the royal family's loyalty to the occupied lands in the north. Step carefully there."

"I'm always careful," Charis said, but she replayed her conversation with Lord Pellinsworth all the same. The obligatory observation that it was unseasonably warm for early autumn. A comment about the delicacies available on the refreshments table. And a subtle dig for information about whether the queen would be open to negotiating a cease-fire if it meant annexing enough of north Calera to keep King Alaric of Montevallo happy. It was no more than anyone else in the antiwar faction had tried, and Charis had deftly turned his inquiry aside and steered their conversation toward safer topics.

A bell rang from the orchestra pit—the signal that intermission would soon be over. Charis rolled her shoulders to remove some of the tension and massaged her aching cheeks. Just one more hour, and she could gracefully exit the ball and return to her chambers to make notes on the conversations she'd had tonight. So far, she hadn't found any obvious solutions for peace with Montevallo—at least, not for a peace that didn't involve sacrificing the Calerans who had already been enslaved by the invading army—but if she saw everything on paper, she might find something she'd missed. At the very least, she might find an inroad to shoring up support for the royal family so the queen could face enemies outside the kingdom without worrying about those coming at her from within.

"Your Highness!" A quiet voice filled with warmth spoke just behind the princess.

Charis turned to find Lady Channing, one of the members of the royal council and the closest thing Queen Letha had to a friend, standing there. Eyes twinkling, Lady Channing smiled and curtsied.

"I'd heard you were back from your trip to the middle kingdoms, but I didn't expect to see you tonight." Charis returned the lady's smile easily. "The journey can be very tiring."

Lady Channing sighed. "Are you trying to call me old?"

"Never."

"Come now, Your Highness. You aren't a liar." Lady Channing's smile widened.

Charis laughed. "You're only a few years older than Mother. If I called you old, I'd have to say the same about her, and I think we both know how well that would go."

"Quite." Lady Channing's graying brown hair was pulled into its usual no-nonsense updo, and she wore a simple silk gown in dusky blue.

"I trust your trip to Thallis, Verace, and Rullenvor was productive?" Charis asked as, from the corner of her eye, she caught a middle-aged man anxiously hovering as though trying to find an opening to ask her for the next dance.

Couldn't he let her finish intermission before swooping in? She hadn't even visited the ladies' parlor yet to have Milla reapply fragrance and check that her towering updo was still firmly intact. With that thought in mind, Charis began moving toward the southeast exit, gesturing for Lady Channing to walk with her.

"The trip was productive enough." Lady Channing moved closer and lowered her voice. "I will continue my relationship with those kingdoms through their ambassadors in the hope that we may rely on them as we seek to end this war. Things look favorable toward that end."

Charis's guards kept pace with her from the sidelines as she neared the exit. "I look forward to hearing the details of your journey. I'm sure Mother already has a meeting with you on her calendar."

"Tomorrow, Your Highness." Lady Channing stepped back as a pair of footmen opened the door to allow Charis into the corridor that held the ladies' parlor.

Behind them, the bell to signal the end of intermission sounded. Charis was going to be late for the third hour, but as Mother was still in the parlor herself, she could hardly fault her daughter for wanting a two-minute reprieve from the crowds.

A frisson of unease spread through Charis.

It wasn't like Mother to spend so long in the ladies' parlor or miss the start of the ball's final hour. Had she eaten something that disagreed with her? If she was indisposed, Charis would have to abandon any hope of even a brief reprieve. One of them should be on the dais overseeing the festivities and making sure the guests of honor were impressed with Calera and her ruling family.

Strange that Mother hadn't sent a messenger to let Charis know what was going on.

"Until tomorrow," Charis said to Lady Channing.

Reuben and Elsbet, hands on their swords, flanked her as she left the ballroom and hurried toward the open door halfway down the corridor. She was nearly to the threshold when a scream tore through the air.

It was coming from the ladies' parlor.

THREE

CHARIS FROZE, A millisecond of hesitation as the scream echoed into the corridor. And then she lunged for the doorway.

Reuben got there first. Thrusting his short, wiry body in front of her, he barked, "Secure the princess!"

Elsbet wrapped a strong hand over Charis's upper arm and pulled her firmly away from the door as Reuben rushed into the room, sword out.

"Let go of me!" Charis tried to jerk her arm free, but Elsbet kept her grip.

Who had screamed? And where was Mother?

An instant later, Milla rushed into the corridor, her hands covered in blood. Three more maids followed on her heels, their eyes wild.

"Mother!" Charis strained against Elsbet's hold, expecting at any moment to hear the queen's cold, imperious voice spitting orders and organizing the chaos into something manageable before the guests in the ballroom took notice.

"Your Highness, I'm sorry!" Milla's voice shook as she pressed against the wall to let another maid rush past. Charis yanked against Elsbet's grip.

"I have to keep you secure, Your Highness." Elsbet's tone was calm, though she watched the princess warily. "Reuben's orders."

"Reuben isn't your princess. I am. You answer only to me." Charis softened her voice, though it took effort. Elsbet was simply doing her job. "Unhand me so I can assess the situation and help the queen manage it."

Milla made a noise like a wounded puppy, and Charis stepped toward her. Elsbet released her but stayed by her side.

"Are you injured?"

Milla shook her head, sending fresh tears down her cheeks. A crash and a shout echoed from the parlor. Without wasting another second, Charis crossed the threshold.

Cushions littered the floor. Chunks of broken glass from a smashed bottle of embyrvale perfume glittered among a spill of finely ground rice powder. A wave of sweet floral fragrance mixed with something sharply metallic filled the air.

Reuben stood in the far corner beside an open window, his sword buried in the chest of a man dressed in the finery of a ball guest. Beside them, stretched out on the rug, lay the queen, her hands pressed to her abdomen. Blood poured from her stomach, a dark stain spreading across the dusky purple of her dress.

"Mother!" Charis ran, skidding through the powder and perfume, and threw herself down beside the queen.

"She's alive." Reuben grunted as he yanked his sword free. The man collapsed against the wall and slid down, his eyes glassy.

For an instant, Charis waited, expecting Mother to do what she always did: take charge. Think three moves ahead, already anticipating what might happen so that the solution was well in hand before it was needed.

But Mother lay, ashen and shaking, her breath coming in hard pants, her eyes glazed in pain. Charis would be the one taking charge. Grabbing a nearby cushion, she pressed it gently against Mother's stomach to stanch the bleeding. Then she swallowed hard against the fear that clogged her throat and forced herself to think.

"He's Montevallian." Reuben gestured at the dead man's throat, where a silver emblem gleamed against a leather cord. "Wearing one of their marriage tokens. Must have a family back home."

"Yet he came all this way to kill mine." Her stomach pitched, and she snapped, "Send Elsbet to check on Father. *Now.*"

As Reuben called the order, Charis met Mother's eyes and found a glimmer of awareness behind the pain.

"The ambassadors . . . ," the queen whispered.

"I have it handled." Turning to Reuben, she spoke in the kind of crisp, emotionless voice that would make Mother proud. "Leave the body. Send a maid for Dr. Baust. Instruct the footmen at the ballroom entrance not to allow any guests into this corridor. And whatever you do, make sure every single maid who was in this room stays quiet about what just happened. We cannot risk the ambassadors knowing the queen is vulnerable."

They couldn't risk their own nobility knowing it either. Not when half of them seemed to be circling the throne like a pack of starving wolves.

"I want four of Mother's personal guards brought here to watch over her while Baust treats her wound. Send your most trusted to search every inch of this palace. If there's another Montevallian spy in our midst, I want them caught."

"I'm not leaving you here alone and unprotected," Reuben said, his dark eyes challenging her to argue.

"Then use one of the footmen to get you the help you need. And send Milla back in here."

As Reuben hurried to obey her orders from the doorway where he could keep an eye on her the entire time, Milla crept back into the room and knelt beside Charis.

"I'm sorry." The handmaiden's voice caught on a tiny sob.

"How did this happen?"

Milla leaned forward and pressed her hands against the cushion, taking over the duty of treating the queen without Charis having to ask.

"That man—" Milla jerked her chin toward the dead Montevallian. "He was in the closet. The queen came in and was finishing up with her maid when the closet door opened, and he rushed out with a knife." A tremor shook her body. "He stabbed the queen so fast, we didn't realize what had happened until she went down. Then he ran for the open window, but maids and tables of toiletries were in the way, so it was a mess. I tried to stop the bleeding, Your Highness, I tried, but—"

"Hush now, Milla," Charis said gently. "You did nothing wrong. I'm grateful you tried to help. There's Baust."

Charis rose and stepped back as the palace physician hurried in. He was a short, round man with a face as smooth as a sea-worn pebble and tawny skin. Several maids accompanied him, each carrying linens or bags of medical supplies.

"I leave the queen in your capable hands," Charis said, meeting Mother's eyes once more and satisfying herself that, though the queen looked shaky and weak, she was still alert. King Alaric of Montevallo should know it would take more than a single knife to bring down the indomitable Queen Letha Willowthorn.

Milla walked with her into the corridor, and Charis said quietly, "Wash the blood from your hands and the tears from your face, and then visit the kitchens once more and order a drink sent to my chambers. Be sure to mention that the queen has become ill from eating something that disagreed with her."

Rumors spread through the palace staff and to the servants of other noble houses with remarkable speed. Hopefully this one would be no different.

Satisfied that she'd managed the crisis as well as she could, she checked herself for blood in the mirror mounted above the room's fireplace. There. A trio of droplets beneath her blue eyes, like crimson freckles. And another fleck on the white hollow of her throat. She dabbed at them with a clean cloth and then, once she was sure she'd removed every trace, returned to the ball, Reuben at her side. A few well-placed comments to the always-indiscreet Lady Vera Shawling was all it took to have half the ballroom buzzing with the news that the queen had taken ill. Suspicious glances were thrown at the sumptuous buffet table. Charis sent a silent apology to the head cook, smiled graciously at Ambassador Shyrn, and accepted another dance.

As the final dance was drawing to a close, Charis whirled away from the firm grasp of Ferris Everly, her fourth cousin and the boy many in the antiwar faction were hoping would one day be her husband. Charis would rather swim naked in the freezing waters of the Draiel Sea than spend the rest of her life with Ferris, but she could hardly risk offending the son of a council member when unrest among the nobility was on the rise.

"If I didn't know better, I'd think you were avoiding me tonight, Charis." He tugged her hand, and she spun back toward him, stopping just shy of his chest.

"Hmm, let's see." She kept time to the music, her aching feet protesting every step. "I gave you my opening dance, I talked with you for at least two minutes during the first intermission, and here you are at my last dance. If you ask me, I may have erred on the side of giving you too much, Ferris."

"People ought to see us spending more time together, Charis." He sounded like he was chiding a schoolgirl. Her chin lifted.

"And why is that?" Her tone was sugared ice, and he blinked, his blue eyes narrowing as he met her gaze.

"Because Father has excellent relationships with many in the antiwar faction and has assured them we are close to the Willowthorns and can help bring their grievances to the throne." He bent forward, dipping her toward the floor as other couples whirled past, feet tapping out a rhythm to the lively tune spilling out of the orchestra pit.

"They can bring their own grievances to the throne," Charis said, her jaw setting as his gaze dropped from her face to linger on her bodice.

"But can they be sure that the queen will listen?" He lifted her slowly, his eyes once more finding hers. "Besides, you and I are an obvious match. We should be working together. I saw you talking to Lord Pellinsworth earlier. What did he say?"

Under no circumstances was Charis going to divulge the outcome of her political maneuvering with Ferris, but she also couldn't risk offending him. He was telling the truth about his father's connections, and while Charis wasn't convinced that Lord Everly was all that stood between the Willowthorns and outright rebellion from the nobles who were sick of the cost of war and wanted to let Montevallo annex the northern quarter of the kingdom, she didn't want to lose the scraps of goodwill the Everlys brought to the table.

She marshaled a response that was both firm and conciliatory but found his eyes once more on her bodice. Heat flushed beneath her skin, and her voice sharpened to a dagger's point.

"See something you like?"

He lifted his gaze, slow and insolent, and a smirk played around his wide mouth. "I would have followed Father's direction to pursue a potential marriage with you no matter what, but it doesn't hurt that I find you attractive."

"Maybe you should be far more worried about whether I find *you* attractive than about what I look like in this dress." She took a step back as the dance ended. "Good evening, Ferris."

He froze for a millisecond, absorbing both her words and her dismissal, and then, his gaze burning into hers, he bowed. "Good evening, Your Highness."

The look in his eyes said he believed she had no choice but to marry him, but if he thought his words had increased his chances of being king consort one day, he could think again.

She wanted more than a political match. She could wear a shield of icy composure and manage a contentious nobility in public, but in private, she wanted safety, true companionship. Love.

It was impossible to imagine Ferris offering any of that.

Keeping her expression cold and remote, she moved through the ballroom, Elsbet and another palace guard by her side. Reuben had left the ballroom shortly after the third hour began. Charis assumed he was still busy following her orders to contain the truth and hunt for additional spies. She would go back to her chambers, get a report on Mother's condition and the search conducted throughout the palace, and make notes about both the assassination attempt and her interactions with various nobles while Milla removed the wire cage from her head.

She nodded regally to Ambassador Shyrn and several matrons

who were near the western entrance and exited the ballroom to see Reuben standing near the main staircase in discussion with another guard.

As soon as he saw her, Reuben ended his conversation and headed her way, his hand on his sword hilt.

"Any news?" she asked as he reached her side.

"The last report I had said the queen is resting and is expected to fully recover, though it will take time." His dark eyes hardened. "We found one additional spy."

Her heartbeat kicked hard against her skin. "Where?"

"Your bath chamber."

"My . . . what?" Her thoughts whirled into chaos as a shiver crept over her skin.

"Hiding in your bath chamber, Your Highness." Reuben's voice was a snarl of fury.

"But how—"

"Someone must have snuck her into the wing. Luther and Fada were both on duty, and both swear they didn't see anything out of the ordinary."

She blinked and frantically tried to grab one of the wild thoughts in her head and force it to make sense.

A spy. An *assassin*. In her private wing. Her bath chamber. She could've gone upstairs after the ball with Milla and been attacked while she slept.

"Funny thing, though," Reuben said, his hand gripping his sword hilt like he wished he had a handy target. "She didn't have a weapon."

"Then how was she going to kill me?" The words sounded logical. Calm. Totally at odds with the fear unspooling within her.

"Maybe she wasn't sent to kill you. Maybe she was simply a spy."

That didn't make sense, but neither did being in the princess's private chambers without a weapon. Charis drew in a shaky breath and nodded as though she were still in complete control. "Very well, Reuben. Put her in the dungeon, and we'll interrogate her tomorrow. Let's get to the bottom of this quickly."

Reuben scowled. "Can't put her in the dungeon, Your Highness."

"You most certainly can."

"She's dead."

Charis glared at him. "Are you telling me you killed an unarmed woman?"

"She was in your chambers. That made her a threat."

"That was foolish. We could have learned something from her." Charis pressed her fingers against her brow in a futile attempt to stave off the headache that was forming. Mother was going to be absolutely furious when she learned of this.

Reuben's jaw tightened, but he held his tongue.

"What's done is done. Be absolutely certain every staff member who knows the truth understands they must keep quiet, and assign extra security teams for the palace tonight." Charis began moving toward her chambers.

Luther and Fada were on duty patrolling the corridor. She thanked them, bade Elsbet and Reuben a good evening, and retired to her chambers.

Milla was in the bath chamber, scrubbing blood from the tub. She looked up as Charis entered, her eyes tearstained, her freckles standing out against her pale skin.

"They killed her right here in your bathtub." Her voice caught on a hiccupping sob. "And Reuben left such a mess. I didn't want you to see it."

"Oh, Milla." Charis hurried to her side and squeezed the girl's shoulder. "I'm sorry you're having to deal with this. Here, let me help."

Milla looked scandalized. "A princess does not scrub her own bathtub!"

"She does when someone's been murdered in it."

Milla swallowed audibly and plunged her dirty rag into a bucket of clean water. Charis grabbed a second rag and followed suit.

"Reuben scares me," Milla whispered after a moment of the two of them working in silence.

"It will be all right." Charis infused the words with confidence and watched Milla's shoulders slowly relax as they finished scrubbing the tub and then tossed the dirty water down the drain.

An hour later, Milla was asleep in the little room beside the bath chamber. Charis had refused to let Milla wash the sticky pomade out of her hair—more because she couldn't stand the idea of getting into the tub than because she was too exhausted to allow her hair to be washed. Instead, Milla had plucked the jewels free, removed the mesh cage from her head, and helped her into her nightdress.

The vanity chair was a solid weight beneath Charis as she collapsed into it. With nothing left to do, the memory of Mother lying on the rug, pale and shaking, blazed to life in her mind and refused to leave. There had been so much blood. What if Mother hadn't survived?

Her heart shuddered, an erratic beat that thundered in her ears as she struggled to breathe past the sudden tightness in her chest.

She was going to lose Father someday soon. It had never occurred to her that she might lose Mother, too.

King Alaric Penbyrn must be desperate to force Calera to accept his terms if he'd decided assassinating the queen was the only way to do it. And why send an unarmed assassin into the princess's chambers? Or had the woman simply found a convenient place to hide from the guards without knowing whose chambers she was in?

Perhaps she'd been the one to help the assassin sneak into the palace and then became trapped and couldn't get out.

Charis's vision swam, and she bent at the waist, hugging her arms around herself and forcing her breathing to slow.

Mother was going to be bedridden for days. Maybe weeks. That meant the entire weight of ruling Calera, running the war, and managing the nobility rested on Charis alone.

Slowly, she straightened, pressing cold fingers against the vanity as she climbed to her feet.

She'd been trained for this from birth.

Be smarter. Strike harder. Never falter, never waver, never break.

She left the lamp lit and crawled into bed. By tomorrow, she'd have a plan. A way to navigate the crisis with strength, composure, and the ruthless will to do whatever was required.

But tonight, she needed to curl up under her blankets, ears straining to hear any whisper of sound that might be a threat, and breathe past the noose of panic that was wrapped around her neck.

FOUR

A WHISPER OF sound drifted across the early morning air. Charis startled awake, heart pounding, blood roaring in her ears. Snatching the dagger she kept on the nightstand, she slid out of bed, her movements silent and smooth.

Another sound. Somewhere to the right. Hushed and secretive.

Charis's fist tightened on the dagger, and she crept across the floor, muscles tense and ready. If another Montevallian spy had somehow managed to get into her rooms, she was going to make him wish he'd never set eyes on Calera's princess.

And then she'd do the same to the guards who were supposed to be keeping her safe.

A quiet footfall brushed the floor inside Charis's closet, and her eyes narrowed. The closet had been fully closed the night before. Now the door stood slightly ajar.

She didn't dare turn her back on the closet to summon her guards. Rolling to the balls of her feet, she adjusted her grip on the dagger, kicked the closet door open, and yelled for her guards all at the same instant.

"Your Highness!" Milla squeaked, and stumbled back, clutching handfuls of sage and sweetgrass to her chest.

"Milla, for seers' sakes, I could've killed you!"

The girl's already pale complexion went pasty, and she made a strangled noise in the back of her throat, her wide eyes locked on the dagger the princess still held in her hand. Charis dropped her arm, hiding the dagger in the folds of her nightdress even as a pair of guards crashed through the door of her room, swords raised.

"Stand down!" Charis kept her eyes on Milla, who was shaking like a leaf caught in a windstorm. "All is well."

"Your Highness?" Fada stepped forward, her wide shoulders still braced, her sword still raised.

"Weapons down," Charis snapped. "It's just Milla."

"Yes, Your Highness." Luther sheathed his sword and nodded for Fada to do the same. He bowed. "Morning shift will be in soon to discuss your day's schedule with you." He stepped out of the room, Fada on his heels.

Charis blew out a long, slow breath and tried to get her heartbeat under control. No assassin. No threat. Just a terrified young hand-maiden who looked close to fainting.

"You're up early," Charis said as calmly as she could manage.

The girl's eyes were red-rimmed, the skin beneath them bruised with exhaustion. "I couldn't sleep. Not after . . ." Her gaze darted toward the bath chamber and then found Charis again. She shook the bundles of sage and sweetgrass she held. "I thought I'd burn a little of this and leave the ashes in the corners of your chambers to help pro-tect you." She stopped, her eyes huge. "You pulled a dagger on me."

"I didn't know it was you," Charis said, the cold metal of the dag-ger's handle digging into her skin as she clenched her fist. "And I didn't sleep well either."

"You think another spy will try to sneak in?" Milla's voice shook.

"Once King Alaric hears the first one failed, yes." Charis's voice was still calm, but something dark and dangerous skittered beneath her skin.

The assassin had dressed as though he belonged at the ball. Arrived early enough to sneak into the ladies' parlor without being so early that he'd seem out of place in the palace. Stood in the darkness of the closet waiting to deal a killing blow, even though he had to know he'd never get out of the palace alive.

It was bold. Daring. She almost admired it.

What made no sense was the second Montevallian, weaponless and alone in Charis's rooms.

"My lady, you've been staring at that door for several minutes." Milla's words broke through Charis's thoughts, and she turned to find the handmaiden standing in front of her, a look of determination on her freckled face. Her voice shook, but her tone was firm. "There's no need to be afraid of the bath chamber. I'll go in ahead of you and make sure no spy is in there."

The dark, dangerous thing that was scraping at Charis quieted, and she smiled. "Brave Milla. What would I do without you?"

Milla's matching smile wobbled at the edges but stayed in place. "No Montevallian scum is going to kill my princess. Not while I'm alive to protect you."

Charis took a long look at the way Milla's hands trembled even as she glared at the bath chamber like it was a dragon she meant to slay with nothing but the bundles of herbs in her hands.

This was why Charis had the will to do what was necessary. Why she manipulated the nobility into filling the war coffers and remaining loyal while working toward a solution that rescued their northern territories and stopped the war.

The beating heart of Calera was its people. Its handmaidens, farmers, merchants, and sailors. The people worked hard for their bread and trusted their rulers to keep them safe.

People like Milla didn't hunger for power or position. They only wanted to go home to their families at night and rise again with the sun, secure in the knowledge that those who stood between them and Montevallo's soldiers wouldn't falter.

Charis never faltered.

Even when she wanted to.

"We'll conquer the bath chamber together," she said, looping her arm through Milla's. "And then we'll figure out what dress and hairstyle I need for the day."

Milla caught her breath as they walked into the bath chamber, but her grip on Charis's arm was solid. If she stared too long at the gleaming white tub in the center of the room, Charis couldn't blame her. It was hard to look at it without imagining blood running down its sides.

Moving past the tub, Charis faced the mirror and groaned at the tangle of curls and sticky beeswax pomade clinging to her scalp. "I should've let you wash my hair last night."

She should have, but she hadn't been able to face the thought of getting into the tub.

"We can sort that out quick enough, my lady." Milla approached the vanity, her movements more confident now that she was focused on her familiar tasks. "But first, let's choose a look for you. What's on your agenda today?"

Charis turned away from the mirror and began ticking items off on her fingers. "Meeting with the palace steward during breakfast, working with Darold to answer correspondence immediately after, checking on the queen to discuss what happened last night and deciding on a response, tutoring with Nalani and Holland, high tea with the Everlys, where I'm sure I'll be prodded for insight into my mother's plans while also enduring the not-so-subtle matchmaking efforts of Lady Everly, and finally, dinner with Father."

"If I may be so bold, I think Ferris Everly would make an awful husband," Milla said.

"And an even worse king," Charis agreed. "But I can't come right out and repel his advances when his father needs to work well with my mother on the royal council. And besides, he *is* my fourth cousin, and his family is in line for the throne if both the Willowthorns and the Farragins are killed. I have to play nice while making sure he knows he's dealing with a well-sharpened dagger."

Milla frowned. "You're going to need to look both approachable and out of reach. Everyone on your list today except for your father needs to look at you and remember who they're dealing with. Wait here, my lady."

While she waited, Charis forced herself to approach the bathtub. Let a sick sense of horror fill her at the memory of the spy with the silver necklace and Mother lying crumpled on the floor. At the thought of another spy violating the sanctity of her rooms. Made herself hold on to the horror until it became fury.

How dare King Alaric send a spy into the heart of the palace to assassinate the queen. He ought to be flayed alive, one small piece at a time, for the atrocities he'd visited upon their northern territories. And now he'd added attempting to kill Calera's ruler to his list of crimes.

If he'd thought removing the queen would make overtaking Calera much easier, then he was about to get a lesson he'd not soon forget.

Charis climbed out of her nightdress and stepped into the tub. The porcelain was cold beneath her bare feet, and she imagined the bits of blood that might still cling secretly to its sides.

"My lady, I found the perfect dre— Oh." Milla came to a stop at the entrance to the bath chamber, her eyes wide as she took in the naked princess standing proudly in the center of the tub.

Charis swept her gaze over the dress in her handmaiden's arms and bared her teeth in a vicious smile. The silk was the swirling deep blue of the sea just before a hurricane hit. The bodice was covered in filigree crafted from the same silver used to make the royal swords. The long sleeves ended in metallic points at the tops of her hands. And bright shards of the same silver were sewn into the hem so that it sounded like a sword being drawn every time the dress brushed the floor.

Milla was right. It was perfect.

"Draw a bath, Milla. And I'll wear a general's braid today. It's a fitting hairstyle for a dress made to win battles."

As Milla began working the pomade out of the princess's hair, Charis leaned against the tub and let rage become her armor.

The Willowthorn family was hard to kill. Harder still to break. King Alaric Penbyrn was going to find that the one thing worse than killing the royal family of Calera was being foolish enough to leave any of them alive.

FIVE

CHARIS LEFT HER bedchamber, flanked once more by Reuben and Elsbet, and found Tal, one of Father's nighttime guards, waiting beside the guards' station at the end of the hall.

"Tal?" She glanced around quickly, but he seemed to be alone. The early morning sunshine spilling in through the windows gleamed against his pale blond hair. He was about her age with the lithe muscles of a farmhand and the shoulders of a swordsman. He'd joined Father's staff last year—another refugee from the war-torn north. Charis didn't see him often—she rarely had evenings free to spend with Father—but it wasn't like Tal to come to the princess's chambers unless Father was with him.

"He isn't with me," Tal said, and her gaze snapped back to his. "I refused to let him come."

"You refused . . . What is going on?"

"The king is very anxious. It's affecting his health, Your Highness." Tal sounded worried. "I thought it best not to have him walk all the way to your wing, but he only stayed behind because I promised I would bring you to him."

"Of course." Charis turned toward the passage that led to the east wing.

Reuben shifted beside her, a subtle move that still managed to appear threatening. "No one brings the princess anywhere. Especially this morning."

Charis waved him off. "If Father wants—"

"*Especially* this morning." Reuben glanced at Charis and then said, "Pardon my interruption, Your Highness."

"I never suggested she should come alone," Tal said, his quiet voice steely with determination. "But the king is very anxious. Ilsa is out doing the shopping, and he refuses to allow me to send for her. I can't get his heart rate or breathing under control."

Charis began walking swiftly. She didn't blame Reuben for his worries. If two spies had made their way into the palace, there could very well be another. But she trusted that Reuben and Elsbet would stay by her side. If it was a trap, both Tal and the spy were as good as dead, though she'd have felt more secure if she had her own weapon.

Making a note to alter all future attire to include either her daggers or her sword, Charis hurried down the long hallway. Elsbet and Reuben hurried to keep up, and Tal moved past her to lead the way, his hand on his sword hilt as well.

Father lived in a wing on the third floor of the eastern side of the palace. He and Mother had been estranged for as long as Charis could remember, and the queen cared so little for what her husband did with his time that the only guards on this side of the palace were members of the king's own staff who'd been handpicked from his beloved northern territory. Besides a half dozen guards who split coverage between a day shift and night shift, he kept a maid and his nurse companion, Ilsa, and that was it. None of them reported to the queen.

"Why is he so anxious?" Charis asked as they moved past the bank of floor-to-ceiling windows overlooking the distant blue ribbon of the Draiel Sea.

"He learned about last evening's attack," Tal said as they approached Father's wing. A single guard stood watch at the entrance. The woman nodded to Tal and then resumed slowly looking from the stairs to the long hall that ran from one end of the wing to the other.

Tal pushed open the heavy carved door that led into Father's chambers.

"*How* did he find out?" It wasn't like Ilsa to give the king upsetting news and then leave him alone to go shopping.

Tal met her gaze as she moved through the doorway. "A page arrived this morning with a message."

Charis rounded on Reuben, her voice vibrating with fury. "You sent a report about the attack to my father? Are you trying to kill him?"

Reuben's lip curled. "Are *you*, Your Highness?"

She drew back as if struck. "How dare you speak to me that way!"

"My apologies, Your Highness." He didn't sound the least bit sorry. "But we have no idea how the spies slipped past security yesterday. We have to assume more could be coming. I had to operate under the belief that every member of the royal family was a target, and I acted accordingly."

"Then you should have told me what you were doing so I could go to his chambers immediately."

"We needed you contained and safe." Reuben held her gaze, his hard, brown eyes unflinching. "Don't worry. I said nothing about the woman in your chambers, so he doesn't have that additional worry."

Charis leaned closer and let the rage that crouched in the corner of her heart flicker to life in her eyes. "My father's health and peace of mind are more important than whether I am contained. You do not make decisions without consulting me, Reuben. I promise you do not want me as your enemy."

He held her stare for another second, and then nodded deferentially. "Yes, Your Highness."

She turned to Tal. "I assume you and the rest of Father's staff have already searched his chambers to secure it this morning?"

"Yes."

"Then Reuben and Elsbet will stay here to guard the entrance while you and I go see Father." Without waiting to see if Reuben would dare argue with her, she pulled the door out of Tal's grasp and closed it with a dull thud.

"Father?" Charis hurried through a parlor decorated in soft blues and whites, a small library with a pair of bronze lanterns gilding the spines of the king's treasured books with gold, and then into a sitting room where the king sat on his favorite gray sofa, a thick yellow blanket draped over his lap.

"Charis!" He struggled to stand, his body shaking.

Charis rushed toward him, but Tal got there first. Wrapping an arm around the king's back, the boy held him steady. Charis reached him an instant later and gathered Father's cold, frail hands in hers.

"There's no need to worry, Father. I'm well."

"You're hardly well." The man who knew her best and loved her most let go of her hands to press his palms to either side of her face as he gazed into her eyes, hunting for the truth behind the shield of strength she tried so hard to never be without.

His breath ended in a wheeze that pierced Charis's heart with a pain that refused to be ignored. She settled down next to the king's abandoned blanket. "Sit with me?"

When Father was settled beside Charis, the blanket fluffed over his legs again, she said, "I'm so sorry you worried. If I'd known Reuben was going to send out that report, I would have come here much earlier. There's no need to be upset. Mother is going to fully recover."

"Of course there's reason to be upset." The sternness in Father's usually gentle voice was a surprise. "There was an assassin in the palace! How did he get there? Why weren't the guards aware of the threat? What if he'd struck Letha's heart? Or what if his target was any royal who entered the room, and she just got there before you? My sweet Charis, this isn't something to brush aside and ignore."

His breathing hitched as though there was something caught in his throat, and the pulse along the side of his neck beat rapidly. Charis cast around wildly for something to say that would calm him.

"I'm not ignoring it, Father. I promise." She kept her voice soothing and patted his hand.

"What is being done?" He looked from her to Tal, who stood a few paces from the couch, staring at the wall as though not at all interested in their conversation. "What is being changed to keep you better protected?"

"Changed?" She frowned.

"There was obviously a terrible breach in security, and we cannot take the risk that it will happen again." His voice rose, thin and unsteady. "How can you sleep when we don't know how this happened?"

A shudder seized Charis, and she sucked in a little breath, desperate to keep her composure. If Father knew the depths of her own horror and fear, there would be no calming him. She imagined every rapid heartbeat, every harsh breath of his giving the illness a stronger foothold and stealing a few more minutes of the time she had left with him.

"My guards will search my chambers—"

"The same guards who allowed a Montevallian spy into the ladies' parlor where you and Letha were supposed to be safe? No, I won't allow this."

"Father, now that we know there's a breach, my guards will be even more careful."

His voice shook. "Letha's security has been increased. We should increase yours as well."

"That can be arranged."

He went on as if she hadn't spoken. "We should move you into this wing. There's a set of rooms across the hall. Or better yet, I'll take the couch and you take my bed. They'd have to get past me before they came for you."

And put Father directly in the line of fire? Absolutely not. There'd been other attempts to harm both the queen and Charis over the years, though none within the palace itself. But no one had ever tried to hurt Father. Even his enemies must have known he was a gentle soul who held no political power and whose death would gain them nothing.

All that would change if Charis appeared to be under his direct protection.

"Tal, send a message—" He broke off into a fit of coughing. Charis rubbed her palm against his back, wincing at the press of his bones against his skin.

She could still see echoes of the man who'd carried her on his shoulders, who'd tucked her in at night and read story after story until she was lulled to sleep by the sound of his voice, and who'd softened the harsh reality of her life as the heir to a kingdom at war with unexpected picnics or trips to the sea. But the echoes of that version of him were fading, faster by the day, it seemed. Consumed steadily by the illness that was devouring him voraciously, an insatiable enemy Charis and every physician she'd hired had been unable to defeat.

"Take a minute," Charis said firmly when Father's coughing finally stopped. "Nothing is going to happen to me in the next few moments while you get settled."

"I'm not an invalid, Charis." His voice was as firm as hers, though it was threaded with exhaustion. "I'm your father. I realize I rarely interfere with the decisions you and your mother make, but I will not back down on this."

Charis blinked. Father never made demands. Never. She couldn't possibly refuse him when the cost of worrying him was further ruin to his health.

But she couldn't possibly agree when the cost of protecting her could be his life.

Father spoke with a note of finality. "You will move into my chambers tonight. If Letha wants to argue about it, she knows where to find me. Tal, send Charis's guards to pack up some of her things and bring them here."

Charis shot Tal a look of panic before she could think better of it and found a similar worry in the boy's eyes.

"I love you, Father." Charis leaned close and pressed a delicate kiss against his cheek. "And I appreciate that you want to protect me. But I can't stay here."

"You most certainly can."

"Not if I want to maintain the impression that the Willowthorns are unassailable and cannot be stopped in our quest to end the war without annexing the north."

"At what cost?" He was already shaking his head. "I won't lose my daughter over some political power play."

"You won't have to," Tal said.

Charis and the king turned as one to stare at Tal. The boy

swallowed hard, but there was resolute determination on his face as he said, "I'll guard Princess Charis."

"What? No. Father needs you—"

"No one ever bothers me." The king waved a hand to sweep away Charis's objection, his eyes still on Tal as though weighing the boy's words. Finally, he said, "I would expect you to be with her at all times."

"I understand."

"Wait a minute—" Charis began, but Father ignored her.

"On your afternoon off, you would personally hand her security over to the guard you trust most."

"Of course."

"There is the matter of your living arrangements. I'm not sure what rooms are available in Charis's wing. I'll check with Letha."

"Both of you just stop." Charis looked from Father to Tal and back again. The only thing worse than worrying about the possibility of another attack in the palace would be having a near-stranger at her side every moment of every day. When would she ever be able to drop her shield and just breathe? "You can't simply decide to assign me a full-time bodyguard and tell him to move into my wing."

"You'd rather move in here with me?" Father asked.

She pulled the one excuse she knew he couldn't argue with. "Mother will never agree to something like this."

"She would if she'd thought of it first." Father patted Charis's hand as if he'd neatly solved the issue.

"But she didn't think of it, and she isn't going to want a guard she barely knows hovering over me every second of the day."

Father folded her hands into his, and she was grateful to realize they no longer trembled. "She will see the benefit in this. She wants you safe as much as I do. Don't worry, Charis. I'll win this argument."

Charis blinked. Her parents' marriage was one of convenience—twenty-eight years ago Letha had needed a suitor who would unify support for the royals in the northern territories, and Father had come from a long line of proud northern nobility. It had taken nearly eleven years for the marriage to produce an heir, but once Charis was born, the queen had ignored Father's presence unless she couldn't help it, and Father had settled comfortably into his wing in the palace and poured his heart into Charis.

In all her seventeen years, she'd never once seen them argue, and it was impossible to imagine Father swaying Letha to do things his way. Nobody ever pushed Mother into following their plans unless she saw a definite political gain in the outcome. Even when she was bedridden and recovering from a knife wound.

Charis smiled gently and squeezed Father's hands. "Whatever the outcome of your discussion with Mother, please don't worry about me tonight. Reuben is on duty and will search my chambers before I enter. If necessary, I'm sure he'd even sleep in the hall outside my door."

"Odious man, but loyal," Father said. "I'll speak with Letha this morning. Tal, thank you for volunteering to guard Charis."

Tal inclined his head and said nothing.

Charis leaned against Father's shoulder, ignoring the way his collarbone pressed against her cheek, and whispered, "I love you." Then she left his chambers and headed off to start her day, sure that Mother would refuse such a ludicrous arrangement.

SIX

CHARIS SWEPT THROUGH the grand hall of the main palace wing, her secretary hurrying to keep pace while Reuben and Elsbet stalked on either side of her, hands on their sword hilts. The metallic hem of her dress struck the white stone floor with the rattle and scrape of a hundred tiny swords. Charis felt ready to chew through metal herself.

Her meeting with the palace steward had revealed that several noble families—Lord Pellinsworth's included—had failed to pay their taxes to the crown this past quarter. Taxes that were due a week ago. Apparently, Lord Pellinsworth and his ilk thought it acceptable to protest the war by refusing to pay the crown its due but didn't have a problem with attending a ball paid for by the taxes of loyal Calerans and partaking in the food, drink, and merriment there.

Charis would like to personally shove the irony of it right down Lord Pellinsworth's throat.

The royal coffers were stretched dangerously thin. They could hardly afford to miss out on tax money that by law should be theirs. Especially with ambassadors from their allies watching every move. If even a whiff of insolvency, of an inability to manage both the war and Calera's booming trade market, were to reach the wrong ears, the perception of Calera could turn in a heartbeat from favorable equal to wounded prize pig ripe for the taking.

Her teeth set as heat flushed her body. Every single one of the families who'd withheld their taxes should be called before the queen and immediately stripped of their titles unless they paid every cent owed, plus a hefty fine for the trouble. If they were allowed to get away with this, the rest of that faction would follow their example.

"Your Highness, there is the matter of the ceremonial launching of our newest naval vessel." Darold puffed as he hurried to keep up with her. "I've put that on your schedule for Sunday afternoon. And the Society for the Advancement of Orphans has requested that you make a speech at the groundbreaking of their new property just outside Arborlay. They wanted next Tuesday, but you're already scheduled to visit the refugee center, so I've suggested that Thursday instead."

"That's fine." Charis struggled to keep her tone even. It wasn't Darold's fault she was in a terrible mood. Still, if he persisted in droning on about her various engagements, she wasn't sure she could hold her tongue. What did it matter which day she attended a groundbreaking when so many things were going wrong?

"We've also received a request from Lady Ollen for a brief speech at her next formal dinner, and another from—"

"Yes, very well, Darold. Please put a list of requests on my desk and add the approved engagements to my calendar. I'll leave you to it."

"Of course, Your Highness." Darold bowed and turned toward the stairs that led to the princess's study.

Anger knotted in her chest, a dagger of heat that burned as she moved. First Montevallian spies in the palace last night, and now noble families, grown bold on antiwar sentiment, refusing to pay their taxes. She needed a new strategy for dealing with Montevallo and an effective way to bring the antiwar faction in line, and she needed it fast.

Turning from the main hall, Charis moved into a long corridor that hugged the eastern edge of the palace. The floor of golden, sun-warmed wood glowed comfortably in the wash of light pouring through a wall of windows.

The palace sat on a hill at the southern edge of Arborlay, surrounded by fields and orchards that stretched out to an eastern bluff's edge overlooking the sea. To the west, just past the palace borders, cottages and farms dotted the landscape. To the north, neighborhoods full of mansions and manicured lawns lay in neat rows until they reached the main road that led down into the city proper, where cobblestone streets lined with small houses, shops, and businesses slowly wound their way down to the busy port.

Today, the sea was the bright blue of sapphires and summer skies. Several merchant frigates slowly approached the port. Sea hawks swooped through the air and came to rest on the stone ramparts that lined the shore at regular intervals. White foam-capped waves crashed against the water and then spent themselves on the golden sand.

Charis turned from the windows and continued toward Mother's wing.

Arborlay was the picture of security, sharply at odds with the wreckage that littered the northern territories, where Montevallo had captured town after town, killing those who were strong enough to resist them and enslaving the rest. The antiwar faction would have the royal family abandon those people to their fates and let Montevallo have unfettered access to the northern seaport in exchange for their own safety.

But then what? Setting aside the horror of consigning their own people to a life of captivity, Montevallo would know they could bully Calera into giving them anything they wanted. What would they ask for next? And how could Calera, cut in half, continue to defend itself?

Charis slowed to a stop outside the wide, iron-hinged door that led to the north wing and took a deep breath.

Anger wouldn't help her here. Neither would frantic thoughts that skipped from one problem to the next. She needed icy composure and ruthless calm.

"The queen is waiting," Reuben said as if chiding an errant child.

Charis locked gazes with him and let her mouth curl into the cruel smile that never failed to remind her of Mother. Reuben's eyes hardened, but he stepped back and said quietly, "Your Highness."

Turning on her heel, she nodded to the footman and walked into the room as he opened the doors.

Mother's study was the picture of elegance. A pair of large arched windows graced the far wall, bathing the dark blue rug and semicircle of ivory upholstered chairs with golden sunshine. A graceful writing desk carved with summer vines and sculpted wooden flowers rested against the northern wall, surrounded by bookcases. Framed portraits from famous Caleran artists were mounted on the walls.

A maid was bent over the hearth, scrubbing the stones until they shone, and a pair of guards stood at attention beside the door that led to Mother's bedroom.

"Stay here," Charis said to Reuben and Elsbet as she left the study behind and entered the queen's private chambers.

The room was done in shades of ivory and pale blue. A settee and a pair of armchairs were arranged before the hearth, where a cozy fire burned. Beyond the sitting area, the queen's massive four-poster bed rested on a plush Solvanish rug. Charis half expected Mother to be sitting up, dressed and ready to command the kingdom from her bed.

Instead, she found her lying against her pillows, still in her night-dress, with gray circles under her eyes.

Charis bowed her head toward Mother and said, "Your Majesty. I have several things we need to discuss if you feel up to it."

"I have something to discuss as well, but please, continue." Mother's voice was a shadow of its usual strength, but the fury in it sent a prickle of alarm down Charis's spine.

She imagined her skin was impenetrable, a shield that would hold fast no matter what came for her, and took the offensive. "Before we get into the events of last night, I'd like to set an agenda item for the upcoming royal council meeting."

The queen waited, her breathing shallow as she pressed a hand gently against her bandaged abdomen.

"I've just learned that four families who've made their antiwar sentiments clear failed to pay their quarterly taxes." Charis raised a hand and ticked the names off on her fingers. "Pellinsworth, Silving, Robill, and Perch."

"Have they, now?" Mother's whisper could cut glass.

"Three were in attendance at last night's ball."

"How bold of them." The queen coughed and winced.

"A bold crime deserves an even bolder punishment," Charis said.

"Indeed it does. What did you have in mind?"

"I propose we call them before the council, levy a fine against them, and sell enough of their lands to cover what is owed unless they can immediately pay their debts. If they refuse to cooperate in any way, we strip them of their titles." Charis folded her hands to keep from worrying the silver pieces sewn into her bodice. "To stop the antiwar faction from spreading the rumor that we are punishing those families to quash dissent, we send out a proclamation that explains our actions and reiterates that we welcome civil discussion but that no one is above the law."

Mother was quiet for a long moment, her eyes closing as beads of sweat dotted her brow. Finally, she nodded. Charis moved quickly to the main purpose of the meeting.

"My top priority is to learn how spies got so far into the palace without being detected and to find a path toward peace with Montevallo before King Alaric decides to send another assassin after you. To that end, I've instructed the head of the palace guard to quietly put feelers out into the city to see if there are any rumors that could provide useful information. It's a shame Reuben killed both spies, or we might have learned something."

Mother coughed again and hissed in pain. "You should have stopped him."

Charis's voice sharpened. "I wasn't in the room when either killing happened. If you disagree with Reuben's handling of the situation, you should make that clear to him."

The queen's lips tightened. Looking at her mother was almost like looking in the mirror—curly brown hair, slim, strong figure, and always, always the touch of cruelty lurking at her mouth. But now the queen's hands trembled, and her skin had taken on a waxy sheen.

"I had a great deal to say to Reuben this morning while you were with the palace steward. He has redeemed his mistake, but I expect my daughter..." Her voice faded, and her eyelids drooped. She seemed to open them again with effort. "I expect my daughter to maintain absolute control over her staff at all times. If you can't do that, how can you control a kingdom?"

Charis held Mother's gaze, grateful for the press of sharp silver filigree against her ribs to remind her that she wore armor outside and in. Letting a hint of her own viciousness coat her words, she said, "I can control my staff. And I have the management of the kingdom well in hand." Charis's chest tightened at the look in her mother's eyes, but she knew better than to show it. A wolf respected another predatory wolf but tore out the throat of an animal too weak to hold its ground.

"We need to understand King Alaric's motives." Charis lowered her voice, though they were alone. "His army continues to conquer our territories. We've made no successful invasion on Montevallian soil. Given enough time, if nothing changes on our end, he will win the war. So why kill you? And why send an unarmed spy into my chambers?"

The queen nodded, her lips pressed together in a thin line, the only outward sign of emotion she would permit herself. "We're missing something, Charis." Her voice was thready with exhaustion.

"I agree. Either he feels threatened, though I'm not sure how, or he needs the war to end quickly, and he believes your death is the way to accomplish that. Which means he will probably send assassins after you again. He must believe that if he removes the queen, he'll throw the kingdom into chaos, and he'll get what he wants much faster."

"He's underestimated you if he thinks dealing with you as queen will be easier for him." There was a tiny glimmer of pride in Mother's eyes, and Charis's shoulders straightened. Earning kind words from Father was as easy as breathing, but Mother dispensed approval like crusts of bread during a famine. "But we cannot ignore that these spies were able to get into the palace, past multiple guards and servants, and hide where we would be most vulnerable, which means the guards and staff who were on duty last night in or near the ladies' parlor or your chambers failed us."

Her voice had a sharp note of finality in it, and the breath left Charis's body as if she'd been struck.

Milla.

"Mother—"

There was a knock at the door, and the queen said, "Enter."

Charis's fingers shook as she pressed them against her sides. Please let her have misunderstood Mother's meaning for once. *Please.*

A footman opened the doors and stood aside as Reuben entered, followed by Tal. Both guards bowed their heads to the queen and said, "Your Majesty," and then turned to Charis and did the same while murmuring "Your Highness."

As soon as the footman closed the door behind the newcomers, the queen said, "Your father and I have spoken about the matter."

Mother waved a hand weakly in the direction of the guards. Tal stepped forward, his eyes on Charis, though his expression revealed nothing. "Tal will be your personal guard from now on. Your father trusts him implicitly. He is to be at your side wherever you go, and he will sleep in the room adjacent to your chambers." Her voice faded.

"But that's Milla's room." Charis locked eyes with Mother.

The queen's chest rose and fell rapidly as though her pain was becoming unmanageable. "As I said, the staff responsible for protecting the ladies' parlor and your chambers failed us last night." Her voice was a dagger drawing blood with every word. "At least one of them must have been complicit in showing the spies where to hide."

"Mother . . ." Charis's voice shook at the edges, and she struggled to draw a breath past the weight that was settling into her.

"Harming a member of the royal family, being complicit in that harm, or knowingly spreading information that could harm the family is treason."

"But we need to figure out *which* of them committed treason," Charis said, pushing as much strength into her voice as she could, though the shield she wore was cracking, the emotion leaking through. "We should imprison them. Question them until—"

"What do you think I had Reuben doing while you were in meetings this morning?"

Charis stared at her mother in silence.

"I was unsatisfied with everyone's proclamations of innocence," the queen said faintly. "A message had to be sent."

Charis's knees threatened to buckle. "What did you do?"

Mother held her gaze, and the flicker of compassion Charis thought she could see in the queen's eyes died beneath a veneer of unreachable calm. "As you said yourself, a bold crime deserves an even bolder punishment. Every member of our personal security teams who wasn't within our sight the entire night and every maid within the parlor have each received a traitor's reward. The bodies will be buried in a prisoners' lot to make sure our message is received by all who need to hear it."

A sharp bolt of pain struck Charis, weakening her knees and twisting her stomach into a knot.

The queen's gaze landed on her, full of implacable expectation, as the pain sank into Charis's blood like acid, a searing ache that wanted to swallow her whole.

She couldn't grieve. Not here. Not where emotion was a weakness and hesitation a failure.

Charis imagined a coat of ice covering her heart. Rising up, slick and untouchable, to mute the pain until it was a faint echo she could ignore. She was hard. Cold. Forged in duty and sacrifice and nothing more. Raising her chin, she met her mother's gaze and held it, all emotion wiped from her expression.

Mother inclined her head in approval and said, "You are dismissed."

Charis left the room, dry-eyed and silent, Reuben and Tal at her heels.

SEVEN

ELSBET AND BAUST, the palace physician, were waiting in the queen's study. Charis focused on putting one foot in front of the other. On breathing past the impossible pressure in her chest.

"Your Highness."

Had Milla known what was coming? Had it been quick? Or had Reuben drawn out the torture, hunting for information to redeem himself in the queen's eyes?

"Your Highness?"

And how many members of Charis's own security team had also died? Luther and Fada had been on duty. Had they been deemed traitors because their patrols through her wing hadn't revealed the spy?

"Your Highness, I really must speak with you."

Charis pulled up short, halfway to the exit, as Baust stepped in front of her and bowed.

"The queen is stable, but I fear her recovery may be an arduous process. The blade entered here"—he tapped a place on his own stomach—"and did damage to her liver and intestines. There is the worry of infection, of course, and the blood loss she suffered was significant. At my best estimate, she will be bedridden for several weeks."

"Thank you for your report." Charis's voice was remote, the words disconnected from the pain that spread through her veins with every heartbeat.

"I . . . The queen is displeased with this diagnosis." Baust's forehead gleamed as sweat appeared. "It's possible she may try to rush the healing process or disregard it altogether if she feels she needs to be seen publicly doing her royal duties."

The pressure in Charis's chest was a stone crushing her from the inside out. There was no room for grief. For taking a moment to just breathe until the pain settled. There was only Calera's need for a capable ruler and the implacable expectations that had been etched into Charis from birth.

Lifting her chin, she said quietly, "Rest assured that I have her royal duties well in hand. Spread the news that the queen's illness from last night lingers, but that you expect a full recovery soon. That will be all, Baust."

Without waiting for him to finish bowing, she left the study, Tal at her side, Reuben and Elsbet at her back. She was due for tutoring in the fifth-floor library with Holland and Nalani, but the thought of facing her friends, who would surely see something was amiss and ask questions, was more than she could bear. Besides, Mother's prognosis meant Charis needed to be seen managing the affairs of the kingdom in the queen's name. She could start with sending a notice of the queen's illness to the council members and then speak with Mother's secretary to see which engagements over the coming weeks needed to be moved to Charis's calendar and which could be postponed until the queen recovered. As a bonus, staying busy would help keep her grief over Milla locked safely behind the shield of icy composure she was desperately clinging to.

She was halfway down the corridor that led from the queen's private wing to the main palace when a page approached and sketched a quick bow.

"Your Highness, Lady Channing is here for her meeting with the queen. The butler put her in the north parlor and sent me to fetch you as the queen is ill."

"Thank you. Please give notice to Tutor Brannigan that I am unable to come to class this morning. He can send any missed assignments to my secretary."

She'd meet with Lady Channing and then summon Mother's secretary, go through the queen's calendar, and then draft an agenda for the next royal council meeting. One that focused on strengthening Calera's alliances, finding a way to open peace talks with Montevallo, and dealing with those who'd failed to pay their taxes. With any luck, that would take up the rest of the morning and leave her no room to think of anything beyond the task of running the kingdom in Mother's absence.

No room to think about returning to her chambers to find Milla gone.

Her eyes stung, and she blinked rapidly as she forged ahead down the hallway, her battle dress striking the floor with every step. Maids dusting framed artwork and pages scurrying about with messages from the head housekeeper or palace steward bowed as she passed. When she reached the north parlor, she waited while Reuben and Elsbet checked it for spies and then took up positions outside the door. Tal followed her inside, but he was so unobtrusively quiet, she could simply pretend he wasn't there.

"Your Highness!" Lady Channing curtsied, her simple gray dress a somber contrast to the soft rose, yellow, and ivory décor.

"Lady Channing." Charis's voice felt like it was coming from a distance. From some other part of herself that wasn't trapped beneath the crushing pressure within.

The woman met her gaze, and Charis was shocked to find tears in her eyes. She couldn't remember ever seeing Lady Channing cry.

"Are you well?" Charis asked as she crossed the pale yellow rug to sit in a high-back chair embroidered with delicate summer flowers.

Once the princess was seated, Lady Channing sat opposite her on a plush rose settee and wrung her hands. "My dear girl, I'm simply heartbroken. You poor thing. But of course you know I'll do whatever I can to help during the transition. Anything at all."

Charis drew back, her skin prickling with unease. "What are you talking about?"

Lady Channing frowned. "Your mother, of course."

"What exactly about my mother?"

"The assassination." Lady Channing folded her hands, her knuckles white as she watched Charis's face. "I've upset you. I'm so sorry. Of course you're not ready to discuss this yet, but there is the coronation ceremony to manage, the council to inform, and a plan must be made to—"

"Lady Channing, the queen is very much alive."

Lady Channing's mouth dropped open, and she stared at Charis for a moment, eyes wide, and then she slowly leaned against the back of the settee, her hands pressed to her cheeks as tears shone in her eyes. "Oh, thank the seers."

A pit of dread sank into Charis's stomach. Lady Channing shouldn't have heard about the assassination attempt. Not if Reuben's quest to silence every witness had been as successful as Mother believed. Which meant the story of the queen's illness would be lost in the wake of the assassination rumor unless Charis quickly nipped it in the bud.

Refusing to consider the methods Reuben would employ against the offender, she said quietly, "How did you hear about it?"

Lady Channing wiped her eyes and sat up straight. "I told the butler that of course I knew the way to the north parlor, no need to escort me, so I was walking in silence, and I overheard a pair of guards talking."

Her eyes widened as she caught the expression on Charis's face. "They were being most discreet, Your Highness. I wouldn't have heard them had I not been passing so close to the alcove they were in, and there was no one else about."

"What precisely did they say?"

"That there was a serious breach in palace security if an assassin could stab the queen and that heads would roll if that breach wasn't found and fixed." She drew in a fortifying breath. "Naturally, I assumed that meant the queen was . . . that she'd died. I apologize for upsetting you."

Charis nodded, her thoughts settling. A pair of guards, most likely tasked with quietly searching the palace to be sure another assassin hadn't entered that morning and not hearing Lady Channing approach, could hardly be punished for quietly discussing the situation between themselves. A thread of relief unspooled within as she shelved any plans to discuss the matter with either Reuben or the queen.

"Your Highness, if the queen is . . ." Lady Channing paused as if waiting for Charis to supply the word that would fit the story the palace was telling.

"Ill?"

"Yes. If she's ill, then I assume you are stepping into her duties for the time being." Lady Channing's eyes were clear, and her tone was once again the calm, unflappable one she always used. "If you find yourself in need of an advisor, I humbly offer my service. If you would prefer a younger advisor, I am happy to work with the council to recommend someone suitable."

Charis considered the offer. Mother had often relied on Lady Channing's pragmatic council throughout the years. And having someone so well respected by all factions approve of Charis's decisions while Mother recovered would be invaluable.

"Thank you, Lady Channing." She paused and looked out the trio of windows at the distant rooftops of the town below them. Today was market day for the kitchens. Milla would have been hovering near the hearth, ready to snatch a pastry or bar of chocolate from the incoming foodstuffs to bring up to Charis's chambers for the two of them to share later.

"Your Highness?" The infinite gentleness in Lady Channing's voice yanked Charis back into the present.

She was mortified to find tears in her eyes. Blinking them away, she forced herself to speak briskly. "Mother will be recovering from her illness for a few weeks. During that time, it's imperative that I act swiftly and decisively on several matters."

Lady Channing folded her hands quietly in her lap and waited.

"First, I must levy consequences against a few noble families who've refused to pay taxes this quarter, but I must do so without losing the loyalty and faith of the rest of the antiwar faction."

"Perhaps a quiet example could be made. One that shows restraint and mercy while still reminding them that you hold the sword that is poised above their necks."

Charis's jaw tightened. "I agree. Mother and I thought to demand immediate payment, including an additional fine for their treasonous behavior, with the understanding that if they don't pay, we will strip them of their titles and confiscate their lands. We also thought to issue a proclamation welcoming the civil discussion of dissenting ideas but reminding our people that all must pay their fair share to maintain our armies and our infrastructure."

Lady Channing inclined her head. "A good idea, though I wonder if instead of a proclamation, which could be seen as defensive, we could simply plant a rumor with the right person."

"What kind of rumor?"

"Oh, perhaps . . . the scintillating tale of how the queen had every right to throw the offenders into the dungeon for forcing other nobles to carry their tax burden, but how instead she chose to offer them the chance to make things right or risk losing their titles. The right person could spin that into a delicious bit of gossip that paints the royal family as firm but fair, and leaves the offenders with a very shaky social standing."

Charis nodded slowly. "I like it. I'll have Darold summon the lords before the council this week."

"And I'll be ready to invite Lady Shawling to tea that very afternoon so she gets all the juicy details."

Charis rubbed cold fingers against the raised embroidery on the arm of her chair. "Thank you. With that handled, I need to figure out a show of strength against Montevallo. This assassination attempt cannot go unanswered, and we need leverage to have any chance of brokering peace. Which brings me to my final item. We need to assure our allies that Calera is a good business risk. Any sign of weakness could undo help that we'll desperately need if we are to survive the war and turn the tide. Already I hear that there will soon be a shortage of medical supplies due to the sinking of the Rullenvor trade ship. We cannot risk any of our allies turning their backs on us, or worse, deciding we're weak enough to be conquered."

Lady Channing looked thoughtful. "My trip to the northern

kingdoms yielded strong relationships with their rulers and ambassadors. Let me see what I can do."

The pressure in Charis's chest refused to ease, and she rose, unable to bear the effort of carrying the conversation for a moment longer. "Thank you, Lady Channing. I'll look forward to hearing your results."

Turning, she left the room, chin high and back straight. Not a single sign of weakness for her enemies or allies alike to pounce on and use against her.

EIGHT

CHARIS HELD HERSELF together for the rest of the afternoon by sheer force of will. Meetings with Darold and Mother's secretary, high tea at the Everlys', and a long session with her weapons trainer gave her something to focus on, but every unguarded breath burned the back of her throat. Every stray moment in between tasks cut her to the bone.

Milla—sweet little Milla with her earnest smile and her cheerful ways—gone.

Not gone. *Taken.*

Taken because she'd had the terrible misfortune of being in the ladies' parlor when the assassin attacked. Because the queen believed she might have been the one who betrayed them.

Charis's eyes stung as she made her way from the training yard to her chambers, Reuben and Elsbet walking silently several paces back, and Tal just behind her to the left. He'd followed her in silence all day, his dark eyes carefully taking in their surroundings before focusing on her again. Charis would bet her crown he deeply regretted being assigned to protect her now that he'd seen the cost of failure.

She dug her nails into her palms before grief could destroy the calm she was fighting so hard to keep.

"Your Highness, I regret to announce that Luther and Fada were part of the staff members who bore responsibility for allowing a spy to hide in the palace. We have two new guards assigned to your night shift," Reuben said as they climbed the stairs that led to Charis's wing and entered her hallway. "I would ask that you stay in your rooms this evening until I've had a chance to fully brief them on—"

Charis stepped into her chambers, followed by Tal, and shut the door in Reuben's face.

Fada and Luther had been her guards since she was ten—it was hard to imagine that one of them had betrayed her.

"Your Highness, can I get you anything?" Tal spoke for the first time, and Charis jumped. She'd been so caught up in her thoughts, she'd forgotten that even in her private chambers, she had to deal with someone watching her every move. His voice was cautious but kind, which somehow made it worse.

She met his gaze and winced inwardly at the wary concern in his eyes. A near-stranger who already pitied her and who would see her grief if she couldn't hold it in a little longer. Unacceptable.

"I'm fine." Her voice hitched, betraying her, but he didn't question her statement. "There's Milla's . . . I mean, your room." Her throat closed over the words, and she turned away, leaving him standing beside the door that led to the small bedroom her handmaiden had used. It was a bright, cheery space nestled between the outside corridor and the bath chamber, just off Charis's bedroom. If he wanted to, he could stand in the doorway and watch her sleep, a thought that gave her no comfort at all.

"I'm sorry," he said quietly as she moved away.

She kept walking until she'd entered her closet and closed the door. Drawing a shuddering breath, she changed out of her training clothes into a simple blue dress for dinner with Father. Her heart felt hollowed out, her knees weak. She wanted to curl into a ball and let the pain consume her. Instead, she dressed woodenly, icy fingers fumbling with the dress's sash until she simply jerked it into a knot and left it hanging limply at her side.

Tal wasn't in her bedroom when she exited the closet. She heard the sound of drawers opening and closing from his room. Perhaps he was putting his things away. Perhaps he was packing up the small pieces that remained of Milla.

Pain stung the back of her throat, and she swallowed hard as she sat in front of the vanity. Her hair was a windblown tangle of wild curls, and there was no Milla to comb it out and pin it in place. Charis's hand shook as she reached for the hairbrush and tugged viciously at the snarls.

Outside her window, the sky was a swirl of purple and gray with lingering streaks of gold as day crept into night.

She could send her regrets to Father and stay locked in her rooms for the rest of the night. He would understand. He always did. Unlike Mother, he had no expectations for Charis to meet. No rigorous agenda for her to perform.

Sitting at her desk, she reached for a fresh piece of paper, then paused, her fingers hovering over a small list written in Milla's sprawling loops and loose swirls. Letting her hand come to rest on the paper, she pressed her fingertips into the tiny raised lines of ink.

Silk rosette—Lady Ollen
Tuuberstone brooch—Lord Westing

Embroidered scarf—Lady Channing
Bronze hairpin—Lady Rynce
Lace handkerchief—Lord and Lady Perch

Charis stopped reading. It was a list of the gifts that had been left for Charis's use at the ball last night. The last thing Milla ever wrote. It was useless now, with the ball past. More gifts would arrive before the next formal event. She ought to throw it away.

Instead, she slipped it in a drawer and reached for fresh paper. She'd already dipped a quill into her inkpot, ready to send a note to Father, when she paused.

The room felt wrong. Charis's battle dress and training clothes still lay on the closet floor where she'd let them fall. Her brush was tossed haphazardly onto the dresser, strands of her hair still caught in its teeth. There was no patter of light footsteps in the bath chamber. No cheerful humming filling the space. Charis had never realized just how large her rooms could feel even as the walls seemed to close in on her.

She couldn't stay here with only a stranger for company. Not while every shadow, every whisper of sound made her heart jump with hope that it might be Milla. That somehow Mother had been wrong, and Milla hadn't been killed in the dungeon that morning. It had been some other girl, some stranger who hadn't quietly taken a piece of Charis's heart when she'd forgotten to guard against it.

The quill fell against the paper, leaving a smear of ink across its surface as Charis turned away from the desk. From the discarded clothes and the treacherous shadows and the silence. Drawing in a ragged breath, she schooled her face into cold indifference and knocked on Tal's door.

He opened it seconds later, bowed his head, and said softly, "Your Highness."

"I'm going to have dinner in Father's rooms."

He nodded and followed her as she opened the door to her chambers and entered the hall.

Her new pair of guards stood at the head of the corridor in front of the guardroom listening to Reuben. Charis ignored them. Turning on her heel, she strode toward the small spiral staircase at the far end of the hall. The one the staff used as they moved through the palace attending to their duties.

"Your Highness!" Reuben's voice barked from behind her.

For an instant, Charis was tempted to pretend she hadn't heard him. But whatever she did now would be reported to Mother. Giving in to emotion over her handmaiden and her guards was a weakness the princess of Calera could ill afford. Not if she wanted everyone to believe she would ruthlessly cut down any who betrayed her. Even if it destroyed her own heart to do it.

Turning sharply, she met Reuben's gaze. The fury in her heart became fire in her blood as she stared into his dark eyes.

He had killed Milla, Fada, and Luther. Charis would be willing to stake her life that he'd enjoyed it.

"These are your new nighttime guards," Reuben said, watching her closely. "Vellis and Gaylle. They will accompany you to the king's chambers."

Vellis was a tall woman with sharp, angular bones and a raw, windswept look to her pale face. Gaylle stood eye level with Charis, his eyes watchful, his brown skin gleaming in the dying light of the sun as it streamed through the windows.

"Wonderful." Charis turned and continued to the staircase, trying to ignore the sound of footsteps in her wake.

She didn't want to know their names or memorize their faces or hear them share stories about their families with each other when they thought she was otherwise occupied. The aching hollow within seemed to expand, pressing against her skin until it was difficult to breathe.

"Remain here," Charis said to the new guards as she reached the door to Father's chambers. Opening the heavy wooden door, she stepped inside with Tal just behind her and closed it.

The lock slid shut with a satisfying click, and she leaned against the door for a moment, her eyes closed as she prepared to be the Charis her father expected to see.

The rage she wore like armor subsided. In its absence, the aching space where Milla had been seeped into her veins and spread. She pressed her lips together and tried to push the pain back where it belonged, but it had taken on a life of its own and refused to be diminished.

"Good evening, Your Highness. Tal." A quiet voice interrupted Charis's thoughts, and she opened her eyes to find her father's companion standing in front of her. Ilsa held a tray of thinly sliced apples and cheese arranged around a small loaf of hearty oat bread. Her black hair was pulled into a tight bun, and strands of silver sparkled at her temples.

"Good evening, Ilsa. How is he?"

The older lady's smile creased the corners of her brown eyes. "Seems a bit stronger today than usual. Follow me, Your Highness."

Ilsa led the princess to the living room. A gentle breeze blew in from an open window to Father's left, ruffling his graying blond hair as he leaned toward the low table in front of the couch.

Father looked up, his blue eyes bright with joy when he saw his daughter in the doorway. "My sweet Charis! You're just in time for predinner snacks." A frown marred his brow as he studied his daughter. "Are you well? Still shaken from last night?"

The ache within her sharpened to something white-hot and dangerous, and she swallowed hard.

"I'm fine." Closing the distance between them, she bent to kiss his face. Two spots of pink flushed his cheeks, and his skin was dry and papery beneath her lips.

"Is she lying to me?" Father asked Tal as the boy took up a position just inside the doorway.

"Difficult to say," Tal said, his voice gentler than Charis had heard yet. The affection on his face when he looked at Father warmed a small piece of Charis's heart, though she knew firsthand it was impossible to spend any amount of time with the king and not love him. Unless you were Mother, but that hardly counted, as Mother made sure she didn't get attached to anyone except Charis.

The king smiled at Tal. "But you'd tell me if she was."

Tal returned his smile. "Between the two of you, she is far more intimidating, so I'm afraid if you want to question your daughter's words, you're on your own."

"How do you like that?" the king asked in mock affront. "He spends an afternoon with you and suddenly he forgets a year of loyalty to me."

"Who could ever be disloyal to you?" Charis settled onto the couch beside him and fussed with his blanket. "I heard you were feeling stronger today."

"Truly!" He smiled and patted her hands until they stilled. "I think this new medicine is working miracles."

The pang of knife-sharp hope that sliced into her left a trail of despair in its wake. Ignoring the fevered glint in his eyes and the tremble in his limbs, she made herself smile brightly. "You'll be join-ing me for a swim in the sea before you know it."

The king looked longingly out the window. "I don't know about swimming, but I would very much like a walk on the sand. Perhaps you and Ilsa can take me when it's warm enough."

Summer had already faded. The winds that blew in from the sea at night were full of mist and skin-piercing cold, and the leaves on the thesserin trees were lined with gold and turning crisp at the edges. It wouldn't be warm enough for the king to go outside for more months than Charis was convinced he had left.

Brushing her fingers over his, she focused on breathing past the sudden thickness in her throat before saying, "That would be lovely, Father."

Charis leaned against her father's side, blinking away the sting of tears when she felt the edges of his bones pressed against her. Once upon a time, he'd been the strongest man in her world. Lifting her over his head to spin her in circles in the garden, racing her across the sand to plunge headfirst into the water, laughing with delight when she proved stronger, fiercer, and far more competitive than any of her tutors expected.

The fact that she'd been so much like her mother had never both-ered him, even though he and his wife had barely been on speaking terms since Charis was little. Would he still appreciate the ruthless-ness in his daughter if he knew just how much like the queen she'd become? If he could see the fury in her heart, would he still call her his sweet Charis?

"What troubles you tonight?" he asked gently, his thin fingers brushing over her cheek.

Too late, she realized she'd allowed tears to fall. Quickly sitting up, she looked out the windows at the darkening sea as the first jewel-bright stars flared to life in the night sky. Obviously, Mother hadn't shared with him that she'd sentenced three of Charis's staff members to death.

"Charis." He waited in silence until she finally looked at him. "There is no shame in hurting."

Her mouth twisted into a miserable smile. "Tell that to Mother."

His eyes darkened. "I tried years ago. She would never listen."

Charis sniffed and blinked back more tears. "To rule is to be alone." She repeated the words she'd heard fall from the queen's lips a hundred times or more.

"No." He shifted his weight and pressed one frail hand over hers. "We choose whether we walk through life alone or not. We choose to let people in or to shut them out."

"If you let people in, it only hurts worse when they leave." Her voice shook and the hand Father held felt like ice.

"Sometimes grief is the price of love." His hand trembled a bit, and she turned hers over so she could lace her fingers through his. "But it's always a price worth paying."

"Is it?" The ache in her chest sank into her bones until she felt brittle enough to break.

"Who left you, Charis?" he asked quietly.

She shook her head. If she said Milla's name, it would be real. It would be final. There were no lies between her and Father, and she couldn't bear to speak the irrevocable truth.

"That's all right." He gathered her close, and she leaned against him once more. "Let the grief hurt for as long as it needs to, sweet girl. Just breathe your way through it."

A sob shook her and then another. He rubbed her back gently as she cried until the last streak of light was long gone from the sky and the blue light of the sister moons danced across the distant ribbon of the sea. Even when the tears stopped, she remained in his arms, breathing past the ache until she drifted into sleep.

NINE

THE WEEK FOLLOWING Milla's death passed in a blur. Charis attended luncheons, sat through meetings, shouldered Mother's obligations along with her own, did homework for her tutor, and checked on Mother daily. She sent supplies to the army stationed in the north, pulling from the palace's own budget to pay for extra guards to make sure they arrived safely, and sent gifts to the ambassadors of Rullenvor, Verace, Thallis, and Solvang in an effort to keep the picture of a prosperous Calera firmly intact. She demanded daily reports from Reuben on the progress of shoring up palace security and discussed rumors of Montevallo's spy network with the head of Mother's guard. Every moment was filled, every second accounted for. She smiled when it was necessary. Held eye contact when someone needed a reminder of her power. And spoke the right words at the right times.

Tal woke early each morning and stayed by her side until she'd climbed, exhausted, into bed at night. She was almost used to his silent, watchful presence, but it was impossible to escape the fact that there was nowhere she could go to be alone. Nowhere she could drop her defenses and let the loss of Milla knock her down in one devastating blow.

Instead, it took pieces of her, bit by bit, a sly, poisonous knife that cut into her when she least expected it.

When a mukkel bird perched on the balcony early one morning and sang its shrill, piercing song, and she remembered the last time a mukkel bird visited and how Milla had marveled at the brilliant purple of its feathers.

When she caught a glimpse of a redheaded girl moving through the busy market streets of Arborlay and had to ask the coachmen to stop the carriage so she could stare long enough to convince herself it wasn't Milla she was seeing.

When she stepped into the bath chamber or sat at her vanity or heard Tal moving around in the room that should still be Milla's.

There was no end to the little reminders lying in wait for her, and bracing for the next cut was exhausting.

"Will there be anything else, Your Highness?" Tal asked as he always did just before she dismissed him to his room so the temporary handmaiden Mother had assigned could help Charis into her nightdress before leaving for the servants' quarters where she slept.

"No, thank you," Charis answered as she always did, the words pushed past wooden lips as she busied herself with removing her shoes, refusing to watch him enter Milla's room.

Her fingers shook a little as she fumbled the buttons on her dainty pair of boots—whether from weariness or because she couldn't stand to swallow more than a few bites at meals of late, Charis didn't know. Didn't care. All she wanted was the sweet oblivion of sleep.

Moments later, she curled up under her blankets, staring at the ceiling while the maid turned down the lanterns and left the chamber. Her thoughts moved sluggishly from one thing to the next.

Father's failing health. The factions that had split the nobility. The woman in her bathtub. The assassin burying his dagger in Mother's stomach.

Milla paying the cost.

Her eyelids fluttered closed, and she sank gratefully into the darkness.

There was a sound—a steady *drip, drip, drip* like fat raindrops gathering at the end of a tree branch and then plummeting to the ground. Charis tried to follow it, but it remained just out of reach. Now in front of her. Now behind her. Now just a faint echo she could barely hear.

Her feet sank into the plush rug of her bedchamber, except it wasn't her rug anymore. It was a carpet of bones, crisp and brittle, that crackled when she stepped on them.

She turned back toward her bed, but it was her bathtub instead. The assassin lay within it, grinning at her though blood poured from his wounds.

"You can't run, Princess." His teeth lengthened into fangs. "There are more of us and only one of you."

Blood from his neck gathered at his collarbone and then plunged to the floor. *Drip. Drip. Drip.*

"You can't run," a soft voice whispered from behind Charis. She spun toward it, and was inside her closet, her dresses thick as a forest of trees closing in around her while the walls echoed the horrible sound of the assassin's blood hitting the floor.

"Milla?" She pushed through a billowing cloud of silk and lace that shredded at her touch like jewel-toned fog.

Her feet slid on something viscous and wet, and she was back in her bath chamber, her knees striking the tub as she struggled to keep her balance. The walls tilted, and the steady *drip, drip, drip* burrowed beneath her skin and thrummed within her like a second heartbeat.

A hand reached out from the tub and wrapped around her wrist. She looked down to see Milla, pale and broken, her mouth a wide slash of red in her too-white face as she whispered, "You can't run."

A scream tore its way past Charis's throat as she tried to free herself from Milla's grip, her feet skidding through the blood on the floor.

She was going to be pulled into that tub, and there was nothing she could do to stop it.

"Your Highness!" A firm voice broke into her thoughts, and the dream disintegrated. Her eyes flew open. Tal sat on the side of her bed, his hands on her shoulders, his face hovering just above hers. His eyes blazed with worry. "Are you hurt?"

"I can't run," she whispered as the sound of dripping blood faded along with the feel of Milla's death grip on her wrist.

He frowned. "Run from what?"

She shrugged his hands away and sat up, her heart thundering.

He leaned back but still watched her closely. When she said nothing, he said quietly, "Bad dream?"

She nodded without meeting his eyes. She ought to reassure him that it was nothing and then dismiss him, but the sound of the blood was still too near. Her voice was faint as she said, "Could you . . . I thought I heard something."

They both knew she hadn't heard anything, but he didn't hesitate. "I'll check your chambers immediately, Your Highness."

Her heartbeat settled as he moved through the bedroom, the closet, the sitting room, and finally the bath chamber, checking any place that could possibly hide an intruder. The ache within eased, and she drew a deep, cleansing breath as he returned to the bed.

"All clear, Your Highness. It's just the two of us."

She blinked as his words settled in.

Just the two of them.

Glancing down at herself, she snatched a blanket and drew it up to her neck. For seers' sakes, she'd been sitting there in her lacy nightgown in front of a guard. It was a small mercy there were no lanterns lit so he could see the flush of mortification burning in her cheeks.

And then she looked properly at him for the first time and realized he was wearing loose linen pajama pants and no shirt. The flush in her cheeks spread down her neck.

He seemed to realize their predicament at the same moment and took a step back, turning his face toward the wall as if to give her privacy.

There was nothing left to do but dismiss him to his room. She would be regal and remote—a princess establishing clear boundaries and erasing all evidence of her previous vulnerability. With this plan in place, she opened her mouth, but he spoke first.

"I had terrible nightmares after I arrived here." His voice was quiet and steady. "Sometimes reading a book helps. Gives you something else to think about."

"Oh."

So much for responding like a regal princess. She clutched the blanket higher, though he'd yet to look at her again.

"Do you want to talk about it?" he asked.

Put words to the images in her head so they could become real and haunt her during the day the way they did at night? Absolutely not.

"I think I'll just try to go back to sleep."

He hesitated for a moment and then said, "Yes, Your Highness."

As he walked toward his room, the quiet echo of the assassin's blood dripping from his wounds scraped against her thoughts, and she bit her tongue to keep from asking him to stay.

She barely knew him. What possible comfort could his presence bring her? The belief that a warm body in the room with her could somehow stave off the darkness that lingered in her mind was foolish. He needed his sleep, and she could at least have the courtesy to pretend she was going to be able to fall asleep too.

But when he reached the doorway that led into his room, he paused and said, "With your permission, I'd like to leave my door open, just for tonight. That way if you need anything, I'll be able to hear you immediately. Would that be all right?"

Relief flooded her, leaving her hands shaky and her throat tight.

She could stay connected to someone—someone real and present and alive—and maybe that would be enough to keep the nightmares at bay, at least for the night.

"That's fine, thank you, Tal." Her voice wasn't quite as steady as she'd hoped, but it didn't seem to matter. He entered his room, and this time, instead of flinching as she heard him moving around its space, she took comfort in the fact that she wasn't alone.

TEN

CHARIS KEPT HERSELF busy for the next two weeks. Every moment was filled with something to do. She woke to the somewhat clumsy ministrations of Mrs. Sykes, the much older handmaiden Mother had assigned to her, skipped breakfast on the excuse that she didn't have time, threw herself into weapons training or horse rides, and then put poor Darold through his paces as she demanded he fill any opening on her calendar with *something*.

Something to keep her mind occupied.

Something to keep her body moving.

Something to fill the unexpected quiet moments when grief over Milla and worry over Mother's slow recovery could find her.

There were committee meetings to chair, tutoring sessions with Holland and Nalani, royal council sessions where she levied sanctions against the four families who hadn't paid their taxes and worked to find an acceptable response to Montevallo's actions, visits to struggling merchants to help spread the word that the princess herself shopped there, christenings of new buildings, the launching of the latest naval vessel, military parade reviews to observe, refugee assistance to oversee, horse races to bet on, ballet or theater performances to view, and a host of teas, dinners, or other social visits that quickly cluttered up her calendar.

She barely ate. Barely slept. Her clothes needed to be taken in at the waist, and her fingers shook when she hefted her sword, but she refused to slow down.

The latest group of injured soldiers had returned from the war-front the previous day, among them the daughter of the palace weapons master. He'd left his post to nurse her back to health, and while Charis sincerely wished them both well, his absence left a gaping hole in her morning schedule. A hole she desperately needed to fill with something other than sitting in her little parlor ignoring both breakfast and the ache of Milla's absence.

Sinking into a plush chair in her parlor, she tapped her fingers on the small marble table in front of her while she ran through her options. She could call Darold up early for their morning meeting, but it wasn't fair to deny him his breakfast. She might get an early start on the essay her tutor had assigned the previous day, but that would require concentration, and it was hard to focus when she hadn't yet had any physical exercise.

Maybe she would just take a horse and ride the grounds. Visit the lonely bluff overlooking the sea on the far southern edge of the property. If she left now, she could be back before—

"I've brought you breakfast, Your Highness." Tal startled her by placing a tray in front of her. A bowl of creamy porridge sprinkled with ground nuts and spices sat in the center with a sliced nectarine to the left and a steaming cup of tea to the right.

"I didn't order breakfast. I'm not hungry."

"Yes, you are."

She froze and lifted her gaze to his, all thoughts of her schedule abandoned. "*What* did you just say?"

He'd been the soul of discretion and polite protocol. She'd gotten used to having his quiet, watchful presence with her wherever she went. She hardly needed her silent guard dog to start voicing opinions.

He looked determined. "You need to eat, Your Highness."

Her eyes narrowed, but he held her gaze. She didn't know him well enough to read his expression, but she was absolutely sure he could see the anger in hers.

"I realize you are rather new to working with me, and that Father maintains a more relaxed protocol with his staff, so I will give you this one warning." Her voice was chilly. "Nobody talks to me like that."

"I realize that, Your Highness, but maybe someone should." His voice was as steady as his gaze, but there was a steely hint of stubbornness in it. "I wish it didn't have to be me, but here we are."

Her chin rose. "You are perilously close to finding yourself without a job."

"And you are perilously close to a full breakdown." He inclined his head and said quietly, "Your Highness, you will either hear this from me, or you will be hearing it from your father, and I think we both want to spare him the worry of seeing you like this."

She'd drawn a breath to give him a scathing retort, but her words dried up as his hit home. She'd avoided Father for most of the past two weeks on the excuse that she was so busy, though if she was brutally honest with herself, she knew it was because he would see right through her. He'd worry over her weight loss and fuss about her running herself into the ground. His love would shatter the shield she wore, and she would be undone.

Tal, as if sensing that she was softening, bent closer. "I don't know what to say to you to help you feel better, Your Highness. I don't think there are words for your loss. But I can bring you food. I can help you clear your schedule so you can get some rest—"

"I don't want to rest." The truth left her mouth without permission, and she flinched inwardly.

He crouched beside her. "I know you don't, but you aren't going to have a choice soon."

"I can't afford to slow down." She'd meant her voice to be dismissive, but instead it came out weary, wearing pale shades of the grief that lived within.

"You can't afford not to."

She looked out the parlor windows as the pale light of dawn warmed into the golden haze of an autumn morning. "I know. My kingdom needs me. My mother expects me to . . . well, she needs me too."

"They can do without for a few days," he said flatly.

She glanced at him in surprise.

"What do *you* need, Your Highness? Besides breakfast." He looked pointedly at the tray.

No one other than Father and Milla had ever asked her that. She hardly knew what to say, but she knew sharing her innermost thoughts with her bodyguard was a terrible idea. Never mind that he'd seen what was happening to her and had cared enough to intervene. She'd let herself become friends with Milla, and that had been a mistake she was still paying for. She couldn't afford to let another staff member get close.

He was still patiently watching her as though expecting she would give him the truth. She reached for the first thing she could think of that would give him something to do besides wait for her to unburden her heart while eating breakfast.

"The palace weapons master has taken a leave of absence to care for his daughter, which leaves me with no one to spar with in the mornings. I need a replacement for him." She turned away, satisfied that he would at least leave the parlor to—

"Done."

"What do you mean *done*?" she demanded.

"I'll spar with you."

She clenched her jaw. "You'll do no such thing."

"Afraid of losing?" He gave her a crooked little smile, and something in her flared to life for the first time in two weeks.

"I'm not afraid of anything."

"Does that include eating breakfast?" He looked pointedly at the tray.

They stared at each other for a full minute, and Charis waited for him to break. To incline his head and murmur "Your Highness" at the very least. Instead, he held her gaze, a challenge in his, and she found herself rising to the bait.

Not because he'd intrigued her.

Because if she didn't, he'd tell Father.

Grabbing the spoon, she shoved it into the porridge and said, "I want it clear that I know you're trying to manipulate me, and it isn't working."

He raised a single brow as if to cast aspersions upon her statement as she took a bite, but said simply, "Of course."

"And I also want it clear that Father doesn't hear a single word of your concerns."

"Happy to oblige as long as those concerns are being addressed."

He caught a glimpse of her expression and tacked on a hasty "Your Highness."

She ate three more bites, irritated to discover that the food tasted good. "One last thing, Tal."

"Yes?"

"No one goes easy on me in sparring practice."

His crooked little smile returned. "I wouldn't dream of it, Your Highness."

Forty minutes later, they stood facing each other in the courtyard outside the palace armory, their swords corked to avoid causing fatal injuries. Charis had more energy than she'd had in days, thanks to the breakfast her bodyguard had practically forced her to eat. He'd been right to insist on it, not that she was going to admit that to him. A collapse would've sent a message of weakness to Calera's allies and enemies alike, and that simply couldn't happen while the queen was recuperating and unable to leave her chambers.

Plus, she'd have scared Father, and she couldn't bear that.

"Ready when you are," Tal said.

Charis hefted her blade. She knew he must be skilled, or Father would never have installed him as her bodyguard. It was time to see just how good he was. "Each touch counts as a point. Best two out of three wins the round."

He adjusted his grip on his sword hilt and slid his feet into attack position.

Lunging forward, she jabbed her blade toward his chest.

He pivoted, lightly nudging her blade with his own as he danced out of the way.

Graceful, then. And quick.

She anticipated his follow-through and ducked just as his blade whistled over her head. Spinning, she struck his side. Or she would have if he'd still been in front of her.

Whirling, her blade rising, she met his attack, her pulse racing as the grooms called to each other in the nearby stables, the palace smithy hammered out an ax-head with a sharp *clang*, and the distant call of a flock of gulls disappeared. All that was left was the fight. Anticipating his next move and the three beyond that even as she planned out her own. The scrape of sword on sword and the huff of her breathing.

He grinned and swept out of the way as she attacked again. His feet shifted like a dancer's, sweeping, intricate movements that pulled his body gracefully in and out of attack range, his blade moving ever closer to getting the first touch.

How was he doing that? It was taking all her considerable skill to keep up with him, and she had the sudden, stomach-squeezing worry that he was going to beat her.

She was the princess. She had to be the strongest.

Her jaw set, she parried his next blow and then attacked, pivoting, thrusting, and swinging her blade in a series of lightning-fast moves. He met her, blow for blow; the air filled with the metallic hiss of clashing blades.

Lunging forward, she jabbed, and then yelped in surprise as he disappeared beneath her sword and rolled to his feet behind her, his blade tapping her back before she could recover.

"Your point," she said, graciously enough, though it was an effort not to bare her teeth at him.

"You're really good," he said. The admiration in his voice sounded sincere.

"So are you. Where were you trained?"

He shrugged. "It's a long story."

"I'm listening."

He paused, as though choosing which memories to share, and she had the uncomfortable realization that once again she was inviting friendship from a member of her private staff. Except this wasn't friendship. This was polite conversation, and she could easily leave it at that.

"I grew up in the north." His voice was soft, and she thought she caught a hint of longing in it. "We had plenty of opportunities to see Montevallo's soldiers practicing. We'd creep out to their camps and watch them. I would go home and mimic what I saw until I was proficient at using their fighting method."

"You know the seven rathmas?" She looked at him with new interest. No wonder he was so difficult to beat. The rathmas were a combination of dance and fight moves, highly prized in Montevallo and guarded fiercely by all its citizens. Not a single person interrogated in the palace or Calera's military outposts had ever given up its secrets. They'd claimed to, but when the Caleran swordsmen tried to imitate what they'd been told, the method had always been a failure.

"I do." He gave her that crooked smile. "Why? Having trouble beating me because of it?"

"I'm not worried." She feinted left, dived right, and swung her blade at his knees.

He leaped over the weapon, danced beyond her reach, and then whirled back so close, the tip of her braid brushed against his arm as she parried his blow.

This was getting ridiculous. She couldn't lose their first sparring session.

He pivoted and came for her, and she lunged sideways, stumbling as if she'd injured herself. Gasping, she doubled over, her free hand clutching her leg.

There was more than one way to win a fight.

"Are you all right?" He sounded worried as he lowered his sword and approached.

He leaned down to look at her injured leg, and she whipped up her blade, pressing its corked tip beneath his chin. Slowly they straightened, her sword held steady, his eyes on hers.

"You cheated." He sounded amused.

"There's no such thing as a fair fight. There are simply those who live to fight another battle, and those who don't."

He looked at her for a long moment as though hunting for something in her expression. Finally, he said quietly, "Your point."

They fought hard for the third point. Charis's muscles were starting to burn, and Tal was breathing heavily. Finally, ducking and feinting, she raised her sword as if to strike from above, and as his eyes followed her arm, she slid her leg behind him, hooked it beneath his knees, and brought him down onto his back. Hard.

Instantly, she knelt on his chest and pressed the corked edge of her blade to his neck.

"My point," she said.

"Your point." He gestured at his chest. "Mind if I take a breath?"

She surprised herself by laughing. Standing, she reached down to help him to his feet. His callused hand was warm in hers.

"Shall we do this again tomorrow?" Tal asked.

"Only if you promise to teach me the seven rathmas."

"Of course. As long as you promise to eat three meals a day."

She glared at him, and he bowed his head and said, "Your Highness." She could swear she saw the hint of a smile on his lips.

ELEVEN

AN HOUR LATER, the palace was bustling, guard shift change had happened, and Charis was bathed, dressed, and staring in dismay at the severe updo her new handmaiden, Mrs. Sykes, had insisted was proper for a princess.

Really, Mother had some explaining to do. This handmaiden appointment was an unmitigated disaster. Perhaps allowances could be made since Mother was still bedridden and barely had enough energy for more than a few conversations a day, but still.

Charis ought to dismiss the older woman on the spot, but along with terrible taste in fashion and hairdos, Mrs. Sykes was a talker. Charis had learned the names of each of the woman's five children and seven grandchildren. The fact that her husband was too ill to work anymore, and that getting a promotion from chambermaid to handmaiden had given them enough income both to get his medicine and heat their cottage through the winter, rather than having to choose between the two.

Charis couldn't possibly send her back to chambermaid status now.

"There, now." Mrs. Sykes patted Charis's hair, which strained against the hairpins that held it but dared not spring free under the woman's watchful eyes. "And with that lovely brown dress, you look most suitable." She lifted a basket and went into the bath chamber to gather up the day's laundry.

Tal, who'd bathed in the chamber after Charis had finished, yelped and hurried out, shirtless, his blond hair dripping, a towel clutched in his hands.

"It's nothing I haven't seen before, dearie," Mrs. Sykes said comfortably as she snatched the towel out of his hand and added it to her basket. "I'll be back in your chambers this afternoon if you should need to refresh your hair, Your Highness. It does like to do its own thing." She gave Charis's head a pitying look and left.

"That woman needs to learn how to *knock*," Tal said, glaring at the door that had shut behind the handmaiden. "I barely got my pants on before she— Oh, seers preserve us, what has she done to you?" He was staring at Charis.

"That bad?" She lifted a self-conscious hand to pat the painfully tight bun that rested high on the back of her head.

"No! I mean, it's not . . . you look . . ." He glanced around wildly as if the appropriate word was simply waiting in midair for him to find. "You look nice?"

"It always inspires confidence when a compliment has a question mark at the end of it."

He winced. "My apologies, Your Highness. I just . . . your new look took me by surprise."

"That makes two of us." Charis sighed as she stared at the high-collared dress the color of dirt. "I didn't even know I owned something like this."

"I suggest burning it immediately."

He stood behind her in her mirror, water running in small rivulets down his bare skin, and Charis was suddenly aware of the rise and fall of his chest. The way his muscles rippled as he moved. And then, to her horror, the way he was watching her stare at him. Wrenching her gaze back to her own face in the mirror, she said, "You are awfully free with your suggestions today."

"You must admit that this one is my best."

She grinned before she thought better of it. Immediately she wiped her expression clean and said stiffly, "You were so quiet for the past two weeks that I'd become used to it. You must take care not to become overly familiar, especially in front of others."

A frown marred his forehead. "I apologize for overstepping, Your Highness."

She ought to leave it at that. A simple rebuke to put him back in his place. No harm to either of them, and she could safely move through her life without allowing him to leave a mark on it.

But there was something in his eyes that reminded her of the nights when she'd creep out of the palace to her favorite bluff because she was sick of being surrounded by nothing but those who wanted her to fail and those who wanted her to succeed only so she could use her power for their own benefit. Nights when it was hard to convince herself she could trust anyone.

When the loneliness of her position became unbearable.

What would it feel like to be so far from home—a home that was now occupied by the enemy—and to spend every waking moment with a princess who refused to even be friendly with you?

She could at least let him feel comfortable with her. She didn't have to truly be friends with him.

She sighed as he turned toward his room. "Tal."

"Your Highness?"

"Do you think you could do a better job of finding a suitable dress for my day while I try to rescue my hair from this unfortunate bun?" Meeting his eyes, she let some warmth enter her face. "And you aren't overstepping in my chambers with just me here. But if you were to speak that way in front of Reuben or the queen, we would have a problem."

He gave her a small smile, though there was still a shadow of sadness in his eyes. "Thank you, Your Highness. Give me a moment to finish getting myself ready, and we'll see what we can do about"—he gestured from her head to her feet—"that."

Twenty minutes later, Charis was wearing a dress in bold green with intricately embroidered brambles at the hem and a sash in lighter green that looked like snake scales. Tal had helped her button it, a process slowed significantly by the fact that he refused to look at her naked back and kept fumbling for the next button.

"Better." Charis looked in the mirror and patted her hair, which was now back to its usual curls. She'd swept it over one shoulder and pinned the opposite down to give it a sense of style. It was the best she could do. She was already late for tutoring.

"Better," Tal agreed with a smile. "Ready?"

She assumed a cold expression and lifted her chin. "Ready."

"You're late, but just in time to help me win an argument with Holland." Nalani met Charis at the doorway of the fifth-floor palace library. Her sleek black hair fell in a sheet down her back, and her golden skin glowed in the morning sunlight pouring in through the narrow windows that rose from the top of the shelves to the ceiling.

Caleb Brannigan, tutor to the princess and her cousins, raised his eyes to the ceiling as if searching for patience. His tightly coiled black curls were precisely coifed, his serviceable day coat didn't dare show a single wrinkle, and his plain cravat remained stiffly at attention around his throat, its snowy fabric gleaming against his dark brown skin. Only the ink stains on his fingertips betrayed his meticulous appearance.

"Good morning, Your Highness," he said in his deep baritone, the slight creases at the corners of his eyes deepening as he smiled at her. "Tal."

"Good morning, Mr. Brannigan," Charis said politely as Reuben and Elsbet took up positions outside the library, while Tal entered the room and stood beside the door.

Brannigan had been their tutor for the past three years and had never displayed even a whiff of interest in anything the three of them did outside of his rigorous assignments, but still, Charis was careful in his presence. He reported directly to the queen, and as far as Charis was concerned, that meant he was yet another pair of eyes watching her every move, ensuring that she met Mother's rigid expectations with perfection every moment of every day.

"So what argument am I solving today?" Charis asked as she took a seat beside Nalani at the library's table.

Holland sat across from them, his papers already organized in front of him. "Apparently, I'm not supposed to wear my sword to the tea Mother is insisting I attend later today." He sounded aggrieved.

"Holland, if I've told you once, I've told you a thousand times: you cannot wear a sword to teas, brunches, dinners, or balls." Nalani opened her leather satchel and took her own papers out.

"You didn't have a problem with it when I wore it to Lady Channing's dinner party last night."

"You wore your sword to the dinner party?" Nalani's voice was faint as she slowly sank back against her chair. When he looked askance at her, she waved a hand weakly in his direction as if somehow absolving him of guilt. "No, no, I blame myself. I was too preoccupied with a tear in my dress to properly look at what you were wearing beneath your dress coat."

"I wasn't wearing a dress coat." Holland sounded offended.

"Well, when you go to tea today, you're going to wear something nicer than what you have on now. I am *this close* to getting a sizable donation from Lady Shawling for the refugee center, and you are not ruining that," Nalani said in a voice that brooked no argument. "And you'll leave the weapon at home. Nobody wears a sword in polite company."

"There's nothing polite about an afternoon tea at Lady Shawling's house," Holland said.

"Charis, help me." Nalani shot her cousin a pleading look.

Charis's lips twitched, though she was careful to hide any hint of amusement when Nalani's eyes met hers. She reached for her own papers as Brannigan cleared his throat in a signal that it was time to get started. "At this point, anyone who invites Holland to an event knows exactly what they're getting themselves into," she said.

"While I hate to interrupt what is truly a fascinating discussion," Brannigan said, "I must insist that you hand in your mathematics and your outlines for your papers on the history of Calera's relationships with the other kingdoms of the sea. Once you've given those to me, you will conjugate the following list of verbs in Solvanish and then use them each properly in a sentence." He placed a neatly written list of fifty words before them on the table and collected their papers.

"Doesn't the fact that our father is Solvanish get us out of this assignment?" Nalani grumbled.

"No, it does not." Brannigan looked stern.

For the next two hours, the only sounds in the library were the soft scratching of quills against paper as the three students worked to master the intricacies of Solvang's language, the rustle of star maps as they charted the next month's placement of the sister moons in the night sky, and the drone of their voices as they read aloud historical accounts of ancient battles written in old Caleran, a language that always felt to Charis as though she was adding too many syllables to every word.

They'd just put away the old texts and reached for their mathematics work when there was a sharp knock at the door, followed immediately by the entrance of a page who gave a short bow toward Charis and then handed her a piece of paper sealed with the queen's purple wax, which was still slightly pliable to the touch.

Charis pried the wax seal apart and quickly read the queen's note. Heat flooded her veins, and her heart thundered in her ears as she read it again, slowly, letting every word sink in.

"Your Highness?" the page prompted, her eyes wide and anxious. Clearly, the queen had instructed her not to leave without a response.

Charis looked up and found the page, Tal, Holland, and Nalani watching her closely. Brannigan was, as usual, examining the stack of papers in front of him as if he wasn't paying the slightest attention to anything Charis did that didn't directly relate to his instruction.

Her throat tightened, and she had to swallow hard before speaking. Forcing her voice to sound quiet and steady, though she couldn't quite rid it of the horror that gripped her, she said, "Tell the queen I'll be there shortly."

When the page closed the library door behind her, Charis turned to the others. "Mr. Brannigan, I'm afraid I need to cut this session short. If there are homework assignments, please send them directly to my secretary. I'll get to them as soon as I'm able."

"What's happened?" Holland uncoiled in his seat, his hand on the hilt of the sword strapped to his hips.

"Charis?" Nalani sounded worried, though, like her brother, she looked ready to stand at the princess's side and face whatever was coming.

"Last night, Montevallo raided farther into our territory than they ever have." Horror tightened around her throat like a noose. "They ignored our military outposts and bypassed the southern flank of our army. Instead, they attacked a town called Irridusk."

"A town? Were any soldiers stationed there?" Holland rose to his feet as if he could take Montevallo in that instant.

"No." Charis spat the word out. Let its terrible truth fall, a dead weight that shattered on impact.

"But then . . . who defended the town?" Nalani looked from Charis to Holland as if one of them could give her an answer that would wipe out the horror she knew was coming. Even Brannigan dropped his pretense of paying attention to his papers and watched Charis closely.

"No one." Charis let her fury scorch the noose around her throat and drew a breath that seared her lungs like fire. "They were massacred. A village of farmers, and there's nothing left but destroyed homes and the bodies of the older men, women, and children who lived there. A few escaped and brought word to the nearest military outpost, but by the time our soldiers arrived, it was too late."

Tal made a noise in the back of his throat, and Charis met his stricken gaze for a moment.

"I'm joining the army." Holland drew his sword. "I don't care if I'm a year away from being of age."

"Mother will never allow—"

"Well, we can't just keep doing nothing but going to useless balls and teas and lessons as if half of our kingdom isn't a smoking ruin." Holland's voice shook.

"What we're doing isn't useless," Nalani said quietly. "We're learning to help Charis lead the kingdom. We're forging relationships with those whose coffers we will need, whose connections we will exploit, and whose children we might very well send to war one day. We're building their trust, learning their secrets, and putting ourselves in a position to be of use when Charis takes the throne. And seers forbid, if something happens to Charis, you're next in line and need to know what to do."

"There won't be a throne to take if Montevallo isn't stopped." Holland raised his sword to emphasize his point.

Charis rose too, her movements fluid and precise, her body craving the feel of a weapon in her hand, though she knew it was more complicated than that. If weapons alone could win the war, it would already be won. But fighting a kingdom that could hide in the mountains and see the Caleran army coming from any direction, a kingdom that had started the war by assassinating Charis's grandmother, that had enslaved a swath of northern territory, and that killed innocent farmers and soldiers alike as if there was no difference required more than weapons. It required strategy. Cunning. And a ruthless will to do whatever had to be done to protect Calera's people.

Charis let rage sink into her blood until it felt like courage.

Whatever it took to find justice for her people and bring Montevallo to its knees, Charis was going to do it.

TWELVE

CHARIS MARCHED ACROSS the grand hall, Tal one step behind, while Reuben and Elsbet flanked them both. Her blood ran hot. Her thoughts felt sharp as knives.

Montevallo had to be stopped. Her people couldn't continue to survive such atrocities, and if King Alaric kept sending assassins, the royal family might not be able to survive either. But how could they stop Montevallo when they couldn't effectively take the fight to them? Every other solution proposed by the council involved giving King Alaric the territory he'd already taken in the north, and that was unacceptable.

"Your Highness." Reuben interrupted her thoughts as they neared the door of the war room.

"What is it?"

"This latest act of aggression from Montevallo, coupled with the attempt on the queen's life three weeks ago and the presence of another spy in your chambers, underscores the need to be sure we surround you only with staff we absolutely trust."

Something hot and razor-tipped unfurled in Charis's chest, and she stopped walking to face him. "Very well. I accept your resignation."

He blinked, and there was fury in his eyes. "I'm not offering it."

"Oh, then what were you offering to do?" Charis's words sliced the air, full of rage and grief. "Kill more of my staff?"

A vein throbbed in his neck, but his voice was even. "If necessary."

She wanted to argue. To dismiss him on the spot. But they both knew the person who ultimately decided if Reuben would kill again, the person who kept him in his current position, was the one person in the kingdom who outranked Charis.

Charis changed tactics. "I fail to see how an invasion of a small town in the north has anything to do with my staff."

Reuben's gaze slid to Tal. "Under the circumstances, I think it best to only have staff who come from the city of Arborlay or the surrounding countryside."

The hot, sharp thing in Charis's chest grew. Tal, who'd done nothing but faithfully serve her father and then her. Who'd seen that she was falling apart and had stepped in to make sure she took care of herself. Who seemed to want nothing more than some friendly conversation and to do his job well. This was the boy Reuben had decided shouldn't be trusted?

"I disagree," she said in a tone that brooked no discussion. "Under the circumstances, I think our people from the north have the most reason to be loyal to me."

Tal shifted on his feet, but Charis only had eyes for Reuben, whose lip was curling in scorn.

"Unless they blame you for the loss of their families and property. Or unless they have loved ones enslaved by Montevallo, making them ripe for bribery." Reuben waved a hand at Tal as if dismissing him.

"You barely know him. There's no loyalty or relationship built here yet. I'll find you a bodyguard who—"

"I've known Tal for over a year. And my father chose him." Charis took a step toward Reuben and imagined it was his head sliding off his neck. Her sword making the fatal cut. She let her wicked thoughts play on her face, and Reuben rolled to the balls of his feet as if sensing a threat closing in.

"Your father is a good man, of course, but he is also from the north." Reuben sounded regretful, as though sorry to admit that the king couldn't be trusted either.

Charis had her dagger in her hand before Reuben could react. Pressing it against the guard's throat she said softly, "If you ever disparage my father's character again, I will kill you myself. And I'll make sure it *hurts*."

"The queen wouldn't allow—"

"The queen wouldn't be fast enough to save you, and I'm her heir." Charis spat the words at him. "Do you really think you matter more to her than me?"

Silence fell on the corridor. She held his gaze and waited until he looked away. Without another word, she sheathed her dagger and entered the queen's chambers, Tal at her heels. The door closed behind her with a snap.

Mother lay propped up against her pillows, a scarlet robe wrapped around her. Her hair was pulled back and papers lay scattered on the bedclothes around her. Charis was grateful to note that while she still looked pale and wan, she was no longer trembling at the slightest bit of activity.

Drawing in a slow, deep breath, Charis pushed her fury back into a corner of her heart and reached for the icy calm necessary for surviving interactions with the queen. "Your Majesty." She bowed. "Before we talk about Irridusk, we need to discuss Reuben."

"What is there to discuss?" Mother locked eyes with her.

The fact that he reported everything he saw to the queen. The fact that he'd effectively sentenced Milla, Fada, and Luther to death and had then carried out the sentence. The way he enjoyed bloodshed and the censure in his voice when he spoke to Charis.

A list of things she didn't dare bring to Mother. Instead, she said, "I don't trust his judgment."

"Reuben is your head guard."

"Reuben is a man who craves violence and fear and constantly needs to be reminded that he has no power over me."

Mother's smile was sly. "I would think delivering a reminder like that would be child's play for you."

"I grow weary of it." Charis took a seat beside the bed. "I'd prefer for those closest to me to be people I can fully trust."

Something dangerous flashed in the queen's eyes. "There is no one you can fully trust. To rule is to be alone. Every person in your life wants something from you. Every person would turn on you for the right price. Everyone loves power more than they will ever love you, and if removing you will give them more power, they'll do it. You must be the most ruthless, most cunning, most dangerous person in the room. Always. I thought you understood that."

"I do." Charis turned away, her gaze skimming the maps on the wall. Of course she knew she wasn't supposed to trust anyone. Mother had made sure to carve that lesson deep into Charis's heart. She knew to keep her guard up and her sword sharp. Was it wrong to wish that, just once, she didn't have to?

"Even your closest friends cannot be fully trusted." Mother's voice was cold. "You can never be sure if they love you, or if they love the idea of being close to the throne."

"I understand." Charis kept her voice as icy as the queen's. "But I must be able to trust my head guard's judgment of others, and I do not."

"Well, I do, so that is the end of that."

Charis nodded obediently, despite the anger that seethed within her.

"Now—" The queen coughed and quickly snatched a pillow to press against her abdomen, her mouth tight with pain.

"Can I help?" Charis leaned forward.

"I'm fine." The queen set the pillow aside, but now her hands trembled slightly. It wouldn't be long before she would need to rest. "The council members have been summoned."

"I'm heading to the war room after this."

"We need a strong response to King Alaric Penbyrn . . ." The queen's voice trailed off, and she sank deeper into her pillows.

"Don't worry, Mother." Charis stood. "I'll make sure of it."

Thirty minutes later, Charis left Reuben and Elsbet stationed in the corridor and entered the war room. It was Tal's afternoon off, and she'd overridden his protests that the attack on Irridusk meant she needed extra protection in favor of sending him to the stables or the kitchens or wherever it was he spent his few free hours a week. Guarding her nonstop had to be a taxing job. She wasn't going to force him to go without a break, especially when the current threat was so far away.

The war room was a long rectangle with an enormous window at the east end overlooking the streets of Arborlay, where homes with white stone walls and colorful roofs wound down the hill below the palace until they reached the shore. Maps of Montevallo, Calera, and the vast sea with its six other kingdoms, the basilisk cave, and the warren of treacherous islands, outcroppings, and whirlpools that littered the northern waters beyond the kingdom of Embre were mounted to the south wall. Battle plans, known troop outposts, and the locations of Montevallo's biggest towns were mounted to the north wall. In the center, a long oval table surrounded by chairs sat waiting for the council members to arrive.

The door opened, and Lady Channing entered, her sensible green dress devoid of all frills except for the sea glass brooch she wore at her throat. Lord Everly entered just behind her, his expression as dour as his dull gray doublet and vest. He was Mother's third cousin. He was also firmly in the group who advocated for annexing the north to Montevallo and being done with the war.

The ladies Whitecross and Ollen walked in soon after, their bold dresses, one in apricot and one in sunset orange, giving the impression that they were two sides of the same flame. Lady Whitecross's bold sapphire necklace glowed against her brown skin, and Lady Ollen wore a trio of ostentatious rings on her pale hands to complement her outfit. Both ladies advocated fiercely for Calera to invade Montevallo, raiding and pillaging until there was nothing left of the mountain kingdom but ash and regret.

The last pair to enter the room was Admiral Peyton, her high cheekbones and golden skin reminding Charis of Nalani, and Lord Jamison Thorsby, the head of the council, his black curls perfectly positioned, his blue cravat tied just so, and a matching blue handkerchief in his hand to dab at the gleam of sweat on his dark brow.

Mimicking her mother's sword-straight posture and cold expression, Charis nodded a greeting to each council member and then went straight to the heart of the issue.

"General Thane left this morning to assess the situation in Irri-dusk," she said. "All of you received the information we have at present. The farming town was attacked in the middle of the night. Every building was burned to the ground. Every inhabitant who didn't manage to run away when the fighting started is dead."

Her voice was a winter storm, cold and deadly. "We will not waste our breath decrying this monstrosity and raging at its injus-tice. Instead, we will look closely at Montevallo's strategy so that we can understand their motives for doing this. And we will formulate a response that will have King Alaric wishing he'd kept his army in the mountains where it belongs."

"I want it on record that I believe we should invade Montevallo and burn one of their cities," Lady Whitecross said, her brown eyes glowing with fury.

"So that our soldiers can be picked off one by one with bows and arrows from atop that city's walls?" Lord Everly's voice was heavy with scorn. "We've tried for years to breach Montevallo's strongholds and failed every time. They have the high ground. We cannot—"

"We cannot allow the destruction of Irridusk to pass without a response!" Lady Whitecross slapped a hand against the table.

"And we cannot send our troops into the mountains to be slaugh-tered," Lady Channing said sternly. "That could be exactly what Montevallo is hoping for."

"We haven't sent troops into the mountains since the Balrusk battle twelve years ago," Lord Thorsby said, still dabbing at his brow with his handkerchief. "Montevallo has continued to encroach on our borders since then, including the terrible attack on the Fynrose outpost that killed so many civilians as well as soldiers. Do we really believe they'd attack a village thinking it would goad us into another invasion?"

Charis studied the map of Calera tacked to the wall across from her. Fynrose, the site of the most brutal battle in the past decade, was far to the north, directly between Montevallo's border and the port of Ebbington, which King Alaric was so desperate to control. Red slashes marked the spots of other deadly skirmishes. All of them were on or near the line from Montevallo's northernmost military outpost and Ebbington. All of them were now captured territories that brought King Alaric closer and closer to the port.

Except Irridusk.

Irridusk was in the direct path between Montevallo's army and the city of Arborlay. If Charis didn't send a response, swift and brutal, what would stop Alaric from ordering an invasion upon the capital itself?

"This has gone too far." Lady Ollen's voice shook with fury. "Women and children were slaughtered. We have to take the battle to them. If we cannot send our soldiers, then we dig a trench to protect our own lands and light the entire mountain on fire."

"Montevallo is comprised of a host of mountains, Lady Ollen." Lord Everly sounded annoyed. "Burn one and we might damage a few outposts, maybe flush out a village or two. But we'd have barely affected the majority of their population, and we'd destroy any forest cover we could ever hope to use in an invasion."

Charis leaned forward, studying the map.

"Then we send in spies to poison their water supply and burn their food storage," Lady Whitecross said.

"A good idea," Lady Channing said in her calm voice, "though we have had great difficulty getting spies into their cities since each is surrounded by a high stone wall and manned by guards. How do you propose we get past that?"

Charis frowned. According to the latest information from the north, the bulk of Alaric's army was stationed near the center of the northern territory, equal distance from Montevallo's border and the port Alaric wanted to take from Calera. The cities on either side of the army had long since been destroyed. There was nowhere to stage an attack, nowhere to shore up defenses and take the fight to his army. Nothing but ruined cities and . . . her finger traced the distance between the army's outpost and the northern edge of Calera.

A blaze of furious triumph kindled within her as she turned to the council and cut through their arguments with a single sentence. "I know how to punish Montevallo."

"How?" Lady Ollen leaned forward, her face eager.

"We're going to set fires to the east, west, and south of their central outpost, hemming their soldiers in. And we will keep those fires going, keep them spreading north until they reach the outpost, leaving the army no choice but to flee." Charis slowly looked around the room, meeting each gaze.

"There's nowhere to run except to the northern cliffs," Lord Thorsby said, horrified awe in his voice.

"Exactly." Charis turned back to the map. "We will drive the majority of his army straight into the sea."

THIRTEEN

AN HOUR LATER, the plan hammered out and orders sent, Charis decided she would make a trip to the refugee camp that was several hours north, where Irridusk's few survivors had fled. King Alaric Penbyrn wasn't the only one who needed to see a swift response from Calera's ruling family.

She sent a page to the stables to arrange a trio of carriages, another page to Nalani and Holland inviting them to come along, and a set of pages to Lady Channing's and Lord Everly's houses to instruct their staff to pack an overnight bag and return it, along with a single staff member, within the hour so the council members could also join the trip. She then sent the head housekeeper on a mission to pack enough food, blankets, and toiletries for everyone.

When at last she reached the privacy of her chambers, she found Tal waiting.

"You're supposed to be taking the afternoon off."

"I was." His eyes found hers. "And then a page arrived at the stables with orders to put together a caravan to a refugee camp. I figured I should come along."

She wasn't going to argue with that.

"May I have a word, Your Highness?"

"If you can talk while packing." She moved toward her closet, making a mental list of everything she needed to bring. It would be a simple matter to ring for Mrs. Sykes to do the packing for her, but Charis would rather not discover another old-fashioned, dirt-colored dress as her only option for the morning.

"Your Highness." Tal's voice was firm.

Charis turned to find him still standing just in front of the closed bedroom door, something burning in his eyes. "What is it?"

He opened his mouth. Closed it. Took a deep breath as if to speak and then stood in silence looking miserable.

She frowned. "Are you ill?"

He shook his head. "No, Your Highness. I'm sick over the atrocity at Irridusk. I'm . . . I don't have words for how I feel about that. But that isn't what I wanted to say to you."

"Well?"

He hesitated, and then finally said quietly, "Thank you."

Her frown deepened. "For what?"

"For defending me to Reuben this morning. You didn't have to, and I'm grateful. I . . . You surprised me."

"Why would that surprise you?"

He paused again, and then said carefully, "Because I thought you were like your mother, but it turns out there's a lot of your father in you as well."

Warmth spread through her, tugging her lips upward in a shy smile. What was she supposed to say to that? Turning away before he could read her expression, she reached for a small travel chest. "We meet at the stables in less than an hour. Better get packing."

By midafternoon, the trunks and supplies were loaded onto

luggage racks, and Charis had divided up the group—Lady Channing and her staff in one carriage, Lord Everly and his in another, and Charis with the Farragin twins and Tal in the third. Six royal guards were mounted on horses to ride on either side of the carriages for safety.

As she approached her carriage, the groom responsible for riding on the back of the vehicle and caring for the horses on their journey saw her and instantly bowed, a bag of currying tools in his hands. He looked about her age, with a mop of dark hair, freckled skin, and brown eyes.

"Your Highness, I will be caring for the horses, but if there's anything I can do for you, please let me know." His dark eyes skipped from her face to Tal's, and he nodded to her bodyguard as well.

"Thanks, Grim," Tal said. When Charis gave him a look of surprise, Tal grinned. "Grimson and I started here at the palace around the same time. We're friends now. We play a few rounds of roshinball when we have spare afternoons."

"Not lately, though," Grim said. "Figured he got tired of me winning."

Tal snorted. "Tired of letting you win, more like."

"Your Highness." Nalani bowed and then said, "I've added a wagon to the procession, if that's all right with you."

Charis turned to find a sleek merchant's wagon in glossy black with a matching black tarp covering a stack of chests three high and five deep. "What is this?"

"Medical supplies, though not nearly as many as I would've liked. Until we get another shipment from Rullenvor, those are hard to come by. Blankets. Food." Nalani frowned. "I wanted to include building materials in case any of the structures need repair, but I couldn't fit it on."

"The camp is well stocked with building materials." Charis smiled at Nalani. "This is very thoughtful of you. Now let's get going."

She entered the carriage, followed by Holland, Nalani, and then Tal. They'd settled in seats with the twins facing Charis and Tal, when the carriage door swung open, and Ferris Everly stepped in.

"Ugh, why are you here?" Holland asked.

Ferris sniffed and ignored Holland. Inclining his head toward Charis, he said, "Your Highness."

"Ferris, we're about to leave, so I'm afraid I can't give you much of my time." And thank the seers she had that excuse, because spending more than a few minutes in Ferris's presence always made her want to hit something. Preferably him.

"Of course, Charis," he said in his smooth, ingratiating voice. "I simply thought it best that I ride in your carriage rather than in Father's."

"And what gave you that ridiculous idea?" Holland demanded.

"I hadn't extended an invitation to anyone in Lord Everly's household," Charis said, keeping her voice courteous, though she could already see what game Ferris and his father were playing: Make sure Ferris was seen as part of the inner group tasked with a goodwill mission. Put him in proximity to Charis to reinforce the idea that they would make a good match. Drop a name or two of connections that could serve the crown well. The perfect example of someone who only wanted what he could take from Charis without any thought for Charis herself.

"As the person who has been raised to help you rule Calera, we felt it important for me to be seen caring about the refugees. At your side, of course." Ferris smiled, and Charis's hand curled into a fist.

Burying her hand in the blue velvet of her traveling skirt, she matched his smile with an icy one of her own. "How lovely of you to want to appear to care, Ferris."

"Some of us are going because we actually care," Nalani muttered.

Ferris gave her an impatient look. "Those of us who are concerned with ruling the entire kingdom can't afford to care about individual subjects. We have to see the bigger picture."

Charis's jaw tightened. She couldn't afford to alienate Ferris and his father because it meant agitating the antiwar faction. She could, however, make sure Ferris remembered his place.

"You there." Ferris motioned to Tal. "Go sit with the coachman on top."

Tal made no move to get up.

Ferris's cheeks flushed. "How dare you ignore a direct order?"

"He doesn't take orders from you," Charis said crisply. "And the bigger picture, Ferris, is that a ruler who can't care about the plight of her individual subjects doesn't deserve to hold the throne. Now, I'm sure you'll have much to think about as we travel—not the least of which is how you might use your considerable wealth to help some of those individual subjects who need it—so I will ask that you return to your family's carriage for the journey."

Ferris hesitated as though briefly considering disobeying his princess, but then he gave her a perfunctory bow, turned on his heel, and left the carriage.

"I loathe him." Nalani glared at the door. "Surely you won't have to marry him to secure the throne, Charis. He would make a terrible husband and an even worse king."

"I don't even want to think about it," Charis said, slowly uncurling her fist now that there was no Ferris in the vicinity.

"If you do have to marry him, I can make sure he doesn't survive past the wedding night." Holland sounded cheerful at the prospect.

The coachman cracked the whip, and the carriage lurched into motion. Charis settled against the seat and tried to keep her leg from brushing against Tal's.

"You can't marry him," Nalani said as if she'd made up her mind. "He's a leech who scuttles out from his puddle of scum when he thinks there's a chance he can get a taste of your power. We'll find you someone you can fall madly in love with and have babies with and be happy with all your life. Holland, who do you know who might be a good fit?"

Holland looked faintly ill.

Charis smiled wistfully. "That's a nice thought, but it isn't practical. I'll have to consider what the kingdom needs, just like Mother did. Whatever match will heal wounds and unite factions is the match I'll have to make."

Nalani made a grumpy noise, but then got distracted by the sight of the docks as they took the main road out of town. Charis let her cousin's lengthy discussion of dock workers' rights and the opportunity to unionize wash over her. The carriage was warm, the company safe, and they'd hardly left Arborlay behind when her eyelids fluttered shut. She fought sleep for a moment, trying in vain to resist the gentle sway of the carriage and the rhythmic tapping of the horses' hooves on the cobblestones, but then her eyelids closed again, and she slid into comforting darkness.

Charis woke slowly, her mind filled with the cobwebs of dreams already half forgotten. Voices swirled around her, and her head was resting on something firmer than her pillow. Her body was stiff, and sleep was slow in releasing her from its grip.

"I've always preferred a cavalier hilt. I like the grip across the back of my hand as I fight." Holland's voice, filled with enthusiasm, prodded Charis further awake.

"That's a nice one, but I like a simple hilt in case I want to switch hands or need to twirl the weapon at a moment's notice." Tal's voice rumbled against Charis's cheek.

Her *cheek*.

Charis's eyes flew open.

She was slumped against Tal, her head resting on his shoulder. His arm was spread across her stomach as if he'd been acting as the brace that kept her sleeping body from hitting the floor of the carriage.

A hot flush of mortification spread beneath her skin, and she jerked away from him as if she'd been burned.

"She's awake!" Nalani grinned, a light of mischief in her eyes. "I was going to wake you up ages ago, but Tal said you needed the rest. I think he just enjoyed being your pillow."

Charis sent Nalani a look designed to shut her cousin's mouth, and Nalani's smile grew.

"You snore," Holland informed her cheerfully.

"But not loudly," Nalani said hastily. "It was kind of cute, wasn't it, Tal?"

Charis dearly hoped Tal didn't answer that. She was already having trouble looking at him.

"Are you all right, Your Highness?" Tal asked quietly.

She nodded once and leaned away from him to look out the carriage window. They were well into the rolling hills of central Calera, and the sun was drifting toward the distant horizon. They'd be stopping at the camp soon, and she'd be faced with the suffering of her northern subjects. How she wished she could tell them she had a plan to bring Montevallo to its knees, but she and Mother had learned the hard way that King Alaric's network of spies in Calera was vast, and the success of Charis's plan depended on absolute secrecy.

"Charis?" The mischief was gone from Nalani's voice.

She turned to her cousin.

"I got mad at Holland earlier for saying you've looked ill lately, but . . . for once, my brother was right."

"I'm often right," Holland protested.

"You're often the business end of a donkey." Nalani leaned toward Charis. "You look too thin. And you slept for hours just now. It's not like you to let down your guard like that, no matter how tired you are. Are you sick?"

Tal shifted, his leg brushing against hers. She kept her eyes on Nalani. "I'm fine."

Holland laughed, looked around when no one joined him, and then said, "Oh, that wasn't a joke?"

"I have a feeling we aren't going to get the truth unless we can get her to go back to sleep so we can ask Tal." Nalani said the words lightly, but there was a shadow of hurt in her eyes.

Charis hadn't meant to hurt Nalani, but how much could she really share? She hadn't told them about the assassin, Milla, or the grief that had threaded itself through her heart as if it meant to stay. If Mother was right, to rule was to be alone in the most intimate sense of the word. No one could truly be trusted with her emotions because emotions were weakness and weakness was the crack in her shield that would invite a knife in her back.

But if Father was right, Charis could choose whether she was alone. She could rely on her instincts about others and give trust where it was earned.

Holland and Nalani had earned her trust a hundred times over and had never once asked for her to use her position to benefit them. And Charis was so tired of feeling like she had to be on her guard every time she left her bedroom.

Drawing a deep breath, she tried to shove Mother's warnings into the corner of her heart.

"I've had a rough couple of weeks, and I haven't been sleeping well."

"Or eating." Holland swept her with a disapproving look.

She pressed her lips together and shot Tal a look to see if he was confirming anything for the twins. He was watching her with an unreadable expression. Mortification threatened again, and she looked away.

This was stupid. She couldn't be embarrassed to look at her bodyguard. She hadn't meant to fall asleep against his shoulder, and it should be no more awkward than if it had been Holland sitting next to her instead.

"What happened?" Nalani asked quietly, compassion already swimming in her eyes.

The carriage rumbled over a rough patch in the road, and Charis gripped the seat cushion to keep from sliding forward. Tal's arm shot out, a brace across the front of her again.

"Thank you," she said, making herself look at him.

He gave her that crooked little smile. "I'd be a pretty poor bodyguard if I let you go flying out of your seat and into Holland's lap."

"Seers forbid." Holland looked mildly panicked at the thought.

"Charis, what happened?" Nalani reached across the carriage to squeeze Charis's hands as the road smoothed out and curved around a vast gray-green swamp, half obscured by ribbons of fog. In the distance, small creatures, no taller than a ten-year-old human, with dark green skin and twiglike brown hair moved across the swampland, digging and raking and farming the mushrooms and moss they lived on.

"It's supposed to be good luck to see a Kirthin, and I think I see three," Charis said.

Holland and Tal instantly craned their necks to look for the creatures who cared for Calera's swamplands, but Nalani kept her focus on Charis. "Please tell us what happened, Charis."

She tried to keep her voice calm and steady. "On the night of the ambassadors' ball, a Montevallian spy was hiding in the ladies' parlor. He attacked the queen and stabbed her. Another spy was found in my bath chamber, though she was unarmed, so we don't believe she was there to kill me. More likely she was the assassin's cover—she was also dressed in ball finery—and she ran and hid when the palace guard began their search."

Holland swore. Nalani made a noise like a wounded bird, her eyes wide.

"The queen is recovering well," Charis assured them. "And I'm fine."

"Well, obviously you're fine." Holland sounded furious. "I mean look at you! Too thin, sleeping in the middle of the day, and keeping terrible secrets from your best friends. You're the picture of *fine.*"

Charis blinked. "I handled it, Holland."

"Clearly."

"How did you handle it?" Nalani asked.

"I . . ." Her throat closed on the words. On the explanation that the woman had died in Charis's bathtub and that she still had nightmares about blood filling her chambers until she drowned in it. That the cost of the spy's attack had been the lives of people she'd loved.

Her heart was beating too fast, a caged bird trapped within, and her fingers felt like ice. Somehow the thought of talking about it, of putting it all into words that couldn't be taken back, felt like a test of courage she wasn't sure she could pass.

"Charis?" Holland's voice had softened, and it was his uncharacteristic gentleness that loosened her tongue.

"Reuben killed the assassin in the parlor and then killed his accomplice in my bathtub."

"In your own *bathtub*?" Holland sounded impressed.

"How can you even face going into your bath chamber now?" Nalani asked.

Charis lifted her chin. "It's my bath chamber. My rooms. My life. I'm not going to cower in fear because some Montevallian dogs attacked the royal family and paid the price."

"Good for you." Holland nodded his approval. "But then why aren't you eating or sleeping well?"

She couldn't answer him. Couldn't push the truth past her lips without letting the grief out at the same time. If she let the grief take her now, how could she be calm and collected in time for the people at the refugee camp who needed a pillar of strength in their princess?

Tal adjusted his seat, his leg once again brushing hers. She looked to him, and his dark eyes found hers and held. There was a shadow of grief in them that matched what lived in her, and for the first time she wondered what memories kept him up at night. What pain pressed against his heart, haunting his nightmares and driving his choices.

"Your Highness, would you like me to explain further?" His voice was soft.

She shouldn't. It was unthinkable to rely on him instead of finding the strength within herself to speak with the calm dispassion Mother required of her. But her throat was tight with unshed tears, and they were just minutes away from a group of weary, terrified people who needed her strength.

"Please," she said.

He inclined his head and then turned to the twins. "The queen decided all staff on duty in the ladies' parlor and in Charis's wing that evening had failed to keep the royal family safe. As a result, they were each executed the next morning. This included her two evening guards and her handmaiden, Milla."

Nalani sucked in a little breath. "Oh, not sweet Milla!" Her eyes swam with tears.

"I now live in Milla's old room with the job of making sure another assassin doesn't get a chance to hurt the princess." He risked a quick glance at Charis. "And I've expanded my duties to include making sure she eats and gets some rest because these past few weeks have been a nightmare for her."

"I'm so sorry, Charis." Nalani knelt on the carriage floor and gathered the princess's hands in her own. "I can come stay with you too, if that would help."

"I'll sleep on the floor across your doorway," Holland said. "I welcome any Montevallian to try crossing the threshold."

Charis swallowed past the knot of tears in her throat. "Thank you both, but just offering your friendship and support is enough."

"I'm glad you're with her now, Tal." Nalani let go of Charis to take Tal's hands instead.

Tal's brows rose as he stared at his hands in hers. "I . . . that's very . . . thank you."

"Be sure you don't fail to protect her," Holland said. "I'm just starting to like you. I'd hate to have to kill you."

Tal grinned. "I'd hate to be killed."

The carriage rumbled to a stop, and voices cut through the afternoon air. Nalani clambered back into her seat as the door opened and a footman bowed. "Your Highness."

Turning to Tal, Charis said, "Thank you." And then she climbed out of the carriage and prepared to face the sea of refugees who were desperately hoping their princess could give them hope.

FOURTEEN

Hours later, long after darkness had fallen, Charis held the hand of the last in a long line of people who had waited to meet their princess. Tal stood beside her, constantly scanning their surroundings for potential threats. Other royal guards stood nearby, though not close enough to overhear what the princess was saying. The rest of the delegation had already retired to the inn, with the exception of Nalani, who was busy assessing the camp's needs and making notes.

Charis focused on the person in front of her, whom she could see in the golden glow of torches lit along the path that led from the three-story inn behind Charis to the neat line of tents that formed the refugee camp. The woman's eyes were filmy with age, and her wrinkled skin felt paper thin.

"Your Highness," she whispered as she bowed her head.

"What's your name?" Charis asked.

"Lourain, Your Highness." The woman grasped Charis's hand in both of hers. "Thank you for coming."

"Will you tell me your story?" Charis asked.

"I've lived in Irridusk all my life." Her hands shook, and Charis shifted her grip so that she was holding Lourain's hands instead of the other way around.

"You're from Irridusk?"

The woman's eyes shone with tears. "It's all ruined. Hilmer and I had a farm at the outskirts, though he's been gone three winters now. My granddaughter was out helping me with the evening chores. We saw the smoke from town, and the neighbor boy came running to tell us. . . ."

"Oh, Lourain." Charis ached to somehow wipe away the woman's pain.

"Saved us, Noah did. Smart little thing. Eight, I think. No, nine. Had a birthday a month ago." She looked at the tents that were staked in the field behind her. "His sister made it out, but he didn't. Too busy running from farm to farm trying to get everyone else safe."

The woman looked beseechingly at Charis. "My granddaughter and I ran south, but I can't find my daughter. It took us nearly a day and a half to get from Irridusk to the camp, so she might still be on her way. Her name is Ellis. She's a bit taller than you, with red hair, and the baby is almost one. Have you seen her?"

Charis bent over their clasped hands. "I haven't, but I'll let the staff here know to look for her. And I'll give her description to those who run the refugee center in Arborlay as well."

The woman nodded. "Thank you, Your Highness."

"I'm so very sorry for what's happened to you, Lourain. You deserve justice and safety, and I will do my best to get that for you."

Lourain kissed the princess's hands and then left to return to the camp. Charis stood in the dark for a long moment, the weight of every story she'd heard settling on her shoulders like stone.

The suffering of her people was palpable. The loss they bore nearly unbearable. There had to be an answer that would free those who were still captives and return land to those who'd been displaced. An answer that would satisfy the blood debt Montevallo owed but still achieve lasting peace so that her people could remain safe.

If an answer existed, it didn't present itself to Charis as she stood there surrounded by the hum of voices from the camp, the smell of food cooking, and the distant sister moons bathing the hills in pale blue light.

"Your Highness," Tal said quietly beside her.

She looked at him.

"You're shivering."

He was right. A brisk autumn breeze scoured the hills, sneaking past Charis's travel dress and tracing goose bumps across her skin.

"The rest of the party has retired to the inn," he said. "If you'd like to remain here, may I send a guard to get your cloak?"

"They're suffering," she said, as if that was the answer to his question.

"I know." There was misery in his voice. "But you shivering in the cold isn't going to help them."

"Then what will?" she demanded, wrapping her arms around her as much for the warmth as to restrain the grief in her chest, grief that was echoed in the faces of her people a hundred times over. She hadn't planned to spill her thoughts to Tal, but she couldn't face Lord Everly, Ferris, Lady Channing, or even the twins when everything inside her was raw and bleeding. She needed firm footing. A plan. Something she could bring to the discussion that would point her kingdom in the right direction.

It wasn't enough to drive a portion of Alaric's army into the sea.

They'd never be able to catch him unaware like that twice, and they'd already proven they couldn't take the invasion into Montevallo's mountains. She needed leverage. Some way to force Alaric to begin talks of peace.

"I don't know if there's a simple answer," Tal said.

"But there has to be *an* answer, even if it isn't simple. There must be. I can't carry the suffering of my people and do nothing about it." She turned to him. "You've been with me at meetings and events for the past few weeks. You know that I have Lord Everly and the rest of his supporters pushing hard to annex the northern territories to King Alaric."

"Which would end the war." He sounded cautious, as though worried she might be seriously thinking of consigning those who remained in his village to permanent captivity.

"At what cost? Leaving our people to be captives of Montevallo? Showing King Alaric that with enough violence, he can take whatever he wants from us? What if he decides he wants more than the north?"

Tal was silent.

"And then I have Lady Ollen, Lady Whitecross, and the rest of their faction demanding that we take the war into the mountains and burn Montevallo to ash, but that's a foolish proposition. Montevallo has the high ground, and their cities are fortified behind walls. We'd lose more people and gain nothing."

Tal made a noise of agreement.

Charis began pacing. "There has to be another solution. Something that pacifies King Alaric but gives justice and safety to our people."

"I'm not sure justice and King Alaric belong in the same sentence."

There was a shadow of bitterness in Tal's voice.

Charis turned to him. "What if we could grant Montevallo usage of Ebbington's port and safe passage there and back? But only if they withdraw troops and return our lands and our people?"

"And why would he do that when in another year or so of battles, he will take the port by force?"

"Because it spares the lives of his soldiers as well as ours."

"I'm not sure that motivates him the way it motivates you."

Charis frowned. "What do you mean?"

Tal ran his hands through his hair and stared at the star-flecked sky. "Living in the north, I spent all my life in the shadow of Montevallo. I've eavesdropped on their camps, watched them in action, and had a front-row seat to their conversations, the orders the king sends, the way their minds work. King Alaric isn't just fighting because he wants to use our port without paying tariffs to the Caleran throne."

"Then why is he fighting?"

Tal paused as though thinking, and then said in a carefully neutral voice, "Because your grandmother, Queen Rhys, broke the terms of her trade agreement with King Alaric's father, King Orwen. She decided she wanted higher tariffs on goods transported to and from the port, and when Orwen said no, because his people couldn't survive tariffs that high, she offered to make Montevallo a colony who would pay tax to Calera in jewels mined from their mountains in exchange for free trade at the port."

"That's what Montevallo thinks happened?"

Tal stared at her. "What do you think happened?"

"King Orwen stopped paying tariffs altogether, and Queen Rhys sent him a demand for back payments, plus a fine for failing to give

Calera its due. Instead of paying, Orwen had her killed, and we went to war."

There was a long moment of silence, and then Tal said, "Montevallians believe in Queen Rhys's treachery. They believe they were cut off from the port, and thereby unable to trade the jewels they mine for goods they need, because of Calera's greed and dishonor. Their people are starving and have been for years. There are shortages of basic goods in every Montevallian city." He met her gaze, starlight glittering in his eyes. "They aren't fighting to avoid paying tariffs, Your Highness. They're fighting for their honor and the honor of their starving people."

Charis shivered as someone shouted from the inn at her back and a nearby guard answered. "If they believe they're fighting to avenge their honor, they won't stop until we're utterly broken."

"I know." The misery was back in Tal's voice, and Charis reached out to place her cold hand on his arm.

"Don't despair, Tal. You've given me good information. The first step to winning a game, even a game as bloody and terrible as war, is to understand how your enemy thinks. Thanks to you, I have that now." She looked across the hills toward the north, where somewhere far from her, Montevallian troops huddled around fires, polishing weapons they planned to use against her people. "There's an answer here. I just have to find it."

His hand, warm and callused, briefly covered hers. "If anyone can find it, it will be you. Now, may I send for your cloak?"

She pulled away and rubbed warmth into her arms. "That won't be necessary. I'm ready to return to the inn. Let the coachmen know I expect us to leave for Arborlay at dawn. And don't even think about telling me to get my rest. I can't do anything more sitting here at the camp. I have to get back to the palace so I can get to work."

"I wouldn't dream of telling you what to do."

"Liar."

He laughed as they turned toward the lights of the inn, and she found that the weight of the stories she'd heard from her people was a little easier to carry.

FIFTEEN

CHARIS SPENT THE next week mulling over Tal's words while she kept up with her relentless schedule. Understanding what drove King Alaric and motivated his soldiers and spies was the key to stopping the war. She just had to find the connection between what he wanted and what Calera was able to give. And to do that, she needed the factions that divided Calera's nobility to give her a little bit more time before demanding she and the queen declare a new course of action.

If today's committee meeting was anything to go by, time was something many weren't willing to give.

"Now that we've resolved the repair schedule for the roads leading north from Arborlay, perhaps we could discuss just how far north we are expected to go." Lady Pellinsworth pursed her lips, painted bold pink to match her nails, and looked around Lady Shawling's sitting room at the rest of the Infrastructure Expansion and Repair committee.

"Certainly not too far," Lord Abbington said sternly, wiping crumbs of pumpkin pastry from his fingers. "Our taxes cannot be expected to support infrastructure in places where tax collection has been limited or nonexistent."

"Are you forgetting that tax collection has been affected by the invading troops?" Lady Ollen's voice rose, and she stabbed a short finger in Lord Abbington's direction. "We ought to take a portion of funds earmarked for northern infrastructure and use them to make inroads into Montevallo instead."

"So our crews can get killed?" Lord Abbington gave Lady Ollen a look of mild disgust, a frown wrinkling his dusky brow. "I think not."

"So then how far do we truly want to repair the roads?" Lady Pellinsworth asked. "After all, Montevallo's soldiers could be using them too."

Charis, who was strictly there to make sure everyone remembered who was truly in charge of Calera's infrastructure, figured it was time for that reminder. Leaning forward, she set her teacup on the low marble table before her with a delicate clink. "How far north does the road go?"

Lady Shawling, who wore her customary black, fanned herself as though overcome with excitement at the drama that was brewing.

Lord Rynce cleared his throat. "It extends into the captive northern territories, Your Highness."

Charis smiled benevolently. "Then I suppose you have your answer, *Lady* Pellinsworth." She lingered on the title, a subtle reminder to the woman that she'd been allowed to keep her title and the honor that came with it only after her husband had quickly sold several properties at a loss in order to pay their back taxes along with the hefty fee Charis had imposed. That benevolence could disappear in the blink of an eye, and everyone in the room knew it.

"Of course, Your Highness." Lady Pellinsworth bowed her head in Charis's direction without actually looking at the princess. "It's just . . ." When no one jumped in to finish her sentence, Lady Pellinsworth waved her hand as if dismissing her thoughts. "It's no matter."

"On the contrary," Charis said. "I think it matters very much. There is no need to fear speaking your mind in front of me as long as you are respectful of our laws and your sovereign." Another subtle dig at the Pellinsworths' foolishness.

The woman's face flushed, and Lord Rynce took pity on her. "I suppose the question is how close can we come to the Montevallian occupation and still keep our work crews safe."

"A worthy discussion point, Lord Rynce, but not what I think Lady Pellinsworth was asking." She glanced around the room, noting which committee members met her gaze and which did not. If Mother was here, she'd quash the dissent by instilling fear and by reminding them where their sovereign stood on the issue of the northern territories. But Mother wasn't here, and sometimes honey worked better than a sword.

Besides, Charis was sitting in the parlor of the most shameless gossip in the kingdom. Lady Vera Shawling could spread a rumor with the kind of speed the other matrons only aspired to. What if, instead of a rumor, Charis gave them a taste of the truth? Might that not appease both factions and buy her a little more time to find the solution to ending the war?

It was a gamble, but it was one worth taking.

"It is no secret that some of you wish us to annex the far northern territories and give them to King Alaric in hopes that will appease him enough to end the war." She took another sip of tea and then set her cup down with care. "And it's no secret that some of you oppose any overtures of peace until we've invaded Montevallo and made them pay for their aggression with the blood of their people."

Lady Shawling forgot her fan as she leaned forward, eyes gleaming. Several of the other committee members straightened in their seats, their full attention on their princess. None of the rest would look at her.

"I sympathize with every Caleran who wants this war over, and with every Caleran who wants Montevallo's debt paid in blood." She let a hint of fury singe her words. "Montevallo's atrocities must be stopped, and they must pay for what they've done to us."

Ah, she'd now gained the attention of the entire room. Good. Let them truly hear her.

"But while we stop their atrocities and make them pay, we must not abandon our own. We must keep our word to our northern subjects, who are promised, under the law, the same protection from the crown as everyone in this room." She clasped her hands in her lap and lifted her chin. "There is a way to accomplish peace without losing the north, and I am going to find it. I have new information that will help me do just that. All I need is a bit more time."

"What new information have you found, Your Highness?" Lady Shawling's voice was breathless.

Charis smiled, cold and calculated. "I'm afraid I do not have the queen's permission to share that yet. Rest assured that your concerns have been heard and are being addressed. We must hold the line a bit longer, remain courageous in the face of Montevallo's aggression, and keep faith with all our people. I promise you, I will not rest until I have a solution to the war well in hand."

Now every committee member was looking at her. Full eye contact. Open body language. Immediate bows and murmurs of "Your Highness" when she met their gaze.

She had them. Or rather, the truth had them. With Lady Shawling at the helm, the rumor that the princess was close to finding a way to end the war would be the topic in every drawing room by tomorrow afternoon. She'd made no concessions to either faction. She'd acknowledged everyone's position.

And her army was nearly in place to light the fires that would drive a chunk of Montevallo's army into the sea. That should renew Calera's faith in their rulers for a while.

It was the best she could do. Now she just had to keep her promise and find the solution that would save her kingdom.

The meeting ended twenty minutes later, and Charis settled into her carriage with Tal opposite her. She'd grown more and more comfortable with him as the days of his service had turned to weeks. Part of that could be blamed on her refusal to consign him to a life of silent formality as her constant bodyguard. The rest of it was entirely his fault. He was perceptive and intuitive, and had no compunction about speaking his mind to her in private, whether she welcomed his thoughts or not.

It ought to have been infuriating, but more often than not she found it invigorating instead. He didn't back down from her challenges. He didn't give way simply because she outranked him. He treated her like her mind, her skills, and her feelings mattered. Not for what she could do for him, but simply because he saw her as a person first, a princess second. The times she spent talking to him away from everyone else's watchful eyes were the only parts of her day where she could breathe freely.

Not that she would ever admit that to him. There would be no living with him then.

As the carriage rumbled over the cobblestones on the way back to the palace, Tal said, "You managed them beautifully."

She met his eyes and found him watching her with that inscrutable look he sometimes got. The one that made her feel like a puzzle he was trying to solve.

"I just hope it buys me enough time to find a viable path toward peace."

"What makes you think you can accomplish what your mother hasn't been able to for the past eighteen years?" The genuine curiosity in his voice took the insolence out of his words.

"Because you gave me valuable insight into what drives King Alaric. I can't win the battle if I don't understand the way my enemy thinks." She leaned forward to look out the carriage window as it turned onto the long road that led up to the palace. She'd been cooped up all day, and an inner restlessness pressed against her skin as if it wanted to pry her apart. She couldn't stand another minute of being inside, on display in front of others, perfectly composed while she tried to stay three moves ahead of whomever she was with. "It's a lovely autumn day. What's left on my schedule?"

He pulled a small paper from the front pocket of his uniform and glanced over it. "Discussions with the head housekeeper for the trade delegate reception, homework for Brannigan, and signing winter festival cards to be sent to each noble family in Calera. After that—"

She held up a hand, and he fell silent. "Reschedule the housekeeper. We have five weeks before the delegates arrive. There will be plenty of time for planning. Push the card signing to later this week. And I'll worry about homework later tonight."

"Instead of sleeping, you mean?" There was a definite tone of disapproval in his voice, and she narrowed her eyes at him. "Your Highness," he tacked on, but the disapproval didn't budge.

Impertinent boy. Just because he made her remember to eat and sleep and take moments throughout the day to breathe didn't mean he got to censure her choices.

"I'm going riding." She gave him a look that invited certain destruction if he chose to argue further.

Instead, he grinned. "Great idea."

"I'm glad it meets your approval."

He ignored her sarcasm.

Thirty minutes later, with her schedule adjusted and her riding habit on, they arrived at the stables. Tal had sent word ahead to have two horses saddled and ready. Grim, the young freckle-faced groom who'd traveled with them to the refugee camp, bowed when he saw them and then continued to fuss with the saddle of the large bay Tal preferred.

Charis patted the nose of her favorite black mare and gave her a sugar cube while Tal walked to Grim and slapped him on the shoulder, a wide smile on his face. Charis ignored them as they chatted roshinball or the bay's saddle or whatever it was friends talked about when they didn't have the fate of the kingdom on their shoulders. They saw each other a few hours a week on Tal's afternoons off as well as each time Charis went riding. She hoped it was enough to make up for the fact that every other minute of Tal's days and nights was spent keeping up with her.

If she felt a tiny sting of envy at their easy camaraderie, it was easily ignored. Instead, she mounted the mare, leaned down to pat the horse's shoulder, and then glanced over at Tal, who was laughing at something Grim had said.

She had only an hour before she was due back in the palace for her next engagement. She wasn't going to waste it watching two boys joke with each other in a stable yard. A wicked little smile played about her lips as an idea blossomed and took hold.

Tal would absolutely hate it.

In fact, she was 100 percent sure it would earn her a few lectures muttered under his breath for at least a week.

Worth it.

Wrapping the reins around her fist, she squeezed her thighs and shouted, "Race you to the orchard!"

The mare took off, her long legs eating up the distance between the stables and the hill that eventually led to the far southern edge of the property. Behind her, she heard a shout, and a bubble of laughter burst from her.

Leaning over the mare's neck, Charis urged her on. Hoofbeats thundered behind her, and she risked a look back, her braid whipping across her face. The bay was galloping toward them, Tal leaning forward to help the horse's momentum. She couldn't read his expression, but she imagined the disapproval must be there, and laughed again.

Racing her horse toward the edge of the orchard that spread across the distant hill, she savored the sting of the wind against her cheeks, the thunder of her heart, and the glow of elusive happiness that burned within. It was wild and reckless and more freedom than she'd had in weeks, and it was exactly what she needed.

Tal was at her heels when she reined the mare in a few lengths from the orchard's edge. Her horse danced along the tree line, and Charis laughed when Tal leaped from his mount and grabbed her mare's bridle.

However, when he looked at her, there wasn't any disapproval on his face. Instead, there was warmth in his eyes. "Feel better?" he asked.

"I always feel better when I beat you at something."

"I will endeavor to lose more often." He grinned at her expression. "But not at horse racing. I'd have beaten you if you hadn't cheated."

"Bold words."

"True words." He held her horse steady so she could dismount. "I once tried to impress a girl by racing a horse across a field and jumping a stream. Unfortunately, I ended up *in* the stream, and she ended up kissing another boy behind the barn while I went home for a pair of dry pants."

"Ouch." She dismounted and patted the mare's neck appreciatively. "Good girl," she murmured.

"The blow to my dignity was far worse than the blow to my backside. However, I vowed to never end up in a stream again, and I worked hard on my horsemanship. If you want a real race, we can do that on the way back, though I'm afraid the blow to *your* dignity might be more than you can take."

She laughed. "We'll see about that."

"Do you hear that?" He frowned and stepped closer to the orchard.

She followed his lead, listening closely. A soft, high-pitched cry came from somewhere to their left. Tal looped both sets of reins around the nearest branch and set off into the orchard. Charis hurried to keep up.

Two rows in and six trees down, Tal suddenly stopped and crouched by the thick tufts of grass that grew at the base of the trunk.

"What is it?" Charis asked.

Tal settled onto the ground, his back against the tree trunk, and scooped a ball of fluff into his arms. "A kitten." There was a note of boyish wonder in his voice that made the happy glow inside Charis brighten.

She examined the kitten. It was a patchwork of orange, gold, and black with a big black smudge of fur across its face and orange fur surrounding its ears. Two golden eyes peered up at Tal, and it opened its tiny mouth and mewed pitifully. He carefully smoothed its fur and scratched behind its ears, and a little rumbling purr came from its throat.

"Where's the rest of the litter?" Charis checked the surrounding area but couldn't find any other kittens. "It must have gotten separated. We can take it back to the stables. There are plenty of barn cats there, and . . ."

Her words trailed off as she focused on Tal again. He had the kitten cuddled up just beneath his chin and was whispering to it. There was an aching vulnerability on his face—a sadness in his eyes that caught Charis unaware. It brushed against her own grief, and she found herself swallowing hard and looking away until she was sure she wasn't going to do something foolish like spill her own pain to her bodyguard.

He looked up as she crouched beside him. "She reminds me of my favorite cat." His voice was nostalgic, but she heard the pain beneath it.

She settled on the ground beside him and brushed a hand over the kitten's fluffy back. "You had a favorite cat?"

"Grismelda."

"That's a very unusual name."

He smiled wistfully. "My sister named her. She got it from a child's story called *The Adventures of Hildegard and Grismelda*. I was afraid of the dark as a child, and she gave me the job of looking after Grismelda at night. I took it seriously and only realized much later that she'd let me sleep with the cat to help me not be afraid."

"Is your sister older or younger than you?" She'd been careful not to ask him about his family or his life before he came to the palace. There was no sense in becoming attached to another staff member who could be removed or killed if Mother decided it was prudent.

But she couldn't leave him alone with the hurt in his voice. Besides, discussing his sister and her cat was harmless.

"Older." He stroked the kitten's face.

"Is she . . . Do you miss her?" What a stupid thing to say. Of course he must miss his family. And as she had no idea if they'd survived the Montevallian occupation of his village, she was prying into a subject that must hurt him. "I'm sorry. That was a careless thing to ask. You don't have to answer."

He gave her another one of his inscrutable Charis-is-a-puzzle looks and then said softly, "I miss her, but I try not to think of her often. It's easier that way."

The kitten lifted its paw and tapped Tal on the chin. He smiled down at it. "This little one needs a bath and some milk."

It was on the tip of Charis's tongue to tell him there were no pets in the palace. And there was certainly no time in their schedule to take on the care of a helpless kitten. The kitten would have to take its chances in the barn with the rest of the cats.

But then he ran a finger down its back and whispered, "I'll name you Hildegard. Hildy for short. My sister would've liked that."

And seers take it, she couldn't manage to get the words out.

He looked up, sadness in his eyes again. "I know we can't keep a kitten in your chambers. We're too busy. And you have all those nice dresses, which don't go well with kitten claws."

He climbed to his feet, cradling the kitten as if she was the most valuable thing in the world, and then reached his hand down to help her up.

"I'll ask Grim if he has time to at least check on Hildy in the barn to make sure she gets enough food to survive the winter." He turned toward the horses, the ache in his voice lingering in the air.

This was ridiculous. It was just a kitten. She shouldn't feel bad about the fact that there was no room in his schedule, in his life, for a pet. There were far more important things at stake in the kingdom than the fate of one kitten and a boy who missed his sister. They'd put it with the other barn cats and go on to her next engagement.

And yet, as she watched him walk back to his horse, whispering to the kitten the entire way, she couldn't make herself force him to give up the little ball of fluff. Instead, she said, "Father would love a kitten."

Tal turned, his face bright. "Do you think so?"

Charis shook her head at her own softhearted foolishness. "I'm sure of it. He loves nothing more than to fuss and care for those who need it. Ilsa too. And that way, you can visit Hildy often. She'll be spoiled rotten in no time."

He gave her his crooked smile as he tucked Hildy into the front of his jacket and freed the reins from the tree limb. "Thank you."

She took her mare's reins and mounted. "Don't thank me yet. You've once again lost a horse race."

And before he could finish mounting his bay, she was galloping toward the stables.

SIXTEEN

THE TRADE DELEGATES were due to arrive in less than two weeks. Reinforcing those alliances remained crucial as Charis still hadn't come up with the leverage she needed to convince Alaric to stop the war. Two sections of her army were in place, ready to light the fires that would drive the bulk of Montevallo's invading forces into the sea. Only the western flank had yet to report back as being in position, but it shouldn't be longer than a few more days before Charis could give the order to deal a crucial blow against her enemy.

It wouldn't end the war, though, which meant until she found the leverage she needed, Calera's alliances were more important than ever. Several other trade ships bound for Calera had gone down in the northern seas over the past few weeks, causing shortages in medical supplies, paper, fabric, and several types of metal used to forge weapons.

Lady Shawling had lived up to her reputation, and the rumor that the princess was close to achieving peace for the kingdom had spread far and wide. It had given Charis a modicum of breathing space, but even that was starting to disintegrate as no new developments had been reported to the kingdom gossips.

For proof that the factions were getting impatient, Charis had only to look to her right, where Lord Thorsby sat at Lady Rynce's sumptuous banquet table dabbing his gleaming forehead with a purple silk handkerchief and fussing with his place setting until every utensil was lined up like the ruler-straight rows of a military parade. The more he tried to balance the competing views of Mother's royal council, the sweatier and more fastidious he became.

To her left, Ambassador Shyrn from Rullenvor ate with gusto. Lady Channing and Lady Everly sat across from her.

Ferris's mother had already made three attempts to corral Charis into agreeing to outings alone with her son. Lord Thorsby was cutting his food into tiny, perfectly symmetrical pieces in between forehead dabs. Ambassador Shyrn was vocally critical of the food even while he ate as if he'd been starving for a week. And Lady Channing was watching Charis with a thoughtful expression.

As far as Charis was concerned, the luncheon to raise money for new army uniforms couldn't end fast enough. But until it did, she had a job to do.

She took a bite of puffed fish pie, savoring the delicate cream sauce and the hint of spice before turning to Lord Thorsby. "My dear sir, does the food disagree with you today?"

He set his knife down, carefully lined up with the rest of his cutlery, and dabbed his upper lip. "Not at all, Your Highness. The food is quite delicious."

"Then why aren't you eating?"

His hands fluttered over his plate as if trying to find one thing he might want to put into his mouth, and then he said, "I'm afraid I'm a bit distracted, and it's taken away my appetite."

Charis nodded in understanding. "You have an unenviable job, Lord Thorsby."

"Just so." He mopped his forehead enthusiastically. "I have Lord Pellinsworth in my ear at least once a day demanding to know why we aren't ending the war, no matter the cost to the north. And then there are Lady Ollen and Lady Whitecross, who, as you know, grow very impatient to invade Montevallo."

Charis sipped her sparkling mulberry wine. "It must be quite difficult to listen well and still remind them that a problem that has been growing for eighteen years can't be solved overnight."

"Do you really think you'll be successful?" Ambassador Shyrn asked, his mouth full of braised golden leeks.

Charis lifted her chin and cut him with a look. "I have no doubt."

"You may not have doubts, but plenty of your subjects do." He reached for his glass.

Lady Channing leaned over her plate and addressed the ambassador. "You forget your place, Ambassador Shyrn. You are new to your appointment here in Calera and cannot possibly be expected to fully understand the complexities of the situation."

"I may be new to Calera, my lady, but you forget I served for three years in Montevallo before this. I am no stranger to this war."

"You are an outside observer, no matter which court you serve in," Charis said, a hint of frost in her voice. "And while we welcome you to discuss Rullenvor's interests with us, that is the extent of your responsibilities here."

Servants flooded the room to remove plates and set the third course before the attendees. Tal stepped forward as one of Lady Rynce's servants approached Charis. Raising a hand to halt the servant's progress, Tal took Charis's plate himself and handed it to the servant in exchange for the bowl of chilled cucumber and dill soup with little rosettes of flaky spiced pastry puffs decorating the side of the plate. He set the food before Charis, bowed to her, and stepped back.

Ambassador Shyrn stared at Tal, who stood quite close behind Charis to make sure no one could approach her without his permission, and then looked back at the princess. "Perhaps we should discuss such matters at another time, Your Highness. This is hardly private."

Charis raised a brow as Ambassador Shyrn shot another suspicious look at Tal. "I assure you, Ambassador, my bodyguard is with me everywhere I go and is the soul of discretion."

He frowned in Tal's direction. "Never trust the help, Your Highness. You can't be sure of their loyalty."

Charis set her teeth, but before she could respond, Lady Everly said firmly, "Every servant knows better than to cross Charis. If they fail, the queen has them beheaded. It makes for an astonishing degree of loyalty."

Something dark and dangerous flared to life in Charis. How could Lady Everly so casually mention sending servants to their deaths? As if their lives meant nothing?

"Well, that is certainly an expedient way to manage things," Ambassador Shyrn said, grudging approval in his voice. "She might consider simply cutting out their tongues, though. That way you don't lose a servant who's already been trained to your standards."

Rage simmered in Charis, bright and burning, and she gripped her knife handle until her palm ached. Time to change the subject before she said something she couldn't take back. "Ambassador Shyrn, I would like to hear more about the unrest in the northern seas."

"Unrest?" He took his time scraping his spoon against the bottom of his bowl to get the last of his soup.

"Yes. We've heard rumors of strange ships. Merchant vessels reporting hearing odd things at night. There have been three more supply ships sunk within the last few weeks, which hardly seems like a coincidence. What have you heard?"

"I've heard nothing." He set his spoon down. "Now, about this war—"

"How can you have heard nothing?" Charis asked, her voice sharp. "The northern seas are right in Rullenvor's backyard."

"Perhaps because there is nothing to hear." He met her gaze and then looked askance at Tal as if irritated by her bodyguard's close proximity.

"My secretary was very clear about the reports we've received." The rage was in her voice, just a shadow of it, but still Ambassador Shyrn drew back as if struck.

Lady Everly leaned forward as her plate was cleared and a slice of ginger apple cake with frothy whipped cream was set down. "This is exactly why you must allow Ferris to come to these appointments with your secretary, Your Highness. He has quite the head for politics and can help you discern which things deserve your attention."

Charis bared her teeth in a semblance of a smile, her hand aching as she clenched her knife. "Are you suggesting I don't have a head for politics, Lady Everly?"

The woman blanched. "Of course not, Your Highness. Merely saying that Ferris could be utilized in a much more prominent role than he currently has. Lord Thorsby himself said that very thing last week at a brunch with Lord Everly."

Lord Thorsby appeared to choke on his drink.

"Your Highness?" Tal's voice was louder than usual as he bent to her ear. Loud enough to carry to those who surrounded her. "I beg your pardon, but you've received an urgent summons from the queen.

I'm afraid you will have to skip dessert."

His fingers brushed her shoulders as he placed his hands on the back of her chair to help scoot it away from the table. She anchored herself to the steady pressure of his hands and drew in a fortifying breath. Wiping her expression of any trace of emotion, she smiled at Ambassador Shyrn, Lord Thorsby, Lady Channing, and Lady Everly.

"If you'll excuse me, I must take my leave."

She stood and walked away before they'd finished getting up to bow and murmur "Your Highness."

Once they were inside the carriage and had left the Rynce house behind, Charis flexed her aching palm, where the shape of a knife handle was still imprinted. The fury that had erupted within her at the casual mention of killing her staff still pulsed through her veins with every heartbeat. The nerve of them—all of them. Treating the death of servants like it was nothing more important than the soup they were served for lunch. Acting as though Charis hadn't been training all her life to manage a war-torn kingdom and the politics that came with it. Insinuating that a spineless, ingratiating boy like Ferris Everly could ever—

"Please breathe, Your Highness." Tal's voice broke through her thoughts.

Instinctively, she drew in a slow, deep breath, feeling the tightness within expand painfully as she forced air past the noose of fury that held her captive.

"And you might think about releasing your skirt before you tear it."

She looked down and found her fists clenched around the pale gold silk. Slowly she released her grip and took another breath. The fury still simmered, a beast escaped from its cage. She reached for something normal to say. Something to help her regain the thread of her control so she could be the princess she was expected to be by the time they reached the palace.

"I wonder what this summons is all about."

"There is no summons."

Charis froze, staring at Tal. "Then why am I in this carriage?"

"Because you looked two seconds away from stabbing Ambassador Shyrn with your butter knife and then using your spoon to carve out Lady Everly's heart. And I really didn't think poor Thorsby's handkerchief could take the sweat that would surely have appeared once you decided to go after him as well." Tal's voice held a flicker of the anger that lived within her.

"You made up a summons to get me out of the luncheon?"

"I apologize for lying, Your Highness." He held her gaze. "But I don't apologize for getting you out of there. Bunch of vultures circling with no thought for anyone but themselves." He whipped an imaginary handkerchief out of his pocket and dabbed his forehead. "Oh, this is awful. Just terrible. I have one of the most esteemed responsibilities in all the kingdom, but I'd rather people were always happy with me than take a stand on anything of principle."

Charis was surprised to find herself smiling. "That is a rather accurate assessment of Lord Thorsby."

He pretended to shove a large bite of food into his mouth. "This is the worst thing I've ever eaten. No, no, don't take the plate. I haven't licked it yet. And by the way, I know more about running your kingdom than you do, but strangely enough I have no idea what's happening in my own backyard."

"Ambassador Shyrn is insufferable, isn't he?"

"It's a wonder he can fit through a doorway while carrying such a lofty opinion of himself. And then there's Lady Everly." He raised a hand and pretended to fan himself while speaking in a high, simpering voice. "My sweet Ferris simply *must* come to your meetings and help you understand things. And take you for walks. And pick out your frocks. He has such a talent for grasping at power that isn't his. It would be a shame not to give him what he wants."

Charis laughed, and the burning fury within subsided to a dull ache. Tal looked closely at her, and then smiled. "Better?"

"Better." She yawned. "But exhausted. What else do I have on my schedule this afternoon?"

"Maybe you wouldn't be exhausted if you'd kept to your schedule yesterday instead of putting your correspondence off until late at night."

"Maybe you should mind your own business."

His eyes found hers and held. "You are my business."

The dull ache within her softened. They spent the rest of the ride in companionable silence. Once they were back in the princess's chambers, Tal told her to change into something comfortable while he arranged for the next item in her schedule. One that, apparently, didn't require her to leave her chambers.

She took him at his word and rang for Mrs. Sykes to help her into a simple blue day dress in a light, comfortable fabric. A chambermaid lit a fire in her fireplace to ward off the afternoon chill, and Charis let her hair down, settled into a chair beside the fire, and sent Mrs. Sykes back to her other duties while she waited for Tal.

The flames were mesmerizing, and she was having trouble keeping her eyes open when Tal returned. He smiled when he saw her curled into the chair beside the fire, and there was a bold light of approval in his eyes when he took in her tumble of curls and casual dress.

"Perfect," he said.

"What am I doing next?"

"The most important job of the day." He set a mug on the table beside her. A ribbon of steam rose from it, and the delicious smell of hot cocoa filled the air. Then he leaned over her and deposited a sleepy, fluffy Hildy into her lap.

She frowned at the kitten, who blinked at her and began purring. "What is this?"

"It's called relaxing. Drink the cocoa. Pet the kitten. Breathe for a few hours."

"But don't I have something else I need to do?" She ran an experimental hand over Hildy's back. The purr intensified and tiny, razor-sharp claws pricked her legs as the cat began kneading.

"I've handled it. All you need to do is rest for a bit. Recover your equilibrium. It will make the evening much easier for you to manage, trust me." He crouched beside her and scratched Hildy's chin.

"But—"

"Your Highness, wouldn't you rather use your energy for kitten petting and cocoa drinking than for arguing with me?"

She shook her head. "You're impossible."

"You're welcome."

She laughed and sipped the cocoa. It was smooth and rich and perfectly delicious. Maybe he was right. The luncheon had taken its toll. She would rest here just long enough to drink the cocoa, and then she would force herself to get up and move forward into the next responsibility on her list.

Curling deeper into the chair, she sipped her cocoa and stared into the fire, a purring kitten on her lap. Soon the flames became a distant crackle, and her head lolled against the back of the chair. Dimly, she was aware of Tal taking the mug from her fingers, draping a blanket over her, and rearranging the kitten, and then she slid peacefully into sleep.

SEVENTEEN

THREE DAYS LATER, Charis was just finishing up her daily meeting with Darold when a note arrived that Lady Channing was downstairs requesting an audience. Charis spent another ten minutes composing a letter to General Thane, who'd been authorized the previous day to begin lighting fires on three sides of the Montevallian outpost, and then sent word to her seamstress about the dress she needed for the upcoming trade delegation ball. Once she'd tidied her desk, she rang for a page to bring Lady Channing to her private office.

"Should I send for tea?" Tal asked from his position beside the study's door.

Charis shook her head. "I can't spare much time for Lady Channing."

"I wasn't thinking of Lady Channing." His tone was perhaps a bit more pointed than was strictly appropriate for a servant. "I was thinking you've pushed yourself hard all morning and barely eaten any breakfast."

"I'll be fine."

He sighed.

When the door opened and both Lady Channing and Ambassador Shyrn entered, Charis rose and stepped out from behind her desk, her thoughts racing.

"Your Highness." Both visitors bowed.

"Welcome, Lady Channing. Ambassador Shyrn, this is an unexpected honor." Charis shot a look at Lady Channing. It was unlike her to forget to mention something as important as an ambassador in her request for an audience. Charis would have received them in a far more formal setting had she known.

"Thank you for making the time to see me," Lady Channing said. "I was unaware that Ambassador Shyrn would be joining me. He arrived after I'd already sent word to you." She sounded mildly displeased.

"I felt it best to present my kingdom's interests to Your Highness personally," Ambassador Shyrn said, bowing once more.

"I can grant you both no more than a few minutes." Charis remained standing, forcing the other two to stay on their feet as well.

"Thank you, Your Highness. I'll make this brief." Lady Channing folded her hands in front of her waist and spoke with the measured calm that always marked her words. "Rullenvor is allied with a kingdom far to the north, and as such has access to a formidable army capable of helping us protect our interests at sea. With those interests protected, Rullenvor would be prepared to join with our army to push Montevallo back into the mountains for good. Ambassador Shyrn can answer any questions you may have."

The silence that followed her words was ripe with tension. Charis's thoughts raced. Who was the kingdom to the north? Certainly not Embre, the farthest northern kingdom on Calera's map of the sea. They were an insular people who rarely dealt with outsiders. And why would this other kingdom be willing to help either Rullenvor or

Calera protect their trade vessels at sea?

"Ambassador, which kingdom are you referring to?" Charis met his gaze.

"Te'ash."

Charis blinked, scouring her memories for Brannigan's thorough lessons on the peoples and creatures who populated the outer reaches of the sea. Te'ash was the kingdom of the Rakuuna—humanlike sea creatures who generally had nothing to do with people. Why would they change their minds now?

Finally, she spoke. "The kingdom of the Rakuuna? I thought they never came ashore or had dealings with humans."

"Just so, Your Highness." Ambassador Shyrn adjusted his collar. "However, they have recently decided to align their interests with ours, and as we are aligned with you, this is an opportunity to create the kind of kinship that no one could stand against, least of all King Alaric Penbyrn, despite his apparently having some help at sea."

A chill crawled across Charis's skin. "King Alaric has help at sea?"

Ambassador Shyrn spread his hands wide. "What else could explain key merchant vessels sinking on their way to Calera? I thought long and hard after our discussion at the luncheon, and this is the only conclusion that makes sense. Alaric must be using an ally to attack ships bound to and from Calera. It's troublesome, especially as two of those vessels belonged to Rullenvor citizens. Our people demand protection. Your people need trade. Montevallo must be put in their place. With the Rakuuna's assistance on the open waters, that can be accomplished. I've already sent a palloren and received confirmation that they are willing to assist."

"And what is the price of this assistance?" No one did anything for free, and Charis couldn't see how the Rakuuna, isolated for so long in their distant underwater kingdom of Te'ash, could possibly gain anything from interfering with the affairs of Rullenvor or Calera. Plus, it would take weeks to send a palloren bird to Rullenvor and receive a response, so either Ambassador Shyrn had negotiated this deal with Te'ash as soon as the Rullenvor ships sank, or he was lying about gaining their full cooperation in hopes that looking like Calera's hero would benefit him here.

Though if either of those were true, why hadn't he discussed it at the luncheon when she'd brought it up? Too many eavesdroppers? Or perhaps there was a third option. Perhaps a representative from Te'ash was in palloren distance out on the open sea, and the ambassador had simply done his job.

"That's the best part of the offer, Your Highness," Ambassador Shyrn said smoothly. "What they want are Montevallo's mountains full of jewels. It costs you nothing but an agreement to give their allies unfettered access to Montevallo for as long as it takes to mine the jewels they need."

Charis held his gaze, her mind racing. Everything had a price. If the Rakuuna were offering help for free, then they simply hadn't been honest about what they truly wanted of Calera.

"What exactly does unfettered access mean?" Charis asked. "And how did they hear about our situation or about the jewels in the Montevallo mines? Montevallo hasn't had access to sea trade since the war began, and the Rakuuna don't travel this far south."

In fact, Charis was straining to remember what they looked like. Surely there had been an illustration in one of Brannigan's textbooks. Something... slightly taller and skinnier than a human, with unnaturally long legs and arms? Maybe with gills or fins? If she remembered correctly, the Rakuuna could breathe out of water for short periods of time, but it was dangerous for them to remain on land for long, so they kept to the sea. It had been at least two years since her test on the reclusive, rarely spotted sea creatures, but she was nearly certain the Rakuuna hadn't surfaced near any of the kingdoms on Calera's map for over one hundred years. Not since they'd once had dealings with Embre, though details on that relationship were sketchy at best.

"We discussed the Calera–Montevallo war with them when we became aware of their need for jewels." Ambassador Shyrn straightened his coat, his fingers worrying with the buttons for a moment before he noticed Charis watching him closely. "We live far to the east of you, Your Highness. It's a different world over there. Forging alliances with species you never see down here is a matter of some priority."

"We have our own alliances with nonhuman species." She thought of the mild-mannered Kirthin who farmed Calera's swamps, and admitted that a friendly agreement with nonlethal creatures who thrived on moss and mud was a far cry from understanding the need to build a relationship with a kingdom as dangerously violent as the Rakuuna were rumored to be.

"I still don't understand their motivation for this offer. What underwater kingdom needs jewels?" Charis frowned. "Kingdoms need food, medicine, weaponry, cloth, and building supplies. Unless they need jewels to pay for those things, this doesn't make sense. And why would they need jewels now when they've apparently been doing well without them for years?"

Lady Channing spread her hands out as if to show that she was holding nothing back. "I cannot answer for their needs. I'm sure they're as discreet about their true situation as we are. But we have an opportunity here to end the war."

"By giving warlike strangers access to our ports, our roads, our cities, and our people for an unspecified amount of time." Charis's voice was flat.

"No, Your Highness." Ambassador Shyrn bowed his head deferentially when her gaze landed on him. "They do not come ashore. Rullenvor would mine the jewels for them. You would simply need to grant us safe passage from your ports to the conquered mountains of Montevallo and back again."

"And what do you get out of the deal?"

"A portion of the jewels and the continued goodwill of a fierce and formidable ally."

"We can negotiate boundaries." Lady Channing remained as unflappable as ever. "But this gives us protection at sea and additional soldiers and weapons from Rullenvor on land to take the fight to Montevallo and finish this."

"How do we know they would honor their agreement?" Charis looked from Lady Channing to Ambassador Shyrn.

Lady Channing smiled. "An excellent question. Ambassador Shyrn, can you offer assurances of their intentions?"

The ambassador hesitated. It was a millisecond, a fraction of a pause before he matched Lady Channing's smile and hurried to assure her of Te'ash's honor, but Charis saw it.

Charis held up a hand to stop Ambassador Shyrn's words, and he stuttered to a halt, a frown digging into his brow. "Your Highness?"

She held his gaze for a long moment, and his fingers reached for his coat buttons again. Calera desperately needed to remain on good terms with Rullenvor, especially with the growing shortage of medical supplies they were facing. She couldn't afford to offend him by turning down the offer out of hand. Neither could she agree to it when it seemed clear Ambassador Shyrn was holding something back.

"Thank you for sharing this offer with me," Charis said courteously. "You've given me much to consider. Of course, I will need to take this under advisement from the queen and our council. If I have more questions, I will send for you."

It was a dismissal, and Ambassador Shyrn immediately bowed, thanked her for her time, and left.

Lady Channing made to follow him but stopped before she reached the door. Quietly she said, "King Alaric has escalated things, Your Highness. We have only to look at the assassination attempt and Irridusk for proof. He must be stopped, and we should look at every option available to us."

"Even one that puts us in debt to both Rullenvor and the Rakuuna?"

"When both allies want nothing from us and everything from Montevallo, I think it must be considered. But of course, it's far easier being an advisor than it is being the one responsible for the decision."

But did both Rullenvor and the Rakuuna want nothing from Calera but access to Montevallo? She knew little of the Rakuuna's culture or value system. Without that understanding, she had no way to gauge their true motivations and intentions.

All she had was the certainty that Ambassador Shyrn had been nervous and was holding something back.

She glanced at Tal and found his expression troubled. Perhaps he'd noticed the same thing she had.

There was a knock at the door.

"Enter." Charis looked past Lady Channing to find a page standing in the doorway. He hurried over, bowed, and handed her a message in an envelope smudged with black dirt. The blue wax seal was off-center, as though hastily applied.

"A missive from General Thane," the page said, bowing once more before leaving.

The instant the door closed behind him, Charis tore open the envelope and pulled out the single sheet of paper inside. She scanned the words once, leaned heavily against her desk, and read them once more.

"Is something amiss?" Lady Channing stepped closer.

Charis looked up, the black dirt from the envelope staining her hands.

No, not dirt.

Ash.

"It worked." Triumph blossomed, a hard, brilliant light that burned within. "My plan to trap the central Montevallian outpost with fire and drive them into the sea *worked*."

Tal sucked in a breath from his place against the wall, and Charis met his gaze for a moment before looking back to Lady Channing. She'd forgotten that it had been his afternoon off when she'd met with the council and come up with their response for Irridusk. And though she'd talked with him in-depth at the refugee camp about Montevallo's motives, she hadn't yet been comfortable using him as a confidant with sensitive information, so she'd kept the plan quiet. He hadn't known the attack was coming, but perhaps hearing that Calera had extracted vengeance for Alaric's atrocities would bring him a measure of peace.

Lady Channing's face looked like Charis felt. Relief and triumph at this definitive victory tinged with horror at the tremendous loss of life.

"That will certainly send a message to King Alaric."

"And fill our people with hope." Charis folded the general's letter and tried to wipe a smudge of ash from her hand.

"You have him reeling, Your Highness. Now would be a good time to strike even harder."

Charis considered her for a moment. "You mean by using Rullenvor and the Rakuuna."

"I mean by whatever methods are necessary."

"I appreciate your advice, Lady Channing. This victory has given me hope that we can forge ahead and find a solution without relying on outside help. At least for the moment." Charis moved toward the door.

Lady Channing bowed. "Your mother will be very proud of you."

Once Lady Channing was gone, Charis turned to Tal. "Ambassador Shyrn was hiding something, wasn't he?"

"Absolutely." His voice sounded subdued.

She paused. "Are you all right?"

He squared his shoulders. "Yes, Your Highness. I was just picturing fire burning my city. I'd always thought I'd have something to one day come home to."

She stepped close and laid a hand on his arm. "You will have something to come home to. I will figure out a way to end this war and rebuild the north. I swear it."

King Alaric Penbyrn had his answer to the atrocities in Irridusk, and to any notion that killing Queen Letha would make Calera an easier prize to conquer. Now she simply needed enough leverage to bring him to the table to discuss peace.

EIGHTEEN

"HOLD STILL, PLEASE," the seamstress said for what seemed like the hundredth time in an hour.

Charis bared her teeth in the closest thing to a smile she was capable of after holding still for most of the morning while Merryl and her staff circled her, pins in their mouths, measuring tapes slung over their shoulders and wide swaths of sea-blue silk in their hands. If Charis had known being fitted for Merryl's new dress design was going to be so tedious, she'd have found someone in the servants' quarters who was her approximate size and sent that hapless girl in her stead.

She could have been pressuring Lady Shawling for another sizable donation to refugee relief. Brainstorming with Mother for ways to end the war without relying on Rullenvor and the Rakuuna. Discussing Mother's prognosis with Baust after yet another setback in her recovery, this time caused by a bout of pneumonia, though Mother had improved enough to insist that she was going to attend the upcoming ball. Sparring with Tal and practicing the seven rathmas, which he made look disgustingly easy, but which were, much to Charis's chagrin, incredibly hard to master.

Tal was in the shop with her, standing just outside the door of the large fitting room. It had been nearly two months since he'd become her bodyguard, and they'd fallen into a comfortable routine. He brought her breakfast each morning. They sparred, and he did his best to teach her to combine dance and swordsmanship. Then they moved through each day together, his silent presence the shadow at her back, until they returned to her chambers, either to get her ready for an evening event or to spend the night in, discussing the day, the war, or whatever topic took their fancy.

She would have given a lot to be able to talk freely to him right now, but Merryl and her two assistants were never out of earshot as they measured the princess for a gown to wear to the ball that would honor the trade delegates from Solvang, Rullenvor, and Thallis, who were due to arrive in another three days.

Charis had to look and act every inch the capable princess at that ball. It was crucial that she and Mother inspire confidence and a willingness to continue partnering with Calera in trade, despite the loss of a few merchant vessels in the northern sea. Without those trade relationships, there would continue to be shortages in medical supplies, and there would be no metal for new weapons. The war would be lost for certain if trading ceased.

She'd be a fool not to assume Montevallo's spies had already reported the importance of these negotiations to their king, which meant it was also crucial that Charis arrived at the ball ready for a fight.

"Make sure to leave room for my weapons," she said as one of Merryl's assistants circled her waist with a measuring tape. "And give me a way to reach them quickly."

The assistant glanced at Merryl as if to see whether the princess's order should be obeyed, but Charis didn't give the older woman a chance to respond. Leaning forward, she locked eyes with the assistant and said, "Either this dress accommodates my weapons, or I will go elsewhere."

The assistant nodded quickly and slid back a step. Charis stretched her neck, feeling the muscles pull after standing still for so long. Honestly, how many measurements were needed for this? It was just a dress.

She closed her eyes as Merryl began pinning swaths of fabric across her shoulders. Her mother's warnings echoed in her head, and she reined in her discontent.

It wasn't just a dress. It was another weapon in her arsenal. A message that Calera still held on to some of their wealth, even though the Montevallians had tried so hard to ruin them. That the princess was powerful, confident, and bold. That Calera was both a force to be reckoned with and a worthy ally.

Less than an hour later, Charis was free. She stepped out of the fitting room to find Tal standing beside the door, looking as alert as ever.

"Don't you ever get tired of standing around waiting for me?" she asked as they moved toward the front of the shop.

He shrugged. "I could see out the front windows, and it's a busy street, so it was entertaining enough. Though not nearly as entertaining as listening to you try to hold your temper for three hours of fabric pinning and measurements."

She rolled her eyes and kept walking.

Reuben and Elsbet stood just outside the shop door. Elsbet hurried to open it as Charis approached. "Your Highness," she said with a bow.

"Thank you, Elsbet."

The afternoon was steeped in pale sunshine and the light, crisp scent of the sea. Charis lifted her face to the sky and drew in a slow, deep breath as Elsbet whistled for the royal coachman to bring the carriage around, and Reuben took up his position at Charis's left.

People bustled along the sidewalks, hurrying from one shop to another, their conversations humming through the air beneath the distant crash of the waves and the occasional piercing cry of a sea hawk. Wagons moved down the street, loaded with wares as farmers and merchants made their deliveries.

Several people close to Merryl's shop noticed the princess standing on the sidewalk and rushed to curtsy or bow. Charis inclined her head graciously and motioned for them to rise and go about their business.

"The carriage is approaching," Reuben said.

A trio of farmers in homespun peasant clothing walked behind her as she stepped toward the street. The carriage rolled to a stop. Elsbet moved forward to open the door, and then a shout echoed from a rooftop behind her.

"Death to the warmongering princess!"

Charis whirled toward the sound.

Reuben reached for his sword.

Charis heard a faint twang—a plucked wire vibrating. Her mind screamed *arrow* an instant before she saw it streaking toward her heart. Too fast to avoid. Too fast to do more than flinch in anticipation of the agony that was to follow.

There was a blur of motion to her right, and then Tal slammed into her. The arrow struck him, a shock of violent force that ripped a cry of pain from his lips.

Charis went down. Tal landed heavily on top of her, the arrow sticking out of his upper left shoulder. Blood poured out of the wound and dripped onto Charis. For an instant, she locked gazes with him, and then Reuben grabbed Tal and dragged him roughly off Charis.

"Into the carriage, Your Highness," he said, his voice clipped. "Move now."

Charis struggled to her feet but kept one hand on Tal. Her eyes scanned the surrounding rooftops even as she registered the panic that had swept the street. People ran, yelling for loved ones as shop doors slammed shut. No one wanted to be out in the open if Montevallo was attacking.

"Are we being invaded?" Her voice was sharp with fear, but it didn't shake. Not yet. Not until she had everything under control. Not until she was alone in her chambers, where she could let the horror wreck her.

"Elsbet and the city guard are chasing down the shooter. I don't know if there are more enemies around us. Your Highness, get into the carriage now. We need to get you to safety." Reuben yanked none too gently on her arm, and Charis's gaze snapped to him.

"Bring him too." Her hand gripped Tal's uninjured shoulder. His face was deathly pale, and his eyes had closed.

"You are my priority." Reuben glared at the surrounding area, his sword held ready in his free hand. "We need to leave. *Now.* We'll send help for Tal."

"A fine way to repay him for saving me. He could bleed to death while he waits." Charis ripped her arm free of Reuben and bent down toward Tal, whose lips were pressed tight with pain. "Tal, open your eyes. Can you stand?"

"Your Highness—"

"We aren't leaving without him," Charis snapped. "You want me in that carriage, Reuben? Then you bring him, too."

The guard swore under his breath, sheathed his sword, and helped Charis lift Tal off the sidewalk and into the carriage. The instant

Charis followed Tal inside, Reuben slammed the door, and the carriage began moving.

"Stay still." Charis dropped to her knees beside Tal, whose breath was coming in awful, desperate gasps. He lay on his right side, the arrow still sticking out of his left shoulder. Blood soaked his clothing and pooled on the carriage floor. Charis lifted his head and placed it in her lap, keeping one hand firmly on his shoulder to stabilize it as the carriage jostled over the cobblestones.

Clenching her muscles to keep herself from shaking, Charis said, "You're going to be all right. Are you listening to me? Don't you dare close your eyes—that's an order from your princess."

Tal's eyes fluttered open, but it seemed to take too much effort to keep them that way. He let them close and reached for his injured shoulder with his good hand.

"I've got you." Charis held Tal as still as possible as the carriage turned up the long, winding drive that led to the palace. "You were incredibly brave. I'd be dead if it wasn't for you. I won't forget the debt I owe." Emotion crept into her voice, and she swallowed hard against the image of the arrow burying itself in her chest. Of lying on the cobblestones, bleeding as she struggled for air until her heart gave out.

Leaning close, she brushed a few errant strands of Tal's blond hair away from his ear and whispered, "I won't let you die, Tal. I forbid it."

As the carriage rolled to a stop and Reuben opened the door, she began spitting orders to every staff member in sight.

"Call for the royal physician. Have him meet us in my chambers. Gather up a few of the stable boys and have them carry Tal to his bed. And notify the queen of the assassination attempt. Tell her I will meet with her about the matter once I'm certain Tal is all right."

As the staff scrambled to obey, Tal groaned and tried to reach for the arrow. Charis bent swiftly and gathered his large hands into her own. "Be still just a little longer. The physician will know how best to remove the arrow without causing more harm. I'll personally see to it that you receive the best possible care."

"Your mother will want to meet with you immediately," Reuben said.

"She can wait until Tal's wound is bandaged."

As stable hands arrived to carry Tal through the palace, up the stairs, and into Charis's private wing, the princess climbed out of the carriage. Her dress, damp with Tal's blood, clung to her as she wrapped her hand around his and willed him to endure the pain just a bit longer.

"Your mother will expect you," Reuben said.

"Then you can inform her otherwise."

His eyes narrowed, lip curling in disdain, though he took a step back. Perhaps the lesson she'd taught him outside the war room a few weeks ago was still fresh in his mind. Or perhaps he felt confident as soon as he reported the incident to Letha, she'd give Charis no choice but to leave Tal in favor of a meeting with the queen.

If that was the case, then Reuben and Mother were both in for a reminder that Charis had a sword for a spine.

Baust met Charis, Tal, and the stable boys at the entrance to Charis's wing. He followed them into the small bedroom just off the entrance to Charis's bath chamber, his physician's bag in hand.

"Set him down on the bed. Gently." Charis whipped the coverlet off the bed and tossed it aside. "Put him on his right side so the arrow doesn't touch the mattress. We can't risk it going in any farther."

When the stable boys had Tal situated to Baust's satisfaction, Charis sent them on their way and rang for a trio of maids to gather supplies for the physician. Hot water. Rags. And a list of things from his office.

"I can help," Charis said.

"The maids can help, Your Highness." Baust gently probed the skin around the arrow. "It went pretty deep into the muscle, but I don't think it hit bone. That's good."

"The maids aren't going to help. I am." Charis's voice was firm, but her touch was gentle as she crouched in front of Tal, whose mouth was pressed into a thin line of agony.

"Your Highness, this is unseemly work—"

"This boy saved my life. Tell me what you need, and I'll do it."

"Cut his shirt away from the arrow and then take it off." Baust turned to direct the maids, and Charis used his scissors to carefully cut Tal's shirt away from the arrow wound.

"Give him a swallow of this for the pain. And then hold him steady." Baust pushed a small jar of red liquid into Charis's hands and dipped a rag into hot water and then into a bowl of something that looked like brown water and smelled sharp and unpleasant. Charis poured a swallow of the red medicine into Tal's mouth as Baust began packing damp, medicine-treated rags around the buried arrowhead. Was it wrong to be thankful that the shortages that had every other physician in the city rationing their supplies hadn't yet touched Baust's considerable stockpile?

"Hold him steady," he barked as he pressed down on the rags with one hand and grasped the arrow's shaft with the other.

Charis wrapped her arms around Tal's shoulders, pulled his head against her neck, and held on tight as Baust slowly and carefully worked the arrow free. Tal's body went taut, his breath stopping in his throat as he clenched his fists into the back of Charis's dress and hung on. When the arrow finally slid out of his shoulder with a slick, wet sound like that of the sea gently slapping against a rock, he slumped against Charis, his body shaking.

Baust pressed the rags over the wound, and they quickly soaked through with blood. "We have to get this wound stitched quickly. Keep him still."

Charis held Tal steady as Baust's nimble fingers pulled the wound closed with his needle and thread. Tal bit his lip and closed his eyes but gave no other indication that he was in agony. When Baust had finished cleaning, stitching, and bandaging the wound, he wiped his face with his handkerchief and then set another bottle of brown medicine on the side table.

"Red medicine with every meal for pain management. Brown medicine at night to help him sleep. I don't know how much blood he lost, but I wouldn't recommend strenuous activity for at least a few days. His body has had quite a shock."

"Thank you." Tal's voice was hoarse with pain and fatigue, but he turned to meet the physician's gaze.

Baust's smile creased the smooth roundness of his face. "Anything for the boy who saved the princess."

When Baust left, Charis called for some maids to clean the chamber and left briefly to discard her ruined purple day dress, wash her face and hands, and then dress in a simple green frock before returning to Tal's room. She found the floors gleaming, new sheets on the bed, all evidence of Baust's tools removed, and Tal lying down, his face still unnaturally pale.

As the door closed behind the maids, leaving Charis and Tal alone in her chambers, her knees went weak. Sinking to the floor beside his bed, she laid her head on his blankets and fought the tremors that shook her.

She could have died.

Tal could have died.

Death to the warmongering princess! the archer had screamed.

She closed her eyes as she once again heard the terrible wet *thunk* of the arrow striking Tal. Felt his weight crash down upon her as she hit the ground, expecting another arrow to find its mark.

How long did she have before someone else tried to kill her? Weeks? Days? And what if the arrow had missed Tal's shoulder and struck his heart instead?

Nausea rolled through her, and she swallowed hard as she felt Tal's hand gently come to rest on the top of her head.

"Your Highness?" When she didn't respond, he shifted in the bed, sucking in a little gasp of pain, and said, "Charis?"

It was the first time he'd ever used her name, and she lifted her head, though the room swam at the edges. His hand fell to the blanket again.

"You could have died." Her words came out sounding like an accusation, and Tal smiled weakly.

"Comes with the job description."

"This is not a time to make jokes. I think I'm going to be sick."

He blanched. "Don't you dare. I'm a sympathetic vomiter. If you start, I'll start, and then where does it end?"

"Where does it end?" She threw the words back at him. "With me dead. Or you dead after trying to save me. I can't . . . you shouldn't have made me eat breakfast." She glared at him.

"I . . . what?"

"You made me eat breakfast." She pointed at him to emphasize her list of grievances. "And became my sparring partner. You let me sleep on your shoulder in the carriage. You brought me hot chocolate and Hildy when I'd had a bad day, and you made me laugh at your terrible impersonation of Lady Everly. *And* you told me about your sister and your favorite cat and sneaking out to eavesdrop on Montevallian soldiers and about the time you fell off a horse trying to impress a girl, and you shouldn't have done *any* of that."

He opened his mouth, apparently decided reclining in bed wasn't the most effective position to argue from, and struggled to sit up. His face went gray as he bumped his injured shoulder against the wall, and Charis whipped her hand into the air, palm out.

"Stop it. Stop moving."

"You don't tell me what to do."

"Of all the foolish nonsense—"

"All right, fine. You tell me what to do. But not while we're arguing." Tal managed to get himself halfway up, and Charis leaped to her feet and hurriedly stuffed pillows behind his back before he could collapse.

She fisted her hands on her hips. "We aren't arguing."

"We most certainly are." He glared at her.

"Nobody argues with me."

"Maybe someone should."

She threw her hands into the air. "This is exactly what I'm talking about! You said the same thing when you made me start eating three meals a day again. And then you made me interested in listening to you. And before I knew it, I felt safe around you."

"Clearly, I am doing an awful job at being your bodyguard if you feel safe around me."

Heat flushed through her, driving away the nausea and leaving something else in its wake. Something like anger, but softer and far more fragile. "I don't feel safe around you because you're paid to protect me. Reuben is paid to protect me, and I would never dream of falling asleep against his shoulder or talking to him about ways to stop the war or . . . I don't care about Reuben's favorite cat."

Tal blinked. "Reuben has a favorite cat?"

Charis's voice rose. "How would I know?"

"Because you brought it up!" He raised a finger to aim it at her, and they both ignored the way it trembled. "If we're making a list of foolish reasons to be upset, I have a few I'd like to add."

"*We* aren't making a list."

"First, you're supposed to be just a job. A favor to the king, whom I like very much."

His words stung, and Charis didn't want to consider why.

"Second, nobody asked you to be more than the ruthless, cunning, rather terrifying princess you show most of the world. Nobody!" He looked around the room as if to prove that there was, indeed, no crowd of people asking Charis to be something beyond her reputation.

"What does that even mean?" she demanded.

"And third, I told you about my sister and that stupid horse trick and my cat because you made me care about you. You made me see you as a friend, and then you walk out of that shop today, as regal as you please, and you nearly get yourself killed! If you think I signed up for this job so that I could lose a friend, you're wrong." His hand fell to his lap, and he pinned her with his gaze. There was an intensity in his eyes that made something in her ache. "I could have been too slow. Or I could've been at the wrong angle. Or—"

"Or you could have died, and if you hadn't made me eat breakfast or laugh at your jokes or listen to stories about your cat, I might have been able to survive that." The words left her lips and hung in the air between them, their honesty scraping Charis raw inside. She swallowed hard and whispered, "I didn't want to be your friend."

"I didn't want to be your friend either." His voice was soft, and when he patted the edge of the bed, she sank down beside him, her hands shaking more than his.

"You scared me today."

"You scared me too." He leaned back against the pillows as though too weak to manage anything else.

She fussed with the blanket covering him, and then finally whispered, "Whoever tried to kill me might try again."

"They'll have to go through me, Your Highness." His voice was fading as the pain medicine and blood loss took their toll.

She scooted farther onto the bed and leaned against the pillows beside him. A crooked little smile tugged at his mouth briefly before he slid into sleep.

NINETEEN

It was unseasonably warm outside later that evening, so Charis arranged to meet Mother in the private courtyard outside the queen's chambers for dinner. Not only was Charis heartily sick of being in her quiet chambers, where the memory of the awful twang of the archer's bow could haunt her, but Baust had mentioned that Mother needed more fresh air to aid in her recovery. Dinner outside was a handy solution to both problems.

Mother arrived as a maid began arranging dinner on a small table beside the double doors that led to the queen's sitting room. Vellis and Gaylle, Charis's evening security team, were stationed nearby, as were four more guards for the queen. Three additional palace guards stood watch on the ivory stone walls that surrounded the courtyard. Charis felt both smothered and exposed.

The queen waited in silence as the maid set out dishes of vegetable barley soup, roasted quail on a bed of seasoned rice, and apples baked and dipped in spiced sugar. A pitcher of fresh water with lemon curls floating inside and two place settings finished the table.

"Leave us," the queen said. The maid hastened to obey. Once the door shut behind her, Mother gestured at the courtyard. "We could have eaten in my parlor."

"I needed to be outside." And a glance at Mother's pale cheeks and sunken eyes in the lantern light said that she did, too.

"I would think you'd have had enough of that after today." Mother glanced at the guards pacing the courtyard walls. "However, I've doubled our security presence throughout the palace."

"Very sensible of you, Mother. That will send the appropriate message of concern to our people." Charis settled into a chair and began portioning the food onto two dinner plates.

"I was rather hoping my actions would send the appropriate message of concern to my daughter as well."

Charis hesitated in the act of pouring a glass of water and nearly overfilled the glass. Hastily setting the pitcher down, she said, "Of course."

Taking the seat beside Charis, the queen pressed her fingers against her forehead for a moment as if staving off a headache. When she spoke, her voice was uncharacteristically gentle. "How is Tal?"

"He's resting. I got him to eat some soup, but I think the blood loss really took its toll. He can't stay awake for more than a few minutes at a time. Baust says that will improve greatly in the next few days as long as we keep him eating and drinking."

Slowly, Mother raised her head. "The city guard caught the shooter."

Charis set her fork down, a chill raising gooseflesh across her arms. "And?"

"Montevallian."

"How did King Alaric know I'd be at Merryl's today?" Charis's gaze was as hard as the pit that was forming in her stomach.

One person might have the answers. The fury that was always lit in Charis's heart rose to flood her skin with heat and her thoughts with venom.

"Where is the Montevallian we caught?" Charis's tone was as uncompromising as the set of her mother's jaw.

"In the dungeons. We'll let her sit for a few days. That should be long enough to let her start rethinking her situation. And then we'll question her."

"We?"

Mother's gaze cooled. "You failed to get information from the spies who snuck into the palace and instead allowed Reuben to kill them. We can't afford any mistakes this time."

Charis narrowed her eyes. "If you accompany me to the dungeon, you will undo all the work we've done to make sure my reputation is as fearsome as yours. One day, I'll be queen. I can't afford for anyone to think I'm not capable of doing everything that is required of me."

"Then *be* capable of everything that is required of you."

The words stung, but Charis kept her expression smooth. Above them, the last remnants of the day disintegrated into darkness, and silvery stars pricked the night sky. "I'm capable, Mother. But it would help if Reuben stayed away from the dungeon. I'll take different guards with me."

"Whoever you take, we need to get to the bottom of these assassination attempts," Mother said. "King Alaric obviously has spies with access to the palace and to your schedule. That means you aren't safe until we discover his network, and if that was an easy job, it would've been accomplished years ago."

An owl hooted mournfully nearby as Charis straightened in her chair. "What do we know?" She raised her hand and began ticking items off on her fingers. "Someone with knowledge of the palace helped a Montevallian man sneak into the ladies' parlor and hide until he could attack you. On the same night, an unarmed woman was found in my bath chamber. The ball was a well-publicized event, so it stands to reason that Montevallo's spy network would have known about it."

She took a sip of water and set her cup down. "Someone with knowledge of my personal schedule helped an assassin know exactly where to be and when today. Only my secretary and the council members had copies of my official schedule for the week, but Merryl could have told any number of people that the princess was coming to her shop for a fitting, which means, again, Montevallo's spy network could have easily learned the information."

"To be safe, your secretary can be replaced immediately." Mother's eyes sparked with rage.

"There's no need to kill Darold," Charis said, her voice steady though her stomach felt as if she'd swallowed worms. Darold had been in charge of her schedule, her correspondence, and the various minutiae that came with being a very busy princess since she was seven. She couldn't imagine a scenario in which he would betray her, but perhaps this was yet another example of the weakness Mother was constantly trying to stamp out of her.

The ache that had blossomed within her at the loss of Milla, Fada, and Luther sent a sharp spike of pain through her, and she lifted her chin. Maybe it was weakness, but she couldn't face being responsible for the death of another person she cared for. Not unless she knew for sure that he'd betrayed her.

"Explain." Mother's tone warned Charis to tread carefully.

"Darold has given us no reason to distrust him. What motive

would he have for wanting me dead now, after all these years?"

"I've told you. People will either want to use your power or take it from you."

"Or they just want to serve me well because they believe I can stand between them and Montevallo and keep them safe." Charis leaned forward. "Darold has never once tried to use me to gain anything. And what if removing Darold is the goal here? What if removing those closest to me, to *us*, is the plan? Isolate us, surround us with strangers who are easier to bribe or threaten, and we would be far easier to kill."

The queen sat back, her expression thoughtful as she considered Charis's words. Finally, she nodded. "I see the wisdom in that. The truth is that it doesn't matter how many spies we catch and kill. If he's determined to kill us, he'll keep trying. What we need to understand, and quickly, is why Montevallo's strategy seems to be changing. What does King Alaric want? Why invade Irridusk when it's so far from the port he's been fighting to claim? Why try to assassinate you when I'm the one who is opposing him?"

"Because I'm the one who authorized General Thane to drive more than half of Alaric's army into the sea."

Mother's smile was vicious. "Indeed you did."

"But now that his generals know that strategy, we won't be able to repeat it. We're back to defending territory without being able to make any headway on Montevallian soil." A soft breeze stirred Charis's hair, and she pushed it out of her face. "We still don't have leverage. We still don't have a way to bring Alaric to the table to discuss peace. Unless we take Rullenvor's offer—"

"Absolutely not. I don't trust it."

"I don't either."

Charis sipped her water and considered the problems facing them. War was like a giant game of chess where the board was full of shadows and a knife could enter your back as easily as a sword could cut through your front. But for all the answers she didn't have, one thing was clear.

"King Alaric wants to punish us for what his kingdom perceives as Queen Rhys's treachery and our continued dishonorable treatment of them. His people are starving, and he has to deliver something that restores their honor and reputation. He wants power over us." Charis set her glass down and leaned forward. "He doesn't just want the Ebbington port. If he did, all his troops would be focused there. He'd be negotiating with us for trade routes and tariffs."

"Montevallo doesn't negotiate." Mother's mouth set in a hard line.

"No, they don't. But maybe that's because we haven't offered them what they truly want." A terrible idea was forming, and the weight of it felt impossible to carry.

"They want to annex the northern section of our kingdom so they can have a sea lane without paying any tariffs for it," the queen said, though she was frowning thoughtfully.

"It's more than that. I've been listening to our refugees from the north. Some of them overheard conversations between Montevallian soldiers. They are on a zealous quest to punish us for the treachery they believe happened years ago. But as a result, their people have gone nearly two decades without access to trade beyond what the smugglers have managed to sneak in and out of small, seldom-used harbors. They might have repelled our invasions, but that doesn't put food on their tables or clothes on their backs. Like you, Alaric's entire reign has been overshadowed by war, and his people must be suffering greatly as a result."

"It's no longer enough for him to gain access to the port." Mother nodded slowly. "His pride demands more. Maybe his people demand more."

"So he attacks farther in. Destroys a farming village. Sends his spies to assassinate us."

"Irridusk is in a direct line between Montevallo's southern border and the palace." The queen straightened. "He wants to destabilize us and clear the path for an invasion of the capital. He wants the throne."

The idea forming in Charis's mind settled into place with stark clarity, and she dug deep for the courage to say quietly, "So let's give it to him."

The queen's gaze snapped to her daughter, starlight glittering in her eyes.

"Or at least let's make him think we have." Charis folded her hands in her lap to hide the way they wanted to tremble. She'd always known she'd been forged in the fires of her mother's indomitable will for one purpose only—to protect the Caleran people. She'd just never dreamed that protection would come at the cost of the quiet longings of her own heart.

Mother's eyes sparked. "Give him the illusion of power."

"Yes."

"There's only one way to do that." Mother watched her carefully.

"I know." Charis lifted her chin, silenced the whisper inside that had dared to hope she might one day find someone to truly see her and love her while wanting nothing but her own love in return, and said with icy calm, "We offer King Alaric my hand in marriage to one of his sons and the use of the Ebbington port in exchange for an end to the war."

Slowly, Mother leaned across the table and took Charis's hand in her own. Her skin was soft, and Charis let herself relax into the touch for a moment. "We are surrounded by enemies. That will never change. But this . . . this might just work. And we both know you can keep the prince in line. He'll be nothing but a consort, though we'll be careful not to refer to him that way lest that get back to Alaric. And in case he doesn't accept the offer, we'll still work to get the trade delegates to commit to helping our war effort."

"And I'll question the assassin in a few days to get a lead on Alaric's spy network."

"We'll begin work on the treaty proposal tomorrow. Report directly to me once you've interrogated the assassin. And Charis"— Mother stood and held her daughter's gaze—"don't fail."

Once she'd returned to her own chambers, Charis locked the door behind her, leaned against it for a moment, and then slowly made her way to her bath. Climbing into the tub, her dress trailing over its edges, she wrapped her arms around her legs and pressed her face against her knees.

Something dark and aching spread through her veins.

She was going to pledge herself to her enemy. Every moment of her life would be spent watching for his knife to come at her back. She would never be able to fully trust him. Never be able to let down her guard.

There was no way to survive that without being what Mother expected—the most ruthless, dangerous person in the kingdom.

TWENTY

The next morning dawned gray and gloomy. Rain pattered against the windows as Mrs. Sykes fussed about which dress the princess should wear. Charis put her foot down when the woman brought out a black dress with a full skirt and gray lace that crept up the throat.

"That's for funerals," Charis said firmly. "I have a meeting with the queen, a visit to the refugee soup kitchen, lunch with Lady White-cross, tutoring, and then tea at Lord Everly's. I need to look both regal and approachable."

"Black is always a suitable color, Your Highness." Mrs. Sykes ran a reverent hand over the stiff satin of the dress.

"Indeed it is. If someone has died." Charis swallowed against the sudden rush of nausea as she remembered the wet *thunk* of the arrow striking Tal. "But since I have no funerals to attend today, I need something different."

"Yes, Your Highness." Mrs. Sykes turned to Charis's massive closet, a frown puckering her brow as she considered the racks of dresses.

Charis sighed. Might as well choose her own dress or this was going to take all morning, and she had precious little time before

Mother expected her. "On second thought, Mrs. Sykes, I will manage my own dress. I need you to fetch warm water, soap, and fresh bandages. Are you skilled at dressing wounds? Tal will need his bandages changed and the wound area cleaned."

Mrs. Sykes hung the dress back on a rack and turned to face the princess, her eyes glowing. "I've a fair bit of nursing skill, Your Highness. It would be a great honor to care for the boy who saved your life. I'm sure he'd be more comfortable with new dressing and perhaps a sponge bath as well. It's always best to be clean."

Sending Tal a swift mental apology, Charis said, "Thank you, Mrs. Sykes. I leave him in your capable hands." The door had hardly closed behind the handmaiden before a voice said weakly, "Who are you leaving in her capable hands?"

"Tal!" Charis turned to find him leaning against the doorframe, his face pale. He still wore the pajamas he'd worn to bed. A small bloodstain marred the tunic near his injured shoulder. "What are you doing out of bed? You're supposed to rest all day."

"I thought I'd use the chamber pot. Unless you'd rather I somehow accomplish that from my bed?"

"Very funny. Fine. You can use the chamber pot."

"How gracious of you, Your Highness." He grinned and then swayed on his feet.

"Do you need help?"

"From *you*? I'd rather fall into it face-first. I'll manage."

"As you wish." She turned back to her dresses and dearly hoped he'd forget the question he'd asked when he walked into the room.

"What are you doing? You have a meeting soon, don't you? Why aren't you dressed?"

"Mrs. Sykes brought out funeral attire for my day." She reached for a dress in gorgeous russet velvet, a perfect match for the thesserin leaves outside her window. Creamy lace ruffles peeked out from a diagonal split down the front of the skirt, and golden embroidered birds of prey decorated the bodice. Ivory ribbons laced up the bodice, which took care of needing anyone to button her into the garment. It was regal enough for the meetings she must attend yet approachable enough for the soup kitchen, and the beautiful birds on the bodice would send a subtle message to everyone that their princess was the predator, not the prey.

"Good choice," Tal agreed when she turned with the dress in her arms. "And so wise of you to distract Mrs. Sykes before she could . . . wait a minute." His eyes narrowed. "You never answered my question."

"That seems very unlikely."

"Your Highness—"

"Tal, I really must get dressed. I believe you said something about using the chamber pot?"

"If you assigned that woman to take care of me, I will never forgive you."

Charis waved a hand in the air, dismissing his concerns. "She's just going to clean the wound area and give you a new dressing."

Tal sighed. "Fine."

"And maybe give you a sponge bath," Charis muttered half under her breath.

"*What?*"

Charis gave him an apologetic look. "She came up with the idea on her own. It all happened so fast. I'm sorry. But it *would* be good to be clean, and you're hardly in any shape to do that for yourself today."

He glared at her for a moment, and then said, "You owe me for this."

"Is this how you talk to your princess?"

"When she turns her enthusiastic, geriatric, no-respect-for-privacy handmaiden loose on me, yes." The door to the chambers opened.

"Tal, you brave boy, what are you doing out of bed?" Mrs. Sykes's voice filled the room.

Tal shot Charis a look that promised retribution and then turned toward the handmaiden. "I'm going to use the chamber pot. No, I do *not* need help with this."

Charis hadn't told him about her plan to offer King Alaric a betrothal in exchange for an end to the war. He'd be proud of her, she was sure of it. Relieved that his people would be free if Alaric accepted.

But talking to Mother about the idea required her to be cold and calculating, and the reality of it was easily held at a distance. Sharing it with a friend was something else entirely. Forming the words would make it real, permanently silencing the quiet longings of her heart, and she couldn't bear to do that until she had no choice.

Twenty minutes later, with Tal back in bed and being ministered to by Mrs. Sykes, Charis arrived at Mother's study, a massive room lined with bookshelves and art from centuries of Calera's best painters. To the right was a receiving area with two long couches in dark blue velvet and several high-back chairs. To the left sat Mother's heavy desk, carved with ornate roses up the sides and the seal of the Willowthorns in the center. Four high-back chairs with ivory satin cushions faced it.

"Your Majesty." Charis bowed and then joined Mother at the desk, where she sat looking weak but regal. A parchment lay in front of her.

"Good morning, Charis. Read over this. If you have no changes to make, we'll send it by palloren bird to King Alaric."

Charis leaned over the parchment. Her mouth went dry as she

read the proposal to marry one of King Alaric's heirs to the princess of Calera to form a truce between the two kingdoms for as long as both parties were alive. The document ended with an invitation for both sides to negotiate items into the contract, such as port usage and rebuilding fees.

It was one thing to offer the idea to Mother. It was quite another to see it spelled out in stark black ink, a thing that couldn't be erased, couldn't be undone once it had left the palace.

Her heart ached for a beat, whispering its longing for a chance to be loved by a boy simply for herself and not for her title, and then Charis called up the shield of ice necessary to be what her mother and her kingdom needed.

"It's just right. Don't you think we ought to use an official courier rather than a palloren for this?"

"We'll use both. And because your idea to drive more than half of his army into the sea went so well, we are now negotiating from a place of equal strength." The queen rolled the parchment into a tight coil and reached for her purple seal. An additional parchment with identical writing lay beneath the first.

"Good thinking." Charis looked away as Mother softened the wax and pressed her seal into it. "When do we tell the council what we're doing?"

"When it's to our best advantage."

A knock sounded at the study door, and then a footman entered, bowed, and said quietly, "Your Majesty, Ambassador Shyrn from Rullenvor is here and requests an audience."

Charis swallowed against the sudden tightness in her throat as the queen handed the sealed parchments to the footman and said, "Send one of these to King Alaric by palloren and one by courier. And allow Ambassador Shyrn to enter."

The footman bowed again and left. Charis pressed her hands against the desk to feel something solid and real as her world spun.

It was done.

The palloren would take no more than three days to reach King Alaric's castle. Would he send a reply immediately or make them wait? And what would they do if Alaric decided the offer to put one of his sons on the Caleran throne beside the kingdom's next queen wasn't enough to restore his people's honor?

"Your Majesty." Ambassador Shyrn bowed to the queen, then turned and bowed to Charis as well.

"Ambassador Shyrn, please sit." The queen stretched out an arm to indicate one of the couches in the receiving area and then chose a high-back chair for herself. Charis chose another chair so that they were both sitting higher than the ambassador as he sank into the cushions. "To what do we owe this visit?"

"Your Majesty, I believe in getting right to the point. No pretty words to dress up the message. I pray you will not take offense." He paused as though waiting for reassurance.

"How can I know whether I will take offense when you've yet to say anything of import?"

"Very well." The man took a deep breath and then said briskly, "Rullenvor has concerns about our allyship with Calera."

"We're listening."

"This war." He spread his arms out, palms up, as if to say, *Surely, you know what I mean.*

"What about the war?" The queen's blue eyes bore into the man before her. "Your offer of help is up for discussion at our council meeting, but these things take time and should have no bearing on our trade relationship. Our trade with Rullenvor continues to be as strong as ever. Our coin retains its value."

"But for how long?" He leaned forward. "I was Rullenvor's ambassador to Montevallo for three years. I know King Alaric and how he thinks. He will not stop fighting until he crushes your kingdom and takes your throne."

Unless he thought he was being given the throne without the years of additional bloodshed it would take to win it. Charis held herself absolutely still as she watched Ambassador Shyrn. The parchments that were on their way to Montevallo now felt like golden keys that would unlock the solution her people so desperately needed. A solution that wouldn't involve Rullenvor's interference, which was clearly where this conversation was heading.

The queen apparently shared Charis's thoughts, for she cocked her head as if studying an ant on the cobblestones and said, "I don't believe I've asked for Rullenvor's advice in forming battle plans, but I'm happy to hear that you're supportive of us remaining on the throne. When your trade delegate arrives in a few days, we can all meet and discuss our mutual interests and how to accomplish them."

Ambassador Shyrn's smile reminded Charis of Reuben's expression when tasked with interrogating a prisoner. "You misunderstand, Your Majesty. We value our partnership with *Calera*."

With Calera. Not with the Willowthorns.

The temperature in the room seemed to drop several degrees.

"Explain yourself, Ambassador Shyrn." There were daggers beneath Queen Letha's words.

"The High Emperor of Rullenvor believes that Calera is a jewel among the sea kingdoms. Your land is perfectly suited to farming all manner of foods and raising all manner of animals. He would be loath to lose trade with you, and he understands that should Alaric take the throne here, a new trade agreement would not be as favorable for us."

"And the High Emperor believes it benefits his trade agreement with us to take the help of your ally Te'ash?" the queen asked.

Ambassador Shyrn drew in a breath as though determined to get through something unpleasant. "Your Majesty, it is the High Emperor's view that you have had eighteen years to establish dominance over King Alaric and restore your borders, and you have not been able to do so. You have also not responded to his ally's offer of assistance. These are not the actions of a leader who is able to protect her people. Therefore, the High Emperor graciously offers to make Calera a protectorate and establish rule here under the auspices of a regent from Rullenvor, in exchange for bringing the full might of our army and that of Te'ash to bear against the Montevallians, both on land and at sea. The High Emperor believes he could quickly defeat the enemy forces and restore the peace and prosperity that Calera was once known for."

The silence that followed his words settled over the room like a shroud. Charis kept her expression cold and emotionless as she waited for Mother's response. They couldn't afford to alienate a powerful ally like Rullenvor, but they would have to be truly desperate to give up the throne and allow strangers to rule Calera.

And with the betrothal offer on its way to Alaric, they weren't yet desperate.

"This is most unexpected," the queen finally said.

"I realize that, Your Majesty, but—"

"I wasn't finished."

The ambassador took one look at the queen's face and hastily bowed his head. "My apologies, Your Majesty."

"This kind of offer takes careful consideration. I'm sure the High Emperor doesn't expect an immediate response and will understand that I will need to meet with my council and take advisement. An issue like this could take several weeks to decide, perhaps more." The queen stood, no sign of weakness evident. Immediately, Charis and Ambassador Shyrn followed suit. "I will send for you when I have an answer. In the meantime, we look forward to welcoming your trade delegation and to continuing the friendship between our two kingdoms."

"Thank you, Your Majesty." Ambassador Shyrn bowed and left the room.

The instant he left, the queen collapsed into her chair and turned to Charis. "That is no benevolent offer."

"No, it isn't." Charis shook her head. "Rullenvor and the Rakuuna see us as an easy conquest because we've got our hands full with Montevallo. When we turn down their offer, they might decide to send their warships and take what they want. We can't fight a second war, Mother."

"I've bought us some time," the queen said, cold fury on her face. "Now we'd better hope Alaric accepts the betrothal offer. If we reach peace terms with Montevallo, Rullenvor will have to either let go of the idea that we can be conquered or understand that a marriage between you and a Montevallian prince means Rullenvor would be facing their army as well as ours."

"In the meantime, we need to have everything ready for the trade delegations, and we have to be certain of our own people's loyalty," Charis said, the queen's rage a match for her own. "We will shore up our alliances, ferret out the spies, and be in a position of strength when Alaric replies."

"Let's get started."

TWENTY-ONE

TWO DAYS LATER, Charis rose early, ate the bowl of fruit that a kitchen maid had brought up, and then knocked quietly at Tal's door, his breakfast in hand.

A floorboard squeaked and Tal's voice, husky with sleep, called, "Come in."

Charis entered to find Tal struggling into a loose shirt that still strained against the bandage on his shoulder.

"You shouldn't be out of bed," she said sternly.

"I'm sick of lying around all day, Your Highness." Tal sounded stronger than he had since being injured.

"It's not lying around if you're recovering from an injury."

"I don't think I have enough energy for another argument with you." He eyed the bowl of spiced plum porridge she set before him and smiled. "Then again, I might feel differently after I eat."

"Your friend Grim from the stables has sent a message every day since your injury asking after you."

"Probably feeling good about his chances of beating me in our next game of roshinball."

"Do you need pain medicine?"

"Not if I want to stay alert." He ate a bite of porridge. "And don't even think about sending Mrs. Sykes in to give me another sponge bath. I will manage on my own today."

"Duly noted. How does your shoulder feel?"

"The shoulder hurts, but it's healing." Tal took another bite and then paused. "Did you eat breakfast already?"

Charis laughed. "I did. And the fact that you're checking up on me today tells me you are truly on the mend."

"I'm not up to full strength yet, but I can manage a few hours of activity before I'll need to rest again."

"That's good news." A knot of tension in Charis's stomach eased. "I've had Reuben shadowing my every move while you recovered, and I'll be glad to relegate him to his regular duties instead. Especially this morning. In fact, I may need your help choosing a dress."

"Ah, clothing advisor. One of my favorite duties." The fact that he said it with absolute enthusiasm made her laugh again.

"You're particularly good at it."

"My sister would be proud to hear it. She always was selective when it came to her dresses." A shadow passed over his face, and not for the first time, Charis wondered where his sister was and what had happened to the rest of the family. The ones he never talked about.

"Did you help your sister choose her dresses?"

He looked at the window, at the silvery streaks of rain that ran down its length, and finally said, "Sometimes. She was kind to me. She was born from my father's first wife, but sometimes she reminded me of my mother."

Charis frowned. "Were others in your family unkind to you?"

His jaw clenched, and for a long moment, she thought he wouldn't answer. Then he said, "I suppose you could call it that. Now, what kind of impression do you need to make today? Let's find you the perfect dress."

Charis met his gaze and thought of what she'd like to do to the assassin who'd dared to send an arrow at her heart. Heat ignited, burning through her veins at the thought of Tal risking his life for hers. At the terrible memory of the wet thud of the arrowhead striking flesh. "They caught the woman who shot you," she said.

"Did they?" Tal's voice hardened. "I hope we're about to pay her a visit."

"We are. I want to look both approachable and absolutely dangerous. See what you can do with that."

An hour later, after bathing himself and donning his regular uniform, Tal had chosen a gown for Charis and then disappeared into his room as Mrs. Sykes helped the princess dress. When the handmaiden had been dismissed to her laundry and mending duties, Charis stepped closer to the mirror in her bath chamber, a small smile lifting the corners of her mouth.

The dress was a bold crimson, the color of freshly spilled blood, but the style was soft and feminine. A fluttering skirt with multi-length hems, an upside-down rose whose petals were gossamer thin. A fitted bodice with delicately embroidered snakes in cream and gold circling the wrists and the neckline. Thorny vines in the same cream and gold were embroidered on either side of the dress's corset lacing. And a cream-colored sheath with thorny rose vines etched onto its surface was ready to attach to whichever wrist she'd prefer to house a dagger.

Her hair fell down her back in a riot of curls, wild and untamed, and her eyes glowed with fury. The woman who'd dared to lift a bow and arrow against Calera's princess was going to wish she'd never set foot in Arborlay.

"Did you want one dagger or— *Oh.*" Tal stopped in the middle of the doorway staring at Charis, her daggers held in his hands but apparently forgotten.

"The dress is perfect," Charis said.

"Perfect," Tal breathed.

Charis turned toward him and froze. The light in his eyes made a flicker of heat blaze to life within her. They stared at each other for a long moment, then Tal looked at the daggers in his hands.

"These are yours. I mean, of course you know that. It's just . . . I . . . did you want them both, or should I go put one away? I should go put one away. I'm going." He disappeared into her bedroom before she had a chance to respond.

She took a deep breath, willing the strange flicker of heat to go away. She had an assassin to interrogate, and it was going to take every ounce of focus she had to make sure she got the information she needed. There was no room for anything else in her head.

When she was certain the rage she felt at the woman who'd shot Tal was all that burned within her, she left the bath chamber.

Tal stood by the door that led to the hall, a single dagger in his hand. His expression was remote. "Your Highness," he said as he handed her the weapon.

She slid it into its sheath. It was time to swallow any hint of softness and sympathy. Time to reach for the rage that would shield her as she marched to the dungeons to extract the truth from someone who wanted her dead.

She was Charis Willowthorn. Let everyone who crossed her path today know that she was the most ruthless player on the board and tremble.

"Ready?" Tal asked.

Charis lifted her chin and let fury kindle throughout her veins. "Ready."

She swept from her chambers, Tal at her heels. The bloodred dress swayed gently as she moved. The sheath at her wrist was a comforting weight, but the steel of her dagger was no match for the steel in her spine.

Charis would get what she came for, and seers help anyone who stood in her way.

Reuben and Elsbet instantly flanked Charis as she moved toward the main staircase. "Your Highness, I will happily manage the interrogation," Reuben said.

"You will not even enter the prisoner's cell."

"With all due respect, a princess in a dress is hardly the kind of intimidation we need for this job."

The fury in Charis's blood sent a flush of heat over her skin. Stopping at the top of the staircase that led down to the back of the palace where the entrance to the dungeon was located, Charis turned, her movements slow and deliberate. Her gaze landed on Reuben, and she imagined pulling her dagger, slicing through muscle, and carving Milla's name into his bones.

Her mouth curved into a smile, vicious and cruel. Reuben swallowed hard.

"I am precisely what this interrogation needs." Charis's voice was just as vicious as her smile. She stepped closer to Reuben, her heart pounding as anger flashed across his face even while he slid back. Lowering her voice, Charis said, "And I will cut your tongue out of your mouth if you ever argue with me again."

She caught a glimpse of Tal's face and found that strange intensity burning in his eyes again. Tearing her gaze away from his, she turned and descended the staircase, her guards and Tal hurrying to keep up. The dungeon was a long, well-lit corridor carved from the white stone that formed the bedrock of Calera. The hallway had eight cells on either side—small rooms with a thin pallet for a bed, a bucket for necessities, and a hook in the wall with chains attached to it for prisoners deemed dangerous enough to require shackles. Thick wooden doors reinforced with iron bars kept prisoners securely in their cells.

A small office with a desk, a bookshelf, and several chairs was located at the dungeon's entrance, and at the far end, past the last cell, was the huge iron door that led to the firepit.

Charis didn't plan for the day's visit to end with her prisoner's body being thrown in the firepit. She needed to gain information—solid information—and then to keep her source alive in case she proved useful. Charis could think of several interesting ways to use the would-be assassin, but until she spoke with the woman, she wouldn't know which path was best to explore.

Meredith Giordan, one of Charis's favorite guards, was seated at the desk. Her skin was the dusky gold of her Veracian ancestors, and her voice still carried faint traces of the musical lilt of her parents' kingdom. She rose to her feet when she saw the princess. "Your Highness." She bowed.

"I'm here to speak with the Montevallian prisoner."

"Yes, Your Highness. And may I be forward enough to say that I'm grateful she failed in her mission." The guard reached for her keys and stepped around the desk.

"Thank you, Meredith. She would have succeeded if it hadn't been for the courage of my bodyguard." Charis nodded toward Tal, who looked slightly uncomfortable when every gaze landed on him.

The woman who'd shot an arrow at Charis looked to be only a few years older than the princess herself. Her red-blond hair was pulled into a messy braid, her clothes were rumpled, and there were bruises blooming on her bare arms and along her jawline courtesy of the city guard who hadn't taken kindly to her treatment of their princess.

"Stand guard outside the door," Charis said to Reuben and Elsbet. Reuben stared at her, and the anger in his eyes shivered through Charis until it met the shield of her own rage.

Maybe Reuben needed more than a lesson in what happened when people failed to respect Charis. Maybe he needed to become an object lesson for others who might want to follow his example.

"Tal, you're with me."

He followed Charis into the cell, stood beside the door, and glared at the woman chained to the far wall.

"I hope you're enjoying your accommodations," Charis said, her voice soft and almost friendly.

The woman spat at her. Tal took a step forward, but Charis raised a hand to stop him and smiled as she approached the woman. "It must be frustrating to hate me so much and have so little ability to hurt me."

"You didn't think that when you were looking down the end of my bow and arrow." The woman sounded proud.

Charis settled herself on the edge of the pallet that was lying on a stone slab about chair height. "You're right."

The woman's eyes lit with fervor. "Bet you were terrified."

"Absolutely."

"Perfect little warmongering princess almost cut down right in the heart of her own kingdom. Just shows that you aren't as safe as you think."

Charis flicked an invisible wrinkle out of her skirt and met the woman's gaze, her lips slowly curving into a smile. "I never believe I'm safe. Do you?"

The woman blinked and shot a look toward Tal, as if the bodyguard could supply the answer to Charis's question. When Tal remained silent, the woman looked back at the princess and said, "I'm safer than you."

Charis's smile gentled, and she infused her voice with sympathy. "Are you?"

The woman drew back. "I don't have a target on my back. You can do anything you want to me here, but it won't change the fact that a lot of people want you dead. One day soon, they'll succeed."

Charis tilted her head as if studying the woman and said, "Forgive me. I've been incredibly rude. I should have introduced myself when I first entered."

The woman laughed, harsh and loud. "I know who you are."

"No." Charis's voice was quiet, but rage flickered in it now. "You know my name. You know my title. But you have no idea who I am."

Charis rose in one fluid motion. In the next instant, her dagger was in her hands.

"Go ahead. Cut me. Torture me. You won't learn who I am or who hired me. You won't get anything from me at all."

"I already have all I need." Charis stepped toward the woman, fury in her heart, ice in her eyes. "I had it the moment I walked into your cell."

She closed in on the woman, who backed up until she hit the cold stone wall behind her. Charis's smile was a feral baring of her teeth. "You made a terrible mistake when you thought you understood who you were going up against. All you know of me is my name and the rumors you've heard."

"I know enough." Bravado laced the woman's voice, but a thin thread of fear shivered beneath it.

"Did you know that I killed my first spy when I was nine years old? A man who thought he could snatch me out of the palace gardens and take me to Montevallo." Charis raised the dagger, and the woman's eyes latched onto it. "I clawed out his eyes and crushed his windpipe. *Then* I screamed for help."

The woman swallowed, her gaze locked on the dagger.

"When I was twelve, someone tried to drown me while I was swimming in the sea. I let her think she'd succeeded, then when she dropped her guard, I rose from the water and cut her jugular with a sharp bit of coral. I think she bled to death before the sea predators came, but I can't be sure."

Charis let the dagger come to rest above the woman's heart, its point pressed lightly against her skin. "I was raised on the understanding that for every bloodthirsty Montevallian who came for me, another two would be right behind. I've executed every one of them."

The woman lifted her chin as if to bravely accept her fate. "And now you're going to kill me."

Charis laughed, a venom-laced breath of cruelty that chased the courage off the woman's face. "Oh, I'm not going to kill you. I'm going to let you go."

The woman barked a laugh. "Sure you are."

"I'm going to unshackle you and personally escort you out of the palace." Charis set her teeth. The woman tried to draw back as Charis slowly dragged the tip of the dagger from the assassin's heart to the base of her neck. A thin, red welt rose in the weapon's wake.

"Why would you do that?" Her voice was breathless.

Charis cocked her head, keeping her eyes locked on the Montevallian scum who'd dared to shoot an arrow at her. "Because I am the nightmare you won't see coming. I am the last gasp of air in your lungs. The final beat of your treacherous heart. And once you've made an enemy of me, I won't stop coming for you until everything you love lies in pieces at your feet."

"But . . . then, why not just kill me now?"

"Because you aren't begging for death yet." Charis pressed the dagger until the tip punctured the woman's neck, drawing a thin line of blood that slid down her skin, a perfect match for the dress the princess wore.

"I'll never beg you for death." The woman's voice was scornful, though the tendril of fear within it had widened.

Charis smiled, and the woman shivered. "I'm going to let you go. And I'm going to spread the rumor that you gave me information about the entire network of Montevallian spies within our kingdom. That you told us exactly how to find them and kill them. Any who are part of that network will worry that their name crossed your lips."

The woman shook her head, her eyes wide, but Charis wasn't finished.

"And then I'm going to let Alaric know you gave us his secrets and that the peace treaty offering we recently sent is now off the table."

Locking eyes with the woman, Charis said, "Who do you think will come for you first? Your king? Or the other spies in my city?"

The woman fell silent.

"You'll run," Charis said softly. "Maybe to friends in Calera who are sympathetic to your cause. Maybe to your family in Montevallo. You'll run, and I'll be the shadow at your back."

The dagger dug in, and more blood poured down her neck. "Those friends who shelter you? Dead. The homes you sleep in? Burned to the ground. The family you love? Utterly destroyed. By the time I'm done with you, there will be no one left to welcome you. No one left to care what happens to you. There will only be your king and your fellow traitors coming for your head, and I promise you, when that happens, you will beg for death."

Charis held the woman's gaze and watched in grim satisfaction as the truth of her words hit home. The assassin's bravado crumbled before sheer terror as the princess sheathed her dagger and reached for the shackles.

"No, wait. Wait!" The woman's voice was desperate.

"Why should I?"

"Please. Don't let me go. Don't start rumors. My family . . . they can't be punished for this."

"Give me one good reason why I should stay my hand."

The woman's gaze darted to Tal and then back to Charis. "Because I'll tell you who paid me to kill you."

"Who?" Behind her, Tal stirred against the wall, but Charis kept her focus on the assassin.

The woman hesitated. People always did right before they turned traitor on their own. A last, desperate attempt to convince themselves they had no choice. Charis waited, holding herself as still as a predator stalking its prey. Finally, the woman whispered, "My orders don't come directly from my king. They go through a man called Bartho. He stays near the docks. That's all I know."

Charis smiled. "For your sake, I hope Bartho exists and is easy enough to find. He's your one chance of staying safely in this cell."

TWENTY-TWO

CHARIS SPENT THE rest of the morning meeting with Mother, then attending a shortened tutoring session, and finally hosting a luncheon for members of Arborlay's performing arts committee. She then forced Tal to rest for the afternoon with the promise that she would meet with Darold in her own parlor rather than her office in the main wing so that she wouldn't have to keep Reuben as her bodyguard while Tal slept.

When he slept through tea as well, she decided to have a maid bring him a late dinner and let Mrs. Sykes begin preparing her for the ball to welcome the trade delegates. Two hours later, after firmly refusing the woman's suggestions that a high, tight bun was always the best hairstyle for a formal event only to realize that was truly the only updo Mrs. Sykes knew how to arrange, Charis graciously thanked her handmaiden and sent her home to her family.

The dress was stunning. Merryl had outdone herself. With its plunging neckline, dramatic sweep of a skirt, and silver embroidery that resembled tiny knives stitched into the blue silk, it gave the impression that Calera's princess wasn't one to be trifled with.

But unlike the dress, Charis's hair was an utter disaster. She stared morosely at the lopsided updo that was slowly sliding down the side of her head. If she rang for another maid to help, Mother would hear of it, and then Mrs. Sykes would lose the job she desperately needed to get her family through the winter. But if Charis showed up at the ball looking anything less than perfect, it would ruin what she and Mother needed to achieve with the delegates.

Maybe she could shore it up on the side that was drooping and then wear a crown to cover most of it. She scooped a handful of hairpins from the vanity and planned her attack.

"Starting a new trend, are we?" Tal's voice startled Charis, and she dropped the hairpins. They scattered across the floor at her feet.

She bent down to retrieve them. "Yes. It's called the Price a Princess Pays for Refusing a Simple Bun. I'm thinking it will be all the rage by the weekend."

The hairpins retrieved, she stood and found herself face-to-face with Tal. His gaze swept her from head to toe, and when it returned to her face, the bright intensity she'd seen in his eyes that morning was back. A hum of pleasure swirled through her, and heat rose to her cheeks as he stood staring at her in silence.

"Do you like my dress?"

"Yes." He answered so fast, he almost cut off the end of her question.

The heat in her cheeks rushed into her veins. "I wanted bold, elegant, and dangerous."

"Just like you." He said the words like a prayer, and something kindled to life in her chest. Something sweet and wild and tender to the touch.

Something she absolutely should not be feeling when her bodyguard looked at her.

He took a small step forward and closed the distance between them. Charis's heart fluttered as he reached out a hand and then stopped, his palm hovering beside her hair.

"Do you want—"

"Yes," she said, her cheeks burning when she realized she hadn't let him finish his question. When she knew that the question she'd hoped he was asking was something she could never accept.

"Charis." Something burned in his eyes—a twin to the flame that was consuming her from the inside out.

"I..." Her hair slid down and brushed against her ear. Quickly she reached for it, brushing against Tal's hand in the process. She moved back, her knees bumping into her vanity chair.

He drew in an unsteady breath and looked at the ceiling. She sank into the chair and ordered her heart to stop pounding. When he looked back at her, there was a rueful little smile on his lips.

"Do you want my help with your hair?" he asked.

"I don't know if that's a good idea." She met his eyes and forced herself to hold his gaze, though the sweet, wild thing within her felt utterly exposed.

He settled his hands on the back of her chair and kept his eyes on hers. "I solemnly swear that I will do nothing but help you fix this disaster on top of your head. Furthermore, I apologize for making you feel uncomfortable. I wasn't prepared for how stunning you look, and I didn't have my guard up so that I could keep my reaction from you. I'll try hard not to let that happen again."

"You didn't make me feel uncomfortable. You made me feel . . . I don't know how to describe it." Her cheeks burned again, but she kept going. "And that feeling, it's dangerous. It's a distraction, and worse, it isn't something I'm free to give to you."

His eyes closed briefly as if her words had landed hard, and then he opened them and smiled, real and genuine. "Definitely a dangerous distraction for us both. Let's agree that you should strive to let Mrs. Sykes dress you from now on so we can be sure you will look a mess, and that I should remember you can cut out my tongue if I displease you."

She laughed, relieved to be back on normal footing. "I'm saving the tongue removal for Reuben. I'll think of a different punishment for you."

A shadow crossed his face, but it was gone before she could identify it. "Make it legendary, please. Surely I deserve nothing less."

Twenty minutes later, Tal made a noise of frustration as several jeweled pins sprang free of Charis's hair and clattered to the floor. As she bent to retrieve them, Charis glanced swiftly at the clock resting on her bedside table.

The ball to welcome the trade delegates started in less than an hour. It would be the height of disrespect not to be standing at her mother's side to greet them as they entered the ballroom, but she could hardly go looking like this.

"Your shoulder makes it hard for you to manage this mess by yourself," Charis said. "Perhaps if we do it together."

Tal craned his neck as if stretching muscles that were tight with pain and said, "Good plan."

Together they worked Charis's thick, unruly curls into a semblance of order, but one glance at the mirror told Charis it would never do. It was far too simple, no better than she would wear for a picnic at the shoreline or a lazy afternoon riding horses where she wanted her hair out of her face. It didn't match the stunning, dramatic elegance of her dress in the least. And it was already starting to spring free of its pins.

Tal seemed to realize this as well. Frowning, he said, "This is a disaster."

"I wouldn't go that far." Charis kept her tone light and began hunting through the jewelry box on her vanity for something that could hide her hair and become the focal point instead. Perhaps she could wear a jeweled headpiece. Or a crown, though dancing while wearing a heavy crown would leave her with a raging headache.

Tal raised a hand to push an errant curl back into the updo, managing to dislodge three more curls in the process. "It would help tremendously if your hair didn't have such a stubborn mind of its own."

"I'll keep that in mind. Meanwhile, I have very little time left before I have to be there to greet the delegates. I simply need to show them I'm strong, capable, and someone they'd far rather have as a friend than an enemy." Charis turned back to the vanity. "I'll just wear a crown. There are five in the velvet boxes—"

"Anyone can wear a crown." Tal looked thoughtfully at Charis's hair and then pulled the hairpins free, sending her curls tumbling down her back.

"Well . . . not *anyone.*"

Tal hardly seemed to be listening. Instead, he turned Charis away from the vanity and prowled around her, tugging at curls and running his long fingers beneath the mass as if encouraging it to rise from Charis's scalp and become something wild and free.

Charis closed her eyes as his warm hands pressed against her temples and then gently tugged at her hair. He smelled like soap and the black-leaf tea he preferred, and somehow those scents together sent an ache of longing through her veins.

"Please don't look at me like that," Tal whispered.

Her eyes flew open to find him bending toward her, his hands still in her hair. The pulse in his neck beat rapidly.

"I didn't even have my eyes open, so I couldn't possibly have been looking at you," she said, but her voice was breathless.

He drew in an unsteady breath and tugged once more on her hair, lifting it away from her scalp until her curls were an untamed mass. "I'm just going to concentrate on your hair, and you are going to make sure your thoughts don't show up on your face." He met her eyes briefly. "Please."

Charis played along. Looking in the mirror, she said, "This is going to make it harder to force my hair into an updo."

"Everyone will be wearing an updo."

"Because it's a ball."

"But you aren't everyone." Tal spun away from Charis and headed to the closet, calling over his shoulder, "You're Charis Willowthorn, destroyer of assassins, ruiner of enemies, and future ruler of Calera, and everyone in that room should feel that in their bones the instant they see you."

Charis blinked and turned to look in the mirror. Her hair rose in a wild halo around her head and fell, free and untamed, to the center of her back. She looked fierce, beautiful, and dangerous.

A tiny smile played at the edge of her mouth as Tal returned, a bit of metal filigree in his hands. "This is certainly going to get everyone's attention."

Lifting a thick strand of hair from either temple, Tal pulled them to the back of Charis's head, where he secured them with the strands of metal he held. Charis watched, fascinated, as Tal bent the metal, unspooled it from its original design, and then wrapped it around the curls he'd pulled into place.

"What are you doing?" Charis asked.

"Making sure you make the right impression." Tal's jaw set in a rigid line as he concentrated on his work. Charis made herself ignore the feel of his hands in her hair and the way his chest brushed against her back. Finally, he looked up and said, "There."

Charis turned in her chair so that her back faced the larger mirror, and then lifted the hand mirror to study the end result. Tal had woven the silver wire into the shape of a dagger and used that to secure the strands he'd pulled back. It looked as though the hilt of a weapon was resting atop the knot of curls while the blade pierced it and came out the other side.

It was perfect.

"Tal," Charis breathed. "You're going to need to add 'hair accessory design' to the list of things you're good at. This is spectacular."

Tal grinned and gave her an extravagant bow. "At your service. Shall we go down to the ballroom now?"

Rising, she shook out her skirts and turned toward the door. "Yes."

Charis paused a moment at the top of the grand staircase, a stunning piece of art that began at the third floor of the palace and plunged toward the ballroom floor in an ever-widening swath of gleaming marble bracketed by spun glass banisters in the pale blue of a winter's sky. The ballroom itself was a decadent picture of Calera's bounty—banquet tables heaped with delicacies, nobility dressed in their colorful finery filling the air with the sound of merriment, and the glorious sea showcased by the wall of windows.

Tal stood beside her, already scanning the room, hunting for threats. Vellis and Gaylle would also enter the room with her, but would stay at the edges, moving where she did so they could reach her quickly if necessary. Only Tal would shadow her every move.

It was ridiculous that the thought of Tal as her escort to the ball made something in her stomach flutter as though she was about to win a game she hadn't realized she'd been playing. She packed that thought away in a corner of her heart and focused on the task in front of her.

The antiwar faction needed to see that Calera still had strong allies and plenty of options. The trade delegates needed to feel confidence in renewing trade agreements so that they'd be open to a more aggressive role in helping Calera beat Montevallo if Alaric didn't take the bait. And everyone who'd heard about the assassination attempt needed to believe that the princess wasn't afraid of anything.

"You're on display," Tal whispered as a member of the nobility noticed the princess standing at the top of the stairs and began whispering with his neighbor. Soon the crowd of people closest to the doorway were all staring up at her.

Lifting her chin, she let her mouth curve into a beckoning smile with just a hint of cruelty. Descending the steps, one hand trailing on the banister, she assessed the room with a single glance.

A few maids continued to bring platters of food to the buffet table set up against the far wall. The musicians, all dressed in dark blue, were seated on a small stage in the nearest corner, instruments raised as they watched their conductor. Nalani, Holland, and several other guests Charis's age were drifting toward the buffet table, though Charis knew they'd never fill a plate until the queen had officially started the festivities. And the guests closest to the door had already separated to form a path for the princess, their heads bowed.

Pausing ten steps from the bottom, Charis looked around the room again, this time slower.

No trade delegates yet. And no queen.

Keeping her smile firmly in place, though her mind was racing, she finished descending the stairs and moved toward her friends, acknowledging the murmur of "Your Highness" that spilled from everyone she passed.

Mother was always early to everything. Always. And this was her first social event since her injury, so her presence was even more important.

Perhaps she'd decided to greet the honored guests in her private parlor before escorting them to the ball, but why wouldn't she invite Charis to attend? It was crucial that the delegates feel full confidence in Calera's leadership. They needed to believe Charis would be every bit the queen her mother was if they were going to commit to aiding the war effort.

Even if Alaric accepted the terms Letha had sent, Calera would still need strong allies elsewhere. One never knew when one would need powerful friends outside her kingdom.

Powerful friends within the kingdom were just as important to cultivate.

Charis's thoughts slid easily into the cold calculation that fit her like a second skin and never failed to remind her of her mother. There were gossips to impress, worried title holders to reassure, and politicians to keep in line. She could stay busy until Mother brought the delegates to the ball.

To the right, Lord and Lady Severin stood against the wall, their stiff postures at odds with those of the other nobility, some of whom had already begun dancing. The most recent raids by Montevallo had cost them dearly. Irridusk had been one of their main sources of income.

Huddled against the far corner, a trio of wealthy nobles who shipped Caleran goods to the other sea kingdoms were deep in conversation. They looked agitated.

Spinning on the dance floor was Lady Vera Shawling, her wrinkled mouth painted a bold red as she regaled her partner with whatever rumor she was currently eager to spread across the kingdom. The right story planted with her could yield fruit with Charis's ongoing search for the traitor behind the recent assassination attempts.

"There you are." Nalani, dressed in a stunning pink-and-gold dress, looped her arm through Charis's and whispered, "Lady Delaire is still trying to flirt with my brother. It's downright painful to watch. But good news! I got Lord Morrison to donate to the refugee center." She took a peek at the back of Charis's head. "Oh, your hair is magnificent!"

"Tal did it."

"Tal, you are a boy of hidden talents." Nalani grinned at him and then sized him up in his dress coat and blue cravat. "And don't you look handsome tonight?"

"Thank you, Lady Nalani," Tal said, sounding amused.

Charis let her focus drift around the room again as she sized up her priorities.

The Severins or the ship owners? Quickly weighing her duties, she decided to speak with the Severins first. They needed to know their rulers were working on their behalf to right the wrong done to them. Charis made a mental note to add a massive shipment of jewels from Montevallo's mines to the itemized list of things she would expect as the enemy prince's dowry.

"... and then Holland told her he would prefer to never be invited to tea again, and you should've seen Delaire's face. I thought—are you even listening to me?" Nalani demanded.

"Of course," Charis said smoothly, giving her cousin's arm a little squeeze as she glanced across the room to find Delaire, her brown skin glowing in the candlelight, looking a bit crestfallen. "Holland is incorrigible."

"You'll turn my head with such flattery," Holland said cheerfully as he approached them. Charis's lips twitched as she took in his usual black duster, his plain white shirt without a cravat, and the sword strapped to his hip.

"Only if I let you keep your head attached to your neck," Nalani said. "You know Mother made you promise to do at least three dances tonight."

"Indeed." Holland's countenance fell briefly, then brightened. "But she didn't say who my partners had to be."

Charis shook her head, laughing as Holland pivoted, bowed low to a very surprised matron in a dark purple gown with a pair of glasses nestled in her silvery hair, and escorted her to the dance floor.

"How can he possibly enjoy dancing with a grandmother more than with someone like Delaire?" Nalani asked.

"Maybe he's just doing his best to be what's expected of him even though we all know he's never going to fit that mold." The words stung, a tiny bite of pain in the part of Charis's heart that longed for a different life.

She fit the mold of a princess. If she sometimes wished for more, for connections that were about *her* and not her title, it was nothing she couldn't silence with enough willpower.

"Your Highness, may I have this dance?" a polished voice said in Charis's ear.

She schooled her face into calm disinterest as she turned to find Ferris Everly standing at her elbow. He was dressed impeccably in a fine gray silk dress coat with a red cravat at his neck. His light blue eyes examined Charis from her neck to her feet and back again, looking as though someone had presented him with his favorite dessert. He treated her to a wide smile, and she reminded herself that it was unseemly for the princess to throat punch a member of the nobility in the middle of a ballroom.

Nalani pulled Charis closer. "We were just going to find the queen and the trade delegates."

"I'll come along, then." Ferris offered an arm to Charis, who answered his smile with one of her own.

"I had no idea the queen had asked you to greet the delegates, Ferris. When did that happen?" Her voice dripped sweetness even as her smile grew thin and razor-sharp.

His brow furrowed, though he didn't drop his arm. "As your fourth cousin and the most eligible man for the position of king, it's only right that I meet the delegates with you."

"Who says you're the most eligible?" Holland asked as he disentangled himself from the matron he'd escorted to the dance floor and moved to his sister's side.

Ferris gave Holland's attire a disparaging glance and said stiffly, "I see you still haven't figured out how to be an adequate member of the nobility."

Holland laughed. "And I see you still haven't figured out how to be a decent person."

"You'll want to watch your tone, Holland." Ferris took a step toward the other boy. "A union between myself and Charis makes the most political sense, and as king, I will not look kindly upon those who speak poorly to me."

"If you can't handle hearing the truth about yourself, then maybe you should make a few changes." Nalani wrapped her free arm around her brother's and glared at Ferris. "You could start with keeping your eyes on Charis's face instead of looking at her body like it's a buffet table. And then you could ask yourself why you feel the need to insult my brother, your cousin, when everyone knows he's twice the man you'll ever be."

Holland bumped Nalani's shoulder gently with his own and gave her a little smile. Tal looked as though he was contemplating murder.

"It would be a small matter as king to seize your family's property in the capital and order you north to the battle lines." A vein bulged in Ferris's temple. "In fact, I may have a word with Father to see if we can't go ahead and conscript Holland right now. As council member, he works closely with both the queen and the general—"

"Give me your sword, Holland." Nalani turned to her brother.

He winked. "Told you this wasn't polite society."

"That will be enough." Charis's cold voice cut through Ferris's spluttering response, and he fell silent, frowning at her expression as if surprised to see that she was speaking to him and not to the twins.

"Charis, you know our parents have long discussed the advantages of a union between us. I've devoted my life to learning how to be king at your side." He glanced at Holland and tried unsuccessfully to wipe the animosity from his face. "I apologize for speaking out of turn to the Farragins, but we both know I should be the one to escort you to the delegates."

Once upon a time, Charis would have had to walk a careful line between putting Ferris in his place and leaving the door to a potential marriage open. He was right that many in the kingdom expected a union between them. Fourth cousin was far enough removed to be an acceptable match, and his father's long service as one of the queen's closest advisors put him in a good position to understand the intricacies of governing Calera.

But now . . . now the proposal for a peace treaty that included Charis's hand in marriage to the enemy was in King Alaric's hands. She couldn't imagine he'd turn down the chance to end the war while also gaining port access and placing his son on the throne. If he did, then Charis had bigger problems than a few ruffled feelings on the part of Ferris Everly.

"I escort myself." Her voice was crisp. "I always have, and regardless of who I marry, I always will." She met Ferris's eyes. "Calera has one throne, and when Mother is ready to abdicate, it will be mine, and mine alone."

Movement caught her eye, and she looked past Ferris to see the queen enter the ballroom. The jewels sewn into the rich cream of her silk dress glittered beneath the chandeliers as she moved through the crowds, dispensing nods and brief words to those who quickly curtsied and bowed in her direction. Her spine was sword-straight. Her mouth curved into her familiar cold, distant smile.

And yet Charis knew instantly that something was wrong.

"If you'll excuse me," she said, already moving toward the queen.

"Mother!" Charis smiled widely for the benefit of the nobility and grasped her mother's outstretched hand. "What is it?" she breathed as she reached the queen's side. "Where are the trade delegates?"

"Drowned." The queen's voice was a whiplash of quiet rage.

Charis kept her expression smooth as glass while her heart thundered in her ears and a pit opened in her stomach. *"What?"*

Mother nodded graciously to those closest to them and turned herself and Charis toward the golden throne that was set on a dais against the wall to their right.

"We received a palloren bird from the Rullenvor delegate two hours ago. They were the last in line behind the ships from Solvang and Thallis as they neared our harbor. The message said they were less than twenty furlongs out when they saw the ships ahead of them go down."

Charis swallowed hard, desperately trying to moisten her suddenly dry mouth. "Go down how? An attack?"

"What else could it be?" The queen's fury vibrated through her voice like a plucked wire. "Montevallo must have access to ships.

That's why they hit Irridusk. It wasn't to move toward the capital. It was to create a clear path to the mostly abandoned harbor of Portsmith."

"Then we send out the navy. Chase them down."

"I did. Nine ships." There was a thread of worry in her voice now. "They never returned."

Charis stared at her mother, heart pounding in sickening thuds against her ribs. "How could Montevallo suddenly have the means to sink so many ships?"

"I don't know, but we'd better hope King Alaric accepts our peace terms, because the Rullenvor delegate turned back to their kingdom, and as soon as the rest of our allies hear what happened, they'll refuse to trade with us as well. We're on our own."

TWENTY-THREE

"*ALL THE TRADE* delegate ships went down?"

"Not Rullenvor, though that's not going to help much if—"

"This is a disaster!"

"Nine naval boats lost? How could—"

"Impossible. Simply im—"

"Montevallo must have help. Another kingdom must be—"

"Silence." The queen's voice cut through the frantic din of voices filling the war room as she and Charis entered. The noise stopped immediately. She faced her council, her ball gown glittering in the light of the oil lamps lit along the walls. Far from the war room, the ball continued. The queen and Charis had stayed at the festivities for over an hour, greeting guests, picking at the plates of food their staff presented them, and spreading the story that the delegates had been unavoidably delayed, but that it was no reason not to enjoy the party.

The last thing they needed was a full-blown panic on their hands, though Charis remembered the ship owners who were arguing in the corner of the ballroom and felt sure word of the tragedy was already spreading.

Finally, when the queen had felt confident they could slip out without causing an uproar, she'd sent a page to discreetly round up the council members for an emergency meeting. Now the queen murmured instructions to the page who'd escorted the council to the war room and then closed the door firmly behind the boy's back. Tal took up his position against the wall directly behind Charis, watching each council member with unwavering intensity.

"Be seated." The queen moved to the map of the sea and its kingdoms that was tacked to a wall. There was a soft scuffle behind her, chairs scraping against the floor, silk rustling against wood, and then silence again.

Charis moved to the opposite wall, the better to have an unobstructed view of the entire map. Tal followed at her heels.

Arborlay was located at the southern tip of the kingdom. Calera's sea border was a wavy line of jutting peninsulas and deep curves. There were a few sheltered coves, a handful of small harbors, but nothing of consequence after the capital's port until she reached Ebbington, far to the north, just before the kingdom's borders stopped at the edge of the large expanse of sea.

The other sea kingdoms were ranged across the map with small, neatly printed numbers below their names to indicate their longitude and latitude and their distance from Calera's major port.

There was Morg, a good distance south of Calera with nothing between the two kingdoms but water. Nowhere to hide the ships that had helped Montevallo commit their latest atrocity. To the east, Solvang, Thallis, and Rullenvor were lined up like buttons on the back of a dress, their large borders so close to each other that it would take less than a week to sail from one to the other.

Beyond them, far to the north, lay Verace, with its swift channels connecting its string of islands, and then the kingdom of Embre, its inhospitable coastline and rocky outcroppings broken up by its two small ports. To the west of Rullenvor, the basilisk cave was marked in bold red. And just past Embre were the uninhabitable islands, treacherous coves, and deadly whirlpools that littered the northernmost part of the sea. Somewhere past that was the kingdom of Te'ash, but Charis couldn't imagine the offer to help them was still on the table now that Calera's trade relationship with Rullenvor had broken down.

Where was Montevallo hiding its ships? In the stretch of water between Calera and Solvang? And how had a kingdom that was completely landlocked managed to get both ships and sea access? Was Mother right about Montevallo using the road from Irridusk to Portsmith to access the small fishing harbor?

"Here are the facts," the queen said. Her voice was calm, though fury sparked in her eyes. "A short while before sundown, just as the delegates' ships were due to enter the harbor, they were attacked. Every ship from Solvang and Thallis went down. Rullenvor's ships were far enough behind them to see the ships sink, but not close enough to see who attacked. When I received Rullenvor's palloren with the news, I ordered nine of our naval ships to pursue the attackers and either capture or kill them. None of those ships has returned. I've sent for Admiral Peyton so we can discuss our next steps."

"Did Rullenvor's message say how many ships were in the attacker's fleet?" Lady Ollen asked, her cheeks flushed, her tone sharp. "Because Montevallo can't possibly have a full fleet of ships. They have no harbor, no port, and no way to build ships without water access."

"You think one of our allies turned on us?" Lord Thorsby's voice trembled, and he whipped his purple silk handkerchief out of his dress coat to dab his forehead.

"I think Montevallo doesn't have ships, so that means we have to take a hard look at who does." Lady Ollen stared at the map.

"No one else would have a reason to attack us," Lord Everly said, his tone dismissive.

Lady Ollen glared at him. "Montevallo has jewel mines in several of their mountain ranges. They must be sitting on a pile of wealth, just waiting for the opportunity to open trade relations with another kingdom so they can spend it."

"So you think King Alaric bribed another kingdom to turn against us?" Lady Channing asked, her voice as calm and measured as always. "It's not a bad theory."

"Perhaps Rullenvor attacked the other ships," Charis said quietly. After all, it was Rullenvor who'd offered to make Calera a protectorate and take over the throne. This could be their way of applying pressure to make sure their offer was accepted. The queen hadn't told the council about their meeting with the ambassador. She wanted to wait until Alaric replied to their offer of peace before broaching a topic that would surely cause distress and division.

Everyone in the room turned to look at Charis. She studied the map while her mind raced, sorting through the facts, forging connections, coming to conclusions.

"Rullenvor is one of our oldest allies," Lord Everly said, spreading his hands wide as though inviting others to join his incredulity.

"An ally is only an enemy who believes your interests briefly align with theirs," Charis said firmly. "If Montevallo offered them a wealth of jewels in exchange for cutting us off from trade or assistance, perhaps it was an offer they couldn't refuse." She met Mother's gaze and saw that the queen had also realized the other reason Rullenvor could have been behind the attack. Especially if Te'ash had pressured them into gaining access to the jewels they wanted so badly.

"And what . . . they also managed to take down nine of our finest naval ships?" Lord Everly met her gaze. "Sinking so many ships would require battle frigates. Don't you think the other kingdoms' delegates would've found an escort of Rullenvorian battleships a bit suspicious?"

"Why would they?" The queen stared at the map, her finger tracing the path the ships would have taken to meet up together and travel south. "They're all allies, and there's been rumors of strange ships in the northern seas. If Rullenvor said they had information about risks from those ships or perhaps had heard a rumor that Montevallo had a few ships patrolling the waters near our shoreline, the others wouldn't have protested the inclusion of battleships."

"We're taking Rullenvor's word that the report they submitted was accurate." Lady Whitecross tapped her short nails against the table in front of her. "And while their word has always been good, we'd be remiss not to look at the big picture. As Lady Ollen said"— she inclined her head toward the lady in question—"Montevallo has no way to build ships. No place to house them. While they are the most obvious threat in terms of motive, they don't have the means."

A knock sounded on the door. "Enter," the queen called.

Admiral Peyton, her uniform as crisp as always, but her face drawn and careworn, stepped into the room, one hand firmly grasping the arm of a young man whose uniform looked bedraggled and damp, and whose wide eyes seemed to take up half of his face.

"Admiral, who is this?" the queen demanded, her gaze sweeping the scratches on the man's dark cheeks, the drops of water still clinging to his black hair, and the way his fingers were clenched tightly around the outside seam of his uniform pants.

"Junior Officer Jeremiah Meadows." Admiral Peyton shut the

door behind them and pulled the man farther into the room. He looked once at the queen and then instantly dropped into a deep bow.

"That will do, Junior Officer Meadows," the queen said curtly. "What is your report, Admiral?"

Admiral Peyton straightened her spine and spoke in a brusque, businesslike tone that failed to hide the horror she felt. "All nine ships are lost, Your Majesty. Junior Officer Meadows here was one of eleven sailors who managed to escape their ships before they went down and swim back into our harbor, where patrol boats picked them up. As he is the least injured in the group, I brought him along to answer your questions."

Every eye in the room landed on Junior Officer Meadows. He swallowed hard, his gaze darting from person to person until he finally chose to stare beyond Lord Everly's shoulder at a point on the far wall.

Before Mother could fire a list of questions at him, Charis said gently, "Please tell us what happened."

Junior Officer Meadows tore his gaze from the far wall, glanced at Charis, and had to clear his throat twice before speaking. "We were chasing whatever ships sank the trade delegates, and—"

"Did you see the ships?" Lady Ollen leaned forward, rising halfway out of her chair. "Did you see their flags?"

"I . . . no. I didn't see anything. I was tacking the mizzen. Had my head down to focus on what I was doing." He looked at Lady Ollen and then hastily looked down at his boots.

"And then?" Charis prompted.

"Then the ship trembled. The whole thing just"—he raised his hands to mime a large object shaking violently—"and we were thrown off our feet. Before we could even obey the captain's orders to turn about and fire the cannons, the ship started sinking. The bow was listing, we were sliding along the deck, scraping the wood." He lifted a finger to touch the scratches along his face. "And then I was in the water."

"Did the ship that attacked you come from the north or the south?" the queen asked. There were lines of strain around her mouth, and Charis worried her strength wouldn't last much longer.

He shrugged, looking miserable. "I don't know, Your Majesty. There was debris in the water. The main mast snapped in half and fell near me. And the *noise*—" He drew in a deep breath. "It was the worst thing I've ever heard."

"How did you end up back in the harbor?" Lady Whitecross asked, her fingers worrying the lace collar of her ball gown.

"I grabbed on to a plank of wood that had fallen into the water and used it to stay afloat while I made my way back to shore. I managed to get two of my mates onto the plank with me, but the rest . . ." His voice broke, and he tugged hard at the collar of his uniform.

An answering pang of grief ached within Charis. She knew what it was like to feel responsible for the death of a friend. To feel hollowed out and brittle while others expected you to somehow behave as if you weren't.

"That was very quick thinking. The sailors you saved might have drowned without your help," Charis said. When he raised his eyes to hers, she said quietly, "I'm very sorry this happened to you."

The queen made an impatient noise in the back of her throat, and Charis quickly wiped the sympathy out of her expression before turning to face her mother.

"Is there anything else you can tell us that might be helpful?" the queen asked.

He shook his head, his shoulders trembling even as he firmed his chin and tried to meet his ruler's gaze straight on.

"You are dismissed. Admiral, you will stay." The queen lowered herself into her chair as Junior Officer Meadows took his leave. When the door had shut behind him, the queen said crisply, "We know nothing more than we did before. And we cannot send ships out again until broad daylight. Admiral?"

"Yes, Your Majesty."

"I want to know who is outside our harbor, where they are hiding, how many ships they have, and I want a plan to destroy them. You will send as many ships as you think necessary once there's enough light to properly see any enemy ships approach. Get that report to me as soon as possible." The queen's tone was steely. "If another kingdom has allied itself with Montevallo, they will regret it."

"Yes, Your Majesty." Admiral Peyton bowed and left the room.

The queen turned to the council and said briskly, "If this was Montevallo, then we may already have the solution on the table." She met Charis's eyes as the council members exchanged confused glances.

Charis folded her hands in front of her and assumed a serene expression, as though there were no rage within her. No pain. No tiny whisper longing for a different path.

She didn't dare look at Tal.

"I've come up with a plan for permanent peace with Montevallo," Charis said. She lifted her chin as a whisper of shock ran through the room and every council member turned toward her. "We've sent a palloren to King Alaric offering our terms. If he accepts, the war is over. Including the attacks on our ships, if indeed Montevallo is responsible." And if Montevallo wasn't responsible, they'd have a stake in keeping Calera safe, so it would be two kingdoms against whoever was attacking from the sea.

There was a beat of silence, and then Lady Channing said in a strained voice, "What were the terms?"

Charis spoke past the sudden tightness in her throat. "We offered a trade route from Ebbington and my hand in marriage to one of their princes."

The council erupted.

"We cannot have a Montevallian dog on the throne!" Lady Ollen slapped the table, the large ring she wore making a metallic clinking sound against the wood.

"Preposterous! We need a king we can trust!" Lord Everly rose from his seat. "My own son has been preparing—"

Charis risked a glance at Tal and found him watching her with an inscrutable expression on his face. His jaw clenched when he met her eyes. She looked away.

"Is this how we make them pay for all they've done to us?" Lady Whitecross's voice trembled with fury. "We give them what they want and more? What's to stop them from taking everything from us once they have their prince in our court?"

"You might have run this past the council before sending the palloren." Lord Thorsby patted his forehead in earnest.

Lady Channing sat back and studied Charis, her expression calm, her body a bastion of absolute stillness amid the chaos around her.

"I won't stand for this. Not after all they've taken." Lady Ollen turned toward Lord Everly. "You're upset that your son won't be on the throne? How tragic for you. My son is *dead*. Killed in battle. Montevallo has taken more from me than you can imagine."

"Montevallo has taken from all of us." Lady Channing's voice cut through the room, sharp as a blade, and in the breath of silence that followed her words, she said, "Peace is the only option we have left unless we accept help from an ally. We all know it, whether we want to admit it or not. This is an attractive offer for Alaric because we assume all the risk."

Chaos erupted again, and the queen raised one eyebrow at Charis as if to say, *Are you going to allow them to do this? I raised you better than that.*

Calling on the ice she wore like armor around her mother, Charis let it fill the aching hollow within. Let it silence the whisper of longing within and flow through her veins until all that was left was Calera's future queen, forged in fire and bloodshed, trained in manipulation and brutal control so that one day she could do what was necessary to save her people. It couldn't matter to her that the cost of saving them would be her heart.

"What's to keep this prince from giving his father the rest of our ports? Our ships? Our people as labor?" Lord Everly gestured wildly.

"We're inviting a wolf into our sheepfold!" Lady Whitecross was on her feet as well.

"We already have a wolf in our sheepfold." Charis let the corner of her lips curl into a vicious little smile. "Me."

The council fell silent. Charis slowly swept the room, holding gazes for as long as it took to force each council member to look away. She was the predator. She was the one they should fear, and she was on their side. If *they* feared her, how much more would her future husband?

Lord Everly and Lady Whitecross sat down again, and Charis said fiercely, "You ask what will keep this prince from giving his father more than what is offered? I will. You worry that we need a king we can trust, and yet you forget that we don't need a king at all. Calera has one throne, and it will be mine. We cannot take the war to Montevallo, and so we invite the king's precious son here under the pretense of peace, but a peace we control. From him, I can learn the secrets of his kingdom. With him, I will be welcomed into the heart of Montevallo, where I will note their weaknesses. And should King Alaric ever cross me"—her smile became a baring of her teeth—"his son will be sent home to him in pieces."

The queen gave Charis a look of approval and then said, "I can't imagine that King Alaric won't be open to negotiating peace with these terms, but in case he isn't, we must continue to plan for war. To that end, I must let you know that Charis's published schedule has been altered. It's unavoidable given the current circumstances. We've found that she is often needed in several places at once, and she requires the flexibility to be able to prioritize her engagements."

Charis schooled her expression into bland indifference even as her pulse raced.

This was new, but Charis was grateful. Now Alaric's spy network wouldn't be sure of her whereabouts unless it was a major social event where her presence was a foregone conclusion. It was a measure of safety until Alaric replied to their offer.

Lord Thorsby stuffed his silk handkerchief back into his pocket and frowned. "When will we be apprised of her new schedule?"

"When we have something finalized."

"This is all very unusual." He waved a hand between the queen and the princess as if to sum up both the fact that they'd offered a peace treaty to Montevallo without running it past the council and that they'd changed the princess's official schedule without notice.

"I will remind each of you," the queen said coldly, "that the Willowthorns do not answer to you. You are here to serve us for as long as it pleases us to have that service. If that arrangement is unsatisfactory to any of you, I welcome your resignation and will have you replaced by morning."

When no one spoke, the queen said, "This meeting is adjourned. Mind your tongues. If I hear that anything we said in this room has been shared beyond these walls, I will have your head delivered to me in a crate."

TWENTY-FOUR

"WE'RE SKIPPING TUTORING today and going into town instead," Charis announced as Holland and Nalani stepped out of their carriage at the palace's front steps. Hazy late autumn sunlight drifted down through ribbons of fog that lay over the city like a tattered shroud. Charis pulled her black traveling cloak tighter as a crisp breeze tugged at the sensible green dress she wore.

"After I stayed up half the night to finish my essay on Morg's political system?" Nalani groaned.

"You can leave your homework with Darold." Charis nodded toward her secretary. Darold stepped forward to collect the assignments.

"Something happen to Brannigan?" Holland asked as he handed a stack of papers to Darold.

"He's fine." Charis craned her neck to watch the royal carriage approach, ignoring the restless movements of Reuben and Elsbet, who were scanning the grounds, hunting for a potential threat. Tal stood next to her as usual, but she couldn't read his expression.

He hadn't said anything beyond a perfunctory "good night"

after they'd returned to her chambers the previous evening, and this morning, he hadn't appeared until just before they were due to come downstairs. If he was upset that she hadn't discussed the peace proposal with him, then he was going to have to move past that. Yes, he'd become more than just a bodyguard. And yes, there were distracting moments lately when she'd wanted . . . something . . . from him that couldn't quite qualify as just friendship. But she was the princess first. Her duty was a cage she couldn't escape. And she was under no obligation to discuss anything with him at all.

That rationalization refused to rest easily in her thoughts, and so she shoved it away and turned to the twins.

"It's important that I change my schedule around as often as possible, which means today we skip tutoring and visit the refugee shelter instead."

"Your Highness, please duck your head and move toward the carriage now," Reuben said, already placing his arm against Charis's back, forcing her to bend forward at the waist so that Elsbet, Reuben, and Tal became the most prominent targets for a potential archer.

Charis gritted her teeth and resisted the urge to throw off Reuben's arm. He was simply doing his job, and truth be told, she'd far rather he take the next arrow instead of her.

Two additional guards took up their posts on the top of the carriage, while Charis, Holland, Nalani, and Tal climbed inside. Reuben and Elsbet took positions on the outside of the carriage—one at the back and one beside the door.

Holland raised a brow at Tal and looked to Charis. "You don't usually let Reuben touch you. I thought that was Tal's job."

"Don't be crass, Holland." Nalani nudged her brother with her elbow slightly harder than was strictly necessary.

"Ouch." He frowned at Nalani. "I wasn't being crass. It's a

legitimate observation. They don't even look like they can stand to be in the same carriage together."

Charis held herself as still as possible and refused to look at Tal. She could only assume he was doing the same. The carriage rolled smoothly down the long drive that led from the palace and turned onto the street.

Nalani studied the two of them, and then gave Charis a worried look. "You know how much it pains me to say this, but Holland's right. If this is none of our business, then just say so. But we're about to go into a very busy area of town, and someone out there wants you dead. If Tal is distracted—"

"I'm not distracted." Tal's voice was steady.

"Of course not," Nalani soothed. "But if you aren't really feeling ready to be Charis's shield today, then—"

"I'm more than ready to be her shield."

Charis risked a glance at his face. He met her gaze and gave her a half smile. It didn't exactly reach his eyes, but still, a tension within her uncoiled.

"Any progress on finding out who sank the ships?" Holland gestured at the ocean just visible in the spaces between brick buildings as the carriage wound its way down to the heart of the city.

"You heard about that already?" Not that Charis was surprised. She'd been sure the merchants arguing in the corner of the ballroom had already received reports from the docks.

"Everyone's heard by this point," Nalani said. "Lady Shawling got hold of the information last night."

"Well, here's some new information." Charis folded her hands to keep herself still. "We sent more naval ships out at first light to find those responsible. But they were attacked and sunk just outside the harbor. The last three ships heading out of the harbor saw them go down and turned back. Unfortunately, they didn't see who did the sinking."

"How could they not see who did the sinking?" Holland demanded. "It's daylight."

"A good question, and not one I can answer," Charis said. "We also lost two merchant vessels that left our harbor this morning. The only boats that haven't been attacked are small fishing vessels and, according to Admiral Peyton's reports, the smugglers who bring goods into smaller ports under cover of night."

"I'm amazed anyone on the docks reported anything about the smugglers' ships," Holland said.

"We have far bigger problems than chasing down a few small ships that traffic surplus goods without paying tariffs, and I'm sure the dock officials and other workers realize it," Charis said. "It's in everyone's best interest to get this solved quickly."

"So none of our ships can leave the harbor?" Nalani's knee bounced up and down, and her eyes were wide with worry.

"Yes."

"And none of our allies can come help us?" Nalani asked.

"I wouldn't help us," Holland said. "I like not drowning."

The carriage left the main road and turned down a narrow street that smelled of fish and salt. The buildings here were long rectangles with scrawny patches of grass growing out of the thin strips of sandy soil that stood between them.

"None of our allies would dare sail to us while this threat exists, which means no help and no trade. We're cut off until we either find the attacking fleet and destroy it or learn which kingdom is behind the attacks and force them to stop."

"Good luck with that," Holland said. "It must be Montevallo, either by somehow building their own ships in a northern cove or something, or by bribing another sea kingdom to help them. And I don't see us being able to force King Alaric to stop attacking by sea when we can't even get him to stop attacking on land."

"I have to agree with Holland," Nalani said. "I don't see how we can possibly convince Alaric to stop attacking us when he has us right where he wants us."

Charis sat back and considered her cousins—the closest friends she had—as she chose her words carefully. It was time she told them about the potential peace treaty, but if the council's response was anything to go by, the twins might react badly to the idea of giving Alaric both port access and entry into Calera's royal family.

As the carriage rumbled over the cobblestones and the calls of merchants hawking their wares outside their shops drifted in, muffled by the mist that clung to the city, Charis said, "All we need to stop Alaric is the right leverage, and I think I've found it."

The twins froze and looked at her—Nalani wearing her thinking frown while Holland leaned forward in eager anticipation. Tal looked swiftly to Charis, his shoulders tense.

"Well, don't keep us in suspense," Holland said. "What leverage do you have?"

"Me."

Nalani's frown deepened. "What do you mean?"

Charis kept her spine straight. "I asked myself what Alaric really wants. It isn't just Ebbington. If that was all he wanted, he wouldn't have ordered the destruction of a simple farm village so far south of the land he wants to use."

"Unless he was just trying to cause us such heavy losses that we'd give in to his demands," Nalani said.

"There are plenty of villages full of innocent people farther north than Irridusk. He took an enormous risk to skirt our army and go deep into the heart of Calera." Charis braced her feet against the carriage floor as the wheels jostled over a rough patch of cobblestone. "Either he did it to have a direct line to a tiny, mostly abandoned fishing town on the coast, or he wanted a direct path to Arborlay."

Holland swore, his hand reaching for his sword hilt. "So he conquers Irridusk while our attention is focused on the northern border, and then he has a place to garrison his troops to stage an invasion."

"Except he didn't garrison troops," Nalani said. "He burned everything to the ground."

"There was nothing there but homes, a temple, a few stores, and a small schoolhouse," Charis said. "Perfect structures for a cozy farming town, but nothing he could use to garrison troops. If he wanted to use it as a staging ground, his army would have brought tents. Maybe put up some makeshift buildings."

"But . . ." Nalani frowned again. "They were gone by the time our soldiers arrived, so what was the point?"

Charis rubbed her forehead as the first twinge of a headache bloomed. "I think it was to show us that he could. That he can cut into the heart of our kingdom and strike down innocents. That he can get closer and closer to the capital. We've sustained heavy losses in the past few years. And we don't have enough resources or people to fight two warfronts. Either we'd pull back and defend the path to the capital, or we'd stay north and keep Montevallo from Ebbington."

"And now we have the attacks at sea to contend with as well," Holland said. "If he invaded and truly broke through our army in the north, we'd have nowhere to go and no one to help us."

"Which is why I had to ask myself what he truly wants. It can't just be the port access. Tal helped me figure it out." She stretched her hand out as though to encompass all of the capital. "Alaric wants revenge for what Montevallo views as a tremendous insult to their honor. He wants to show his people that his victory was bold and brilliant."

"We can't give him a bold, brilliant victory, Charis." Nalani sounded shocked.

"No, but we can make him believe we did."

All three of them looked at her as the carriage rumbled to a stop in front of the large warehouse the queen had turned into a refugee shelter for those displaced by the fighting in the north.

"How will you do that?" Nalani asked.

Charis raised her chin. "By offering to marry one of his sons."

There was a beat of silence, and then Nalani said with quiet sympathy, "Oh, Charis."

A shiver of longing moved through Charis, and she suppressed it. "Montevallo won't be at war with us if one of their princes is king."

"That's actually brilliant," Holland said.

"No need to sound surprised." Charis clenched her folded hands so hard they hurt. It was so casual. They could have been discussing a battle plan for the north or an assignment for Brannigan instead of the destruction of her secret dreams.

"And if he steps out of line"—Holland patted his sword sheath—"I'll kill him. Unless you want that honor?" He looked at Tal.

"I would very much like that honor," Tal said in a voice Charis barely recognized.

"You can't kill him," Charis said firmly. "If Alaric agrees to this, then the peace treaty will only be valid while the prince remains alive."

Holland's lips curved upward. "Maim, then."

Charis made herself smile back. "Fine, Holland. If he steps out of line, you get to maim him."

"But this means you have to spend the rest of your life with the enemy." Nalani's dark eyes found Charis's and held. "It means you never get to rest. You never get a break. Even in your private chambers, your quiet moments, you have to always be on guard."

"I can manage it."

"I know you can." Nalani reached across the carriage to take Charis's hand in hers. "But I want better for you. I want a man like your father. Someone who would let you be who you need to be and love you for it without asking for anything in return that you hadn't already offered to give."

Charis's throat tightened, and an ache blossomed in her heart. She wanted that, too. More than she cared to admit. But a princess didn't get to want something for her own heart when the heart of her people needed protecting. Giving Nalani's hand a quick squeeze, Charis said, "Maybe he won't be so bad."

"Can't be any worse than Ferris Everly," Holland said.

Tal laughed, but there was a tinge of misery to it. "I apologize, Your Highness. That was disrespectful."

Holland grinned. "I see you've accurately assessed Ferris's charms."

"At any rate, we can't worry about what kind of person the prince is. First we have to hope Alaric accepts our terms and begins negotiations so that we can stop the fighting, both on land and at sea," Charis said.

Outside the window, her guards were finishing their search of the center, inside and out, to make sure no assassins were lying in wait. A large man with dark brown skin, callused hands the size of bread loaves, and a shiny bald head with a tattoo of a sea hawk on the back of his neck stood at the center's door, his watchful eyes studying the warehouses across the street as though also hunting for any threat to his princess. When he caught Charis looking out the window, he flashed her a quick grin, deepening the creases in his sun-weathered face.

Orayn was another friend of Father's who'd followed his new king from the far north to the capital city so many years ago. Unlike the others, who'd become Father's personal guards and assistants, Orayn had never been one who could stand being indoors for long. Instead, he'd taken a job on a merchant's frigate and become Father's eyes and ears at the docks. When Father became too ill to care any longer about the comings and goings of those at port, Orayn had reported to Charis instead.

"What are we going to do if Alaric turns down your offer?" Nalani asked.

"He'd be kind of stupid to pass up a chance to put his son so near the throne," Holland said as the guards made their way back to the carriage.

"Unless he wants the throne all to himself," Nalani shot back. "My point is that we need an alternate plan. And figuring out who keeps attacking us on the open sea seems like an important place to start."

Charis's thoughts raced.

They needed an alternate plan in case Alaric refused to stop the attacks.

The navy couldn't risk sending out more ships to be sunk.

Orayn knew the waters. Knew his way around a boat. And knew plenty of sailors who were now temporarily out of a job while their ships were docked until the threat was over.

The only boats who sailed unscathed were small fishing vessels and smugglers.

Charis smiled grimly. Maybe she couldn't stop the bloodshed up north right away. Maybe she didn't yet know how to uncover the network of spies. But this? This she could manage.

Turning away from the window, she said quietly, "I have a plan."

"Excellent." Holland popped his knuckles. "Let's hear it."

"We're going to search the sea for the attacking fleet by pretending to be smugglers."

TWENTY-FIVE

MOTHER WAS WAITING in her office when Charis arrived five days after the trade delegate ships had gone down. The queen was wearing a bold dress the color of sea emeralds and there was a dagger strapped to her waist.

The glint in her eyes looked just as dangerous.

She waited until Tal closed the door and took up his position against the wall before saying, "We're in real trouble, Charis." She began pacing. "Fifteen naval vessels lost. Twice as many merchant ships. I closed the harbor yesterday when it became clear that no matter which direction our ships take, somehow the enemy ship finds them and sinks them."

"A closed harbor?" Charis's stomach sank. "But that means we can't accept trade from other kingdoms who hadn't yet severed relations with us. Some of that trade is essential to our survival."

"I know." The queen's voice was grim. "I've quietly asked the city's top physicians, alchemists, herbalists, and blacksmiths to take stock of supplies so we can begin rationing medicine and metal, since we won't be receiving any for the time being. I don't have the entire count in yet, but I can already tell we're going to run into serious shortages within a month, maybe less."

"We need to find and sink those enemy ships," Charis said.

"Agreed. How soon can your smuggler operation start the search?"

Charis risked a quick glance at Tal, but of course he was simply staring at the wall. He'd been distant since the night she'd announced her plan to marry a prince of Montevallo.

"Tonight," she said. "Orayn has a small crew and a boat. We'll go out as often as we can at night until we find who's behind this."

"I don't like you going out to sea. We should let Orayn handle it."

"Not a single smuggler's ship has been sunk, Mother. We'll be cautious and safe."

"It's too risky." The queen's eyes were worried.

"It's no riskier than doing my normal duties in a city full of spies who want me dead. And I don't want to rely on secondhand information about the attacking fleet. We need to be absolutely sure what we're facing."

The queen sighed. "You are as stubborn as I am."

"Thank you."

"Fine. Go get your workload done for the day so that your evening is clear. I have an appointment with several members of the council." The dagger-sharp gleam in her eyes brightened. "And we've got a lead on the man Bartho who sent the assassin to Merryl's. A city guard recognized the name and pointed us toward the warehouse district, where he's rumored to live. Several guards will spend the day searching every single warehouse for him and anyone else staying with him. We'll compare notes tomorrow."

෧ঌ

"This is madness," Holland said happily as he, Charis, and Tal left the plain wagon they'd taken from the back of the Farragin estate for the twenty-minute ride to the small fishing dock at the northern tip of the city.

Charis had to agree with Holland. A princess dressed as a smuggler sneaking out of a fishing dock to search for a fleet of battleships while also waiting to hear if King Alaric would take the bait and accept the betrothal was utter madness, but she couldn't see another move on the chessboard.

Mother had nearly stopped Charis from going at the last minute, but she'd finally agreed to it as long as Nalani stayed back in case the worst happened and the next person in line for the throne was needed. And only if Tal swore on his life to the queen that he wouldn't let anything happen to Charis.

Orayn and a small crew of loyal sailors waited for them at the fishing dock for their first nighttime trip onto the open sea. An older frigate, painted black and flying no identifying flags, was anchored beside the dock. Charis drew in a bracing breath of salt-laced air and nodded to herself as she studied the boat. It resembled the ones used by the smugglers who brought goods into Calera without paying the tariff and who often traded with Montevallian spies, at risk of a long stint in the queen's dungeon if they were caught. Much smaller than most merchant vessels. More nimble. And much harder to see out on the open sea, especially given that the sails were also black.

"Put your masks on," Charis said quietly as they left the wagon and began their trek down the sand dunes toward the waiting dock. "It's crucial that no one on the crew is able to identify us."

"It's going to look strange if we're the only ones wearing masks," Tal muttered as he slipped his on. His hair was tied back, and like

Charis, he wore simple black pants, a plain gray shirt, and a black cloak. Holland wore his usual duster over black pants and a black shirt and had his sword sheathed at his waist.

"Everyone will wear a mask," Charis said. "We cannot risk a spy knowing the princess is out on the water each night. If Alaric doesn't accept the betrothal offer, he could order his fleet to hunt us down and sink us."

"That would be unfortunate," Holland said, though he still sounded happily in his element as their boots scuffed against the aging wooden boards of the walkway that led to the dock.

The sister moons hung low in the star-flecked sky, their soft blue light reflecting against the dark surface of the water, a spill of pale sapphire that undulated with the waves. Orayn met them at the entrance to the dock, a mask tied in place just above his bushy beard.

"It's a fine night for sailing," he said, stopping himself from bowing to Charis when she whipped a hand in the air.

"And for skewering things with a sword," Holland replied enthusiastically.

"We're going out to try to see where the fleet is hiding. Not to board them and try to fight them to the death," Charis said to him.

Holland sighed.

"The rest of the crew is already here. Some of them are deckhands I've known for a while. Some are friends of mine from the city—got us a physician, just in case, and a seamstress to help repair sails and such—and a couple are refugees who've been hanging around the docks for months doing odd jobs for anyone with coin. All aboard that's coming aboard, Captain," Orayn said.

"I can't be the captain, Orayn. I don't know a ship well enough. I don't have the instincts necessary to manage a battle on the water.

And"—she dropped her voice though no one was near enough to overhear them—"no one can suspect I'm the princess. *You're* the captain."

He shifted uncomfortably, and then said, "Well, I'm not giving you orders, Your High—"

"Do *not* call me Your Highness." Charis kept her voice gentle but firm as she placed a hand on his arm.

"He can't exactly call you Charis, either," Tal said dryly.

"It's a common enough name," Charis said.

Holland snorted. "How many other girls named Charis do you think move like a predator who owns everything she touches?"

"That's a little harsh," Orayn said.

"It's a little accurate." Tal adjusted his mask. "She speaks, moves, and acts like the princess at all times. If you call her Charis, it won't be hard for the crew to figure out who she is."

Charis held up a hand for silence and then had to acknowledge that even that act was one only someone used to having everyone obey her would think to do. "We'll have to come up with another name, Orayn."

The big man shrugged, his tunic straining over his muscular shoulders. "How about if you're the captain, and I'm your first mate? A first mate always relays the captain's orders to the crew, so this gives you a reason to look like you're in charge, but lets me take over giving the orders myself if we get into a situation you aren't sure how to handle."

"What crew is going to believe a seventeen-year-old girl is qualified to be a ship's captain?" Charis asked.

"I'll just tell them you're the daughter of an experienced smuggler who is loyal to our cause and that the ship is yours." Orayn smiled.

"None of them are going to question me. They've all known me long enough to trust me."

"All right." Charis checked to see that her mask was firmly in place. "Let's get out onto the water."

Moments later, the crew of twenty-seven was assembled on the deck while Orayn and Charis stood on the quarterdeck beside the helm, facing the group.

"You all know why we're here," Orayn said, his deep voice rumbling through the night. "This is your captain. She might look young, but she makes up for it with a wealth of experience in both smuggling and the Montevallian war dogs. Her family is financing this crew. She has a few words to say to you before we get underway."

Charis stepped forward, gripping the balustrade and looking out over the assembled group.

"Thank you for coming." Her voice was carefully controlled. Soft enough to be slightly disarming, but cold as steel underneath. "Please know that your discretion is imperative. Choosing to join us means choosing to keep this secret, even at the cost of your own life. There are Montevallian spies throughout our city. If the enemy gets word that we're searching for their fleet, they'll turn against us instead. Should any one of you decide to betray us, I will personally hunt you down and make your death as slow and painful as you deserve."

She paused, letting the weight of her words and the vicious sincerity in her tone sink into the crew. When she judged that they were all taking her seriously, she nodded to Orayn, and he stepped forward.

"The enemy fleet won't be the only potential threat we face," he said. "There are monstrous creatures roaming the seas, though most of them leave ships alone unless there's blood in the water to draw them close. There are Blood Mists, as you know, and there are other smugglers who wouldn't think twice about trying to board us, rob us of our cargo, and feed our bodies to the fishes."

A few in the crew shifted on their feet as if anxious about this list of potential threats. Orayn raised a hand and began to tick items off on his thick fingers.

"If a sea monster gets too curious, we'll trim the sails and leave that area. If a Blood Mist rolls through, we'll do what we'd normally do on land when one comes in: lock ourselves in the cabins belowdecks and stay hidden and quiet until the shades within the mist dissipate in the morning sun."

"How would we see a Blood Mist coming?" a woman with a long braid down her back and a strong, sturdy build called out. "You can't tell that a mist is red when you're out on the water at night."

"Maybe not, but the shades aren't quiet," another woman answered from the front of the group. "The souls of those lost at sea make enough noise that you can hear them coming if you're paying attention."

"And we'll be paying attention anytime we see fog," Orayn said calmly. "As for the threat of other smugglers, we'll have to assign some of our group to man the cannons while others are prepared for sailor-to-sailor combat on deck."

A soft murmur rose from the group, and Charis raised her hand for silence. "Those of you who have any combat training, please remain in the center of the deck so we can assess your skill level. The rest of you see our first mate about your assignments. We'll take two hours inside the harbor to learn our jobs and do our practicing, and then I want this ship moving out into open water. We will have a quiet ship when we leave the harbor."

"You heard the captain," Orayn called. "Get moving."

Within moments, Orayn had assigned two sailors to study the maps in the captain's quarters and chart their course for the evening. He had five people on the cannon deck learning how to quickly load, aim, and fire the weapons. The rest were tacking sails, hauling ropes, and scrambling to obey his every order.

Charis stood in the middle of the top deck with Holland, Tal, and four others who'd stayed to be assessed for their readiness to defend the ship with weapons. She already knew how skilled Holland and Tal were. That left the other four.

She studied them as she handed out swords with corked tips. A woman old enough to be her mother held the weapon like she had some experience with a blade. A man who looked to be in his early twenties seemed a little uncertain how to grip the hilt properly. Another woman around his age took the blade gingerly and admitted she preferred daggers.

The fourth volunteer, a boy who appeared to be Charis's age, held his weapon in his gloved hands like it was an extension of himself. There was an ease to his stance, an immediate familiarity with the sword, that made her wonder if he'd ever done training with a swords master.

"Everyone choose a partner. Holland, you work with those three. You." She nodded toward the boy. "What's your name?"

"Dec," he said quietly.

"You'll be with Tal. I'm going to observe and work up a defense plan in case it's ever needed."

The others paired off and began practicing. Charis watched closely. She'd been right about Dec. He had experience with a sword, though Tal was better.

Tal was better than Charis, too, but she was working hard to close that gap. Or she had been before the announcement that she'd offered herself to the Montevallian prince had put such a strain on their friendship.

At first, she'd been frustrated at his apparent inability to realize that as the future queen she had to make decisions that weren't going to line up with what she personally wanted. Then she'd been angry that he'd somehow made her want something with him in the first place—not that she even knew how to put a name to the wild, tender thing that ached in her heart when she looked at him.

But now . . . now she'd started to consider that it might not even be about the attraction that had blossomed between them. Tal had lost everything. He barely mentioned his family, but there was always pain in his eyes when he did. He'd once told her he dreamed about his old home and woke up expecting to see his family when he opened his eyes.

There was grief and bitterness in him, and the cause was King Alaric of Montevallo. And now the girl he'd taken an arrow for had offered herself to the enemy as a prize. No wonder he could barely look at her.

The best move would be to leave things as they were. Tal would keep protecting her until the threat was gone, and then they would simply grow apart. He would go back to her father's employ, or perhaps join the weapons master to help with training. He'd meet a nice girl, tell her his secrets, fall in love, settle down, and get a new favorite cat.

It was the life he deserved. The life she ought to want for him.

She turned away from the sparring and moved to the railing. The *thunk* of ropes hitting the deck, the sharp slap of wind filling the sails, and the soft shush of waves scraping against the ship's sides filled the air, and she closed her eyes as the dark chasm within her opened wide.

She was quick to say she wasn't afraid of anything, but now she knew those words were a lie. It was wrong of her to want to cling to the boy who'd seen her at her cruelest and at her most vulnerable and who still took an arrow for her, argued with her, and sometimes looked at her like he wanted to bridge the distance between them and kiss her. It was wrong of her, and there was only one thing to do about it. All she had to do was let the distance between them grow. In the end, it was better that way.

Her mind made up, she wandered the ship, observing each of the positions Orayn had assigned, trying to soak in as much understanding of sailing as she could. All too soon, Orayn called out, "We're leaving the harbor. Quiet conversations only. No swords. All eyes on the horizon unless I've given you another duty. You see a ship? You let me or the captain know about it."

Charis took up her spot on the railing again as the ship nosed its way out of the bay and onto the open sea. Orayn headed north, staying close to the shore as they'd decided to check the water in grids, dividing up each area so as the nights passed, they could cover every furlong from Calera's capital all the way north to Ebbington if necessary while also searching as many furlongs east as Calera was wide.

"What do you think you're doing?" Tal's quiet voice at her shoulder made her jump.

She shot him a look and then turned back to the horizon. "What are you talking about?"

"Giving me the job of training people to fight with swords and then wandering off alone. Going all over the ship. *Alone.*"

"No one knows who I really am."

"You're sure of that?" There was a thread of anger in his voice, and she gripped the railing hard. "Or did you even stop to think it through?"

"That's not fair." She tried to keep the hurt out of her voice. "I'm surrounded by allies here. Orayn, you, Holland—"

"Holland and I were busy at the center of the ship, and Orayn was at the tiller. So who exactly was watching your back?"

"I was." She turned on him, forgetting that she was trying to hold her temper. "I was watching my back like I always have. Like I'll always have to for the rest of my life. Me. *Alone.* You're right about that."

"You choose if you have to be alone. You either let people in, or you push them away. Any guesses which camp you fall into?" There was anger in his voice too, but beneath it, she heard the hurt.

Drawing in a deep breath, she forced herself to find the courage she needed to do the right thing. "I know why you're angry with me."

"Do you?" He held her gaze, starlight gleaming in his dark eyes.

"Yes," she said quietly as the dark hole within her widened. "Remember when we stood in the dark at the refugee camp, and I told you there had to be a solution? That I just had to find it?"

He frowned. "Yes, but—"

"I know it must feel awful. You've lost so much to Montevallo, and then you risk your life to keep me safe, and what do I do? I offer myself to a prince of Montevallo like some sort of prize. It has to feel like a slap in the face."

"I promise you have no idea what I'm feeling," he said with quiet force.

"I know I can't fully understand, but I also know that this is what I have to do. I can't see another way to forge a truce, and we desperately need one." She swallowed hard against the knot that was forming in her throat.

"And you think I don't know that?"

"Of course you do. Probably more than most of the people in

Arborlay. I just hate that what I have to do to gain a truce must make it feel like I threw your sacrifice in your face. I'm sorry for that."

He took a small step back. "You're sorry for that."

"Yes." There was a long silence punctuated by the creak of the ship's timbers and the slap of the water against its bow, and then she found the courage to say, "I meant what I said about watching my own back. I know your job here is temporary. We'll catch Bartho, and you'll return to Father's staff. And eventually you'll move on to another job, and you'll find a girl to love and a cat to adopt. The wounds Montevallo inflicted will slowly heal, and you'll be all right. And I'll do my duty and watch my back and keep the enemy in line so that your people stay safe."

He stared at her and then said slowly, "Well, as long as you have it all figured out, I guess it's fine."

She frowned. There was something heavy in his voice. Something she hadn't heard from him in all their months of closeness.

A friend would ask him about it. Pull the truth out of him bit by bit. But he would be leaving. He'd already started to, even though he was standing right in front of her. It wasn't fair to either of them to fight it.

He turned away and stood in silence watching the horizon for the next hour until they returned to the harbor having seen not a single ship. He was silent on the carriage ride home, and he didn't say good night as he went into his room.

Charis changed into her nightdress as the ache of loneliness within her cracked wide open and swallowed her. And then she climbed into the bathtub, the last place she'd seen Milla, the place where everything had started to go so terribly wrong, laid her head on her knees, and cried.

TWENTY-SIX

IT HAD BEEN over a week since their first nighttime trip to sea. They'd been out twice more and found nothing.

Charis had filled her time with fittings for her winter wardrobe, tutoring sessions, meetings, and an extremely pared-down social calendar now that they were keeping her schedule as unpredictable as possible. She'd kept pressure on the search for Bartho, the man the assassin claimed had hired her. She stayed vigilant in meetings, playing politics with lethal precision.

And she cried herself to sleep each night after yet another day of silence, or worse, stilted exchanges with Tal, who'd become so distant she felt she hardly knew him anymore.

It shouldn't have felt like her knees had been cut from beneath her. Shouldn't have blindsided her with aching misery that blended into her grief and loneliness until she no longer knew the difference between the hurts.

It was pain, and it was hers only at night. During the day, she drew on rage and called it courage. Kept her expression smooth as glass and made sure not a hint of what ravaged her escaped.

A hundred times she thought of asking Tal if they could go back to being friends, and a hundred times she found the courage to keep her mouth shut.

Exhaustion fogged her mind and slowed her body. The grief she'd kept at bay for so long refused to let her sleep now. Refused to let her eat. She pushed food around on her plate to satisfy Tal, but even that didn't matter because he hardly looked at her when they were in her chambers.

Monday dawned cold and crisp. Autumn was slowly giving way to winter. Charis dragged herself out of bed, let Mrs. Sykes pull her curls away from her face with a jeweled headband, and barely looked at the blue dress the older woman pulled out of the closet.

She cut her roasted fowl into tiny pieces, only eating a bite when Tal walked from his room to the bath chamber. The food tasted like dust. She left the tray on the table and stepped out onto her balcony just so she wouldn't have to bear him ignoring her as he returned to his room.

Wind shook the thesserin trees, tearing away the few remaining leaves and chasing them over the grounds. Charis envied them their freedom. They danced and spun, at the mercy of the wind but still at least they were going somewhere new.

There was a soft knock on the doorframe, and then Gaylle stepped onto the balcony and bowed.

"Night shift guard is leaving, Your Highness. Vellis is giving our report to Reuben now. Do you need anything before I go?"

She smiled politely. "Thank you, Gaylle. You are dismissed."

The man stepped back into her room, and there was a murmur of voices and then silence. She watched the leaves scrape over the stone courtyard, tangle with the dying grass, and then race south. Lifting her eyes, she looked past the stables and the copse of oak trees. Beyond that, at the southernmost point on the grounds, was her favorite bluff. The place she would sneak out to visit so she could think without the pressure of being the princess on display. She hadn't visited since Tal took over as bodyguard. It had seemed unnecessary when she hadn't had to put on a display in front of him. When sharing her thoughts and getting his help working through them had become as easy as breathing.

But she didn't have that now, and her thoughts were a tangle. A mess of grief, anger, and duty with the ax of the proposed peace treaty hanging over her head, just waiting for a response from Alaric.

There was another knock, and then Tal said, "Time to go to your office, Your Highness."

She didn't even try to look him in the eye. He would either be looking past her, or he'd make eye contact, but there would be nothing but cold duty on his face. Instead, she walked past him and out her bedroom door in silence.

Her office was a smaller version of the queen's and housed in the same wing. Charis immediately went to her desk to check her revised schedule for the day. After glancing at it, she handed it to Tal, who memorized it as well and then went to stand by the door to monitor anyone who entered.

Charis was halfway through the correspondence waiting for her signature when angry voices rose in the hall just outside her door. Charis heard the unmistakable tones of Lord Thorsby and set down her quill.

"Please see what's happening," she said.

Tal opened the door to reveal Lord Thorsby and Reuben.

"—and you should watch where you're putting your hands. Careful! That's Solvanish embroidery." Lord Thorsby snatched his pink handkerchief out of Reuben's hands as the guard circled the man, running his hands down Thorsby's back and legs in slow, fluid sweeps.

"Your Highness!" Thorsby dabbed at his forehead, his brown eyes wide. "This is outrageous."

"This is security protocol for visiting the princess," Reuben said in a steely voice. "Unless you have something to hide, I suggest you let me finish my job."

"Well, I've never . . . the very thought that I . . . your tone, my good man, is inexcusable. Watch those hands!" Thorsby jumped as Reuben encircled his waist, tugged at something beneath the lord's coat, and came out with a small bejeweled dagger.

"No weapons allowed near the princess." Reuben made the words sound like an accusation.

Thorsby bristled. "That was my mother's dagger. I carry it for sentimental reasons." He dabbed at his upper lip. "And also one cannot be too careful these days. Montevallian spies under every rock, it seems."

"He is cleared for entry," Reuben said to Charis, his hard brown eyes searching her face as if looking for the answer to a question he hadn't yet asked.

Charis gave him the barest hint of a nod and turned to Lord Thorsby. "Please come in. I can send for tea or chocolate if you prefer."

"Tea would be just the thing." Thorsby shot Reuben a resentful look and then entered the office.

"You may sit." Charis waved to her seating area. She chose a chair covered in ivory silk and rang the bell for tea.

Thorsby smoothed his finely pressed trousers and adjusted his carefully coiffed black curls before taking a seat opposite the princess. They chatted about the rapidly cooling weather, the fact that there had been a lull in battles in the northern territories, and the problem of their merchant ships being trapped in their harbor.

Once tea arrived, Lord Thorsby spooned a generous heap of sugar crystals into his cup, took a sip, and then set the cup back on its saucer.

"Now that we won't be interrupted, it's time to discuss the real reason you came to see me," Charis said.

"Yes, Your Highness." His fingers fussed with the seam of his pants, creasing and re-creasing as if he had something on his mind. When he noticed her watching him, he reached for his tea again.

Charis cocked her head. "Why are you nervous around me today, Lord Thorsby?"

Thorsby choked on his mouthful of tea and reached for the silk handkerchief in his pocket as he coughed. "You are quite direct, Your Highness."

"That can hardly come as a surprise, Lord Thorsby. You've known me for . . . How long has it been since you were appointed head of the royal council?"

"Seven years." Lord Thorsby tucked his handkerchief away. "I've had quite a bit of experience helping to manage the affairs of the kingdom, as you know."

"Certainly." Charis's tone was pleasant, but the inexorable demand for the truth was there.

Thorsby drew in a deep breath and then seemed to deflate before her eyes. "King Alaric has responded to our offer."

The world froze, a crystallized moment where time slowed to the quiet, infinite space between heartbeats, and she was caught between the life she'd thought she might have and the one she would endure if it would bring her people peace. She was exquisitely aware of Tal's silent presence.

"And?" Her voice was calm, a slick coating over the impossible chaos within.

If King Alaric accepted, she was destined for a life with her enemy at her side. No rest. No space to breathe without watching for his knife in her back.

But if Alaric declined, she had no way to save her kingdom.

"He accepted, Your Highness. We are already at work arranging for him to visit Arborlay and sign the treaty." Thorsby's lips thinned as though he'd forcibly closed his mouth before he could say more.

And just like that, everything changed.

She was betrothed to her enemy. There would be no dropping of her guard, ever. No softness. No giving in to the tiny voice of longing in her heart.

A pang of grief stole her breath, and she let it cut her. Let the quiet wishes, the well of loneliness, bleed. Her teacup clattered against its saucer, spilling dark liquid onto the floor. She set it onto the table and folded her hands so Lord Thorsby wouldn't see them tremble.

This was an impossible road to walk. To spend her life married to the son of the man who'd tried to kill her, who'd wrecked her people and who might be responsible for destroying her allies at sea. To give his son a crown and a title, to stand by his side as if they both deserved to rule Calera.

To turn away from the chance that one day she'd fall in love with a man like her father who'd see the best in her and help anchor her to it.

The grief seized her throat in a crushing grip and stung her eyes. She tilted her head back to look at the ceiling, blinking rapidly to keep the tears from falling.

And then, slowly, she straightened her spine. Forced a breath past the tightness of her throat, and then another.

She was her people's rage. Her kingdom's vicious protector.

She never flinched. Even when she wanted to.

"Good," she said, the word falling from her lips with all the finality of a death sentence. "Then we begin negotiations immediately.

The top item on the list is that all attacks at sea must stop."

Thorsby cleared his throat and reached for his tea. Taking a hasty sip, he said, "The queen already sent that demand several days ago as an addendum to the peace treaty offering. King Alaric claims no knowledge of or responsibility for any attacks at sea."

Charis frowned. "Could he be lying?"

Except . . . what would he have to gain? If it was discovered that he was behind the attacks and that he hadn't stopped them after signing the peace treaty, he would lose access to both Charis and the port at Ebbington. Who would take that risk? And for what? She'd already given him what he wanted.

No, it was one of their other allies—possibly Rullenvor. Or it was the strange ships rumored to be in the northern seas. Could it be Te'ash? She hadn't heard of an underwater kingdom using ships, but Calera's knowledge of the Rakuuna was slim at best. She supposed it was possible the Rakuuna had sunk a few ships to try to force Calera into an agreement, but it seemed counterproductive to sink the ships of their ally, Rullenvor. Either way, she—

"I said the very same. He *must* be lying." Thorsby's voice trembled with righteous indignation. "I have brought my concerns to the queen, Your Highness. And I will again. But I'm afraid she isn't listening."

"Not listening?" Charis raised her cup and took a delicate sip. "Or not following your advice?"

"It is one and the same." He pushed his tea aside and leaned forward. "This treaty with Montevallo . . . the council is divided."

"The council will do what Mother and I have decided is best." Charis sounded serene, but she watched him carefully.

"Yes, of course, it's just that . . ." Thorsby seemed to lose his nerve.

The handkerchief made another appearance as he dabbed at his brow.

"Speak plainly, Lord Thorsby, or take your leave."

"This betrothal agreement," the man burst out. "We are ceding land to Montevallo. Making them pay a mere pittance for use of the northern port. Giving their eldest prince access to our throne. And what do we get in return?"

"Peace," Charis said firmly. "Enough jewels to rebuild the northern territories—"

"Territories they destroyed!" He pounded his fist on the table. "They should pay for that, and not just in rubies. Several members of the council wanted to invade Montevallo. Give them a taste of the ruin they brought on us. Teach them that there are consequences for the atrocities they've committed, but instead, we are offering peace. It does not sit right, Your Highness." He sagged against the back of the chair, the handkerchief clutched in his hands.

Charis studied him in silence for a bit. It was unlike Thorsby to come undone, but perhaps he had a reason. Finally, she said gently, "Is this about what's best for the Caleran people? Or is this about Fergus?"

Thorsby crumpled. Tears leaked from his eyes, and his handkerchief was put to use again. "It's been a year since our son was killed in a Montevallian raid, Your Highness. A year this week."

"I'm very sorry about Fergus," Charis said sincerely. "And I understand the desire for vengeance. Truly, I do. Montevallo has been trying to kill me since I was nine."

"And they just keep trying! If that doesn't prove that this could quite possibly be a disastrous course of action, what will?"

"What is more disastrous?" Charis asked quietly. "Refusing to cede some of what we want at great cost to our people, or negotiating a contract both sides can live with so that our people stop dying? And I hardly think Alaric will try to assassinate me again when my death means his son won't get a Caleran crown."

"Your Highness, we didn't need to get to this point. We should have taken the fight to Montevallo last year as Lady Whitecross and Lady Ollen advised. We could have figured out how to breach their walls. We could have crushed their villages before they raided ours, and ended the war before last winter." His voice shook. "If the queen had listened to that advice, Fergus would still be alive."

"Or he would have died in a raid on a Montevallian village instead of protecting one of our own. Where is the honor in that?" Charis's voice was silken steel. "It sounds to me as though you have lost confidence in the queen's governance."

Thorsby froze, swallowing hard as he met Charis's eyes. "Oh no, Your Highness. Never that. I simply brought this to you because there are opinions that are not being listened to. Last year, she didn't listen to opposing views, and look how much we've lost since then. I don't want us to proceed without taking into account everyone's advice. That is all."

Charis inclined her head. "Perhaps the anniversary of Fergus's death is too emotional a time for you to think clearly on how to approach this discussion, Lord Thorsby. I would hate for the queen to get the wrong impression."

Thorsby nodded quickly, stuffing his handkerchief back in his pocket. "Quite right, Your Highness. This is a very difficult time. And I've had Lord Everly and Lady Whitecross in my ear for days. It can sometimes be a trying job balancing the advice of the council and the will of the queen. I apologize for overstepping in this instance."

"Apology accepted. Now, please, be with Lady Thorsby today and remember Fergus. I will make your excuses at the council meeting this afternoon." Her tone was kind but left no room for argument.

"Thank you, Your Highness." Thorsby quickly left the room.

Charis sat staring into her cup of cooling tea. It was done. There was no backing out of it now. No other course her life could take.

It was done and the pain scraping her raw would have to wait until darkness fell and she could be alone.

TWENTY-SEVEN

BY SHEER FORCE of will, Charis held herself together through a strategy session with Mother, a council meeting where the members began the task of hammering out the language of the peace treaty, and a host of other obligations that blurred into one long day that seemed to stretch on forever. With her list of duties finished, she'd retired to her rooms, cut her poached fish into tiny bites and ignored her roasted root vegetables entirely, and then turned off her lights as if she planned to go to sleep early.

Not that it mattered. Tal had gone to his room the moment they entered her chambers.

She was alone, and that was never going to change. She just had to figure out how to survive it.

She waited until she heard the evening guards arrive in the corridor outside her chambers. Waited a bit longer to make sure no one was going to knock on her door. To make sure it was past the time Tal usually fell asleep. And then she changed into black pants, a black shirt, boots, gloves, and a thick knitted sweater to keep out the worst of the chilly air.

The night was cold and clear as she stepped onto her balcony. She grasped the balustrade at the far edge, hauled herself over the side, and then stretched her arm out until she could grab the branch of the closest thesserin tree. Once her grip was secure, she pulled herself into the cradle of the tree and shimmied down its trunk.

The grounds were shrouded in shadows, but the thin crescents of the sister moons, surrounded by a sea of silver stars, gave enough light for her to find her way. She kept to the shadows, though she doubted any staff would be out on the grounds, and made her way through the courtyard, past the stables, and across the field that led to the orchard that covered the southern hill. It took almost an hour to walk what usually took her fifteen minutes on horseback, but she was grateful for the burn in her muscles and the heaviness of her breathing.

Putting one foot in front of the other kept her from thinking.

When she reached the edge of the trees, she climbed the gentle rise of the hill to the bluff overlooking the sea and sat on the cold ground, her arms wrapped around her stomach. The thunder of the waves crashing against the shore calmed her, and she reached for that elusive sense of peace and held on to it with desperate fingers.

Maybe the Montevallian prince wouldn't be a terrible person.

Maybe those who hated her would stop trying to kill her now that peace had been achieved.

Maybe Tal would talk to her again once the idea of peace became real.

And maybe the loneliness and hurt inside of her could be caged the way she imprisoned her rage until she needed it. If she could build a wall strong enough and thick enough to separate herself from the ache, it would be like it wasn't even real.

She lost track of how long she sat gazing out at the sea. The darkness within shivered, and she rocked herself back and forth as something raw and painful blossomed out of it. A tear slipped free, scalding her cold cheek with its heat, followed by another.

How could she survive being the ruthless, dangerous princess every minute of every day if she couldn't even survive losing a friendship or two?

She was stronger than this. Better than this. She had to be.

Something rustled in the trees behind her, and a twig snapped. Charis froze, terribly aware that she'd come out here alone and weaponless.

She scrambled to her feet and faced the orchard as a dark shape raced out of the trees and then skidded to a stop.

"Charis?" Tal's voice, laced with furious worry, echoed across the bluff.

Hastily, she wiped the tears from her cheeks as he made his way up the hill until they were face-to-face. "How did you find me?"

"That's it?" He sounded out of breath. "You disappear out of your locked bedroom almost two hours ago, and that's what you say to me?"

"I guess you're angry with me." She was too weary, too spent to argue. Let him tell her she'd been foolish. Let him remind her that she was his job, and he needed to do that job well to keep his future secure.

"I am unbelievably angry." He took a step closer. "I don't think I've ever been this furious."

She turned away. Starlight danced on the water, tiny sparkles in the vast darkness of the sea. "I understand."

"You don't understand me at all."

She shrugged. Did it matter? He'd chosen distance. She'd honored that. And now her life was permanently on a different path.

The emptiness within ached. She pressed her hands against her heart to still the hurt.

"I'm angry, Charis, but not with you."

She turned toward him. "Who else is there to be angry with?"

He laughed, but it was full of pain. "Me."

"I don't understand."

"No, you don't, and I'm sorry I didn't see that clearly until today. I should have. All the signs were there, but I was too caught up in my own pain to see yours." He began pacing. "You're so used to being what others need you to be. So careful to be responsible and do your duty by others. I thought you were carelessly misunderstanding me, when really you were drowning, and it never occurs to you to call out for help. Instead, you use your last breath to take care of others."

"I'm not drowning." Her voice betrayed her, a hoarse, broken whisper that scraped against the hurt like a knife.

He stopped in front of her and said with infinite gentleness, "You've been drowning since you decided to sacrifice your future for the safety of your kingdom. But you went under for the last time last week when I couldn't look past the fact that you didn't tell me, your friend, about such a huge decision. I thought we were closer than that, and it was like getting tossed into an icy lake when I was surprised by the news in front of the council."

Charis's eyes stung. "I didn't tell you *because* you're my friend. I know that doesn't make sense, but—"

"It makes perfect sense." He moved closer, and she could see his face, limned with starlight, lines of misery on his brow. "At least, it made sense to me once I remembered how you dealt with the death of your friend Milla. How you couldn't put it into words for your father, the person you are closest to in all the world. You cried with him, something you won't do with anyone else, but even then, you couldn't say the words. You couldn't say the words to Holland and Nalani, either."

"Because then it becomes real," she whispered.

"I know." He reached out a hand and waited to see if she would take it. She hesitated, and he said quietly, "You didn't tell me because it felt like a door closing on all the things you'd hoped for, and you could avoid thinking about the finality of that if you never put it into words. And then it became a reality today, and I saw you."

He sank to his knees, his hand still outstretched, and whispered, "I saw *you*, Charis. I saw you lose control in front of Thorsby with the teacup. Saw you fight off tears, and there is nothing that would make you lose your composure like that if you weren't already drowning. And I'm the fool who should have tossed you a lifeline when I first heard you cry yourself to sleep. When I noticed that you were cutting up your food but not eating it. When I saw the light go out of your eyes."

The wind rustled through the oak trees and tugged at Tal's hair. "I needed time to figure out why you kept it from me. And then to figure out that you telling me I would move on when we were on our first boat outing was really you stepping back so that you wouldn't hurt me. And now that I see you clearly, I also see myself, and I am so sorry for failing you. Please, forgive me."

A tremble shook her, and she slowly reached out to take his hand. His fingers closed over hers, and it felt like safety. Like a warm hearth after being out in a winter storm.

A light—warm and golden—flared to life in her heart, and the loneliness shrank a little.

He bowed his head and let his forehead come to rest against her stomach. She placed her other hand on the top of his head and felt him shiver.

"You're freezing." She looked at him properly for the first time. "For seers' sakes, Tal, you're wearing nothing but pajamas."

"You were gone. I couldn't afford to waste time changing my clothes."

She knelt in front of him, and he locked eyes with her. "I forgive you, but really I think we need to forgive each other. I made my own mistakes, and I'll make more. I don't really know how to be . . ." She searched for the right word.

"Vulnerable," he finished for her. "Of course you don't. Your guard has to be up most of the time. You have enemies within your court and without. And your mother inspires many things, but vulnerability doesn't make the list."

"I'm sorry for scaring you tonight."

He leaned forward, gathered her close, and held her. "Please don't ever do that again."

She froze for an instant. Only Father and Nalani ever hugged her, but this didn't feel the same at all. It was warm and cozy, and intimate in a way that made her feel comforted and exposed at the same time. Slowly, she wrapped her arms around him and leaned her head against his shoulder. He laid his cheek on the top of her head and sighed.

"I have wanted to do this since I saw you stay to talk to every single refugee in that camp. I knew you could be fierce and terrifying. I knew you were smart and capable. But that was the day I learned that you are incredibly compassionate. You gave everything you had to those people, and no one gave anything back to you."

"No one needs to give anything to me."

"Yes, they do." He rubbed small circles against her back. "That's what people do for each other when they care."

She was silent for a few moments and found herself relaxing into his embrace. He smelled like mint and black tea and a hint of soap.

She snuggled closer and pressed her nose against his neck. He sucked in a little breath and said, "I'm going to let go of you now, but not because I want to."

"Then why let go at all?"

He laughed. "Because if I don't let go of you now, I am going to do more than hug you, and I don't think that's what either of us needs tonight."

Her breath caught in her throat, and something warm and delicious swirled through her veins, but when he released her, she scooted back to give them space.

"You never answered my question," she said. "How did you find me?"

"I came to my senses before you left, actually. I was in my room working up the courage to come out, wake you up, and apologize properly when I heard you go out onto the balcony. I got out there in time to see you cross the courtyard." He shivered again. "I figured out you'd climbed down the thesserin tree, but by then, you were long gone. It's lucky I remembered you telling me about this bluff. I'd already checked the stables and the armory."

"We need to go back. You need to warm up."

He smiled. "I'm glad we're still friends, Charis. I've missed you."

"I missed you too. But I'll understand if you change your mind about friendship once the Montevallian prince moves in."

He tucked an errant curl behind her ear. "How about if we figure that out when it actually happens?"

"I can agree to that. Ready?"

He glanced past her shoulder at the sea and paused.

"Tal? It's getting late. We should—"

"Lights."

"I beg your pardon?"

He grasped her shoulders gently and turned her to face the sea. "What are those lights?"

On the edge of the horizon, just past the mouth of the bay, a trio of ghostly green lights bobbed gently on the water.

Charis frowned. "I've never seen that color before, but . . . do you see that? Just past the middle light. Is that a shadow or . . ."

"A mast," Tal said grimly. "Those are ships."

TWENTY-EIGHT

"CAPTAIN, WE GO out with a quiet boat right from the start. Agreed?"

"Agreed. Give the orders."

It had been just over two hours since she and Tal had seen the green lights and the vague, smudged shadow of a ship at the mouth of the bay. They'd sprinted back to the palace, climbed the thesserin tree, and scrambled to change into their sailing clothes and grab their weapons as fast as possible. Then they'd snuck back down the thesserin tree. On their usual seafaring nights, Charis entered a fake social engagement in the guards' schedule book but declined their escort. There was no time to make up a story tonight. Not if they wanted to catch the ships they'd seen.

They were running with a skeleton crew. Just Orayn and the few deckhands that he'd roused from the boardinghouse where he lived. If they got into battle, they were going to be easy prey, but Charis was betting they wouldn't be attacked. They looked like smugglers traveling at the time that smugglers traveled. For extra insurance, they were going to take a known smugglers' route to a small port about seventy furlongs away.

Orayn gave the order to be quiet and then they sailed out of the harbor and into the open sea. Charis turned in a slow circle, her eyes scraping the horizon. There was no sign of the green-lit ships. Orayn looked to her for permission to begin the smugglers' route, and Charis nodded.

It made the most sense for the ships to have gone north. That's where all the attacks but one had happened. She was banking on probabilities and praying she was right.

Tal stood at the railing beside her, his hand brushing against hers as they both hung on to the balustrade. They said nothing, but every now and then he bumped his shoulder against hers or pressed his arm close, and she smiled.

They'd traveled forty-six furlongs when Tal said softly, "Maybe they didn't go this way."

"Maybe, but if we—"

A haunting cry rose from somewhere just beyond the ship. It sounded like a woman singing, screaming, and laughing all at once. The noise rose, so high-pitched that Charis's teeth ached, and she lifted her hands to cover her ears.

"What is—"

The noise reached its crescendo and then dropped swiftly into a series of rapid clicks, like a handful of brittle twigs rattling together. From the water to their left, something clicked in response. Then another. And another.

"All hands on deck!" Orayn roared. "Tack those sails! Grab the lines! We are hard to port in thirty seconds!"

Charis ran for the helm as activity exploded around her. Sailors grabbed ropes, tacking to port and securing the lines around the metal handles embedded in the deck.

"What is that?" she asked breathlessly as she reached Orayn, who was straining to haul the ship hard to port.

"Don't know, Your High—Captain, but I'm not taking any chances. They're talking to each other, and we look to be the only topic of conversation available." The helm fought him, and she grabbed it with him to hold it steady.

"You've never heard those creatures before?"

"Never." Orayn completed the turn and set a course back to Calera. Behind them, another cry shivered through the air, followed by a series of rattling clicks.

"What do you see from the crow's nest?" Orayn hollered to the whip-thin boy around Charis's age whose job it was to climb the rigging and keep watch from the tiny wooden deck near the top of the main mast.

"Nothing, sir!"

"Considering how dark it is tonight, that's not very reassuring," Charis said as another haunting cry rose and fell, chasing a shiver down her spine.

The rapid clicking filled the air, swelling from behind them until it flanked the ship.

"They're on either side of us." Tal loped up the steps to the helm. "We need a battle strategy."

"Strategy against what?" Orayn said, his massive hands wrapped firmly around the ship's wheel. "We don't know what's out there."

"You've had years on the water, Orayn." Charis kept her voice calm, though her stomach was queasy and her knees felt weak. "Think. What could this be?"

"I . . . a monster?" He shook his head. "Some kind of creature who likes deserted shorelines? Nothing much sails around here but a few small fishing boats and smugglers. Might be we stumbled into the creatures' nest."

"If that's the case, then sailing away from it should keep us safe," Tal said. He sounded as if his stomach felt queasy too.

"If not, we fight," Charis said.

"What are we fighting?"

"Whatever comes out of the water."

Charis clenched her teeth as the haunting cry rose again, just off the starboard bow, so high-pitched it sent a stab of pain through her temples. "Everyone to their battle stations. If the creatures in the water do more than chase us away, I want us ready to respond."

Orayn nodded once and then bellowed, "Battle stations! Weapons out! Cannons loaded! Be quick about it."

As the crew scrambled to obey, Charis led Tal down to the deck, drew her sword, and planted her feet beside the starboard railing. Tal took up his position on her right with Dec beside him.

She shot Dec a look. "Stay steady, no matter what comes out of the water."

He kept his gaze on the sea and said quietly, "I can hold my own."

Something skittered along the side of the ship, as though bony fingers were scraping against the wood. Charis focused on the space of dark water in front of her and waited for the creatures to show themselves.

Time slowed to a crawl. The crew braced their boots against the creaking timbers of the deck, their weapons held ready. All were silent save for their ragged breathing as they watched the dark waves for a glimpse of what lived beneath the surface.

Another call rose into the air, but this time, it was in their wake. A second call answered the first, and the rattling clicks followed, but as far as Charis could tell, none of the creatures were still beside the boat.

"I think we've left them behind." Tal moved toward the railing as though to peer over its edge, but Dec beat him to it, thrusting an arm against Tal's chest to hold him back and gazing into the black water himself.

Charis raised a brow, though no one could see it behind her mask. Tal laughed and gave Dec a good-natured slap on the shoulder.

"Don't worry. I can swim."

Dec shrugged. "Never know with nonsailors."

Orayn ordered the crew to stand down. Whatever creatures they'd disturbed were far behind them now.

The rest of their journey home was quiet. When they finally dropped anchor at the small fishing dock again, Charis stood on the deck, watching her crew slink away from the dock in twos and threes, and then turned to Tal.

He stood there, blond hair blowing in the chilly sea breeze, his gloved hands jammed in his cloak pockets. "May I walk you home?"

She grinned. "If you must."

He offered her his arm, and she placed her hand in the crook of his elbow. As they stepped down the gangplank, he said, "We need to get back to practicing the seven rathmas, though once you clean up your footwork, your ferocity is going to make you difficult to beat."

"*Impossible* to beat."

"Let's not get ahead of ourselves."

She laughed, and it was almost easy to imagine for a moment that she wasn't the princess of a war-torn country betrothed to her enemy and facing an unknown threat from the vast reaches of the sea. To pretend she was just a girl walking home with a boy, neither of them trying to use the other for anything more than a quiet conversation and some time spent together.

Thirty minutes of pretending wouldn't change her duties or her future, but it might bring her some peace. She leaned against him and let the warm golden light he'd lit within her be the only thing she thought about for the entire walk home.

TWENTY-NINE

TEN DAYS HAD passed since the news that King Alaric had accepted the offer of a peace treaty. The council was nearly done hammering out negotiations and finalizing the precise wording. Charis's busy schedule continued to fluctuate, the ships they'd seen that night at the mouth of the harbor remained elusive, though thankfully they hadn't run into the strange sea creatures again, and she'd managed to eat a bit more, despite the impending betrothal.

There was still the issue of finding Bartho. A search of the warehouse district had yielded a building that was obviously being used as a makeshift home for multiple people, but it was deserted when the guards found it, and though the queen had ordered it watched closely since then, no one had returned to it. Maybe he'd left the city now that his king had agreed to the betrothal and abandoned plans to assassinate the Willowthorns. It wasn't as satisfying as throwing him in the dungeon and letting the queen exact vengeance, but it would have to do.

And of course, there was still the pressing need to learn who was sinking their ships. The queen had allowed another merchant vessel to leave three days ago. It had sunk twenty-four furlongs from the harbor.

Charis had more than enough worries on her plate, but for this moment, in the misty haze of early morning, all that existed was the dance of her body with Tal's, the harsh melody of their clashing swords, and the sound of their breath mingling in the chilly air.

She knew his swordsmanship now. Knew that even though his healing left arm was weaker than his right, his speed made up for it. Knew that he laughed when he lost but fought hard to win. And knew that he never gave her quarter, but instead treated her like an equal.

"Left foot back. Plant, then pivot your hips."

She slid her left foot back, cursing the sixth rathma for always giving her trouble. Something about the transition from the water pose to bowing hawk felt unnatural. Years of traditional sword work had trained her body to move a different way.

"Not quite." Tal sheathed his sword and moved to stand behind her. "Like this."

His hands circled her waist, gently tugging her into position, and then putting slight pressure where he wanted her to bend. Tiny points of heat spread from his fingertips and seemed to sink into her blood.

Her breathing hitched, and Tal stilled. "Are you all right?"

"Of course I'm all right." She had to be. Never mind that she was too aware of his chest at her back and the pressure of his hands at her hips. Too attuned to the expression in his eyes and the warmth of his smiles. It was ridiculous, and she could lay the blame on the fact he challenged her skills, respected her strength, and somehow made her feel like she was *seen*.

His chest brushed against her back, and she leaned against him before thinking better of it. His fingers tightened slightly, and she cursed her traitorous pulse for spiking.

For one glorious moment, she let herself imagine what it would be like to be an ordinary girl. A girl who could flirt with a boy she liked. Who could feel breathless at the touch of his hand and dream of a first kiss.

But she wasn't an ordinary girl. She was a princess with fury for a heart and ice in her veins, and she was betrothed to another.

Stepping forward, she said quietly, "I think we're done practicing for the morning."

He said nothing as she sheathed her own sword, and then as they made their way toward the palace, he said, "I don't think you're all right."

She remained quiet.

"Ah, I see. We get to play Tal Reads the Princess's Mind."

Charis smiled ruefully. "Or we get to play Let the Princess Keep Her Traitorous Thoughts to Herself for Once."

"Traitorous?" He gave her a sidelong look. "You have to know I'm dying of curiosity now."

"I hope you don't suffer on your way out."

He laughed. "I bet I can guess what you consider traitorous."

He could, and they both knew it. Heat flushed her cheeks, but she ignored the tiny spark in her chest. She was so tired. Not just tired, *spent*. The world kept hurtling toward her, and there was never a moment to just breathe. Just collect herself and somehow be ready to face what was coming.

"Hey there, where did you go just now?"

She blinked and looked at him. They were already at the courtyard outside her wing, and she'd lost the past two minutes to her thoughts. His eyes were full of concern.

"I'm just tired."

He studied her for a moment and then said, "I know what you need."

"A nap?"

"Yes. But clear your schedule for dinner tonight, all right?"

"What are you going to do?" She frowned. "You can't take me to dinner."

"You let me worry about what I can and cannot do."

"Tal—"

He leaned closer and said softly, "Have a little faith in me, Your Highness."

She smiled wearily. "I have nothing but faith in you."

He gave her his crooked smile and escorted her back to her chambers, where Mrs. Sykes waited to get Charis ready for her day.

Charis finished with her last meeting as the sun was sinking below the distant horizon in a pool of fiery crimson. Still no news on Bartho, though no one had returned to the warehouse yet. Still no solution for the ship attacks, though the queen had sent word to other kingdoms to see if any of them were having similar troubles. And now the Rullenvor ambassador was requesting another audience with the royals. Obviously, the High Emperor had decided they'd had enough time to consider his offer.

Charis entered her chambers and then stared in shock as Tal dismissed Mrs. Sykes for the evening.

"Why did you do that? I thought you had something planned for me for dinner."

"What I have planned doesn't take fancy hairdos or elaborate gowns. Wear your most comfortable dress and forget jewelry or even shoes if you don't want them." He sounded proud of himself, and so Charis obediently went into her closet and pulled on a favorite soft wool dress the color of pale sunshine. She left her shoes off and exited the closet to find Tal in a simple pair of pants and a gray shirt.

"If you are taking me out of the palace in this outfit, I will personally throw you in the dungeon," she said sternly.

"You wouldn't dare."

"I dare a great many things."

He grinned, and the light he'd kindled within her brightened. "Let's go."

She laughed. Every second of her day was planned down to the tiniest detail. Leaving her chambers without a timetable or a destination in mind felt like an adventure.

Tal led her down the stairs with Gaylle and Vellis just behind them, and then headed toward the east wing. Charis's heart soared.

He was taking her to Father, and he was right—this was exactly what she needed. It had been almost two weeks since she'd seen him. Her brutal schedule had made sure of that.

Tal and Charis entered the king's suite and followed Ilsa into the sitting room, where oil lamps spread warm, golden pools of light across the wood floor, and the bank of windows framed a spectacular view as tiny pricks of starlight twinkled to life in the purple sky.

"My sweet girl!" Father's wan face lit with joy as Charis and Tal entered the room. "Tal, I do thank you for bringing her to me." He struggled to his feet, swaying slightly.

Ilsa rushed to place the trays on the table so she could catch him, but Charis got there first. Wrapping her arm firmly around Father's

back, she took half his weight against her shoulder and stood supporting him while he reached a shaky hand toward Tal.

Tal stepped forward, managing to move quickly without making
it look like he was hurrying. He bowed, and then the king pulled him
in for a hug.

Charis caught a glimpse of Tal's face, of the ache of longing in
his expression, and resolved to share her father with him more often.
It would be good for both of them. Hildy meowed impatiently and
wound around everyone's feet, already purring.

"Your Highness, it's a pleasure to see you again," Tal said.

"My dear boy, the pleasure is all mine." The king trembled as
Charis helped him settle back onto his couch and then perched
beside him. "And you've been taking good care of Charis. You know
she never really thinks about taking care of herself."

"I've realized that, sir." Tal scooped up Hildy and settled into a
chair. The kitten curled up beneath his chin.

The king smiled. "I figured you would." He turned to Charis.
"Very perceptive, this one."

"And bossy."

He laughed, a wheeze that ended in a rattle, and patted Charis's
hand. "About time someone with your best interests at heart stopped
being afraid to stand up to you. Not that you're a tyrant, my dear."

Tal laughed. Charis narrowed her eyes at him, and he tried unsuccessfully to turn it into a cough.

Father beamed. "There, now! I knew the two of you were well
suited."

Tal accepted a plate of fruit, cheese, and crusty oat bread from
Ilsa and then had to maneuver it away from Hildy's inquisitive nose.
He was halfway through a bite of dried spiced apricot when the king

said, "Speaking of well suited, I wonder if you've considered any of the pretty maids who work in Charis's wing?"

Tal choked on his apricot, coughing until he was red in the face. Ilsa ran to his side.

"Smack him on the back," Charis said helpfully.

Ilsa delivered a solid thwack to the center of Tal's back, and he waved the nurse away.

"I'm fine." His voice sounded husky, and he cleared his throat before continuing. "Your Highness, I don't have time to notice the maids. It's all I can do to keep up with your daughter."

The king smiled. "Yes, well, you are one who loves a challenge. I suppose a girl who couldn't match your intelligence, swordsmanship, and stubbornness wouldn't be able to catch your eye."

Tal shot a look at Charis, who was busy trying to decide if the king was being sly or simply making conversation, and said, "I . . . um . . ."

Father laughed again, and Charis winced at the frail, wheezy sound of his breathing. "Perhaps if you haven't found someone who intrigues you, Ilsa and I can get to know some of the maids and introduce you. We've had some luck setting up successful dates between some of the younger staff. Unless, of course, there's someone who already takes up your thoughts."

Twin spots of color burned on Tal's sun-kissed cheeks. "I don't . . . that is to say . . . I'm really not sure I should discuss my thoughts here."

"Oh, don't worry about my daughter's reaction." Father reached for a bite of cheese. "Charis understands the appeal of a handsome stable boy, so surely she would understand if we found a maid or perhaps a page for you."

Charis rolled her eyes. "No, Charis does *not* understand the appeal of a handsome stable boy. Honestly, Father, what has gotten into you?"

Tal looked in danger of choking again, and hastily focused on Hildy as if the kitten required his undivided attention.

The king patted Charis's knee. "One day soon, you'll meet someone who makes you want to sneak out just to steal a few minutes alone with him."

For an instant, Charis thought of the southern bluff, and the feeling of Tal's arms around her as she pressed her face to his neck, and her cheeks heated as if she'd leaned too close to a roaring fire.

"What's this?" The king's voice positively sparkled. "My sweet Charis is blushing? Are you already sneaking out to meet a young man? Please tell me it isn't that oafish Everly boy."

Tal's head shot up, and he locked eyes with Charis. For a moment, Charis thought he'd read her thoughts and was remembering the bluff as well. But then he looked pained, and the truth hit.

The betrothal.

Charis still hadn't told Father the terms of the peace treaty. He'd been delighted to learn that she'd brokered a stop to the eighteen-year war, and she'd been scarce on the details. It was enough to see his pride in her as he learned that his beloved north would finally be free of bloodshed again. If she hadn't wanted his worry, his grief, over his only daughter being shackled to a Montevallian for the rest of her life, condemned to the kind of loveless marriage he had, was that so bad? He could spend his remaining months proud of her, relieved for his kingdom, and never know the pain she carried.

"Who is he?" the king asked as he brushed a frail hand against her heated cheek.

She made herself smile like she hadn't a care in the world and thought of Tal. "He's funny, interesting, sincere, honest, and better at swordsmanship than I am, though I'd rather die than admit it to him."

"Well, now." The king sat up a little straighter. "He sounds a sight better than the Everly boy already."

"He puts the Everly boy to shame in every way," Charis said softly, her heart aching as Tal met her gaze, his eyes dark with something she couldn't interpret. Willing Tal to see that the topic of the betrothal was off-limits, Charis said briskly, "I've never heard the story of how Tal came to be in your service." She leaned toward the table and scooped up a sugared apple slice.

The king eyed Charis for a moment and then said quietly, "All right, we'll change the subject. But, Charis . . ." He waited until she met his gaze. "If this boy doesn't treat you with the utmost honor and respect, then he isn't worth a single minute of your time. And if he doesn't challenge you, you'll grow to despise him. If he doesn't see past your walls, he won't make the effort you need to help you connect to the parts of yourself you keep secret. You make sure of that before you take things any further."

Charis kissed his cheek and leaned against his shoulder while Tal told a very short story about Montevallian soldiers invading his village and days of trekking south on foot until he came to Arborlay.

"There were a few others from various villages in the north who were traveling south too. I joined up with them, and when we arrived at the refugee center, Orayn and several others helped everyone find jobs. I was lucky enough to get a job with the king." Tal smiled warmly at Father. Charis didn't have the heart to ask him if any of his family had survived the invasion of his village.

Later, as Charis sat in front of her vanity removing her hairpins and braiding her hair for the night, she said, "So, going to let Father set you up with a chambermaid?"

Tal smirked. "Somehow I don't think any of them would be enough to take over what's already in my thoughts. Are you going to tell me about your mysterious, charming friend?"

Charis raised one dainty eyebrow. "There's nothing to tell."

"Liar," he said as he came to stand behind her and took her thick hair into his hands. "I'll do it." He began separating her curls into three sections.

"How dare you call me a liar?" Laughter sparkled in her voice.

He bent close and locked eyes with her in the mirror. "Am I wrong?"

His breath tickled her ear, and she shivered, though she was far from cold. When she didn't answer, he smiled as if he was a cat who'd caught a mouse and straightened so he could continue braiding her hair.

After a moment, Charis said quietly, "Thank you for not telling Father about the betrothal. I want to spare him that pain."

Tal's eyes darkened, and he looked down at his hands as he worked with her hair. After a moment, he said, "I hope this is all right to say, but I love your father, too, Charis."

Charis smiled. "Everyone does. Except Mother, but even she doesn't actively dislike him."

"He really loves you. He understands you, accepts you, and truly loves you."

Something dark lingered in his voice, a nameless hurt that cast a shadow over his eyes as he finished the braid and then met Charis's gaze in the mirror.

"I'm sure your father loves you, too," Charis said gently.

Tal's hands stilled on Charis's shoulders, and a muscle along his jaw tensed. Finally, he said quietly, "No, I don't think so. I could never be what he wanted me to be, and no matter what I did, he was never proud of me. When given a choice between saving me and throwing me to the wolves, he chose the wolves."

Charis reached up to place her hand over Tal's and said fiercely, "Well, then, he chose wrong."

"Thank you," Tal said. He squeezed her shoulder lightly and then turned toward his room. "I'm going to bed. Don't sneak out while I'm sleeping."

"Are you going to keep saying that to me every single night before bed?"

Tal stopped and patted his chest. "Let's see. Ah, there it is. The memory of near heart failure. Yes, I will continue saying that to you every single night before bed. If you don't like it, you should think twice before giving me heart failure again."

Charis crawled into bed with a smile on her face. Worries about the betrothal could be shoved into a corner of her mind, along with her fear of losing her father. Those were fears for the future. Instead, she held her memories of the night with Father, Tal, and Ilsa close. Tender, golden moments that would carry her through whatever the week would bring.

Tonight, she would go to sleep comforted by the time she'd spent with people who truly loved her, not because of anything she could do for them but simply because she was their Charis.

THIRTY

THE CARRIAGE MOVED sedately through the long, winding streets that wrapped around the capital's southern neighborhoods. Enormous stone mansions with immaculate lawns, stately gardens full of autumn colors, and golden rooftops that glowed in the late afternoon sun were set at a respectable distance from the cobblestone road.

Charis shifted against the plush velvet carriage seat and smoothed the skirt of her rose-and-ivory dress. Tiny, delicate silver blades were stitched into the hemline like jewels, and a chain of opals wrapped around her waist. She adjusted the dagger sheaths she wore on each wrist and wished she'd insisted on wearing a sword as well.

Mother sat opposite her, dressed in a stunning gown that began as the color of delicate sunshine at the neckline and darkened until her hem was a pool of glowing amber. Mother's latest maid sat beside her, holding the queen's cape, muff, and a small bag of toiletries in case the queen or Charis needed to freshen up between tea and dinner. Tal sat beside Charis in his dress uniform.

"Remember"—Mother's voice was as crisp as the air outside the carriage—"everyone will be wondering how you feel about the

betrothal. This is your first appearance after our official announcement to the kingdom, and it is imperative that all in attendance leave
feeling confident that you are more than capable of keeping the new
king consort in line once he arrives."

Charis nodded obediently. She knew all this. Knew that she was
on display from the moment she left the carriage, even more so than
usual. Every expression, every word, every gesture would be noticed,
analyzed, and then discussed at length, first in the Everlys' drawing
room, and then throughout the city, until it spread to the entire kingdom. She could almost hear their whispers now.

What if the new king takes over?

What if this is a ploy to steal our kingdom and give it to Montevallo?

What if Charis isn't strong enough? Smart enough? Ruthless enough?

What if this ruins everything?

Charis drew a fortifying breath as the carriage turned onto the
lane that led up a gentle slope to the Everly mansion, where a line of
carriages waited in front of the house while uniformed pages helped
nobility disembark and then sent the carriages around back to park in
the field beside the stables.

What would she do if the new king consort tried to take over and
give Calera to his father? What if he proved difficult to manage? Sly
and dishonorable, just like the rest of the Montevallians who'd passed
through the Willowthorns' dungeon?

What if he was a man who craved violence and pain like Reuben,
and every day for the rest of her life she would be forced to use fury as
her armor as she fought to keep him in his place?

Her mouth went dry as the carriage rolled to a stop, her pulse
thundering in her ears. Already, flocks of ladies in brilliant silks and
gentlemen in dress coats and fine cravats clustered near the mansion's entrance, their eyes on the royal carriage, their faces alight with

speculation as they whispered to each other.

As the door opened and the queen stepped regally from the carriage, Tal's fingers brushed the top of Charis's hand and pressed lightly. When Charis turned to look at him, Tal said softly, "You are smarter, stronger, and far more cunning than the lot of them put together, Your Highness. None of them could do what you've already done for Calera. They're lucky to have you. Don't let them forget it."

The pressure building within Charis lessened a fraction, and she gave Tal a tiny smile. "Thank you. Now remember, Elsbet will shadow me for the first hour. I need you to mingle with the staff from other households. Listen closely for talk of Bartho, but don't—"

"Get caught. I know how to be invisible when I need to be," Tal said, a shadow passing briefly over his expression.

Not for the first time, Charis wondered if Tal's father had made him feel invisible. Or maybe he'd been so horrible, Tal had learned to move through his life without leaving a mark in order to escape his father's attention. Giving Tal's arm a quick squeeze, she said, "Be careful."

Then, calling on the ice in her heart to shield her, Charis left the carriage, spine straight, chin lifted, her expression promising ruin to any who dared to cross her.

She nodded imperiously to the cluster of ladies near the mansion's entrance but didn't stop, though she could tell they were dying to speak with her. Let them see that she had more important things to do than be a piece of meat they tore apart with their gossiping little tongues.

The Everlys' drawing room was an ostentatious affair. Blush-colored plaster met ornate, scalloped molding, and a ceiling full of hand-painted water nymphs looked down upon the guests, who mingled in small clusters while maids in starched gray uniforms handed out plates of tiny sandwiches and delicate cups of tea.

Charis watched Tal as he skirted the edges of the massive entrance hall and disappeared into the small sitting room that had been set aside for staff members of the Everlys' guests. Reuben took up his post just inside the drawing room doors, his eyes roving over the guests, hunting for trouble, while Elsbet walked a half step ahead of Charis. She'd much rather have had Tal with her, but they'd decided this was a good opportunity to see if the staff members of other noble houses were sharing any interesting gossip that could narrow down Bartho's location. Charis refused to trust anyone but Tal with the job. He was far too perceptive and observant to be wasted following her around a drawing room.

Satisfied that her staff were where they should be, Charis surveyed the room, quickly sorting through her priorities.

Her hosts first, though she dreaded the inevitable confrontation with Ferris, who would know for certain now that his hopes of being king were dashed.

Next, she'd approach the few members of the northern nobility in attendance. They had the most personal stake in the peace treaty and needed to hear their princess assure them that their villages would be rebuilt with Montevallian jewels once the wedding took place.

The cluster of lords and ladies with Lady Vera Shawling at their center would need attention before tea was over. Charis could put to rest any rumors that weren't to Calera's advantage and start a few that were in a matter of moments.

And finally, she'd make sure to speak to each council member before the night concluded. Her eyes narrowed as her gaze scraped over Lady Ollen whispering furiously to Lord Thorsby, whose green silk handkerchief was in grave danger of being ruined by the anxious sweat dotting his brown face. There were ruffled feathers to smooth, and she would do it in a way that reminded them who was truly in charge of this kingdom.

She bared her teeth in a smile as ice prickled beneath her skin.

"Your Highness, you look lovely. I apologize that Lord Everly isn't here to greet you. He's sorting out a small issue with the additional kitchen staff we hired for today. But he sends his compliments," Lady Everly gushed, dropping into a curtsy while cutting a swift glance to her right at Ferris, who stood beside his mother, his tea coat and cravat perfectly complementing her pale blue dress.

Ferris stepped forward, bowed respectfully, and said in smooth, courteous tones, "Allow me to offer my congratulations on finally negotiating peace with Montevallo."

Charis looked from one to the other, letting her gaze settle on Ferris like a blade poised above his neck. "I'm surprised to hear you congratulate me for allowing a Montevallian into the palace." Her voice was just as courteous as his, though there was a sharp edge to it.

His mother gave him another swift glance freighted with meaning, and Ferris smiled, sly and knowing. "It's not the kind of peace I'd hoped we'd accomplish together, but it is peace, and it gives us a way into Montevallian politics. Perhaps some leverage, if we play it right."

"We?" One brow rose as Charis let the word drop between them, cold as the marble floors beneath their feet.

His smile hardened. "If I can't help rule Calera by your side, then I can be the force at your back. The head of your council. And if the king consort doesn't measure up in . . . other areas"—his gaze swept her body and slowly returned to her face—"then I can help you there, too."

Twin spots of pink bloomed on Lady Everly's cheeks, though

when she looked at Charis, her gaze was just as eager as her son's.

Mother's words echoed in Charis's head as she let any lingering warmth in her eyes die.

Everyone wanted Charis for her power. Either to take it from her or to use it for themselves.

And those who wanted to use her deserved nothing but her contempt.

Her eyes bore into Ferris's as she said coolly, "When I take the throne, I will certainly remember this conversation as I choose my council members. Now, if you'll excuse me."

Turning, she stalked toward the bank of floor-to-ceiling windows that lined the wall overlooking the sumptuous gardens. Guests took one look at her face and moved swiftly out of her way even while they scrambled to drop into curtsies or bows.

So Ferris and his parents thought they could still position him beside Charis. Still pair him with her to share the responsibility of ruling Calera. It was a shame they held so much wealth and influence. Clearly, they were under the impression that being in power was their due, but without concrete evidence that they'd actually moved against the throne, Charis couldn't risk alienating their friends and supporters by banning them from the capital, no matter how satisfying that would be to her personally.

"Your Highness." Lord Severin, a tall, thin man whose clothes hung a bit loosely on his sticklike frame, bowed as she reached his side. He could trace his ancestry on his mother's side to Solvang and had the high cheekbones and golden skin to prove it. Lord Palmer, who barely reached Lord Severin's shoulder and whose shock of red hair was beginning to turn silver, quickly bowed as well.

"I apologize for interrupting your conversation," Charis said with sincerity.

Both northern landowners hurried to assure her they couldn't be more pleased. She smiled. "That's very kind, but the truth is that you must have questions and concerns. Your lands have been deeply affected by the war. I wanted to personally assure you that the plight of your villages was utmost in my mind as we negotiated the peace treaty, and I want to address any misgivings. Now, what questions do you have?"

"When will the Montevallian army leave our lands?" Lord Severin asked.

"And how will we get the resources necessary to rebuild? I have five villages that have sustained heavy damage, not to mention our seriously depleted food stores for winter. And Severin here has lost Irridusk completely." Lord Palmer blinked as the setting sun bathed the garden in gold and sent piercing rays through the windows. Turning his back on the scene, he faced the princess.

"The army will leave once the wedding is final," Charis said, "though they will not attack again. And I've negotiated a generous settlement of Montevallian jewels as part of the prince's dowry. I will use those jewels to pay for the rebuilding of our northern territories. I can't replace the lives that have been lost, but I can give you safety, security, and a chance at prosperity once more."

"Thank you, Your Highness," Severin said. "And please know that those of us in the north support you. Your father is well loved, and you show his courage and his heart. If the Montevallian prince gives you any trouble, we stand at your service for whatever you need."

She smiled, warm and sincere. "I thank you. I am confident I can manage a single prince, but should he prove troublesome, I know whom to call upon for help. Do you have any other questions?"

Lord Palmer shot a look at Severin and then said in a hushed voice, "Lady Merryfin isn't here to tell you in person, but I know she supports you as well. And though her lands haven't received as much damage from the Montevallians, being farther south on the coast than Ebbington, she has concerns that have nothing to do with the peace treaty."

"Speak freely."

"There are . . . strange things happening along the coast, Your Highness," Lord Palmer said. "Noises at night that sound like a woman screaming or crying. And rattling sounds, as though dry twigs are being shaken by the wind, though it all seems to come from the water."

A chill chased itself across Charis's skin, and it took effort not to rub at the goose bumps rising on her arms. She knew that sound. She'd heard it once from aboard the ship.

"That's strange enough, but then there are the bodies." Lord Palmer tugged at his tea coat as though the subject made him uncomfortable.

"What bodies?" Charis asked.

"Lady Merryfin says bodies have started washing ashore. A few one day, one the next, then nothing for a week straight only to find yet another pair. All sailors, I suppose, though by the time they reach the shore, they're disfigured and decaying, so her guards have a hard time knowing for certain."

"Perhaps a ship sank in the area and some of the sailors are being brought to shore," Charis said.

"Perhaps, but . . ." Lord Palmer tugged more insistently on his coat, and Lord Severin took over.

"The bodies are all on the shores of Portsmith, Your Highness." His brown eyes held hers. "It's a small, mostly abandoned fishing town with a very narrow harbor. Inhospitable to bigger ships and certainly not a place any merchant has used for decades. Of course, Lady

Merryfin doesn't have a guard presence there, so most of the reports are brought in by palloren. She's only sent one group to the town to investigate, but still, given the attacks our ships have suffered at sea, she's concerned that the threat is close to her lands."

"Portsmith." Charis's thoughts raced as fast as her pulse. Portsmith's harbor couldn't manage large frigates, but perhaps whoever was sinking Calera's ships also had a smaller attack vessel. One that would be faster, harder to see, and easier to hide.

It didn't explain the strange sounds coming from beneath the water, but Charis would worry about that later. The most pressing issue was to visit Portsmith herself with her crew under the cover of darkness and see if an enemy fleet was using it or the large caves that lined the northern shore as cover.

By the time the tea was over and the crowd was moving toward the dining room, Charis had spoken with every northern landowner, planted a rumor with Lady Shawling that the queen had received overwhelming support for both the peace treaty and her reign from their allies at sea, and had quelled several impertinent matrons who'd openly speculated that having a Montevallian in the palace would be the ruin of Calera.

Fools.

The ruin of Calera would be the continuation of a war they'd long ago proven they could not win. But then, Charis supposed it was easy to say such nonsense when the war had never cost your family anything but increased taxes. Let those matrons spend a few weeks in the north, sifting through the burnt rubble of homes for bodies of children or staring at warehouses nearly empty of grain as winter swiftly approached and see what they had to say about ruin then.

She paused by the ladies' parlor, Reuben and Elsbet at her back.

"What can I get for you, Your Highness?" a plump woman with

bright brown eyes and a wide smile asked as she curtsied from the doorway, her starched gray uniform gleaming in the light of the oil lamps that had been lit along the hallway.

"My guard Tal, if you please. And my mother's maid so I can freshen up."

The woman nodded and entered the room. A moment later, she was back, a slight frown marring her forehead. "I apologize, Your Highness, but your guard isn't here at the moment, and the maid is with the queen. If there's something I can do for you, I'd be happy to assist. I have powders, combs, mints, and an assortment of fragrances for you to choose from if you'd like."

Charis stared at the woman in silence, her thoughts spinning.

Where had Tal gone? Had he overheard something that was concerning enough that he'd decided he needed to investigate it further? And how would he even do that here, unless whatever he'd overheard had something to do with the Everlys?

"Good afternoon, Your Highness," a quiet, calm voice said from Charis's left.

Charis turned to find Lady Channing and her maid, Leeya, a woman old enough to be Charis's mother who'd been at Lady Channing's side for as long as Charis could remember.

"Where did Tal go?" Reuben asked close to Charis's ear.

The last thing she needed was for Reuben to take it upon himself to go hunting for Tal. She didn't trust him while she was present to keep him in check. Having him confront Tal without her was a recipe for disaster, though she was pretty sure the one who'd come out the worse for wear was Reuben.

"Chamber pot," Charis said cheerfully. "Reuben, please go do a check of the dining room."

Lady Channing stepped to Charis's side, neatly cutting off

Reuben's attempts to whisper something else to the princess, and said, "Perhaps I can be of service? I have plenty of toiletry items left in my bag."

Charis moved away from the doorway of the ladies' parlor but stopped before they reached one of the private chambers near the end of the hall. She couldn't go inside without taking her eyes off Reuben, and she needed to see that Tal returned safely before then.

If Lady Channing thought it strange that the princess showed no inclination to step inside a private room to freshen up, she didn't show it. Instead, she nodded to Leeya, who scooped out a glass container of finely ground rice powder and a clean sponge. Reuben passed them on his way to do a check of the dining room, and Elsbet positioned herself just to Charis's left.

As Charis stood still, allowing Leeya to press the powder against her forehead and nose, Lady Channing said softly, "How did tea go? I expect there were some people who feel unhappy with the peace treaty's terms."

Charis considered her response carefully. "There are certainly those who have concerns, but the legitimate worries have been addressed in our negotiations and the rest are nothing but rumors and fearmongering." Charis held Lady Channing's gaze. "If it all comes down to worrying whether I can manage a power grab from the Montevallian prince, then either people will believe I'm capable, or they'll see proof of it once he's here."

Leeya replaced the powder and reached for a bottle of fragrance as Lady Channing said, "That's what I've always admired in you—absolute pragmatism. You understand that the stability of our kingdom is more important than appeasing those who think they know best but don't have a full grasp of the situation. Leeya, I believe the princess would prefer the floramint fragrance instead."

The maid hurried to exchange the green bottle she held for a purple one as Charis raised a brow at Lady Channing. "I didn't realize you knew my favorite scent."

The woman smiled. "It's one of my favorites too, so I recognize it on you."

"How observant."

"We both know that's one of my strengths," said Lady Channing. "One of yours too. I wonder, have you encouraged the Farragin twins to change up their schedules and hire more guards?"

Charis stilled. "Why would they need to do that?"

"Because they're next in line for the throne. My staff have passed along some rather nasty rumors about the plans of those displeased with the betrothal. If someone who is against the peace treaty managed to kill you, seers forbid—"

"If someone kills me, the treaty is dead."

Lady Channing frowned. "No, we specifically worded it that one of their heirs must marry one of ours. It is understood to be you, of course, but should you die, the next heir would qualify."

Charis locked eyes with Lady Channing. "Who asked for that wording?"

The woman's eyes widened, and she looked slightly flustered. "Your Highness, I apologize. I had no idea you didn't realize we'd taken out your name and used 'the heir' instead. It's a smart move, and honestly I thought you had to have approved it because you're always thinking so far ahead."

"*Who* suggested we do that, Lady Channing?"

The woman swallowed. "Lord Thorsby."

THIRTY-ONE

CHARIS STOOD FACING Lady Channing, her eyes on the older woman's face as her thoughts spun. Lord Thorsby, who'd come to Charis because the queen refused to follow his advice. Who was furious that the peace treaty meant his son's death wouldn't be avenged. Had he decided the Willowthorns should no longer rule and then prepared the way to put another heir on the throne without plunging the kingdom back into war? Or had he simply taken the most pragmatic approach in wording the treaty given the attempts on Charis's life?

"Your Highness?" Lady Channing's calm, quiet voice broke through Charis's thoughts, and she focused on the woman again. A slight frown puckered Lady Channing's brow, and her gaze was sharp.

"When did this discussion take place?" Charis asked.

Lady Channing shook her head. "I . . . We had several very long meetings to figure out the terms of the contract before sending it. I'm not certain at which meeting the wording was finalized."

Charis cocked her head. "You remember my favorite scent, though I've never told it to you, but you can't remember in which meeting the wording was finalized?"

Lady Channing's mouth twisted. "The hazards of getting older."

"Indeed."

"Your Highness, if this upsets you, please call a council meeting. All of us would be happy to discuss the issue. I'm positive another council member will recall the exact chain of events."

Charis found it hard to believe Lady Channing couldn't remember the precise details of each treaty discussion. The woman had a mind as sharp as a sword and spent her time quietly observing and cataloging details. So why didn't she want to share it with Charis? Was she trying to protect someone? If so, who? She'd already told Charis that Lord Thorsby had been the one to suggest the wording.

Unless Thorsby hadn't come up with the idea on his own but had instead simply been doing his job—presenting all useful ideas gleaned from his individual conversations with each council member and working toward a consensus. Which could mean someone else had decided to ensure peace whether Charis was alive to fulfill the contract or not. If that someone was Lady Channing, why be the one to accidentally give Charis the information?

Maybe the woman really was struggling to remember the exact details because it hadn't seemed momentous to her at the time.

"Your Highness!" Lady Everly bustled into the long corridor, looking slightly harried. "There you are. We are ready to serve dinner if it pleases you to join us."

Charis began moving toward Lady Everly, and Lady Channing kept pace at her side while Elsbet fell into step behind them. Reuben waited at the doorway to join them. As they neared their hostess, Lady Channing said quietly, "I do know that Lord Thorsby had a long meeting with the Everlys before we began working on the treaty's details. I gather they were none too happy with your decision to marry the enemy prince."

Charis gave a slight nod of her head, the barest acknowledgment that she'd heard Lady Channing as the two of them reached Lady Everly, who quickly curtsied to Charis, her smile strained.

"Who is seated beside me?" Charis aimed the question at Lady Everly. Lady Channing paused briefly in the doorway between the corridor and the formal dining room and then moved forward as if their hostess's answer meant nothing to her.

"Ferris is on your right, Your Highness, and Lady Ollen is to your left at her own request." Lady Everly seemed faintly annoyed. "She doesn't usually ask for favors, and of course I owed her for"—her eyes darted to Charis's and then away—"for her discretion on a small matter last year, so I placed her beside you."

Which meant that if Charis requested to have Lord Thorsby take Lady Ollen's place, she would cause deep offense to both the lady in question and her hostess. It would insult the Everlys to ask for Ferris to be moved as well, which left Charis with few options. Fine. The conversation with Thorsby could wait. Lady Ollen had been present for the treaty negotiations. Charis could aim questions at her instead.

Inclining her head to Lady Everly, Charis moved into the dining room. Two tables stretched nearly the entire length of the room, creating a wide corridor between them. Each was blanketed with table linens in snowy white while pale blue wine goblets and silver utensils carved with the Everly family crest gleamed beneath the chandeliers.

The queen was already seated at the head of the table to Charis's left, flanked by Lord Severin and Lady Whitecross. Charis met her mother's gaze as she moved toward her own seat at the head of the table to the right. She doubted Lady Everly had placed the Severins beside the queen of her own volition. Not when the spot could have gone to one of the Everlys' many friends in the capital who would then owe their hostess a debt she could easily call upon. Mother must have requested it, which meant she would complete the work Charis had begun in the drawing room. By the end of the night, the northern title owners would feel confident in their rulers and hopeful for the future of the people who depended on them.

Ferris stood beside Charis's empty chair, a sly smirk plastered on his face. She would bet the entire contents of her wardrobe that he was the reason Holland and Nalani hadn't received an invitation to the dinner. If he hadn't wanted the competition for Charis's time and attention, he was about to be sorely disappointed.

"Ferris," Charis said briskly as she stepped past him, appearing not to notice the way he stretched his hand toward her as if to help maneuver her voluminous skirts into her chair. She'd been managing skirts for as long as she could remember. She hardly needed a boy's help to do so.

Reuben and Elsbet took up their positions a few paces behind her chair, their eyes constantly scanning the room for threats. Charis allowed herself one swift glance back at the hallway she'd left, hoping to see Tal, and then settled into her seat.

To her left, Lady Ollen rose, curtsied, and then plopped back down onto her chair and reached for her wineglass, which was already half empty. Ferris cut a sharp look at Charis as he, too, took his seat, but she wasn't interested in deciphering its meaning. A bell tinkled from a doorway tucked into the western corner of the room, closest to Charis's table, and waitstaff dressed in gray uniforms began moving along the tables with small plates of aged brullaise cheese drizzled with plum sauce and surrounded with wafer-thin crackers. As a waiter set a plate in front of Charis, she turned to Lady Ollen and found the woman watching her closely over the rim of her wineglass.

"You are a very busy girl these days, Your Highness." She spoke casually, though a spark of curiosity burned in her eyes. "So busy it seems your schedule can never be finalized for the council."

"There is much to be done." Charis reached for her wine. Ferris snapped his fingers toward a boy in gray stationed against the wall at Charis's back, and he hurried to the table. "Taste the princess's food and drink."

Quickly, the boy pulled a small glass cup from his pocket and poured a swallow of wine out of Charis's goblet into his own. His fingers trembled slightly, and he pressed them against his cup until the nails turned a faint bluish-white. Raising the cup to his lips, he swallowed the contents and then stood, waiting for any poison to take effect. When nothing happened, he removed a miniature silver knife from the same pocket, cut a small bite of the sauce-drizzled cheese, placed it on a cracker, and then ate it.

Charis flinched inwardly as the boy again stood waiting for any poison to take effect. It was one thing to know her life was always in danger. It was another to ask an innocent Caleran to possibly die in her stead. She had a taster of her own at the palace for those times when anyone other than her personal maids prepared and served her meals, but waiting to see if someone was going to die in her place never got easier.

When the food didn't affect him either, the boy gave Charis a quick bow and moved back to the wall. Charis took a tiny sip of wine and returned her attention to Lady Ollen as the drink's sweet, nutty flavor spread across her tongue.

"I understand you were very instrumental in helping Lord Thorsby formulate the exact wording of the treaty," Charis said, though she knew nothing of the sort. Giving people credit for something without any warning always caused a reaction. If they deserved the praise, they glowed with pride and were quick to respond with open, frank honesty. If they didn't deserve it, they showed instant confusion.

And if they wanted to hide what they'd done, they froze. Dropped eye contact. Fumbled with their hands, their words, until they cautiously found a response they hoped would steer Charis's attention elsewhere.

Lady Ollen frowned as she pushed a cracker piled high with cheese into the corner of her plump cheek so she could say, "Was I?"

"That's my understanding."

The woman shrugged, reaching for her wine and bumping the dark green stone of the large ring she wore against the glass. "If you say so. I was more concerned with the details of what we were demanding in exchange for the marriage. I still think we should've asked for more." Her gaze caught Charis's, and she tacked on a hasty "I mean no offense, Your Highness."

"Of course." Charis nodded regally. "I do appreciate your work on the matter. But I would like to thank those who worked with Lord Thorsby on the exact wording of the treaty. Perhaps you could tell me whom I should speak to?"

"I'm sure Father had much to do with that," Ferris said smoothly, leaning forward to rest his hand on Charis's arm. She gritted her teeth and resisted the urge to snap at him. She couldn't allow the conversation to become sidetracked.

"If he did, then he must have done it in private," Lady Ollen said, reaching for more cheese.

Ferris's brows lowered as Charis pulled her arm free. "Father had several meetings with Lord Thorsby. Our family is highly invested in the treaty and its outcome."

"As are we all." Lady Ollen sounded stung.

"Of course," Charis said quickly, giving the woman a sincere smile. "Now, in the discussion during council meetings, which members—"

"I don't mean to contradict you," Ferris said, his voice dripping with condescension, "but surely you don't mean to suggest that your family is as affected by this treaty as ours."

Lady Ollen straightened, though her tiny stature didn't lend itself well to intimidation. "Every family has been affected by this war, young man."

"Yes, but every family didn't just lose what they'd spent their lives working toward," Ferris said, his eyes hard with anger. "We've had to reassess our goals and our future, now that I won't be marrying Charis. We had to find a path that would still put to good use my years of training to lead Calera at her side. Father found that path, but I would be lying if I said this treaty isn't going to be hard on us."

A flash of heat blazed to life in Charis's chest, spreading fire along her veins as Lady Ollen puffed up like a billy bird whose nest was being threatened.

"Surely you aren't comparing your situation with losing my son in battle and any chance at revenge against Montevallo once Charis marries their prince." The woman's voice trembled.

As Ferris replied, his gaze fixed on Lady Ollen's face while color rose in his cheeks, and she responded, her ring flashing beneath the light of the chandeliers while she pointed her finger in his face, Charis's hands slowly curled into fists.

The treaty was going to be hard on *them*?

She raised her head and slowly perused the dining room. How many of the nobles in here were complaining as well? Stubbornly clinging to the idea that they could profit from Charis's position or be avenged for what they'd lost to Montevallo. Focused only on what they each wanted without ever truly recognizing that, out of everyone in the room, Charis was the one who'd given up everything.

They weren't going to spend the rest of their lives shackled to the enemy, watching every word, every move, for the slightest hint of betrayal. They weren't going to walk a fine line between keeping Montevallo happy to ensure the peace and keeping the new king consort from taking too much power from the rightful heir. And they didn't have to lie awake every night, slowly smothering the whisper in their hearts that had once hoped to be truly seen and truly loved.

Yet here they were, arguing over which of them was most affected by the sacrifice Charis was making as if her feelings meant nothing. As if she was simply a pawn in a game that had caused them bitter disappointment.

Something dark and painful shivered beneath the fury in her heart, and she struggled to draw a breath past the sudden tightness in her throat.

"Your Highness, are you finished?" A girl with smooth white skin and short brown hair stood at Charis's side, her hand extended toward the princess's untouched plate of cheese and crackers.

Charis blinked.

"Your Highness?"

Slowly uncurling her fists, Charis swallowed hard, forcing the grief, the rage, back into a corner of her heart. She had information to uncover. A kingdom to assure. And a queen to satisfy. Whatever pain her heart carried would have to wait.

"You may take it," she said quietly.

Ferris immediately turned toward her. "But, Charis, you haven't had a bite."

How he'd managed to notice that while he'd been busy arguing over his imagined injuries with Lady Ollen was beyond Charis, but it didn't matter.

"I'm not very hungry," she said, reaching for her wine and turning once more to Lady Ollen, who had grabbed the last of her cheese as the plate was being lifted away. "It must be frustrating to agree to our terms of peace without getting to punish Montevallo the way they deserve to be punished."

The woman smiled slyly as she tapped a finger on the large green stone of her ring. "Serpanicite. Very rare gem mined in the mountains of Montevallo at least two centuries ago. Been in my family for decades. Worth more coin to the other sea kingdoms than the rest of my property combined. Maybe we didn't get to burn their villages to the ground like I wanted, but we are stripping them of an obscene number of jewels. Enough to rebuild the northern territories and refresh the royal coffers while still having some left over to devote to bulking up our military. You'll be able to learn the inner workings of Montevallo and discover their weaknesses by visiting the king consort's home, and that means that once we're in a position of strength again, we can destroy them if we decide that's what is needed."

Lady Ollen's eyes were bright with fervor. Charis swallowed against the sudden dryness in her mouth and sat back as the waitstaff set a plate of roasted hen, pickled beet salad, and creamy golden squash soup in front of her. The taster stepped forward, tried each item, and then returned to his position against the wall.

This woman didn't want Charis dead. Not when she was so invested in using the princess to set Montevallo up for possible invasion. She had no stake in changing the wording on the treaty to "the heir." Not when everyone involved knew that while Charis was capable of managing the enemy prince in a way that benefited Calera, the others in line for the throne didn't have her training, her experience, or her ruthless will to do whatever was required.

Ferris, on the other hand, had revealed something interesting indeed. And the only way to get him to reveal more was to play to his ego. She took another sip of wine to moisten her mouth and then treated Ferris to a dazzling smile and said, "You and your father are truly resourceful, aren't you?"

He froze for an instant—a breath of hesitation in which his hand hovered between his soup bowl and his mouth—and then he leaned forward, his smile matching hers. "I'm glad you see it, Charis. We want only to be the support behind the throne."

Charis kept her lip from curling in derision. Barely. Ferris wanted a good deal more than to be the support behind the throne. The question was just how far he was willing to go to get it.

"I'm so glad Lord Everly was able to make a plan for that. I assume that meant being highly involved in the language of the treaty itself, of course." She said it like she already knew it to be fact, and Ferris nodded.

"I'm sure he was."

Charis cocked her head. "He didn't share that with you?"

Ferris swallowed a bite of soup hastily while a faint pink crept up his fair neck. "Because I'm not yet a member of the council, I, of course, wasn't privy to the details of his meetings with Lord Thorsby. But Father has assured me that our family will continue to be very involved in the running of Calera. I'm sure that gives you peace of mind."

Charis smiled and reached for her soup spoon, though her fingers felt a bit clammy. Why would Lord Everly keep his dealings with Lord Thorsby a secret from his son? Was it simply because he was obeying the queen's orders to be discreet on the matter? Or did he have a plan to put Ferris on the throne and didn't trust his son to keep it quiet?

Swallowing past the dryness in her throat, she said, "I would be interested to hear the details—"

"Let me in. Let me *in*!" a familiar voice echoed from the staff doorway.

A wave of scandalized whispers swept the room as the occupants of both tables turned, craning their necks to see the commotion. Charis half rose in her chair to see Tal struggling to get past the pair of Everly guards who were stationed at the door.

"You don't understand," Tal said roughly. "I have to get to the princess!"

"No one comes through this door who isn't authorized by the Everlys," the guard said firmly, twisting Tal's arm behind his back the better to force him to leave.

Charis stood quickly, intent on reaching Tal before the scene became something the queen wouldn't forgive, but the room swayed and pitched as though she were on the deck of a ship in a storm. Gasping, she grabbed for the edge of the table to keep herself upright, and Tal yelled, "Charis!"

Charis raised her head and met Tal's gaze as the man began dragging him out of the doorway. Her vision went hazy at the edges. The sound of Tal yelling at the guard felt as if it was coming from a great distance. Something dark and dangerous flared to life on Tal's face, and he planted a foot, pivoted toward the guard who held him, and plowed a fist into his throat. As the guard stumbled back, choking, Tal shoved his way past the other guard and ran toward the princess.

Reuben stepped in front of Charis as if he thought she needed protection from Tal, but then Tal snarled in a voice Charis barely recognized, "Get out of my way. The princess has been poisoned."

THIRTY-TWO

Commotion erupted around Charis, and she sank toward the floor as the room became a brilliant swirl of color and sound. Strong arms wrapped around her and cushioned her fall. She blinked her eyes open—when had they closed?—to find her head in Tal's lap. His worried face hovered over hers, with Ferris crouched on her other side.

"Shh, I've got you," Tal said softly. Then, looking up, he called, "The princess needs a physician. Immediately."

Charis swallowed against the dryness in her mouth. Her tongue felt too large. Her airway too small. And her eyelids were so heavy. She would let them close for a moment. Just one moment. That's all she needed.

"Charis, stay with me." Tal's voice, low and urgent, breathed against Charis's ear. "Don't fall asleep."

There was something Charis needed to remember. Some connection she needed to make. But her thoughts were spinning, her body ached, and her eyes refused to stay open. With a little shudder, she slid into darkness.

☙

"She's waking up." A man's voice, deep and frail, said quietly from somewhere left of Charis.

"Are you sure? Call for Baust." A woman's voice, brittle with worry.

"The physician is on his way," said a familiar voice from somewhere by Charis's feet.

Pillows beneath her head. Soft sheets beneath her skin. She was in bed. But that wasn't right. She was supposed to be at the Everlys'. Ferris needed questioning. Or was it Lady Channing? No, she'd already talked to Lady Channing. Lady Ollen, then?

"Charis, sweet girl, can you open your eyes?" the man said again, and this time Charis knew his voice. But that didn't make sense either. Why was Father at the Everlys'?

She drew in a deep breath, slowly stretching her body to feel each muscle tighten and release, and then opened her eyes. The room swam in and out of focus for a moment, but then slowly resolved into the cream and gold of her own bedchamber. Father sat next to her, his thin hand slowly stroking her arm. Mother stood next to the bed on Charis's other side. The dress she'd worn to the Everlys' was slightly rumpled and her hair was sliding out of its rigid updo.

"What…" Charis's voice cracked on the word, and Mother swiftly reached for a glass from the bedside table.

"Drink this. Slowly, now. You want to give your stomach time to get used to it. Make sure it stays down." Mother's voice was firm, but the hand that held the glass shook slightly.

Charis took several swallows, her throat feeling parched. When Mother removed the glass, Charis pushed herself into a sitting position.

"Slowly!" Mother snapped. Charis swayed for an instant before the room righted itself again.

"I'm all right, Mother," she said as the events of the Everlys' dinner rushed back. The food she hadn't touched. The wine she'd drunk. The taster who hadn't died. And Tal . . . Tal striking a guard to get to Charis because he'd somehow known what was happening.

Charis looked toward the foot of her bed and found Tal standing there, his dark eyes pinned to Charis.

"How did you know?"

"I did what you told me to. I paid attention to gossip and then moved through the house looking for anything that seemed out of place." There were smudges of exhaustion beneath his eyes and the shadow of a bruise on his face.

"He saw additional kitchen staff enter the building from a side door without the approval of Lord Everly." Mother smoothed her dress, though the wrinkles refused to leave. It looked as though she'd slept in it in the chair beside Charis's bed. "Tal worried that something might be amiss and quietly followed them to the kitchen, where he saw them make a plate for you separate from the other plates and then send it out to you."

"One of the men added something to your soup," Tal said, his voice thick with anger. "I was going to cause a scene in the kitchen and knock the plate to the floor, but then he said it was just in case you hadn't already eaten enough, and I knew . . ." He drew in a shaky breath and swallowed.

"Our dear Tal knew it might already be too late," Father said softly, smiling at Tal as though he were sunshine after a storm. "So he fought his way to your side, yelled for the Everlys' physician while others were still trying to figure out what was happening, and was able to tell him exactly what the poison looked like. The physician combined that description with your symptoms and figured out you'd been dosed with lisodor. He was able to get the antidote quickly."

"Lisodor," Charis said, reaching for the water again as her scratchy throat caught on the word. "The nutty flavor in my wine."

"Tal saved your life," Mother said quietly, her voice uncharacteristically gentle. "Again."

Charis held Tal's gaze for a long moment, and then said, "You're beginning to make that a habit."

"I'm grateful you're still alive, Your Highness."

"Not for lack of trying on someone's part. And I hardly think we can blame this attempt on King Alaric or his lackey Bartho. You have another enemy." Mother was back to her crisp, icy self. "What do you remember of yesterday's meal that might be useful?"

"Yesterday?" Charis leaned past Father to look out the windows. A heavy golden haze spread across the sky, sinking into amber at the horizon. Twilight was here. She'd missed an entire day.

A sharp pain spiked through her head as she sat up straighter, but she willed herself not to wince. She'd learned much at the Everlys', and none of it could be dealt with from the comfort of her bed.

"Charis, lie back," Father said, patting her shoulder as if that gentle pressure could make Charis submit.

"Mother, we must divide our focus for a moment," Charis said as she wrapped her hand around Father's to ease the sting of having his daughter ignore his wishes. "I learned several things yesterday." She squeezed Father's hand and then let go so she could tick off items on her fingers.

"First, the strange sound we heard out on the ship that one night is happening frequently around Portsmith, and bodies are washing ashore."

The queen frowned. "It's a small port. Inhospitable for merchant ships, but it could work as a staging ground for small battle vessels. Certainly it's sheltered from the sea, and our naval ships wouldn't see them unless they entered the port themselves."

"Which they can't do, because of their size," Charis said.

"Second"—she raised another finger—"we need to know where the Everlys hired their extra kitchen staff and where they got their taster."

Icy fury sparked in the queen's gaze. "I've already sent an inquiry and expect a full recounting, along with a list of names of every person who was involved in any part of the event."

Something nagged at Charis. A small detail she'd ignored at the time because she'd invented a reason for it that made sense.

She frowned and stared out the window at the swoop of sea hawks gliding across the amber skies while the memories of the dinner played in her mind. Ferris's hand on her arm as he interrupted her conversation with Lady Ollen. The clink of Lady Ollen's massive ring against her pale blue goblet. The way the taster had gripped his tiny cup as he raised the tainted wine to his lips.

"Blue fingernails," Charis said, turning back to find Mother, Father, and Tal all watching her. "The taster's fingernails were whitish-blue. I thought he must be gripping the cup tightly because he was nervous, but . . ."

"But fingernails turn white and pink when you grip tightly," Tal said, raising his own hand to demonstrate as he gripped the bedpost.

"So the taster built up an immunity to lisodor. That takes time," Mother said.

"Which means someone put this plan into place a while ago," Charis said, her voice steady though reality was scraping at her veneer of calm. How long did it take to build up an immunity to poison? Had someone been working toward her death long enough to have set this plan into motion in case other attempts failed? Or had they somehow stumbled upon a person who'd developed an immunity and was willing to do what was asked of him for the right amount of coin?

Father ran a hand down her back, smoothing her curls. "We should double your guard. Keep you isolated in your wing until we find the person responsible."

She smiled at him. "Thank you, Father, but I'm afraid that's impossible right now. I have far too many responsibilities, and our kingdom needs to feel utterly confident in me. They can't do that if I'm hiding."

Turning back to Mother, Charis ticked the third item off her fingers. "Finally, I learned that the council changed the treaty wording to say 'the heir' instead of my name."

Tal made a small noise of protest.

"When was this?" The queen straightened her spine as if preparing to go into battle.

"It must have been right before they sent it. We'd already approved the final details, but I remember Thorsby saying they were meeting to draft a clean copy to send to King Alaric."

"Why was your name in the treaty at all?" Father asked as he looked from Charis to the queen. "What have you agreed to?"

Charis drew in a breath. She'd forgotten that she'd protected him from knowing about the betrothal. She could blame waking up with a headache and the confusion of missing an entire day for that.

"Charis is marrying one of the Montevallian heirs in exchange for peace," the queen said in a tone that made it clear he was not to argue with what was already done.

He ignored it.

"No, Charis." He said her name as if it was delicate glass. "Not that."

She blinked against the sudden tears that pricked her eyes and made herself smile at him again. "It's all right, Father. I've already signed the contract."

"But—"

"We need peace, Edias." Mother began pacing as she spoke. "We're losing badly in the north, and now we're losing ships at sea. Charis was raised for this. She can keep the king consort in line and restore Calera to peace and prosperity once more."

"Marriage should be about more than keeping a king consort in line." Father's voice was still quiet, but now there was steel within it.

Mother stopped pacing and stared at him.

"Charis needs someone she can trust. Someone she can be honest with." His hand covered hers. "Someone who loves her more than he loves the idea of her title or how useful she can be to him."

"That's a fairy tale for a different life," the queen snapped. "Charis knows better than to believe in fairy tales. To rule is to be alone. She understands that."

"But she isn't alone." Father's trembling voice rose. "If she was, she'd already be dead. She has a family who loves her, friends who share her life because they want to, not because she's their princess, and she has people like Tal who care enough to risk themselves to save her without asking for anything in return."

Mother pressed her lips into a thin line and said nothing. Charis turned her hand over, palm up, and laced her fingers through Father's. When he met her gaze, tears shone faintly in his eyes. She leaned against his chest, listening to the thready beat of his heart.

"I won't lose any of that, Father," she said, though part of her whispered that it wasn't enough. "I'll still have you and Mother, Nalani and Holland, Orayn and Ilsa and Tal. I'm rich with friends."

Father said nothing for a long moment, and Charis met Tal's gaze. The boy's jaw was clenched, and something dark hovered in his eyes.

Another memory from the Everlys' surfaced, and Charis turned toward Mother. "Lady Channing said she'd heard rumors from her staff about people unhappy about the betrothal. Perhaps unhappy enough to kill me and then go after Holland and Nalani if they support it as well."

There was a quick knock on the door, and then Reuben entered, Baust right behind him. The guard gave the queen a look and jerked his head toward the door as the physician hurried to Charis's bedside.

"The taster was found dead in an alley this morning," Reuben said softly as the queen turned toward him. "Stabbed through the heart. Got Lord Everly in the south parlor with a list of those he hired for extra kitchen staff. Says he used the staffing service all the noble houses use. Nothing unusual."

"Which means whoever did this knew I'd be at the event and knew Lord Everly always uses that service." Something cold and heavy unfurled in Charis as she lined up the facts. "Only someone adamantly against either the peace treaty or me as heir would benefit from killing me now. Someone close enough to me to guess my schedule. Someone quite familiar with how the nobility run things."

"A Caleran." The queen's voice sliced through the air like a sword.

"We have a traitor in our midst. And the fact that we were never able to find a single hint of Bartho outside that empty warehouse makes me wonder if he ever really existed. Certainly a traitor close to us would've known I was going to be fitted at Merryl's the morning of the arrow attack. And would know how to sneak an assassin into the palace during a ball." Charis tried to toss her covers aside, but her muscles felt too weak to allow her to do more than sluggishly push them to her knees.

"Stop moving," Mother snapped. "I will get to the bottom of this. You stay in bed until morning, and then you may resume your duties only if Baust clears you."

Charis raised her chin. "I will resume my duties tomorrow morning whether Baust clears me or not. We cannot afford for a single rumor of weakness on my part to shake our kingdom's faith in me, and we cannot allow Alaric to believe he should put his attention on Holland as the next in line to our throne."

Not just Alaric's attention. The traitor's as well. Charis couldn't believe Holland would try to kill her to take a throne he absolutely didn't want, and it was hard to imagine someone working so hard to remove Charis only to crown a young man who refused to be influenced by politics, convention, or power and would therefore be impossible to control. Which meant that Holland was surely next on the traitor's kill list if Charis fell.

The queen waved Reuben and Baust from the room and then said quietly, "You get your strength up so you can be seen tomorrow, healthy and strong."

"And then I'll take my crew north to Portsmith," Charis said. "Our ship is smaller than a battleship. We should be able to get into the bay—"

"And do what?" Father's shaky voice rose. "Sail straight into a trap? Into a battalion of war vessels?"

"They won't attack us," Charis said firmly, though she wrapped her hand around Father's again. "We look like smugglers."

"Why should they care what you look like?" he demanded. "If you find their base of operations, they'll kill you to keep you quiet."

He was right, though Charis was loath to admit it. She couldn't just take a frigate into the bay at Portsmith without endangering herself and her crew.

"So we take a smaller vessel." Tal stepped to the side of the bed to straighten Charis's covers. "Leave the frigate in deeper waters and take a rowboat. If it's dark enough out, no one in the bay will ever see us."

Charis looked to her mother, carefully watching for any sign of disapproval that Tal had volunteered a plan, but instead, she found a faint light of appreciation in the queen's icy blue eyes.

"An excellent suggestion, Tal. See that my daughter stays safe while you're out there. I believe she's in far less danger on the water than she is in Arborlay." The queen swept from the room, sending Baust back inside to treat Charis.

Charis remained quiet as Baust checked her pulse, her breathing, and her eyes. When he pronounced himself pleased with how fast her body was ridding itself of the poison and prescribed more rest and plenty of water, she dismissed him and turned to Father, whose face was now lined with exhaustion.

"Tal, send for Ilsa, please."

"I can stay," Father said quickly, a forced bravado in his voice that belied the way it shook with weariness.

Charis wrapped her arm around his frail back and leaned her head carefully against his shoulder. "I know, but you heard Baust. I need rest."

Father laughed. "What a diplomatic way to tell me I need rest too."

Charis tipped her head back and smiled. "I'm glad you were here."

"My sweet Charis needed me. Where else would I be?" He laid a papery cheek against her forehead, and a sharp pain stung the back of her throat.

She wasn't going to stop needing him—his gentle strength, his constant love, and his deep belief in the better side of her nature—but they both knew he couldn't be with her much longer.

Before that thought could crush her, she said quickly, "I'll visit you tomorrow."

"Before you take a rowboat into a bay full of warships?"

"Someone has to find the truth, Father."

"And why does that someone have to be you?" His voice broke, and he raised a trembling hand to smooth her cheek.

"Because this is my kingdom. My people. If I'm not capable of protecting them when they need it, I don't deserve the crown."

"Charis—"

"I'll be careful."

He sighed.

Ilsa entered the room and quickly moved to his side. "Your Highness, it's time for dinner. Cook made smoked beef and roasted apples." She gave Charis a quick, sincere smile. "I'm glad to see you up and about."

"Thank you, Ilsa," Father said as he took her arm and struggled to his feet. Turning to look again at Charis, he said quietly, "I love you, sweet Charis. Get some rest."

She swallowed against the pain in her throat and said, "I love you too."

When the door closed behind them, Tal came to the bed and lifted the water glass to Charis's lips.

"I can do that for myself."

"Or you could rest and gain your strength so that tomorrow, two days after being poisoned, you can row a boat into a rocky bay in the middle of the night to see if it's full of warships intent on killing you."

"May I remind you that the rowboat was your idea?"

Tal's eyes narrowed. "I'm aware."

"Besides, you'll be with me. I'll be perfectly safe."

Tal's throat bobbed, and he fumbled the glass as he tried to set it on the bedside table. It struck the edge of the table and toppled to the floor. He muttered something under his breath as water spread across the plush white rug beside Charis's bed.

"Tal."

"I'll get a cloth."

"Tal."

He stilled, though he kept his eyes on the spill soaking into her rug. "Yes?"

"Thank you for saving my life."

He crouched beside the bed and looked into her face. There was misery in his eyes. Finally, he said, "I thought you were going to die, Charis. That I was too late. It was . . . Don't ever put me through that again. I can't . . . I need you to be alive arguing with me and trying to beat me at swordplay, making me laugh and making me proud as you destroy someone who thought they could get the best of you. I don't ever want to catch your falling body and watch you slip away from me again." His voice shook.

She reached for him, resting her hand against his cheek. He leaned into her touch and closed his eyes. She tried to keep her hand there, but exhaustion swooped in as if she hadn't just spent a day and a night asleep.

"I'm sorry I scared you," she said as she slumped back.

Instantly, Tal sprang forward. Plumping her pillow, he pulled the covers into position and smoothed the edges with quick, practiced movements. When he was sure the princess was comfortable, he moved to the window and shut the curtains, leaving the room in a twilight haze of purple shadows.

Charis's eyes fluttered closed. As the heaviness of sleep rushed in, she thought she heard Tal whisper something, but then slumber took her, and whatever Tal was saying drifted into the darkness and was gone.

THIRTY-THREE

"ALL RIGHT, OUT with it." Holland joined Charis as they stood on the ship deck, a damp, frigid wind kissing their cheeks while the bow plowed through the black waters of the sea. They were sailing north, far from the shoreline to avoid running into the creatures they'd heard before, with the plan to weigh anchor outside Portsmith and take a rowboat into the sheltered cove.

It was madness, but Charis couldn't find it in herself to care. Not when it was taking every ounce of strength to remain on her feet, just two days after being poisoned. And not when someone close to her was not only dedicated to killing her but had already managed to change the treaty wording to make sure that Charis's death cost Calera nothing.

"Out with what?" Charis tugged her cloak tighter, glad she'd decided to wear gloves when the wind pried at the gaps between her clothing, chafing her exposed skin raw. Tal was at the helm with Orayn, discussing their approach to Portsmith, satisfied that Holland would keep an eye on Charis for a few minutes.

"The thing that has been churning through your brain for the past four hours."

Charis sighed. "It's that obvious?"

Holland laughed. "You've either been ignoring anything we say or snapping at us like we just suggested you abdicate the throne and move to Morg."

Charis leaned her elbows against the rail, watching long trails of silvery starlight shimmer on the water and then disappear beneath the boat. Behind them, Orayn and Dec were deep in conversation at the helm while the rest of the crewmates either manned a mast or stood along the opposite rail, their eyes searching the dark horizon for the shadow of an enemy ship. There were several crew members belowdecks as well, though not as many as usual. They were running short tonight since Charis had sent a message that tonight's trip wasn't likely to return to port until midday at the earliest. Some of her crew had jobs or families who needed them first thing in the morning.

Charis had understood, but even running with a bare-bones crew hadn't changed her mind. They needed to go as far north as Portsmith so they could check the harbor and the caves. Even if it meant hearing that eerie sound from beneath the water.

"You see?" Holland slapped his hand on the railing, startling Charis out of her thoughts. "Abysmal."

"I'm sorry. I didn't mean to ignore you."

"Probably upset about being poisoned. Terrible way to go. Father has been in talks with the queen," Holland said, his voice rough though the shoulder he bumped against Charis's was gentle. "We've dedicated every guard we can spare to help hunt down those responsible. I've personally volunteered to gut the traitor when he's found, but apparently I need to get in line." He sounded disgruntled.

"In line?" Charis frowned.

"Father says the queen will execute the traitor publicly and doesn't need my help."

"Not if Tal gets there first," Charis muttered. Tal had made a list of truly inventive ways he wished to punish the traitor, and for some reason, knowing he wanted to destroy the one who had hurt her made something warm and sparkling dance through her veins, leaving a trail of heat behind that felt like a promise.

"What's going on with you?"

"I wasn't thinking about Tal," she said.

Holland snorted. "I didn't say you were."

"Oh." The trail of heat threatened to turn into mortification.

"Why would you say that? Has Tal done something to upset you?"

"No! I mean . . . not really. It's not . . . I'm not upset."

Holland shot a look over his shoulder at Tal and said sternly, "Speak plainly. If he's dishonored you in any way, I'll deal with him immediately."

"I can deal with him myself."

"So he has done something wrong?" Holland sounded disappointed. "Just when I was starting to like him, too."

"No! He's fine. We're fine. There's nothing to discuss."

Except the fact that she was far too aware of Tal when he was near her. And she could understand his thoughts by simply glancing at his face. And then there was the troublesome heat in her stomach when she thought of his protectiveness toward her. All of which added up to . . . "Oh no."

Holland slapped a hand on the railing. "Listen, I am going to need you to start making sense. You toss Tal's name in the discussion and then say it's nothing and then say 'oh no' like it's definitely something, and I am not a mind reader."

Never in her wildest dreams had she ever considered discussing something like this with Holland, but of all those on the short list of those she truly trusted, he was the one least likely to tell her what he thought she wanted to hear. Gathering her courage, she said quietly, "I think I might like Tal."

"I just said that I'm just starting to like him too." Holland sounded impatient.

"No, I mean . . . I find him interesting." When he frowned as though he didn't understand, she said, "I think about him. A lot. And I notice things about him that maybe I don't need to be noticing. It's . . . there's the way his smile is a little crooked, and when I see that, something inside me—"

"Stop talking this instant, or I will throw myself overboard." Holland stared at her, panic on his face. "This is clearly a Nalani conversation. Why are you having it with me?"

"Because you'll tell me the truth, no matter how it makes me feel."

He glared at her for a moment and then said, "Fine. What's the question?"

"Am I being foolish?"

"For asking my opinion about whatever this is? Yes."

"No, for thinking about him like this. Or worse, for keeping him as my bodyguard when I'm having trouble viewing him as just a friendly staff member."

He sighed. "I don't like it when Mother and Nalani tell me I have to politely flirt with people at court. I despise having to act in a way that goes against my nature. I don't think it's good for anyone to feel forced to ignore their true selves."

"I'm not sure this is the same thing."

"Do you like having him around?"

"Yes."

"Does he like being around?"

"I'm pretty sure he does, but what about in a few months when I have to marry the Montevallian prince? Is it fair to think about Tal like this when nothing can come of it?"

"Can you just . . . stop? If you decide nothing can come of it, can you turn off that part of yourself and never be bothered by it again?" Holland sounded genuinely curious.

Charis considered his question as Tal began making his way toward them. "No, I don't think I can."

"Then all you can do is decide each day what you will do and what you won't do. Just because you feel something doesn't mean you have to act on it." Holland lowered his voice as Tal came near. "For example, next time you decide to have a conversation about romance, you could hold off on those feelings until you're with my sister."

"You two seem to be discussing something important," Tal said as he stopped beside Charis and leaned on the railing.

Warmth flooded Charis's face, and she studied the water and chose her words carefully. "Holland was asking what's bothering me. I can't stop thinking about Lord Thorsby changing the wording of the peace treaty so that it reads 'the heir' instead of my name. He didn't ask me first. He just ordered Lady Channing to do it. She was surprised to learn that I didn't know."

"He should've checked with you, but it is a smart way to go," Holland said. "That way if something happens to you, the treaty doesn't fall apart."

"I know that," Charis said quietly. "But why not discuss it with me first?"

"Because he didn't want you to argue against it," Tal said flatly.

"This way, the deal is done, and there's nothing you can do to change it."

"I would have agreed to it," Charis said, the words bitter on her tongue. That was the thing that had nagged at her thoughts since her conversation with Lady Channing. She would have agreed to using "the heir" instead of her name. It protected Calera, and that was the entire point of the betrothal.

To take that decision away from her, to be afraid to come to her with it in the first place . . .

"Either he thought you weren't smart enough to see what was best for Calera, or he didn't want you to know he has a contingency plan in place to keep the peace with Montevallo even after you die." Tal sounded furious. "Which makes it look like he's the one who's been trying to kill you all along."

"But why?" Holland leaned on the railing next to Charis and studied the horizon. "Lord Thorsby has been a supporter of Charis for as long as I've been paying attention to court politics. He supports the queen as well."

"Not always," Charis said softly. "He lost a son in the war last year. It changed him. Of course, nearly every council member has lost someone in the war."

"Not Lord Everly, more's the pity." Holland gripped the hilt of his sword as if considering removing Ferris from the world so that all the council members could share an equal measure of grief.

"Someone who would benefit from my death is behind the recent assassination attempts," Charis said, forcing her voice to sound crisp and unaffected. Like she didn't wake in the middle of the night, shaking as she reached for her dagger, convinced she'd heard a whisper of sound in her closet. Like she didn't have to force herself to breathe past a noose of panic every time she walked the short distance between her carriage and a building in town. And as though she hadn't simply pushed food around on her plate for the past three meals until Tal sat down beside her, ate part of the princess's meal over Charis's furious protests that it was dangerous, and then pointedly refused to help her move on with her day until she ate the rest.

"And now you think it might be Lord Thorsby?" Holland asked.

Charis permitted herself a single nod, her eyes fixed on the horizon as the blue sister moons drifted behind clouds, plunging the sea into utter darkness.

"We can toss him in the dungeon," Holland said. "Question him. Find out the truth."

"Or we can look at all angles first and make sure we don't accuse an innocent man and ruin his reputation," Charis said evenly. "That's what I've been telling myself. Lord Thorsby would never survive the type of interrogation my mother would inflict upon him, but if he's guilty, he has to know that. He would have a plan in place. Something that would be set into motion upon his arrest. That's what I'd do, at least."

"You might be giving him more credit than he's due," Tal said. "You plan every word, every gesture, like you're in a duel with the entire world. Most people don't live like that."

"Lady Channing could've been lying," Holland said. "Have you talked to Thorsby?"

Charis shook her head. "Not yet. There was no time today." And she'd barely had enough energy to get herself down to the docks, even after resting for much of the day.

The boat rose over a large swell and then dipped low. Charis's knees shook, and she leaned heavily against the railing while trying hard to keep her spine straight.

Leaning toward her, Tal said softly, "Are you all right?"

"Weigh anchor!" Orayn called. Finn, one of Orayn's most experienced sailors, and a deckhand named Shevvyn hurried to the anchor winch and began letting out the chain.

"Time to face some warships with nothing but a rowboat and our wits," Holland said, excitement practically vibrating through him.

"Wait." Charis's voice shook with exhaustion, and she forced herself to stand up straight and look Holland in the eye.

"What is it?" he asked.

"You aren't going."

"I beg your pardon," Holland said, his voice crisp with indignation.

"We can't risk it."

"What are you talking about?" Holland demanded. "I didn't come all this way just to sit in this boat and miss the fun."

"Yes," Charis said gently, "you did. It's going to be risky, and—"

"Oh, I see." Holland turned to Tal. "It's perfectly fine for the *princess* to get herself killed protecting the kingdom, but seers forbid I get to join the fun."

"Holland—"

"I'm supposed to be with you every step of the way." Holland glared. "We're already taking risks. You don't get to suddenly decide this is one risk too many."

"Actually, I do."

"Now you listen to me." Holland raised a finger and shook it in Charis's direction. "You aren't going out there by yourself. We take the risk together, or—"

"You are not putting yourself in a position where you might die." Charis's voice brooked no dissent, for all the good that did with the twins.

"Then neither are you!" Holland folded his arms over his chest.

"I already am," Charis snapped. "A spy in my bath chamber. An arrow outside the seamstress's shop. Poison in my wine. Every breath I take is on borrowed time until the traitor is caught. If I die, at least you take the crown. If both of us die, the assassin goes after Nalani." She sagged against the railing again, her energy spent.

Instantly, Tal wrapped an arm around Charis's waist, supporting her weight.

Holland clasped her hand in a rare show of affection. "Fine. I'll stay. But you'd better return."

Charis nodded, and when Holland said nothing else, she motioned for Tal to help her get to the rope ladder that led down to the rowboat. Dec and Finn were also waiting there, each with a weapon strapped to their waist. Holland walked with them, and when they stopped at the railing, he looked at Tal.

"I actually like you, unlike most people I meet. But I promise you, if anything happens to her, I will personally disembowel you and throw you to the sea monsters."

"Understood."

Dec made the descent down into the rowboat, and then Charis made herself climb over the railing and onto the rope ladder. Slowly, she felt below her for each new rung, gripping the rope until her skin burned as the ladder swayed in the wind. Finally, she reached the rowboat and felt Dec's wide hands surround her waist and gently help her into the craft.

Moments later, Finn, Tal, Dec, and Charis were rowing west toward the distant smudges that marked the entrance to Portsmith's bay. Finn and Dec sat in the center, each gripping an oar. Tal and Charis sat at the bow, keeping a close eye on the water in case any of the creatures they'd heard before returned.

For a while, there was only the small splash of the oars dipping into the water and the distant roar of the waves breaking against the shore. Then Tal shifted closer to her, his leg pressing against hers on the small wooden plank they shared. Softly, he said, "How are you?"

She lifted her chin, and he laughed quietly. "I see."

He pressed closer still, shoulder to shoulder, hip to hip, the heat of his body warming hers. A clear invitation to lean on him if she needed to.

If she wanted to.

The glow of warmth she always felt when she was with him brightened.

When she kept her spine straight, Tal leaned forward, his face turned toward hers as if wishing he could read her expression beneath her mask. His lips quirked into a smile. "If you get too tired to keep pretending you're fine, let me know. I won't tell the crew. And I would like a warning if you think you're going to pitch over the side of the boat."

She huffed out a little laugh. "We wouldn't want you to have to dive in after me."

"Seers forbid. That's why I brought Dec along. He enjoys rescuing people from the water."

"I wonder if that will count as protecting me in Holland's eyes."

Tal sobered instantly. "There is the matter of my intestines."

"Indeed."

"Perhaps I should take some precautionary steps to ensure your safety." He lifted his arm as though to wrap it around her back and watched her for permission. "For Holland's sake."

She laughed again, though the wind whisked it away instantly. The warmth inside glowed like the sister moons, and it was getting harder and harder to convince herself that she could ignore it. "Who would have thought that the first time a boy wanted to put his arm around me, it would be to avoid a disembowelment."

His arm curled around her back, warm and secure, and he anchored her to his side. She meant to straighten her spine. To pull away just enough to let him know that she wasn't leaning on him. Not really. But his shoulder was warm, and his touch was gentle, and she was just so tired.

Her head tipped against his shoulder, and he leaned his cheek against the crown of her hair. Quietly, he said, "You know quite well it didn't take the threat of disembowelment to make me want to put my arm around you."

The boat rose and fell, rocking gently with the swells of the sea, and all too soon the large, rocky cliffs that flanked the entrance to the bay were just ahead of them. Charis sat up, her exhaustion forgotten as they came closer. The wind scoured the sky above, chasing away any clouds and leaving the sapphire light of the sister moons shining clearly.

Charis leaned forward, her hands gripping the edge of the rowboat as they swept between the cliffs and into the shallow, rocky bay.

"Seers forbid!" Finn whispered. Charis waved a hand at him to shush him as her heart became thunder in her ears.

Spread out before them, tucked beside rocky outcroppings and lined up like miniature war frigates, were at least twenty ships. They were small—even smaller than Charis's ship—with crisp lines that ended in points as sharp as fangs on the top of the masts and at both the bow and the stern. Lanterns that glowed an eerie pale green were hung in clusters of three on the cabin walls. There wasn't a single sound from any of them.

Charis's mind raced as Finn and Dec quietly rowed them out of the bay.

Twenty ships, unlike any she'd ever seen. Capable of navigating shallow water and the tight turns necessary to maneuver around rocky outcroppings. And somehow packing enough weaponry to take down Calera's massive navy frigates before any of her sailors could understand what was happening.

Which kingdom had done this? And why? Or were these the strange ships that had been sighted in the northern seas? If so, she could understand Rullenvor choosing to ally itself with the Rakuuna so they could defend themselves on the water.

"Captain, that's an armada," Finn said finally as they moved quickly back toward their waiting ship. "And we don't have a single war frigate capable of going into that bay to fight them."

"I know," Charis said, feeling slightly dizzy as her racing thoughts picked up one solution and then another.

"We have to let the queen know," Dec said.

"I'll handle that." Charis stared back at the bay, at the terrible secret hiding within it. "She'll need to attack from both land and sea."

"Nothing we have on the water can get in there safely," Finn said. "Nothing with any sort of cannon power, at least."

"We don't have to get in there safely," Tal said, his eyes meeting hers as if they were in perfect harmony. "We just have to make sure they don't get out."

Charis bared her teeth in a vicious smile. "We send flaming arrows from land."

"And cannon fire from the sea," Tal finished.

And once the enemy ships were destroyed, they'd fish some of the survivors out of the water and interrogate them until they knew which kingdom had betrayed them.

THIRTY-FOUR

FIVE DAYS LATER, Charis felt more like herself. The Sister Moons Festival, the day that Calerans celebrated the official end of autumn, was nearing. The weather had been a dense, misty gray with bouts of furious rainfall for most of the week, but this day had dawned sunny and mild. She rose early, ate so much of her breakfast that even Tal was grudgingly impressed, and then sent word to the stables that she and her bodyguard required two horses.

"Where are we riding this morning?" Tal asked as they made their way to the stables. "The bluff again?"

She smiled. "Not this time. I thought we'd ride through some of the surrounding streets. Let people see I'm strong and healthy. Let any Montevallian spies carry that news back to their king."

Tal frowned. "I'm not sure it's a good idea to ride a horse into town when someone wants to kill you."

"The beauty of it is that no one but you and I know where we're going. Hardly enough time for someone to set up an assassination attempt."

"Still—"

"I can't live in a cage, Tal. I'm already going to imprison myself with my marriage. I'm not going to cower in a corner. If someone wants me dead, they are going to have to become bold enough to face me themselves, because I've taken away every predictable opportunity. No more social engagements until the Sister Moons Festival ball at the Farragins', where I will eat nothing, drink nothing, and keep you glued to my side."

"You know I hate to argue with you—"

"I know absolutely no such thing."

He grinned, but the worry didn't leave his eyes. "But this is a risk, Charis."

"My entire life is a risk." She patted his arm as they came to the stables where Grim waited with her black mare and Tal's bay. "The kingdom needs me to show everyone I'm alive and capable. Let's go."

They mounted the horses and headed into the surrounding fields as though once more going for a sedate ride around the palace grounds. When they were out of sight of anyone who could report their movements to a spy, they turned toward the road that led away from the palace and into the streets of ornate mansions owned by Arborlay's nobility.

"Winter's almost here," Charis said as a damp, chilly wind tangled with her hair.

"At least we don't get snow in Arborlay." Tal pretended to shudder. "I enjoy living somewhere that isn't covered in ice and snow for months."

Charis considered this for a moment. The north would start getting snow in a month. Montevallo might be snowbound even sooner. That gave her at least until spring before the wedding could take place. A few more months to pretend the easy friendship she shared with Tal could continue indefinitely. That she could flirt with the spark of attraction between them and hoard the memories to keep her warm when everything changed.

"I lost you to your thoughts," Tal said, giving her a smile as she blinked at her surroundings. They were on the road that led to the homes of the Everlys, the Comferoys, and several other prominent members of the nobility.

"I was just thinking that I'm enjoying this lovely morning ride with you."

"Liar." His voice was tender.

She sighed. "The fact that you can read me so easily is highly inconvenient."

"Out with it, secret keeper. Unless it really is none of my business, in which case we'll just continue to discuss the weather."

She laughed. "Fine. I was thinking that the ice will keep Alaric and the Penbyrns from wanting to schedule the wedding until at least spring. I'm not sure which son he'll choose—Vahn or Percival."

"Do you have a preference?" Tal sounded cautious, as though unsure whether she wanted to dive into this discussion.

She was feeling cautious about it too. If it became too real, the chasm within her would crack open again. But with the buffer of winter standing between her and a wedding, it felt safer to say, "I don't know much about either of them. I think Vahn is a little bit older, but maybe he's already married? Hard to get a spy into a walled-off city to obtain good information. I don't know about marrying someone older than me, but a man can be kept in line no matter his age."

Tal grunted.

"And Percival Penbyrn. Who names their son that? Sounds utterly pretentious. I imagine he's another Ferris, though probably without the sense of entitlement. Most younger sons are too far from the line of succession to expect that kind of power."

"Probably cuts every bite of food into perfectly symmetrical pieces." Tal raised an eyebrow as though inviting her to play along.

Charis grinned. "Carries a handkerchief he uses exclusively to wipe down cloth chairs before sitting in them."

"Oh, not just a handkerchief," Tal said. "He carries his own teacup with him. Has a holster for it on his belt."

Charis laughed again, and the specter of the wedding faded a bit. "Whatever will I do with a pretentious king consort?"

"Threaten to break his teacup if he crosses you." Tal grinned at her, but there was a shadow in his eyes.

She reached across to lay her hand on his arm for a moment. "Thank you for making me laugh about this. I feel better. Especially because winter is coming. Months and months of ice and snow."

"Months and months," he agreed, the shadow lifting.

A carriage rolled down the Everlys' drive and moved past Charis and Tal. Charis was looking at Tal, at the way the weak sunlight gilded his hair with strands of glittering gold. At the flecks of green in his brown eyes and the tiny scar on the right side of his chin.

"I know that man," Tal said.

"What man?" Charis looked around.

"In the carriage. That was Ambassador Shyrn."

"The ambassador from Rullenvor?" Charis stared after the carriage. "Let's make sure."

She nudged her mount into a canter, with Tal by her side. Soon, they pulled abreast of the carriage. As they passed it, Charis looked inside. Ice formed in the pit of her stomach, and she glanced away quickly before the man in the carriage could realize she'd been looking.

All ambassadors were required to submit their schedules to the palace. Social engagements had to be approved by the royal secretary. Charis was absolutely certain no early morning meeting with Lord Everly had been approved for the Rullenvor ambassador, and she couldn't think of a single good reason for them to be meeting in secret.

"We're going home," Charis said as they left the carriage behind them. "Hurry!"

They galloped back the way they'd come, only slowing as the stable yard came into view. Grim and another groom hurried out to meet them. Charis pulled her horse to a halt, slid down, and was already running toward the palace before Tal finished dismounting.

"If you're about to meet the queen and call in the ambassador, you'll need to change into a dress worthy of the occasion," he said as he caught up to her.

"And I'll need my sword."

"Ambassador Shyrn is going to be very sorry he crossed you."

Mother and Charis stood side by side in the queen's office, both wearing bold hues of crimson and gold. The queen wore daggers on both wrists. Charis had her ceremonial sword strapped to her waist, the hilt formed from the bodies of three intertwined snakes. The largest snake's mouth surrounded the blade, its ruby eyes glaring as it sank its fangs into the metal.

Lord Everly stood at attention in front of them. He had not been invited to sit.

"Your Majesty, may I ask the reason for this meeting?"

"I should think you know the reason, Blaise." Queen Letha cut into him with a single look and waited.

"I . . ." He looked around the room as if to check to make sure no one but Tal was there to overhear him. "I admit that I'm a bit confused about being summoned here this early, but I would like to report an inappropriate visit to my home by Ambassador Shyrn from Rullenvor."

"And why did I have to summon you to receive this report?"

Lord Everly adjusted his cravat and looked at Charis. She wrapped her hand around the hilt of her sword. If he thought he'd find mercy in this room, he'd badly misjudged his sovereigns.

"The meeting happened not more than thirty minutes ago—"

"Nearly an hour at this point," Charis said crisply. "Or do you think we aren't aware of what happens right under our noses?"

"No, of course, an hour. I simply lost track of the time." He raised his hands in a placating gesture. "I planned to make my report in person rather than send a note. It seemed important enough to warrant a visit."

"So it is," the queen said.

A knock sounded on the door, and a page hurried in, handed the queen two letters, each bearing a wax seal, and then left. The queen moved to her desk to open the parchments. Charis kept her cold stare on Lord Everly, taking it as a personal victory when sweat dotted his pale brow.

"Interesting," the queen said as she returned to stand beside Charis. "I've just had notes from both Lady Channing and Lady Whitecross that Ambassador Shyrn visited them this morning. Apparently"—she made a show of looking at the parchments—"they felt the visit was unusual enough to warrant my immediate notification. They have both also made themselves available for an interview at my convenience today." She rolled up the parchments. "What have you to say for yourself, Blaise?"

He shook his head. "Your Majesty, a simple oversight. Truly. I wanted to discuss it with you in person. It was . . . a strange meeting. Unsettling."

"Explain," the queen said. "If we're satisfied with your answer, you get to keep your title, your lands, and your head. If we aren't . . ."

Charis drew her sword and held it ready.

"He just showed up! No appointment. No warning. I was barely dressed." His words tumbled over themselves. His eyes stayed on Charis. "He was talking nonsense. Said he'd made a reasonable offer to you to let the High Emperor of Rullenvor make us a protectorate under their rule. Utter rubbish. Begged me to see that convincing you to accept the offer was in Calera's best interests."

"And did you agree to that?"

"Of course not! How could it be in our best interests to give another kingdom control over us? Let a foreigner rule us." He spat the words. "Probably steal our wealth and make our titles meaningless."

Charis shared a long look with her mother and then lowered her sword. Lord Everly's words, full of shock and self-interest, had a ring of truth to them.

"You are dismissed," the queen said.

Lord Everly bowed, blotted at the sweat on his forehead, and hurried from the room. As soon as he left, a footman entered. "Ambassador Shyrn from Rullenvor has arrived."

"What a nice way to say he was summoned," Charis said.

"This ends with him leaving us, dead or alive," Mother said. "Let's get any useful information out of him that we can before that happens."

Charis nodded and kept her sword out of its sheath.

Ambassador Shyrn entered the room and hurried toward them.

His shirt was half tucked, his collar stood up on one side, and there was a tear down one pant leg.

"Your Majesty, I am grateful to finally be called before you again." He bowed low, revealing a stain on the back of his dress coat. His graying red hair looked like it hadn't been properly washed in days.

"Why is that?" the queen asked.

He straightened and smoothed the front of his jacket, completely missing the untucked shirt and the undone collar. "Well, of course, I've been expecting to be able to send your reply to the High Emperor's generous offer back to Rullenvor. I do hope, with these ship sinkings, you have considered their offer and are ready to accept help."

"*Their* offer?" Charis cocked her head. "You led us to believe this offer came from the High Emperor."

"Of course! Yes! From both the High Emperor and the leader of Te'ash." He wrung his hands, then seemed to realize he wasn't doing himself any favors and dropped them to his sides. "Shall we sit?"

"No," Charis said coldly.

"Interesting that you should bring up the ships sinking." Queen Letha's tone was a delicate razor poised above his neck.

He looked from one to the other, prey sensing a trap. "It's all anyone is talking about."

"That's not quite true, is it, Charis?"

"Not true at all." Charis slowly raised her sword. "In fact, I believe the most popular topic of conversation is the news that we've signed a peace treaty with Montevallo and will soon have full use of their army and their considerable stockpile of jewels."

"The jewels . . . you've signed a treaty?" He was back to wringing his hands.

"Indeed." The queen sounded almost sympathetic. "Ambassador

Shyrn, you've been visiting my royal council, trying to convince them to pressure us to take your offer. And you stand before us now clearly upset and nervous. Tell me about that."

"I . . . I had to!" He fell to his knees before the queen. "Please, you have no idea. None. But this can still be fixed. It can still be all right. You have access to the jewels now. You can send them to Rullenvor as payment—"

"Payment for what?" Fury burned through Charis. "For calling off your armada?"

He turned to her, his hands up in the air like a supplicant. "You don't even have to be a protectorate. You can just arrange a regular shipment of the required jewels, and the Rakuuna will protect you. Everything will go back to the way it was."

"We seem to have run into a misunderstanding, Ambassador Shyrn." The sympathy in the queen's voice had turned to stone. "You are laboring under the delusion that we are going to send blood money for the High Emperor to call off his ships, but—"

"Please." His voice cracked. "If you refuse to pay, you are sentencing me and my family to death."

"You were willing to sentence my entire kingdom to servitude, were you not?" Mother's eyes pinned the ambassador.

"I beg you for mercy." Ambassador Shyrn looked wildly from Charis to the queen. "Pay the Rakuuna. I'm sure I can convince them to protect your ships if you just do that much for me. You have no idea what happens if I fail. None. It would be better for me to kill myself than to face them."

Mother's mouth curved into a cruel smile. "I have no interest in paying the Rakuuna or in dealing with Rullenvor at this point, Ambassador Shyrn. You have been insulting and duplicitous, and it's clear the High Emperor and his ally are no friend to Calera. As for your fear of facing them with your failure, you need not worry. You'll be too busy in our dungeons giving us every piece of information we need to ever set foot in Rullenvor again."

Charis met Mother's gaze as she quickly ran through the questions they needed Shyrn to answer. There was precious little information about the Rakuuna in Brannigan's texts, but none of the brief passages described the fearsome underwater creatures as having ships. Did the armada stationed at Portsmith belong to Rullenvor? Had they been sinking Calera's ships all along as a way to force the queen to accept their terms? Or was something else going on? Some sort of dangerous political game between Rullenvor, the Rakuuna, and the owner of those ships? Somehow the jewels demanded as payment were the key, which meant—

"Charis, be careful!" Tal lunged from his position near the wall and sprinted toward her, but it was too late.

Ambassador Shyrn leaped to his feet, took three running steps, and launched himself into Charis's weapon. Her blade pierced his throat and came out the other side as they crashed to the floor. The breath left her body as the hilt of her sword slammed into her abdomen.

Seconds later, Tal was there. He tore Ambassador Shyrn off her and tossed him aside. Kneeling beside the princess, he said, "Where are you hurt? Charis, please. Tell me where to look, sweetheart. There's so much blood. So much."

He ripped his jacket off and pressed it to her chest where blood pooled in the center of her dress.

"Get Baust!" the queen yelled. A guard wrenched open the door and raced inside while the footman ran for the palace physician.

Charis wheezed. Her lungs felt as though they were encased in stone.

"Charis, I can't find the source." Tal pressed his jacket harder, frantically looking for the wound. "Help me. Tell me where it is."

"Not mine," she rasped, drawing in half a lungful of air. "His."

Tal pulled his coat away and examined her dress, his hands shaking. When he was finally convinced that she was right, he rested his hands on her shoulders and curled over the top of her.

"You are going to be the death of me," he whispered as the queen yelled instructions. "This is the fourth time you've nearly given me heart failure."

"Help me sit up before my mother actually does drop dead of heart failure." It hurt to breathe, but she could manage.

"Your Majesty," Tal called over the top of the queen's frantic directions to her staff. "Charis is unharmed. She is well."

The queen hurried to her daughter's side, saw the truth for herself, and then lowered herself shakily into the nearest chair.

"Your Highness!" Baust rushed into the room and headed toward Charis.

"She's fine. The blood is his." The queen waved a hand at the body on the rug. "Get that useless sack of meat out of here and leave us."

The staff promptly obeyed, and then it was just Mother, Charis, and Tal. The queen looked at them both.

"We have two issues. First, you called my daughter 'sweetheart' when you thought she was dying."

Tal blanched, and Charis's stomach pitched.

"Your Majesty—"

"I don't care if you have feelings for her. She's free to take a consort if she is unsatisfied with her marriage to the Montevallian, though knowing my daughter, I'm not sure that's an option she'll exercise. At any rate, your feelings can never be revealed in public again. Even if you think she's dying. Am I clear?"

"Yes, Your Majesty," Tal said.

"Second, and of far more importance, Ambassador Shyrn just deliberately impaled himself rather than answer our questions. That speaks to desperation and danger. We need to figure out why the Rakuuna want a stockpile of jewels from Montevallo, whether those ships belong to them, and how to defeat both the ships and Te'ash, if necessary. It's a small mercy that they never come on land. It buys us time to figure this out. I have no intention of becoming ensnared in an agreement where we have to pay these creatures just to keep our ships afloat. Now go get cleaned up and watch your backs. We still have a traitor to catch."

THIRTY-FIVE

THE NEXT WEEK was spent reaching out to the kingdoms closest to Rullenvor to ask about the High Emperor, the Rakuuna, and the armada of small battle frigates with green lanterns. Every palloren bird brought back utterly useless information.

Thallis had suspicions that the High Emperor wasn't well because he apparently hadn't been seen in some time, but those were unconfirmed rumors. The Rakuuna hadn't been seen in their area of the sea for nearly a century.

Verace hadn't renewed their trade relationship with Rullenvor last spring, though they weren't sure why. It had been Rullenvor's decision. They'd heard rumors that the Rakuuna were back in the northern waters but couldn't confirm a single sighting.

Embre had heard nothing about the affairs of Rullenvor, but that wasn't surprising given how far north they were. They did, however, confirm that the Rakuuna were no longer keeping strictly to the borders of their kingdom, though they'd personally had no interactions with the species.

Abandoning their attempt to get insight into what was going on within Rullenvor, Charis and Mother came up with a new plan of attack. Charis would take the boat out every night for a week, hunting for the small warships with the ghostly green lights, searching for patterns or paths of safety on the waters so that the queen could send a battalion of naval vessels to trap them between the mouth of Portsmith's cove and the army that was heading there now.

They also issued an invitation to Alaric and whichever son he was going to include on their peace treaty to attend a formal contract signing in Arborlay. The meeting had the added benefit of giving them a chance to question Alaric about the type of jewels they mined to discover the connection between the jewels and the war frigates. Charis couldn't think too hard about that impending meeting without feeling something inside start to unravel, so instead she focused on Alaric's reply. His brusque agreement arrived a few days later and included a reminder that they could only stay for two nights due to the arrival of winter in the mountains.

She could survive two nights.

And that would teach her how to survive days that would turn into weeks and months and years. But for now, she could push it to the back of her mind and focus on the last few minutes of their fourth nighttime sail that week. Once again, they'd seen nothing out of place, though they hadn't dared go as far north as Portsmith. If anyone in the armada was watching them, they needed to believe the ship contained actual smugglers who were traveling to viable small ports.

It was all too much to think about. She needed exercise to clear her mind and help her find solutions to the problems that faced her.

Turning to Tal, she said, "We'll be back in the harbor in the next thirty minutes. Perhaps we should practice the sixth transition without swords. I need to build that muscle memory."

His lips lifted, and something warm unspooled in her stomach.

"Are you sure? I thought you said no sparring on the open water."

"We won't be sparring. I'll practice the movement while you watch. You can correct my form from over there." She pointed to a distance several paces away. That should be safe. No fingers at her hips to distract her. No heat at her back to send traitorous thoughts through her head.

His smile widened. "So keep my hands to myself."

"Unless you want to lose them."

He cocked his head as if considering the benefits of taking that risk, and she laughed. "Just go stand over there and tell me what I'm doing wrong."

He took a single step, and something struck the side of the boat.

Charis tumbled forward, slamming her knee against the deck and landing hard on her chest as the ship rocked violently side to side. A man screamed as he was flung from the foremast and into the sea.

"Captain!" Tal threw himself down beside her, his hands frantically running over her head, her arms, and her legs. "Are you hurt?"

"Man overboard," she gasped, her lungs seizing.

Tal whipped around and yelled, "Man overboard!" Turning back to her, he said, "Where are you hurt?"

"Don't worry about me," she wheezed, struggling to sit up as the boat pitched again.

"I wish I could stop," he muttered as he wrapped an arm around her back and helped her to her feet. Pain shot through her knee when she put weight on her leg, but it was bearable, and they had bigger things to deal with.

The crew from belowdecks burst out of the stairwell, weapons drawn.

"Orayn, take the helm!" Charis shouted, her mind racing as she scanned the deck, cataloging her crew and her options. She knew enough about sailing now to at least get them headed in the right direction until Orayn could grab the helm, assess the situation, and take over. "Dec and Arden, trim that main mast and get us back to the docks fast. Sella, Kam, and Rithni, go help Joren get our sailor out of the water. The rest of you, either grab a sword or man a cannon."

"Are we going to sink?" Kam, a whip-thin boy whose mop of red hair reminded her of Milla, trembled as the boat rocked violently again.

"No, sailor, we are not. Go get our man out of the sea."

When the others scrambled to do her bidding, she turned to Tal. "Let's go see what is trying to destroy this ship."

Together, they drew their swords and fought their way across the deck as the ship pitched and tilted. When they reached the railing, Charis peered around, expecting to see one of the small war frigates from Portsmith, cannons aimed at their little frigate.

There was nothing.

"Who's firing at us?" she yelled. "Somebody tell me you see the attacking ship!"

The boat rocked violently, and something snapped in the rigging overhead with a loud *crack*.

"Where is it coming from?" Tal turned full circle, staring out at the dark water. Charis joined him, but the seas around them appeared empty.

"Ship, ahoy!" a sailor called Perrin called from the crow's nest. "Due east."

Struggling to hang on to the railing as the ship shuddered and creaked, Charis glared east, expecting to see an enemy craft bearing down on them. Instead, she saw a string of lights far in the distance with the smudge of a boat-shaped shadow behind it. Merchant vessel, by the looks of it. And much too far away to be shooting cannons at her ship.

"That's too far," Tal said as if he could read her mind.

"And it's a merchant vessel. See the sails? A navy frigate has four sets, each a triple. This one only has three."

"So what is hitting our—"

Boom.

The merchant vessel tilted wildly, its lanterns crashing onto the deck and igniting it in a blaze of fire.

"No. No!" Charis yelled as the heart-wrenching shriek of timbers tearing apart filled the air. "Sail east. Go east! They need our help."

"*We* need our help," Orayn said even as he wrenched the helm to send the boat east.

"We aren't on fire. Nothing has tilted our boat." Charis looked at the water, her stomach feeling as though she'd been struck. "We were just jostled on the way to the real attack."

The merchant vessel tipped, spilling men, cargo, and bits of flaming debris into the water.

"There is no attacking fleet." Horror stole her breath and stung her eyes. "The threat is coming from below the surface. I need to get closer." She sheathed her sword.

"Don't you dare tell me you plan to go into the water." Tal's hand wrapped around hers, anchoring her to his side.

"Not into the water. Just close enough to catch a glimpse of what we're fighting."

"Captain—"

As she rounded on him something broke on the merchant ship with a sharp, wet crack, and the main mast went up in flames. "We thought it was the small war frigates bringing down ships, but this is something different. Orayn will either get us clear of it as we search for survivors, or he won't. The crew will either fight it off with cannons, or they won't. I can't change that now. What I can do is make sure if we survive, we know what we're facing and can figure out how to kill it."

"Then I'll do it."

"Don't be foolish. I'd struggle to pull you back into the boat, whereas you can haul me up easily. It's safer if I'm the one who goes."

He glared at her. "I hate it when you're right."

"I'd think you'd be used to that feeling by now."

His jaw clenched, but he slowly released her hand. "I'll tie a rope around your waist and anchor it to the mast. But if you die, I will never forgive you."

"I won't forgive me either." She unbuckled her sword and placed it on the deck and then pulled a dagger from the sheath at her ankle and stood still while he knotted a rope harness over her chest and around her waist. Cannon fire boomed, and then the unearthly, high-pitched wails that sometimes haunted Charis's nightmares rose all around them, sending piercing pain through Charis's teeth until the cries tapered off into that series of rattling clicks. Orayn shouted for Dec and Arden to trim the sails.

"Ship, ahoy!" Finn yelled. Charis whipped her head up to see three of the small war frigates from Portsmith, their green lanterns glowing as they bobbed in the sea at least twenty furlongs from the smuggler's ship.

"They're too far to be attacking the merchant vessel," Charis said. "Plus, the attack is coming from the creatures beneath the water. So why are they here?"

Tal finished the harness, tied the other end of the rope to the mizzenmast, and then reached her side in three long steps, wrapped his arms around her, and dragged her against his chest. She fisted her free hand into the back of his shirt as he buried his face against her neck for a moment.

Another scream. More cannon fire. And Tal's breath hot against her ear as he said, "I mean it, Charis. Don't die."

She pulled back, her lips hovering a whisper away from his. "I'll do my best."

And then she let go of him, grabbed the railing, and hauled herself over the side. The rope let out swiftly, and she plunged halfway to the water before the harness yanked her to a stop. Keeping her dagger in one hand, she braced herself against the side of the ship with the other and waited.

"Come on," she whispered, her eyes burning from the spray of salt water as she glared at the sea beneath her. "Show yourself."

Orayn yelled, and there was another crash from the deck, but the ship was moving out of the direct line of attack now. As it picked up speed, there was a flash of movement in the water below Charis. Something pale and vaguely human-shaped slammed into the boat once more, and Charis's throat tightened until it felt like she was choking.

She couldn't be certain. It was dark, and the creature had moved so fast.

But it had been humanish, even though the limbs seemed unnaturally long. There was only one sea creature who looked like that.

They neared the wreckage of the merchant ship as it slowly sank, its flames glowing against the moonlit water in streaks of crimson. There was a tug on the rope, and Charis looked up to see Tal above her, his lips set in a grim line as he hauled her toward the deck. When she reached the top, he pulled her over the side, and his hand found hers and squeezed.

"Did you see it?" he asked.

"Just a flash. It seemed almost like a person, though too pale and too fast. I can only think of one sea creature who resembles that description."

He stared at her for a long moment. "Rakuuna?"

She nodded, her heart thudding as she considered the implications.

A blast of sound, like the golden, sonorous notes of a trumpet but so high-pitched it set Charis's teeth on edge, echoed from the distant bobbing green lanterns that marked the location of the small war frigates. Instantly, there was a rush of motion from the merchant ship. Pale shapes that moments ago had been swarming the vessel's wreckage now dived into the water. The wake slapped the side of Charis's boat, though they were some distance away. And moments later, the green dots of light on the horizon bobbed frantically, as if their ships were swaying side to side.

Swaying because the creatures they'd called had returned?

"Did they just . . ." Tal gestured toward the green lights.

"Call the Rakuuna back to their ships?" Charis's mouth was dry. "Yes. I think they did. It seems Rullenvor does have an armada and has been behind the ship sinking all along."

Which meant her plan with Mother to ambush the frigates from both land and sea wasn't going to work. They would have to coordinate an attack from land only and hope they set enough of the ships on fire to discourage the rest from staying. If that didn't work, then she was going to have to figure out how to destroy the Rakuuna before they cut her kingdom off from the rest of the world forever.

THIRTY-SIX

RAIN DRUMMED RESTLESS fingers against the carriage top as Charis returned from a quiet evening at the Farragins' house. It had been three weeks since she'd seen the Rakuuna destroy the merchant vessel, four weeks since Rullenvor's ambassador had killed himself on the point of her sword, and she was still no closer to figuring out how they could defend themselves at sea. No closer to finding the traitor in their own ranks either. And she was running out of time.

Tomorrow Alaric and his son would arrive to sign the peace treaty. She would find a way to question them about the type of jewels they mined and hope something in their answer would give her insight into the Rullenvor-Rakuuna problem. And she'd keep Tal beside her every step of the way in case the traitor tried to kill her after the treaty was signed to destabilize the agreement.

Her stomach clenched, hollow and queasy. The air in the carriage was too thick to breathe, and her heart pounded, a rapid, jarring rhythm that made her feel faint.

How could she keep her composure as she signed away her life to the enemy?

"Hey, now." Tal left his place in the seat across from her and crouched before her. "Breathe. Nice and slow. There you are. Now another."

She tried to breathe past the noose of panic that was closing around her throat, but everything inside was chaos. Her hands shook as she raised them to her flushed face, and Tal took them in his own. He rubbed some heat back into her icy fingers as he peered into her face, worry written on his.

"Charis, what's happening? What's wrong?"

She shook her head. She couldn't say that she wasn't ready for everything to become final. That the specter of living her life beside her enemy kept her up at night and flooded her body with heart-pounding, stomach-clenching fear. Words would give the fear shape and weight and *power*.

Her head spun as the world seemed to rush away from her.

He let go of her hands and gathered her close. Pressing her face to his shoulder, he said gently, "Be here with me, Charis. Just here. Nowhere else. Can you feel my arms around you?"

His arms were a comforting warmth at her back. She focused on that and drew an unsteady breath.

"Listen to my voice," he said, his mouth beside her ear. "You're here with me, and you're safe. Nothing else matters right now. Just hold on to me."

His voice filled her panicked thoughts. His chest was a solid weight she could lean against. She snuggled closer and hung on to him as the chaos inside slowly settled. His breathing was a steady rise and fall, and she tried to match her breathing to his as she silenced the fear that was crouching in the back of her mind.

She was in the carriage with Tal. Nothing was spinning out of control. Nothing was rushing away from her. She was safe in this moment, and that was all she could control.

He held her in silence for the rest of the carriage ride to the palace as her breathing hitched and then grew steady. Slowly, her heart settled into its normal rhythm, and her thoughts cleared. As they pulled into the wide, circular drive at the palace's front entrance, he said softly, "Better?"

She nodded, and he slowly released her.

"I know I'm supposed to look over the luncheon setup and approve the menu with the head housekeeper, but I don't think I'm up to it." It was hard to push that truth past her lips. Hard to admit that there was something she couldn't manage, especially something so small.

He held her gaze. "I'll take care of it and have Reuben take you to your chambers. No escaping out your balcony or spiraling into panic before I get there, all right?"

She gave him a small, weary smile. "I wouldn't dream of it."

"Liar," he whispered as the carriage door opened and light from the entrance spilled across the rain-soaked cobblestones.

She entered the palace and headed toward her chambers, Reuben close behind. When she reached her wing, the night shift guards were waiting at the guards' station. Vellis looked up from the notes she was making in the register.

"Good evening, Your Highness," she said, scooping up a stack of papers. "I have three items that need your approval before I close out the autumn records and file them away."

Charis paused. "Yes, Vellis?"

The guard rustled through the papers and pulled out three pieces.

"I have the visitor log from the night of the first assassination attempt, the notes from the investigation into the archer's background, and a list of medicines Baust provided during Tal's recuperation. Are those still needed for further investigation, or shall I archive them with the rest of the season's records?"

"I . . ." Charis's mind spun, and tendrils of her earlier panic snaked into her thoughts. She simply couldn't think clearly enough to give Vellis the right answer. The guard stood waiting, the papers extended toward Charis. "I'll look these over and get back to you on that in the next few days."

Charis took the papers, waited until Vellis and Gaylle had cleared her chambers for entry, and then bid them all good night. Mrs. Sykes had her nightdress and a cup of hot cocoa waiting beside a cozy fire. Charis made short work of her nighttime routine and then sent the woman home.

Tal still hadn't returned, and so Charis settled into a chair beside the fire, sipped her cocoa, and looked at the papers Vellis had given her.

The investigation into the archer's background hadn't revealed much, but it hardly mattered. The would-be assassin had given up Bartho's name, and that was the clue that mattered. Charis set that sheet aside and looked at the next paper.

The list of medical supplies Baust had used to treat Tal's arrow wound was sobering, but it hardly merited saving out of the archive. She took another sip of cocoa and looked at the final sheet.

She'd studied the visitor log for her wing on the night of the ambassadors' ball with Mother the day after the assassination attempt, but nothing had stood out. No one on the list beyond her own staff—who'd had good reason to be there, not that it had saved them in the

end—and the members of the nobility who'd sent a gift for the princess to potentially wear in their honor at the ball. Nothing out of the
ordinary.

Still, she looked at the list again, her eyes lingering on every name
as Tal entered the chambers.

> *Milla*
> *Fada*
> *Luther*
> *Lady Ollen*
> *Lord Westing*
> *Lord and Lady Rynce*

"I see Mrs. Sykes wisely sent for cocoa this evening," Tal said as he
approached.

"You can have it," she said, setting the papers aside.

He picked up her cup and took a sip.

"What am I going to do, Tal?" She pressed her fingers against her
forehead. "I can't figure out how to beat Rullenvor's armada. Not
with the Rakuuna sinking ships from beneath the water. How can
Calera survive without trade routes?"

He set her cup down and crouched before her. "I can't believe I'm
about to say this, but . . . soon you'll have Alaric's help."

Her lip curled, and she wrapped her arms around her knees and
hugged them to her chest. "I don't want his help."

"I don't know a single person who does, but the fact is the Rakuuna,
and by extension Rullenvor, seem singularly focused on plundering
Montevallo's mountains for jewels." He met her gaze, and for once,
she couldn't read his expression. "I have no doubt Alaric will pay any
amount to assure his son access to your throne and your ports."

"Is that the answer, then?" She frowned. "We pay for the privilege of keeping our ships afloat?"

"I don't like it either, but we can't ration medicine, cloth, and spices much longer before we run out."

She looked at the fire as something dark and painful twisted within her. "I thought I was saving my people by offering up the betrothal, but we're still trapped. What if the jewels run out? Or the Rakuuna demand something else? Something we can't afford to pay? Or—"

"Or what if a payment of jewels buys you enough time to figure out how to stop this?" Tal sounded like he had utter faith in her, and somehow that made it worse.

"But I can't stop this, Tal. I can't. You saw what those creatures did to the merchant vessel. There is no safety at sea if the Rakuuna decide to take it from us. And I still have a traitor who wants me dead, and Alaric arrives tomorrow, and I'm going to sign my life away, but my kingdom still isn't safe. I'm not safe." Her voice shook. "I'm going to be alone with an enemy prince for the rest of my life."

He leaned forward and took her hands in his. "Charis, you will not be facing this alone. I swear it."

She smiled sadly at him. "Months and months of ice and snow, but after that—"

"After that, we move forward into what comes next." His voice was steady. "The only way you can get rid of me is to send me away. I'm not leaving you."

His dark eyes found hers and held. Heat that had nothing to do with the roaring fire unfurled within and spread through her veins, like honeyed sunshine.

"You won't leave?" she whispered.

"I won't leave."

He gathered her close and held her until the worries chasing themselves in circles around her mind settled and all that remained was the crackle of the flames, the scent of rich cocoa, and the warmth of his chest against her cheek.

THIRTY-SEVEN

CHARIS LOST HER breakfast the morning of King Alaric's arrival.

When she stepped out of the bath chamber, her teeth brushed and her stomach empty, Mrs. Sykes clucked her tongue sympathetically and said, "Stomach upset. Probably going around. Expect you'll start up next." She looked at Tal.

Tal shook his head, though he looked just as queasy as Charis felt.

Mrs. Sykes frowned at them both. "I have half a mind to message the queen and have her tell you both to go back to bed."

"We'll be fine," Charis said, though she had no confidence that she was speaking the truth. "I'll start with the blue ombré gown. And I'll need the silver sheath for my sword. Remember, I have three outfit changes today."

"Oh yes." The older woman fluttered happily as she reached for the blue gown. "Won't you make a memorable first impression on your soon-to-be husband? He won't be able to take his eyes off you."

That wasn't a comforting thought.

"What hairstyle are we doing?" Mrs. Sykes asked as if she had more than three at her disposal.

"I'll do her hair," Tal said. His eyes found Charis's and held.

"Well, that's highly unusual." Mrs. Sykes looked flustered.

"He'll be doing metal sculptures around my hair. To match my dress." Charis raised her brows at Tal to prod him into helping her spare the woman's feelings.

"Yes," he said. "She's starting a new trend. We want her guests to know exactly with whom they're dealing."

"Just so." Mrs. Sykes nodded as she finished setting out the petticoat, corset, stockings, and shoes that went with the blue ombré. "Our princess is like a delectable pastry laced with the prettiest poison imaginable. They'll be lulled by her beauty and forget to be careful how big a bite they try to take." She sounded like a proud grandmother.

Once Charis was dressed, she sat at her vanity and waited while Mrs. Sykes left with the laundry, and Tal came out of his room wearing his blue-and-silver uniform. He stood behind her and looked in the mirror.

"She's right." He sounded as though someone had kicked his favorite cat. "He won't be able to take his eyes off you."

She clutched her hands in her lap and tried to breathe slowly. He bent to her ear, still holding her gaze in the mirror. "I won't take my eyes off you either. If you need me, just look for me. I'll be there."

He combed lightly through her curls with his fingers, and she said, "It's Vahn."

His hands stilled.

"That's the one they brought. Not fussy Percival. No teacup to break." She tried to smile but failed.

His hands came to rest on her shoulders, warm and comforting. "Every man has a favorite teacup. You just have to figure out the source of Vahn's pride. Once you know that, you know how to break him."

Her lips lifted slowly, and fire began burning in her belly. "I happen to be particularly skilled at breaking people."

"That's my princess. Now let's make sure everyone who looks at you knows it."

An hour later, Charis stopped outside the queen's drawing room, Tal by her side looking pale and miserable but resolute. For once the queen had decided not to have Charis arrive early to greet their guests, who'd already been received by the council and treated to a sumptuous breakfast. This time, Charis needed a grand entrance. A first impression that would stick.

She took a deep breath, let rage become her armor, and smiled, cruel and vicious.

"Let her in," Tal said. "She's ready."

She swept into the room, bowed to Mother first, and then faced Alaric and Vahn, who were flanked by a trio of guards in red-and-black uniforms. Alaric was a large, broad-shouldered man with long graying blond hair. Silver charms with bits of colorful jewels were tied into his flowing locks. His brown eyes found hers, and his brows lifted as he took in her proud expression.

"You'll have your hands full with this one," he said in a voice that rumbled from his chest. A light of challenge entered his eyes as Charis held his stare. "You ought to bow to a sovereign, girl."

Charis's smile widened. "Indeed, you should."

He barked a laugh. "I like her. A sword for a spine, this one. What do you say, Vahn? Going to bow to your future wife?"

Charis turned, her mouth dry, her heart pounding, and found a young man who looked remarkably like Alaric. His hair was light brown instead of graying blond, and it was just past his shoulders, but there were three charms tied into his locks, and his eyes were the same shade of brown as his father's. He took his time studying her, and then he bowed his head a fraction. Just enough to show nominal respect.

She had no intention of doing the same. She outranked him, and she refused to start their relationship giving the impression that he was her equal. Instead, she softened her smile and said, "Welcome to Arborlay."

"Let's see this contract, then," Alaric said. "I want to send a palloren back to my kingdom once we've signed it and these two have made their vows."

Charis froze, her eyes instantly seeking out Tal. He looked as if he'd been struck. Today was supposed to be a treaty signing only. Not the actual wedding. Had Alaric misunderstood? Or was he trying to push the timetable forward for his own reasons?

Alaric laughed, a cold, cruel sound that reminded Charis of Mother when she'd found proof of someone's wrongdoing. "What have we here?" He walked toward Tal.

Tal straightened, and something dark and dangerous flashed across his face.

"My bodyguard," Charis said, moving to stand between them before Alaric could reach Tal.

"Seems like he can't get enough of looking at you."

"He'd be a pretty poor bodyguard if he didn't watch out for me," she said crisply.

"Alaric, the contract is here." Mother called the king's attention to the table that rested against the far wall between two magnificent windows.

"I want this boy relieved of his duties once the vows are spoken," Alaric said.

"You do not have any control over our staff." Letha's tone could cut glass.

"I haven't signed the treaty yet, have I?"

"Father, it's fine." Vahn's smooth, polished voice lingered a little too long on the Caleran vowels, but overall, his accent was nearly flawless. "Let the boy stay if that's what Charis wants. Once she gets to know our family better, she may get more comfortable with the idea of listening to your staffing suggestions."

Tal's expression looked carved from stone.

Charis inclined her head to Vahn in a silent thank-you. He smiled as if secretly delighted with her.

"Looks like she's already got you bowing to her wishes." Alaric turned away from Tal and slapped Vahn on the back. "'Course I see why, but don't let a pretty face lead you into bad decisions."

"We have refreshments laid out in the adjoining room," Letha said. "Once we sign the contract, we'll have a light lunch, and then we have a few activities planned for this afternoon and evening."

"As long as one of those activities is a wedding," Alaric said as he took the quill and signed his name to the treaty, just beneath Letha's.

Vahn signed next, and then handed the quill to Charis. His fingers brushed against hers and lingered. She fought the urge to yank her hand away. Instead, she kept her expression smooth as glass as she bent over the table, dipped the quill into the inkpot, and signed her name.

As she made the last stroke, Alaric and Letha congratulated each other and then began moving toward the adjoining room. Charis set the quill down slowly and stared at her name.

It was done.

There was no reprieve. No backing out.

Her knees wobbled, and she pressed her hands against the table before she could show weakness.

"Charis?" Vahn stood beside her.

She straightened. "Shall we have lunch?"

"Not yet." He placed a hand on her arm, and then removed it when she seared him with a look. "I've heard so much about you. I almost feel like I know you already, but I can assure you our spies' reports failed to do you justice."

"Did they, now?"

"It's almost as though they wanted me to be less interested in you than you deserve."

"That makes no sense."

He smiled, and the knowing look in his eyes sent a thrill of unease up the back of her spine. "This betrothal was your idea, wasn't it?"

"It was."

"And you aren't the kind of person who backs out of her agreements, are you?" He said it as though he was certain of her answer.

She lifted her chin. "I am not."

He looked from her to Tal, his smile sharpening. Charis didn't dare follow his gaze. If she looked at Tal's face knowing the Penbyrns expected her to say her vows this afternoon, she would break. Shatter right there in front of her enemy. There would be no coming back from that. No way to regain the upper hand in their relationship; and so she kept her eyes firmly on Vahn.

"Then let me do something for you, because I am assured that you are nothing if not loyal to your duty and your word." He looked at her again, a cruel light of mischief in his eyes. "We'll call it a wedding gift."

"I want nothing from you."

"Oh, you want this." He leaned closer. "You see, I am also a man of honor. I keep my word."

Her eyes narrowed as she waited for him to continue.

"You don't want to get married today, do you?" He looked at Tal again. "That came as quite a shock to you both."

It was unnerving how easily he seemed to read Tal. Worse, how easily he read her. He'd mentioned spies. Did he have someone in the palace? Someone who'd observed how close she'd become with Tal?

"I'm waiting for an answer, Your Highness." There was a faint sheen of mockery to his words, and Charis took her turn baring her teeth in a venom-tipped smile of her own. He thought he was going to negotiate their wedding date and hold that over her head, did he? She'd rip that leverage away from him in one fell swoop.

"No, I don't want to get married today. I don't have my wedding dress yet. And in Calera, we have a series of important traditions that must take place before a royal wedding. If you expect to be acknowledged as my true husband, and therefore as a true king in Calera, those traditions cannot be skipped." She shrugged delicately. "Of course, if you don't care about being seen as anything more than a consort, we can marry this afternoon. I will ascend to Calera's throne either way. I'm simply offering you the benefit of true power rather than a lifetime spent in its shadow."

His smile slipped. "Is that true?"

"Would I lie to you? You seem to know so much about me. I'm sure the topic of my truthfulness and honor must have come up."

He looked at the floor as if thinking, and then met her eyes again, his unnerving smile back in place. "We'll postpone it to the spring, then. But understand this." He leaned closer, his tone dripping with courtesy. "When we marry, you are mine in every sense of the word. I don't share."

His gaze slid to Tal and then back to her. "I take what's mine, and I punish those who step out of line."

"How lovely," Charis said with as much icy enthusiasm as she could pack into the words. "I keep what's mine, and those who cross me find their heads removed from their bodies."

He laughed. "You do delight me, Charis. This will be no dull union. Let's retire to the luncheon, your faithful bodyguard in tow—how do you train them to be so silent? It's refreshing—and we can upset my father's digestion by telling him our plans to wait until spring so that I can be a true king of Calera and you can . . . prepare to be mine alone."

He placed his hand against her back and ushered her toward the door. She stepped to the side to break his hold on her, and his smile widened. As she passed Tal, she risked a quick glance at him.

Tal's eyes burned with fury, and pain flashed across his face when their gazes locked. She let her own pain show for an instant, and then as she turned away, she let rage fill the ache within her, burning through her fear and her loneliness until all that remained was her duty to Calera and her refusal to let Vahn and Alaric see her break.

THIRTY-EIGHT

SHE'D DONE IT.

Three outfit changes with flawless hairstyles from a subdued, miserable Tal, who did his best to give her the strength it took to face the Penbyrns again and again. A luncheon, an afternoon horseback ride, a formal dinner with a few hand-selected noble families, and a dance that had nearly been Charis's breaking point.

Vahn's unfailingly courteous voice, cruel charm, and the barbs buried in his words lingered, as did the feel of his hands on her as they'd danced.

She'd stopped looking at Tal for support. Every time she did, Vahn was right there to remark on it. And the more she wanted to run to Tal, the harder it was to stay where she belonged.

Vahn had taken plenty of shots from her as well. She'd made sure of it. He was leaving in the morning knowing that she, and by extension Calera, would not be the easy conquest he'd assumed she'd be. She'd made him work for every advantage, and she'd seen his moves coming before he made them.

It was a victory, but it felt utterly hollow.

She felt utterly hollow.

And so she'd waited until the palace was silent and Tal would be sleeping, and then she'd crept out to her bluff. She needed the wind to scour the feeling of Vahn's touch off her skin. Needed the starlight, cold and distant, to show her how to be remote and untouchable, no matter how much he tried to wound her.

Needed to believe she could survive the rest of her life with a man like him.

Charis wrapped her arms around herself and squeezed until her fingertips dug painfully into her skin. If she held on tight enough, the pieces inside her would settle. Fragments would knit themselves whole again, and the fire that burned in the corner of her heart would turn the hurt to ash.

A soft rustle whispered behind her, and she whirled, a dagger in her hand before she finished lunging for the dark silhouette of the person who'd crept up on her.

Her blade flashed in the starlight as she drove it toward the person's throat, and then a hand whipped up, grasped her arm, twisted firmly, and spun her back to face the sea, her dagger now behind her back. She planted her foot and slid her other dagger into her hand, but then Tal's voice said softly beside her ear, "It's just me. Be at ease."

His grip on her arm lightened, and she yanked herself free and turned to face him as she sheathed her daggers.

"I could have killed you!" And curse him for making her voice shake as she imagined the horror of driving her blade into his throat.

"My life isn't the one in danger." His tone was steady, but there was misery beneath it. "I thought we'd agreed it was too dangerous to creep out to an isolated part of the palace grounds in the dead of night while someone is trying to have you assassinated?"

He truly cared, she could hear it in his voice, and somehow that made the ache within her sharpen.

"No one knows I come here." Her voice was as sharp as the pain in her heart.

He cleared his throat, and she sighed. "No one *else* knows I come here. It's fine. I'm fine."

"Are you?" He waited for her answer, comfortable with the silence between them as he gave her time to decide if she wanted to talk.

But how could she tell him how much it hurt when he'd been hurt today too?

"I . . . it's just . . . I'll be fine." She tucked an errant curl behind her ear. "I always am."

He made a noise in the back of his throat that sounded suspiciously like disbelief, and her brows rose. "You doubt me?"

"Never." He looked past her at the glitter of starlight on the heaving expanse of the sea. "I was just thinking that meeting your future husband might have been . . . difficult."

His voice was carefully neutral. She frowned.

"You don't like him." She didn't make it a question, but he nodded anyway.

"I don't like him, and I don't trust him."

"Why?" The instant the question left her lips, she knew this was what she needed. To hear someone else say that smooth, polite, excruciatingly proper Vahn Penbyrn wasn't what he seemed to be. That his cruel barbs weren't his sense of humor, but indicative of something deeply wrong within him.

Tal glanced at her and then looked away. "It's complicated."

"What do you mean?"

His jaw clenched. For a long moment, she thought he wasn't going

to answer, but then he said quietly, "I think there's something predatory about him. Not just toward me, because that made sense. He saw
me as a threat to his relationship with you. But I felt he was predatory
toward *you*. However, I may not be the best judge of his character."

"I find you to be an excellent judge of character."

He smiled a little, though his voice was sad as he said, "In this case,
I can't see him clearly."

She frowned. "Why not?"

He blew out a breath and looked at the sea again before saying
quietly, "Because he's the man who gets to marry the girl I love."

"Oh." She stared at him in surprise as something delicate and
almost painful unfurled within her.

Silence fell between them, thick as sea mist, and she couldn't figure out how to break it. Her thoughts skipped from one useless thing
to another, but all she could feel was the way her heart beat, fast and
eager, as heat crept into her cheeks.

He squared his shoulders. "I apologize, Your Highness. I over-
stepped. I'm not going to leave you alone and unprotected out here,
but I will move back and leave you to your thoughts." Turning, he
began moving away from the hilltop.

"Wait."

He paused, his back to her, and she said the first honest thing she
could think of that would make him stay.

"I don't want to marry him."

The words, held inside for so long, chained by her forced smiles
and calm assurances that she was ready to do what was best for the
kingdom, spilled from her lips, bitter as wine. He turned, something
burning in his eyes, and the rest of the truth rushed free.

"I tell everyone it doesn't matter. That a princess doesn't get to
choose, but that's not true. I did choose. I chose Calera, and I won't go

back on that choice. But every day"—she swallowed hard and made herself finish, though her voice trembled—"every single day, I wish I could tear up the treaty and be free to find someone who will love me for who I am and not for my title."

He took three steps toward her and stopped an arm's length away. "You deserve to be loved, Charis." Her name was a prayer he whispered, reverent and hushed. "You deserve to have someone who doesn't care about the throne half as much as he cares about you."

Her heart was thunder, her blood lightning, as she took a step toward him. "I wish I could have that."

"You already do." He shifted, a slight movement that brought them closer together. Close enough that she could sense the rise and fall of his chest and feel the warmth of his body. She wanted to lean her cheek against his chest and let the rhythm of his heart soothe her own. She wanted to feel his hands in her hair and his lips on her skin. She wanted him.

Which would be foolish. Incredibly, exponentially foolish.

There were a hundred reasons why she couldn't give in to such a dangerous impulse, and it was his fault that she was having trouble remembering any of them. His fault, with his bossiness, his sense of humor, and his steady belief in her. His dark eyes that met hers across a room and communicated entire conversations with a single look. The way he made the breath catch in the back of her throat when she caught him watching her as though he alone could truly see her.

"Charis?" He placed a finger under her chin and lifted her face to his. His movements were slow. Careful. Giving her plenty of opportunity to step back or order him to stop.

She should absolutely order him to stop.

He leaned closer, his eyes searching hers.

"I don't feel like talking anymore." She'd meant the words to be firm. An unmistakable signal that he should leave her alone. Instead, her voice was soft and breathless, and her traitorous body swayed toward his.

"What do you feel like doing?" His voice was just as breathless as hers.

Her eyes held his, and warmth spilled into her veins, racing toward her fingertips with a delicious tingle. Before she could talk herself out of it, she closed the distance between them and pressed her lips to his.

For an instant, they stood there, lips barely touching, their bodies utterly still. And then his hands slid down her back and pulled her against his chest as he tilted his head and kissed her for real.

His lips were as gentle as his touch, but Charis didn't want gentle. She wanted the pain inside to quiet. The fire to slink into its corner. The fear to disintegrate. She wanted to be so consumed with Tal that she could think of nothing else.

Fisting a hand into the front of his tunic, she took control of the kiss. Her mouth was a fierce demand for absolute submission, but he wouldn't give it. Instead, he met her demand with a fierceness of his own.

A flicker of light blazed to life within her as she slid her hands into his hair and let herself be kissed as if he meant it.

This was the Tal who fought her as an equal in their weapons practice. The Tal who never held back because she was the princess.

He didn't hold back now.

The heat in her veins pooled in her stomach, and her knees went weak. She leaned against him, and he wrapped his arms around her, cradling her as though she were made of glass even as he kissed her as if he meant to conquer the challenge she presented.

When he lifted his face, his eyes searched hers, but she had no words she could give him. Instead, she leaned against his chest, closed her eyes, and listened to the steady beat of his heart.

He held her close, his arms securely around her while his cheek rested on the crown of her head. She wished the world would stop rushing forward and let her keep this one perfect moment. Let her have this one perfect boy, who couldn't help her save Calera, but who might just help her save herself.

But the world refused to give in to her wishes. King Alaric and Prince Vahn were even now sleeping in the north wing and would expect to see her at breakfast. The ink on the treaty was dry. Her feet were set on a path that would free her kingdom and bring her people peace. If her heart longed for the boy with the dark eyes and the crooked smile, she was strong enough to ignore it. The memory of this moment would have to carry her through.

She ought to step away, but instead she lingered, memorizing the feel of his body against hers. The scent of his skin and the way his breath hitched when she traced a finger up the side of his neck and pressed her palm against his cheek. She tilted her head back to look him in the eyes, the wound in her heart already bleeding again.

"Tal—"

"Don't say it." He pressed his lips to hers, his hands tangling in her curls.

She kissed him back, desperate to imprint the moment in her memory. The boy who wanted her not because she was the princess, but despite it. And then, regret sitting in her stomach like a stone, she pulled back.

"We can't," she whispered.

"I know." The heartache in his voice brought tears to her eyes, and she blinked before they could fall.

"I won't break my promises, and I won't take a consort, no matter how much I might want to betray the enemy I'm marrying."

"I would expect no less of you." His voice was steady, though the pain in it hurt her more than the ache squeezing her own chest.

"If it would be easier on you, I can have you reassigned or—"

"Don't you dare." He met her gaze. "I'm not trusting anyone else to protect you. I can handle what you have to do, but not if it means I can't be by your side."

The band around her chest loosened a little, and she drew an unsteady breath. "Thank you. I don't want to do this without you by my side either."

"I told you, the only way I'm leaving is if you send me away." He leaned his forehead against hers, and they stood in silence, their breath mingling, surrounded by the distant roar of the crashing sea.

"I'm sorry," she whispered.

"I am too." He drew her close, holding her as though he were drowning and she was his salvation. Then he kissed her as the stars slowly spun across the sky above them and the edges of the horizon gradually softened into the hazy gray of dawn.

THIRTY-NINE

CHARIS WOKE THE next morning after only three hours of sleep. Mrs. Sykes was bustling around the room, humming as she prepped Charis's dress, deep purple with glittering metallic thread embroidered into the bodice and sleeves in the patterns of Calera's patron constellations. A subtle message to Vahn that she was and always would be Calera, and no amount of posturing about taking what was his could change that.

This time, she left her hair wild, tumbling down her back in unruly curls. Instead of an updo, she reached for a silver tiara made of two snakes wrapped around sharp, thornlike spikes. The snake's eyes were rubies to match the ruby eyes on her ceremonial sword.

Vahn wasn't the only one who needed to see Charis as an untouchable threat. The traitor who was trying to kill her also needed to understand the kind of enemy Charis could be.

Tal stood by the door watching her as she adjusted the tiara. He smiled, wide and real, when she came toward him. "No one in his right mind would underestimate you."

"Vahn must not be in his right mind, then."

"We'll come up with a plan for him." Tal sounded certain. "I've been paying attention, and I have a few ideas."

"Excellent." She smiled fiercely. "Let's go intimidate my future husband and get some answers about the kind of jewels the Rakuuna might want."

"I do love multitasking."

Breakfast was a fancy affair. The council members were there, with the exception of Lord Thorsby, who'd come down with a bad cold. Charis sat between Vahn and Lady Channing, with Lady Ollen and Lord Everly just across from her.

"Blessed morning, Charis," Vahn said with exquisite courtesy. "I hope you had a restful night."

"Very," she said, sharpening her smile and aiming it at him. She needed information from him before he returned to Montevallo, and now that she'd taken his measure, she was prepared to get it. "Now, shall we discuss your dowry?"

He frowned. "My dowry?"

"Yes. I realize we agreed to a rather obscene number of jewels in the treaty, and of course those will be put to good use rebuilding Calera, a project which I'm sure enjoys your full support now." She raised her brows at him and waited until he nodded. "Wonderful. My question is about the types of jewels your father will be sending."

"The types?" He looked from her to Alaric, who sat at the far end of the table beside the queen. "I . . . does it matter?"

"I think every detail matters, don't you? One wouldn't want to overlook something that might later be important."

He laughed under his breath. "If you say so."

Lady Ollen spoke around a mouthful of sugared oat cakes. "I myself have several unique pieces from Montevallian mines. I'm most anxious to see what else your kingdom has to offer. The value of the jewels sent to repay your kingdom's blood debt will have to be significant."

Lord Everly looked faintly disgusted at both the topic and Vahn in general. Lady Channing said nothing as she took delicate bites of her poached egg.

"Obviously you'll send an assortment of rubies, sapphires, and the like. All fairly . . ." Charis waved a hand in the air as if searching for the right word. "Ordinary, am I right?"

"I suppose you could say that." He took a bite of pumpkin muffin and then reached for his glass of sparkling plumberry juice.

Lady Channing brushed against Charis as she reached for her own glass.

"Well, it just seems rather unremarkable." Charis pretended to stifle a yawn and looked away from him as if he no longer interested her.

"Not all the jewels are ordinary, you know." Vahn puffed out his chest, a glimmer of anger on his face. "We have chryllophire, thorall, serpanicite, and zellorite. You can't find those anywhere else. Not a single kingdom on the sea has them."

"Hmm." She brushed a speck of lint from the tablecloth and reached for her glass. "I suppose I'll find those more exciting once I actually see them."

Chryllophire, thorall, serpanicite, and zellorite. Which of those had Ambassador Shyrn been so desperate for Calera to send to the Rakuuna?

She caught Tal's gaze from his place against the wall to her right, and the spark of pride in his eyes warmed the torch he'd lit in her heart. Quickly she looked to Lady Channing as if that's where her gaze had been the entire time and said, "I do hope no one in your household catches the cold Lord Thorsby now has."

Lady Channing smiled, though her eyes were bright as they slid from Vahn to Charis. "I do hope so as well. It always goes through the staff. Very inconvenient."

"Indeed." Charis spooned up a bite of fluffy winterberry compote. "Have you given any thought to your Sister Moons Festival outfit?"

"Oh, it's already done." Lady Channing gave Charis a sly smile that seemed to say she knew exactly the game the princess was playing and was only too happy to assist. "My household is wearing a white-and-pale-blue theme this year. I must say Merryl outdid herself. Did you know she can work live flowers into a bodice? Of course, she can't add them until the day of the ball, but I promise it will be unforgettable."

"How fascinating!" Lady Ollen leaned over her plate. "Our household will be wearing silver and plum. It's a bit of a departure from our usual shades of blue, but my seamstress convinced me no one else would wear the colors of a twilight sky."

Lord Everly, appearing desperately bored, took a bite of his oat cakes.

"I beg your pardon," Vahn said, his courteous voice clipped with anger. "I don't wish to offend, but you can speak with your friends about dresses whenever you wish. You and I only have a few more minutes to get to know each other."

Charis took another bite of compote and savored it. Then she said slowly, "You were very clear yesterday that your spies have told you all about me, so what else could you possibly want to know?"

"I . . . yes, they have. You have no idea the kind of information I've gathered. But I'm sure you want to get to know *me*. You need to understand the man you're bringing into your bed."

Lady Ollen laughed. "My dear prince, if you understand one man, you understand them all."

Charis looked at Vahn and shrugged as if to say she agreed.

"I see," he said. "Then you are in for some surprises."

Charis took another bite. "I am very rarely surprised." She turned her gaze on Vahn. "Especially when I'm already bored."

He flushed. "You weren't bored with me yesterday."

She smiled, slow and vicious, and gave in to the temptation to return every cruel barb he'd landed yesterday with interest. Leaning close, she said softly, "That's because I hadn't yet had the real thing. Now that I have, I find it hard to be interested in anyone who doesn't measure up."

He fisted his hands and turned to look at Tal as though he wanted to tear him limb from limb. Tal, seemingly unaware of what Charis had said, nevertheless tipped an imaginary hat toward Vahn and then looked only at Charis.

"I grow tired of these games," Vahn hissed.

"Tired already?" Charis pretended to pout. "But we've only just begun."

"Where do you see this ending? With his body at the end of my sword? Is that it? You want to drive me to jealousy?"

Charis laughed. "How tiresome. I see this ending with you minding your tongue and treating me with respect. You walked into my home, into my kingdom, with every intention to be cruel and callous. To manipulate and degrade. If that's how you choose to act, then you can be prepared for the kind of war you will never win. But if you choose to be respectful of my people, my kingdom, and me, you will find me a pleasant, intelligent, compassionate companion who will support your interests as long as they do not cross mine."

He stared at her, and then laughed without cruelty or malice. "You really are something. I'd hoped you'd be a challenge. Stars know, I don't want to be bored. And you are anything but boring."

"I imagine you must have things you want to accomplish as king," Charis said. Lord Everly leaned forward as if anxious to absorb every word.

Vahn met her gaze. "Of course."

"Perhaps you'd like to share that with me so that we can be sure our mutual interests are fully aligned." Charis gave him the smile that always had the nobility scrambling to explain themselves so they could stay in her good graces.

He took his time answering, and when he finally spoke, he sounded thoughtful and sincere. "I admit that I came to this kingdom with a great deal of anger and scorn for you and your people."

Lady Ollen hissed and snatched her glass of plumberry juice as if she needed something to distract her mouth before she told the prince what she really thought.

Charis, however, softened her smile into something more sympathetic. "I've also had a great deal of anger and scorn for your father and your armies."

"With good reason," Lady Ollen managed to mutter around the lip of her glass.

Vahn ignored her. "My people are starving. There are shortages of everything imaginable. I'd happily bring an entire mountain's worth of jewels to Calera if it meant we could immediately access a trade route from a major port."

Charis nodded and decided it would be foolish to assume he didn't already know about the ships sinking. The Montevallian spy network would have informed Alaric of it weeks ago.

Strange that he hadn't brought it up before signing the treaty.

Her brow puckered into a frown, and Vahn said, "Have I said something wrong?"

"You consider yourself well informed about Calera, Arborlay, and me in particular, don't you?" she asked.

"I do." He set his fork down and considered her. "Though I have to admit that our spies' reports about the Willowthorns were not quite as comprehensive as we'd believed."

Lady Channing stirred, her sleeve brushing against Charis's, though she said nothing.

"But surely you received reports about trade ships sinking." She watched him carefully.

Now it was his turn to frown. "Of course."

"And that doesn't worry you?" Her voice sharpened. "Your singular goal as king of Calera is to open a sea route for Montevallo's trade, and you aren't at all concerned that those ships will sink when they leave the harbor just like everything else in the past two months?"

He smiled. "My dear Charis, I've just said I'd be willing to pay a mountain's worth of jewels if it means saving my people. Our reports say Rullenvor and the Rakuuna are behind the sinkings and simply want payment in jewels to become allies instead of enemies. Father and I determined before we even set foot in Calera that it was a price we are willing to pay."

Charis blinked. He said it so casually. As if allowing both Rullenvor and the Rakuuna to have power over his people was an easy decision to make.

Maybe it was. If the alternative was starvation and the collapse of their civilization, giving some of their mountains' bounty to save their people wouldn't seem all that difficult.

And if he and Alaric were willing to pay off the Rakuuna, that meant Calera was also free. Trade would resume. Shortages would ease. And her decision to marry the enemy prince truly would save her people.

"In fact"—Vahn patted his lips with his napkin—"I'm happy to send a message to the attacking fleet today and begin negotiations on their price."

"Be sure to tell them not to sink another ship from this moment on," Lord Everly warned. "It's best to force them to put up a show of good faith right from the outset."

Vahn tilted his head toward Lord Everly. "What was your name again?"

"Lord Blaise Everly, third cousin to the queen, esteemed member of the royal council for fifteen years." He puffed up, a light of challenge in his eyes.

"Lord Everly, if you ever again presume to give me advice before I've asked for it, it will go badly for you." Vahn said it simply, as though it was just a statement of fact.

Charis believed his words completely.

She hardly appreciated being caught between instinctive protectiveness toward a member of the council and grudging appreciation for the way Vahn had put dour, presumptuous Lord Everly so neatly in his place.

When the meal was finished and the queen rose at the head of the table, the rest of the attendees got to their feet and bowed until she'd left the room.

"I'll send the message by palloren before Father and I leave for home," Vahn said quietly beside her. "And I suggest you and I begin corresponding regularly so that we can get to know each other and align our mutual interests." He shot a distinctly unfriendly look at Tal, but his smile seemed genuine when he turned back to Charis. Bowing, he said, "I look forward to sparring with you again in the spring, Your Highness."

She inclined her head graciously. Not a bow, but a token of respect for his future rank in Calera. "Until then."

Turning, she left the room, Tal at her side.

"What did you say to Vahn to make him so mad at me?" he asked softly as they moved through the hall.

"I told him it was hard to be interested in him when I'd had the real thing last night."

Tal choked on a laugh. "You're my favorite person. You know that, right?"

She smiled.

"He seemed to have a lot to say today."

"He did." She glanced at Tal as they entered the corridor that led to her private office. "Including that he is willing to pay the Rakuuna jewels to turn them from enemies to allies. He's sending a message to that effect to the armada today."

"That should solve the problem at sea." Tal sounded carefully neutral, and Charis couldn't blame him. It was hard to admit that the cruel, callous Vahn of yesterday had actually volunteered to do something that would save both his people and hers.

"It should. Which just leaves us with a traitor to catch."

"And kill," he said. "Or, at the very least, maim."

"You sound like Holland."

He gave her a crooked little smile. "I'll take that as a compliment."

FORTY

"Is it strange that I'm looking forward to celebrating the Sister Moons Festival?" Charis asked. "I know we still have to find the traitor, and that the odious Vahn Penbyrn will be back in the spring, but right now"—she wiggled in her vanity chair, and Tal rolled his eyes as the hair he'd been trying to style slid free—"the war is over, Montevallo's shipment of jewels should stop the ship sinkings, and we have all winter to be together. I'm happy."

He met her gaze and smiled. "I am too. Who cares if it's temporary?"

A shadow crossed his face, and he looked at her hair again. She raised a hand and wrapped it around his. "All right, it's my turn to invite my handsome secret keeper to tell me what's eating away at his thoughts."

He spun another curl into a rose above Charis's left ear and pinned it into place. "It's . . . complicated."

"What part of our lives these past few months has been uncomplicated?"

"My feelings for you." Another curl was spun into a rose. "Some days they're the only thing I'm sure of." He looked at her. "I had absolutely no intention of falling in love with you."

"Well, I can be pretty irresistible."

"If by irresistible, we mean irritating, fierce, unrelenting, uncompromising, challenging, compassionate, intelligent, and not quite as good at the seven rathmas as me, then yes. You're irresistible." He pressed a kiss to the crown of her head, but the shadow was still in his eyes.

The annual Sister Moons feast was celebrated across Calera to usher out the old year and bring in the new. Dances were held in the streets, merchants sold roasted nuts, spiced pastries, and cups of piping hot cider from tables on street corners, and one noble family in each city hosted a ball. This year was the Farragins' turn to host, and Nalani had been talking about it since their name was drawn at the end of last year's feast.

"You still look sad," Charis said.

He fixed a drooping rose, and then said quietly, "What do you do if you know something is coming, something unavoidable, and there's nothing you can do to change it? Do you confront it early in hopes that somehow ripping the bandage off will start the healing process? Or do you wait until the last possible second, right before disaster strikes, and hope for the best?"

She set down the bracelet she was fiddling with. "Are we talking about my wedding?"

He kept looking at her hair. "Do you ever wish you could be someone else? Just for a night?" The raw pain in his voice brought tears to her eyes.

"Someone who isn't bound by duty and by promises that put others first at the expense of your own heart?" she asked.

He lifted his head. "Yes."

"Yes," Charis whispered.

He adjusted one more hairpin and then let his hands come to rest on her shoulders. When he met her gaze again, the shadow in his eyes was gone. "This isn't the right night to overthink things. You're happy. I get to go to a ball with my favorite person in the world. Life is good right now, and we should savor that."

Charis stood slowly, her eyes still on him. "You can talk to me about how you feel, Tal. I know I'm not the only one who needs to figure out how to live with a very complicated situation."

"I will after we enjoy tonight." He stepped close to drape her fur cloak around her bare shoulders. "I promise. Now, here's the list of items submitted to the guards' station today by various members of the nobility. See anyone you want to show favor to by wearing their gift?" He handed her a sheet of paper.

She glanced over the list, calculating the benefits of showing favor to each person listed. There were sixteen gifts on the page with the name of the benefactor beside each item. It wouldn't hurt to wear the bracelet offered by the Severins, or the lacy scrap of a shawl left by Lady Merryfin. A show of support for the north on the heels of a peaceful end to the war would remind both the battle-worn northern nobility and those who'd tried to annex the north for the sake of peace that the Willowthorns kept their word to all.

Of course, if she slighted Lady Whitecross's offer of a pendant, there was the issue of complicating the message sent to the council members. Still, no one else from the council had sent gifts, so she could simply let Lady Whitecross know her pendant would be worn at Charis's next social engagement.

She ran her finger down the list of items one last time, as

something—some vague memory that felt important—itched in the back of her mind.

Show of support to the north? No, that wasn't it.

"Are you ready?" Tal asked.

Shaking her head, she kept staring at the list. Choosing with care so that she didn't offend a council member?

Not quite, though that felt closer to the truth.

"What's wrong?" Tal sounded concerned.

She set the list down, her mind racing. "Where are the papers?"

"What papers?"

"The ones I had the other night, before Vahn's visit. From the guards' station. I left them on the side table by the fireplace."

He moved to her desk. "I put them here for safekeeping."

She followed him and scooped up the list of visitors who'd come to the guards' station at the entrance of her wing to leave a gift the night of the ambassadors' ball. The night someone had snuck an assassin into the ladies' parlor and a spy into her own chambers.

> *Milla*
> *Fada*
> *Luther*
> *Lady Ollen*
> *Lord Westing*
> *Lord and Lady Rynce*
> *Lady Silving*
> *Lord and Lady Mefferd*

She frowned, running her finger over the list again. There were fourteen names. "Something's off about this."

He peered over her shoulder. "A visitor log?"

"From the night of the ambassadors' ball. These are the people who entered my wing that evening and could have ostensibly helped the spy hide in my chambers." She opened a drawer. "Mother and I studied this already, of course, but that was right after Milla, and I . . . my focus wasn't very sharp."

"Understandable." He watched as she pulled out another sheet of paper filled with Milla's looping scrawl.

"Here's the list of gifts that were left for me that night."

She placed the two lists side by side and slowly moved a finger down each. Her heart kicked hard, and fury burned within her. "Do you see what I see?"

His voice was as unforgiving as the stone floor beneath them. "Lady Channing left a gift, but her name isn't on the log."

"Which means she didn't check in at the guards' station but used the staff stairs to get into my chambers," Charis said. "But she's been free to move about the palace for years. It could be an innocent mistake."

"It could be," Tal said slowly, his eyes on hers. "But she assumed the queen was dead the morning after the assassination attempt. You took her at her word that she'd overheard a conversation, but what if she assumed that because she's the one who smuggled in the assassin?"

Charis nodded as the pieces fell into place, lighting a spark of fury in her heart. "She's the one who tried to broker a deal with Rullenvor and the Rakuuna. She told me we had to do whatever it took to end the war. The second assassination attempt—the archer—that happened the day after I refused to take her advice and make a deal with Ambassador Shyrn."

"There's too much here to be coincidence. Especially when, as you said, she's had free run of the palace. She must have hid the spy in your chambers and then put a gift into your pile to have an excuse for being here if she got caught. She could easily have shown the assassin which room would be used as the ladies' parlor that evening, too." Tal met her gaze, and the fury in his eyes was a match for her own. "Say the word, and I will go haul her in front of the queen tonight."

Charis tapped her fingers on the lists, her mind racing. "It's close to proof, but it isn't absolute. There's a possibility the guards simply neglected to write her name down. We'll confront her at the ball."

"Then let's get going."

The ball was a sumptuous affair. White shryenthian blooms dipped in silver and bound by elegant black ribbons graced the tables that lined the edges of the ballroom. People in glittering clothes the color of moonlight, midnight, or the star-swept sea danced, laughed, and piled their plates with roasted fish, sugared apples, and buttery pumpkin rolls. Every woman wore a pair of glittering sapphires set in silver to represent the sister moons, and every man had sapphire cuff links. There were large vases in pale blue surrounded by quills, and strips of creamy paper set on tables near the ballroom entrance for people to write a wish they hoped the sister moons would grant before the following year's festival.

Charis did her part. Greeted her hosts. Laughed with her friends. Kept an eye out for Lady Channing, who was unusually late. And gave her first dance to Lord Severin to make sure her support for the north was clear.

But beneath it all, Tal's words echoed.

Do you ever wish you could be someone else?

A princess didn't get to choose love over duty. The truth of that was carved into her very bones.

But.

Her heart didn't care what was written on her bones. Her heart wanted, just for tonight, to be lit on fire and consumed. If she had to live in the ashes of it for the rest of her life, at least the burning would've been her choice. Not for her people. Not for her mother.

For her.

She should have told Tal she loved him. He'd said it to her a hundred times by now, and he never expected anything in return. The truth wouldn't heal the pain that was coming for them, but he deserved to hear it.

She curtsied to her ninth dance partner of the evening and excused herself to freshen up. Giving Nalani a little wave when her friend sent her a worried look, she moved off the dance floor and took a small cup of cider from the closest beverage table.

Her guards were stationed throughout the home. Reuben had insisted that every guard be in attendance tonight, even her day shift. Two at the ballroom's entrance. Two near the buffet. Another walking the grounds while still another walked the house, consistently hunting for threats. And of course Tal, always at the fringes, watching his princess to make sure she stayed safe.

She finished the cider and headed for a side hallway. Vellis turned to follow, and Charis said, "Notify me when Lady Channing arrives." Then she entered the first room she found, with Tal on her heels, and let the door shut behind her.

They were in the Farragins' main library. Three walls held floor-to-ceiling bookshelves, filled with leather-bound books and rolls of parchment. The fourth wall held seven pieces of artwork in heavy golden frames. The pictures were as tall as Charis herself, each depicting a seminal moment in Caleran history.

Tal and Charis stared at each other, the ticking of the library's enormous clock and the muted sound of the music from the dance floor filling the silence.

He closed the distance between them. "Could we pretend for a moment?"

"Pretend what?"

"To be just a girl and a boy who care about each other and want to dance at a party. No complications. No duty."

His eyes lingered on her, darkening with something that sent her pulse beating against her skin like a caged bird. "Tonight, I decided that we have no tomorrows. No guarantees. There is only who we are right now, right here. And who I am is a boy who wants to dance with you."

Hope was a frail, impossible thing that refused to let Charis rest.

There was no path forward without duty. No alternative to the road she'd set her feet on when she'd signed that treaty.

But her heart refused to care. She wanted, just for tonight, to be an ordinary girl dancing with the boy she loved.

She took his offered hand, and he swept her into his arms. They swayed and spun to the ticking of the clock and the distant lilt of music they could barely hear. She laughed as he dipped her low and then brought her up against his chest, her hand sheltered in his as the music faded.

Before he could release her, she said, "I love you, Tal."

"Charis," he whispered.

"I don't want to regret not telling you the truth. I don't want to waste a single moment of the time we have left together."

This was it. No tomorrows. No guarantees. Only this one moment.

She pressed her lips to his.

He made a noise in the back of his throat and dragged her closer, sliding his hands up her back. She dug her fingers into his shoulders and let the heat that swirled through her light her on fire.

It was agony. It was magic. It was a lifetime of yearning, of wishes she'd never dared voice, and she couldn't bear to stop.

She kissed him until the feeling of his lips was in her blood, until the taste of him was a secret tucked away in the corner of her heart. Until she could no longer tell where she ended and he began.

He broke away, his breathing ragged. "Charis, I have something to tell you."

"What is it?" She was a breath away from his lips, and everything within her ached to close the distance between them and never let him go.

There was a sharp knock at the door, and then Vellis entered. "Your Highness, Lady Channing has arrived."

FORTY-ONE

CHARIS PULLED AWAY from Tal, all thoughts of romance disappearing as she looked to Vellis.

"Should I send her to you?" Vellis asked. If she thought it strange to walk in on the princess embracing her bodyguard, her face betrayed nothing.

Charis considered the idea of speaking with Lady Channing privately. It would maintain the woman's reputation should this turn out to be an innocent misunderstanding. But if indeed Lady Channing was the traitor, there was at least one other person who needed to be present for the conversation, and Charis could hardly summon the queen away from the most important festival of the year to accuse her friend of treason unless she was absolutely sure.

No, it was better to issue an invitation rather than a summons. It was hardly out of the ordinary for Lady Channing to be asked to spend time with the royal family during a social engagement, though enjoying a private conversation at the buffet table was a far cry from being welcomed onto the royal platform.

"Please invite Lady Channing to join the royal family on the ballroom dais. Thank you, Vellis." A hard, bold light burned in Charis as she considered what she'd say to Lady Channing. In moments, the nightmare that had started the night of the ambassadors' ball could be finished. Charis had found a way to end the war, to use the enemy prince to stop the threat toward Calera's ships, and now if she exposed the traitor who'd tried to destroy the Willowthorns, the host of nearly insurmountable obstacles that had plagued Charis would be resolved.

As the woman left, Charis turned to Tal. "I know we aren't finished with our conversation, but—"

"It can wait." His eyes were bright with the kind of intensity that never failed to flush her skin with heat. "Let's go catch a traitor."

Charis found Mother seated in the Farragins' most comfortable chair on a dais erected in the center of the eastern wall just for this occasion. She looked resplendent in a gown the color of the midnight sea. Tiny diamonds were sewn into the fabric to mimic the shine of starlight, and she wore a silver crown with glowing sapphires worked into the filigree to represent the blue light of the sister moons.

Tal stuck close to Charis, his gaze watchful as they ascended the stairs and greeted the queen. Reuben and Elsbet took up their stations at the base of the stairs, while Vellis and Gaylle hovered nearby, eyes scraping over the crowd of dancers who whirled around the floor to the lively tune the orchestra was playing.

"Your Majesty." Charis bowed. A quick glance showed Lady Channing approaching the dais, a small smile on her face as she found the princess's gaze.

"You've invited a guest onto the platform?" Mother assessed Charis with a swift look.

"I thought we could have a conversation."

Mother's cold, remote expression remained intact, but her chin lifted. It was one thing to spend time talking with a member of the nobility during a social event. It was another to invite someone onto the dais. That kind of preferential treatment would be torn apart in drawing rooms across the city for weeks.

"I trust you have a good reason for this."

"I believe I do." Charis turned as Lady Channing mounted the steps and moved toward them.

"Your Majesty. Your Highness." Lady Channing bowed to each in turn. "I'm most honored to be invited onto the dais."

"The honor is ours," the queen said. "You were most helpful to my daughter while I was unwell."

Lady Channing folded her hands at her waist and smiled. "I was happy to be of service."

"Truly." Charis turned to Lady Channing. "You helped me form a plan the day after Mother took ill. And you were instrumental in our discussions with Rullenvor's ambassador."

Something flitted across Lady Channing's calm expression and was gone in a blink. "Terrible news about the ambassador's untimely death. Quite shocking."

"He certainly didn't turn out to be who we thought he was," Charis agreed. "And I'm sure you join us in counting us fortunate to have turned down his offer now that we understand the Rakuuna themselves are behind the sinking of the ships."

Lady Channing swallowed. "I hadn't heard that news yet, Your Highness. I apologize that I didn't realize early on the duplicitous nature of Ambassador Shyrn."

"We don't blame you." The queen smoothed her skirt and glanced around the ballroom.

"Of course not," Charis soothed. "You initiated discussions with him in good faith and took him at his word. Even the savviest politician can be taken in by a masterful liar."

Lady Channing held herself perfectly still as she too watched the dancers.

"It's my turn to apologize," Charis said. Mother and Lady Channing turned to look at her in perfect unison. "I meant to show favor to you tonight by wearing that lovely embroidered scarf you gave me, but sadly it has been misplaced."

"The scarf?" Lady Channing sounded puzzled.

"Yes. The one you left for me the night of the ambassadors' ball. It would have looked beautiful with this dress, don't you think?"

"I . . . yes, I suppose it would have."

Mother straightened in her chair, an almost imperceptible move, but Charis knew the queen was a predator sensing her prey's hiding place.

"I hope you'll forgive me." Charis smiled warmly at Lady Channing. "There was so much chaos in my chambers that night."

"There is nothing to forgive." Lady Channing matched Charis's smile. "The queen's unexpected . . . illness was quite upsetting."

"Indeed." Charis's smile sharpened. "Our security teams have conducted a thorough investigation of that evening's events. They wanted to bring you in to answer questions, but I wouldn't hear of it."

Lady Channing froze, her folded hands in a white-knuckled grip. "Questions, Your Highness?"

"Just a small misunderstanding, I'm sure." Charis waved a hand as if to emphasize how trivial a matter it was. "In fact, if you wanted to clear it up right now, we could consider the matter closed."

She waited, watching Lady Channing expectantly. Innocent or guilty, she'd rush to assure them she'd be happy to help. But guilty people always had a plan. A rehearsed response for any contingency. They took the offensive, while innocent people waited to be led.

The orchestra moved into a soft, solemn number, and the vibrant crowd of dancers gently swayed and spun to the rhythm. Lady Channing spread her hands wide as if to show she had nothing to hide.

"Of course, Your Highness. In fact, I may know what this is about."

Beside Charis, the queen drew in a deep breath.

"You'll recall that I'd just returned from my goodwill trip to the northern kingdoms. I was quite exhausted." Lady Channing gave a little laugh, and Charis inclined her head as though in understanding. "I was running a bit late for the ball, and after all the groundwork I'd done to shore up our relationships with our allies, I didn't want to be discourteous by arriving late."

"Very sensible of you," Charis agreed.

"I'm glad you agree." Lady Channing glanced at Tal, who stood just behind Charis's right shoulder, where he could pivot to be in front of the princess in an instant. "There was a bit of a line of people at your guards' station waiting to drop off gifts, and I really didn't want to spare the time when it would make me tardy. I used the staff stairs to simply drop the scarf off in your chambers with a little note that it was from me and thought I would check in with the guards' station later that night. Unfortunately, in my exhaustion, I forgot to do so."

"Well, that clears it up." Charis laughed a little, though she watched Lady Channing closely. "You can't imagine how relieved I am that you weren't part of the chaos in my chambers that evening. I told my security team that of course you couldn't be part of it."

Lady Channing laughed too. "The very idea is preposterous. Why would I need a spy in your chambers when I could simply schedule a meeting to discuss with you anything I felt the council needed to know?"

Tal shifted a hairsbreadth closer to Charis as the princess's chin rose. With exquisitely cold precision, she asked, "How did you know there was a spy in my chambers?"

The woman froze for an instant, her eyes darting between Charis and the queen, and then she said, "I . . . we already discussed this. I overheard palace staff talking, and—"

"You told me they were discussing the assassination attempt against the queen." The rage in Charis's heart flickered and burned. "Not once did we discuss a spy in my chambers."

"That's . . . perhaps I failed to mention it at the time, but—"

"Enough." The queen's voice cut through Lady Channing's like a sword. She rose, her icy blue eyes finding her friend's.

"Charis, you must understand." Lady Channing reached for the princess.

"No." Tal stepped between them, his sword out, a dangerous gleam in his eyes. Lady Channing staggered back a step.

Beyond the dais, the dancers closest to the stage stumbled to a stop, staring at the drama unfolding before them. The understanding that something was happening spread through the ballroom in waves until every face was turned to the platform as the music stuttered into silence.

"You must understand, my dear, I have the utmost respect for you. The spy was only there to gather information from your private correspondence in case I needed it to help influence you on the correct path once you took the throne. Don't you see? Only Letha had to die."

She moved toward Charis again, as if by taking the princess's hands in her own, all would be forgiven.

"Stop," Tal snarled from in front of Charis. "One more step and I promise I will make sure your death hurts. One wound for every time you nearly killed her. I'll choose places that bleed out long and slow."

"Your loyalty is appreciated, Tal," Mother said, fury burning in her voice. "But I will personally drive a sword through this traitor's heart."

"No, no." Lady Channing waved her hands. "Charis, please understand. Letha was the problem. We would've been able to end this war a decade ago if she'd had the stomach to do what needed to be done. No one else needed to die! Just the people who'd already been taken captive, and while that's unfortunate, it's sometimes the price of war."

"But you didn't keep trying to remove the queen." Charis's voice rang out in the silence. "You tried to kill me. I thought the first attempt was King Alaric reacting to our response to the Irridusk invasion, but it wasn't. Just before I received news of the successful destruction of Montevallo's central army outpost, you showed up in my office with Ambassador Shyrn and a proposal to accept help from Rullenvor and the Rakuuna."

A murmur of shock spread throughout the crowd. Charis ignored them.

"You strongly advised me to put our kingdom in the debt of two others, one of which has been sinking our ships to try to force our compliance."

"It was a good offer!" Lady Channing looked wildly from Charis to the crowd and back again. "I didn't know the Rakuuna were behind the ships sinking. I was simply trying to end the war. I was doing what was best for Calera."

"And when I said I didn't want us in their debt, when I refused to accept their offer, you tried to have me killed."

"Because you wouldn't listen to reason! Just like your mother, always thinking the Willowthorns, with your absurd loyalty to the north above the interests of the rest of your subjects, know best. I could have ended the war immediately. Kept our ships from sinking. Shored up alliances with two powerful kingdoms. I could have been queen!"

Her voice rang out, echoing across the ballroom as Mother stepped past Charis.

"So that's the price of your treachery. Rullenvor promised you the throne if only you'd subjugate us to them, and you ate it up."

Lady Channing took another step back. "I knew what Calera needed, and you were too stubborn to do what was necessary. I had hopes for Charis, but she turned out to be just like you."

"On your knees." The queen's voice filled the ballroom.

When Lady Channing hesitated, looking out at the crowd as though she expected them to rush to her rescue, Tal took two steps forward, smacked the flat of his sword against the back of her legs, and knocked her to her knees.

"You will never be queen." Mother accepted a sword from her guard and raised it above Lady Channing. "You won't even be a foot-note in Caleran history. But don't worry. By tomorrow morning, you won't be alive to mourn the loss."

The crowd drew in a collective gasp as the blade flashed through the air. Lady Channing cried out as the queen drove the sword into her chest, and then she crumpled. Blood poured from the wound, soaking the pale blue flowers Merryl had painstakingly stitched into the bodice of Lady Channing's gown.

"Justice has been served." The queen's voice rang out. "The war is over, our ships will soon be protected, and the traitor in our midst has been vanquished. Let us celebrate!"

The crowd murmured as the orchestra conductor tapped his baton and then plunged his musicians headfirst into a cheerful tune that whirled through the ballroom, light and airy. Soon, couples were dancing, laughter was spilling out of the groups that gathered along the edges of the dance floor, and even those who couldn't seem to stop staring at the body on the dais had a look of excitement rather than fear on their faces.

Charis turned toward Tal as the queen summoned a trio of guards to remove Lady Channing's body from the Farragin house.

"It's over." Two simple little words, but the relief that unfurled within her threatened to bring her to her knees.

"You're safe." Tal sounded as relieved as she felt.

Charis glanced at the dance floor and then at the corridor that led to the library. It would be unseemly to take another break from the crowd so soon after her last break. Especially in light of Lady Channing's death. She had a duty to the queen and to the Farragins to help lead the celebration on the dance floor. It would be unthinkable to shirk it, and yet . . . and yet all she wanted to do was return to the library and kiss Tal.

"Want to dance?" Tal asked quietly, his voice for her ears alone.

"Yes." She breathed the word, full of longing.

They were silent for a moment as the song shifted to something slow and beautiful. And then Tal said softly, "Put me down for your last dance of the evening, Your Highness."

Warmth flooded her cheeks, and she bit her lip to keep from smiling while the eyes of the kingdom were on her. "I'll have to check my dance card and see if I can fit you in."

He made a noise that sounded as though he'd smothered a laugh, and she turned away from the crowd to meet his gaze. The warmth within her grew bold and dangerous at the glint in his eyes, and she whispered, "I think my dance card for this particular event is completely full."

"How unfortunate."

It was impossible not to smile. "Indeed."

"Whatever shall we do?" He raised a brow.

"I was thinking of visiting the bluff later tonight."

He sucked in a little breath, his eyes darkening. "I suppose I'll have to come along."

"I suppose you will." The dangerous heat in her veins sparkled as she looked at him.

"Time to go do your duty," he said softly. "Before I abandon all common sense and kiss you in front of everyone."

"You wouldn't dare."

He grinned. "I dare a great many things, Your Highness."

She was absolutely looking forward to standing on the bluff with him and seeing what exactly he dared to do, but first, she had a duty to perform. The longer she stood on this dais with him, the more she risked revealing her true feelings to the kingdom. Turning, she began moving toward the stairs, Tal a step behind, but then the doors to the ballroom crashed open, and someone started to scream.

FORTY-TWO

CHARIS WHIPPED AROUND to face the entrance to the ballroom as a haunting cry shredded the air. It rose in pitch until her teeth ached and then tapered off into a series of rapid clicks, like bones rattling.

Horror blossomed, slick and cold, as a pearly white hand with unnaturally long fingers wrapped around the doorframe.

Rakuuna. On land. Where everything Charis had ever learned about them said they'd never go.

Tal grabbed her arm and anchored her to his side as those at the edge of the ballroom began screaming.

Tall, slender creatures with shimmering silver-blue scales, long white hair, and black eyes moved into the room with impossible speed. Their long webbed fingers snatched at people, tearing limbs and spraying blood onto the silvery shryenthian blooms, while their mouths opened, revealing rows of sharp fangs.

One of them snatched Lord Comferoy as he ran toward the exit, leaped onto his back like a mountain cat, and sank their fangs into his neck. He stumbled, went down on his knees, and hit the floor, where he twitched once and then lay still.

"To the queen!" a guard yelled, and a blur of uniformed staff converged on the dais. Charis went for her sword, but Reuben reached her, grabbing her other arm and putting his body between hers and the Rakuuna, who were racing for the dais with terrifying speed.

"Kill them!" The queen's voice was a whiplash of fury.

The first wave of guards raised their weapons and took a fighting stance, but the Rakuuna simply smashed through them, tearing bodies and sending weapons skittering across the floor.

Another five guards stood at the base of the platform, their eyes wild as they raised their weapons.

"Remove the royal family!" Reuben shouted.

Mother's security team closed around her and began moving her toward the left-hand stairs. Charis's team moved her toward the right.

Charis could barely swallow past the fear clogging her throat as she drew the daggers she wore on her wrists. Where was Mother? Holland? Nalani? The ballroom was utter chaos, and as Tal, Reuben, and Elsbet herded her down the stairs, she craned her neck to look for those she loved.

"We can't fight them," Tal said in a voice that shook. "Look at them! We have to know their weakness to even have a chance. Charis. *Charis!* We have to run."

Two more Rakuuna sidled up the sides of the ballroom wall closest to the queen, their webbed hands and feet clinging to the wall as though they were spiders.

Mother's security team raised their weapons as the Rakuuna sprang from the wall straight at the queen.

Charis couldn't breathe.

Couldn't look away as she strained against Tal's hold on her. She stumbled over someone lying in a pool of blood but didn't look down.

Mother was fine. She had to be. Nothing was strong enough to kill Queen Letha.

"Get her out of here!" Reuben barked as he shoved Tal and Charis toward the garden exit.

Mother and her guards collapsed beneath their attackers.

"Mother!" Charis wailed, her voice shredding through the fear that choked her.

More Rakuuna on the walls by the last place Charis had seen Mother cocked their heads, their black eyes finding Charis's across the bloody chaos that spread across the ballroom. One of the Rakuuna, a gaunt creature with long white braids, opened his mouth and let out the unearthly, high-pitched cry Charis had first heard on the water months ago. People fell to their knees, clutching their heads, and the cry trailed off into clicks and rattles. Every Rakuuna in the ballroom froze, swiveled their heads, and locked eyes with Charis.

"Run!" Tal's voice snapped her into action as behind them, the Rakuuna leaped forward, their long limbs eating up the space between them and the princess like it was nothing.

She sprinted for the garden exit, her guards surrounding her. Someone close by screamed, a thin wail of agony that sliced into Charis.

Her people were dying. *Mother* might be dying. And Charis was running because she had no way to fight the Rakuuna. No way to save herself, much less anyone else. Her heart burned with fury while tears poured down her face.

Holland, Nalani, and Lady Delaire were in the garden, bruised and battered but alive. As her guards pushed her into the nearest available carriage, Charis yelled, "Holland, get everyone you can to the fishing port. Hide!" Immediately, he grabbed Nalani and Delaire and disappeared into the depths of the garden.

It was the only place she could think of that might be safe. The Rakuuna had left their smuggler's ship alone, and surely they had more important things to do than worry about searching vessels at a tiny fishing dock.

Rakuuna swarmed out of the house. Several charged for the carriage but shied away when the horses screamed and kicked at them. The groomsman whipped the horses, and they sped away from the Farragin house. Vellis and Reuben were inside the carriage with Tal and Charis. The other guards were up with the coachman or hanging on for dear life as they balanced on the step.

"To the fishing dock?" Reuben asked, frowning as though trying to make sense of the directions she'd yelled to Holland.

"To the palace first," she said firmly, wiping at her tears. "Father is there, and there are other staff members who stayed home from the festival as well. We must get there before the Rakuuna."

Reuben shouted instructions to the coachman, while Tal kept one hand on Charis and the other on his sword.

Charis watched in gut-wrenching horror as the crowded streets streamed by her carriage window. Rakuuna clung to the sides of buildings, leaped from rooftops, and tore through anyone they could reach. People ran, screaming and bleeding, clutching children and loved ones as they fought to find safety.

The screams faded as they turned onto the long, winding drive that led to the palace. Charis's heart was thunder in her ears, and her breathing came in harsh gasps.

She didn't know the Rakuuna's weakness. She didn't know why they'd invaded when Vahn had already sent them a message promising them the jewels they wanted. And she didn't have time to figure it out. She needed out of this dress, and she needed weapons. Then she could get Father and the rest of her staff to the dock, board the smuggler's ship, and make a plan.

When they reached the palace, it was eerily quiet.

Charis's hands shook as she watched the long drive for a moment. Her mother was a force of nature. Practically indestructible. Any minute now, her carriage would come thundering up the drive, and she'd exit, already snapping orders, organizing a defense, and dealing with the crisis.

The road remained empty.

"Did anyone see if the queen made it out?" Tal asked.

"The queen has fallen," Reuben said softly.

"Your Highness," Vellis said firmly, "we need to get you inside and lock the palace."

Charis drew in a breath and forced herself to shove the horror away. Her people needed leading. There would be time to fall apart later. "You're right. Let's—"

A flash of movement caught Charis's eye, and she whipped around to see a long, scale-covered creature leave the row of hedges that lined the drive and begin running toward the palace.

"Inside!" Elsbet shouted. A guard screamed as the Rakuuna reached her, pounced, and tore out her throat.

Charis whirled and ran. Dimly, she registered the sound of a guard slamming the door behind her and sliding the bolts into place, but she didn't slow. Tal kept pace beside her. They had to get weapons. Get her father and any staff who'd remained behind instead of going to the festival. And then get to the ship and make a plan for their safety. For her city's safety.

Taking the stairs two at a time, she and Tal sprinted into her chambers. She couldn't go back to the Farragin house for her mother or any of the rest of her people. There were too many Rakuuna. The knowledge sank into her, slick with despair, and she fought it.

She had to do her best to make sure those who were in the palace stayed alive.

"They're afraid of horses," she yelled to Tal as she tore her dress off and grabbed her sailing clothes instead. "If we can get to the stables, we could be safe until we get everyone ready to go to the dock."

He ran from his room, still buttoning his shirt. "The armory is beside the stables. We'll have weapons, too."

"But no food."

They stared at each other for a blink.

"We'll figure out the food issue once we aren't in danger of being torn limb from limb," he said.

She was pulling on her boots when an idea struck. "The ships!"

"What ships?" He was lacing his boots too.

"Those ships with the green lights. They must have come into the harbor. Or be just outside it." She grabbed her sword and strapped it on. "If most of the Rakuuna are on land, the ships might be vulnerable."

"You're saying we burn them?" He snatched his coat and sword.

"All but the one we take." She strapped her daggers to her wrists and turned toward the door. "We use the boat to get us close enough to board one. Then we use that one to burn down everything else. They'd be stranded here, and we'd have their home away from home."

"What better way to learn their secrets?" He reached for her hand as a scream echoed. "They're inside the palace! Let's get everyone to the stables. We'll plan our way to the docks from there."

She reached up and kissed him. Hard. "Don't die."

"You don't die either. Ready?" He hefted his sword.

"Ready."

FORTY-THREE

THEY WRENCHED OPEN her bedroom door and found pandemonium in the hall.

A Rakuuna clung to the wall, halfway up, her head turning at an impossible angle to follow Tal and Charis as they ran into the fray. The creature wailed, the cry rising and rising until the humans dropped to their knees, clutching their ears.

Answering wails echoed from the stairs below.

"That's not good," Tal said. "Everybody to the servants' stairs. Go!"

Vellis, Reuben, and a tiny chambermaid named Polly ran, leaving three other guards bleeding out in the hallway.

Charis and Tal backed toward the stairs, but the Rakuuna didn't attack. Instead, she crept along the wall above them, her black eyes following their every move while her tongue made rapid clicking noises.

"She's telling the others about us," Charis whispered.

"Why doesn't she attack?" Tal asked.

They reached the stairwell and found Reuben waiting for them. The others were already halfway down.

"Maybe they won't attack me because they think they need the royal family alive?" Charis said.

"Can't be or they wouldn't have killed your mother." Reuben shoved her toward the stairs and kept his sword out, his eyes on the approaching creature.

Charis locked eyes with Tal. "Father!"

Whirling, she sprinted down the stairs, burst into the servants' corridor, and ran for the east wing.

"Look out!" Tal yelled as she skidded around a corner and nearly crashed into another Rakuuna.

She ducked, flowing naturally into the seven rathmas, her feet taking her just out of reach as the monster slashed at her with his unnaturally long, talon-tipped fingers.

"Go!" Reuben yelled as he came up behind them. "Get to the king!"

Most of the palace was deserted—the staff had been given the night off for the festival—but they found the butler, four maids, and a page still alive on their way to the east wing. Yelling at them to follow her, Charis sprinted for her father's chambers, her boots slapping against the stone corridor that led to his rooms.

He was going to be all right. He was going to be all right. *Please* let him be all right.

His door hung askew.

She slammed into the doorframe and launched herself into his chambers. "Father! Ilsa!"

The sitting room was empty. His sofa was torn to pieces and a lamp lay shattered.

Panic hit, stealing her breath, seizing her chest.

"Father!" She leaped over the broken pieces and ran into his bedroom.

The dresser he'd received as a gift from the queen of Solvang lay on its side, an enormous hole smashed into its lacquered wood. The covers were torn off the bed, and one of his heavy bedposts had snapped in two and lay across the mattress like a broken ship mast.

"Where is he?" She scrambled over the dresser, her hands shaking, her heart aching, desperation clawing at her. "Father!"

She turned to his bath chamber, but it was perfectly intact. Perfectly empty.

Turning, she raced back into his bedroom as Tal shoved the dresser aside and ran toward the bank of windows on the opposite side of the bed. When he jerked to a halt, his entire body vibrating as though he'd been struck, the desperation that had been clawing at Charis seized her throat.

She ran, every step an eternity, every second an infinity.

"Charis," Tal whispered, and the grief in his voice was her undoing.

She made it past the bed, past the cheerful yellow-and-gray rug Ilsa had made during long winter nights three years ago, past Tal frozen in place, and then stopped.

Father lay crumpled on the floor, his eyes staring sightlessly at the wall, Ilsa's broken body an arm span away from his.

Charis made a noise like a wounded animal and rushed forward. "Father? Father, look at me." She dropped to her knees beside him and put shaking hands to his cheeks. Blood dripped from a wound in his neck in a steady stream.

"You'll be all right." She snatched a torn sheet and pressed it to his neck. "See? It's all right. Everything is going to be all right." Her voice broke over the words, and tears spilled down her face. "Father, please. *Please.*"

"Oh, Charis," Tal said softly as he knelt beside her. His voice shook. "I'm so sorry."

He reached out to gently close the king's eyes. A yawning darkness opened within her, and she clung to her father.

He wasn't dead. He couldn't be. It wasn't supposed to be like this. She was supposed to have more time. More dinners. More hugs. More moments when the person who'd always loved her best made her feel that she was the most precious thing in the world.

A tiny meow came from under the bed, and then Hildy crept out and onto Charis's lap.

"This isn't . . . he's not gone." She looked up at Tal and found tears in his eyes. "He can't be gone. I wasn't ready." Her voice broke.

"I'm so sorry." He gathered her close. "So sorry."

Something whispered behind them, the faint sound of steps skittering along the staircase closest to the king's chambers, and Tal snapped into action. Rounding on the few staff members they'd collected, he motioned for them to run for the door that led from the king's chambers to the garden.

"We should go with them, Charis," he said as he carefully pried her hands away from her father and pulled her to her feet. She clutched Hildy to her body. "You can't do anything more for him now."

He was right, and she couldn't bear it. Darkness spilled out of the corner of her heart and swallowed her grief, leaving a shell in its wake. She leaned against Tal, her feet refusing to walk away from Father on her own.

Tal wrapped his free arm around her and helped her toward the door, his sword held steady in his other hand.

They'd crossed the sitting room and were halfway to the garden door when the Rakuuna with braids and bloodstained lips exploded into the hall and raced for them, moving with impossible speed.

"Go." Tal hefted his sword and turned to meet the incoming threat. "Charis, *go!*"

And leave the boy she loved? She'd rather die.

"Get to the stables," she yelled to the staff. When Reuben ran to put himself between her and the Rakuuna, she screamed, "No! Get them to the stables."

"Then you go too," Reuben said, backing up until he stood at her other side, his sword dripping blood.

She tucked Hildy into the front of her jacket and hefted her sword.

The Rakuuna stopped a short distance away and opened her mouth. Charis, Tal, and Reuben braced for an attack, but instead, the creature spoke in a high, lilting voice that scraped down Charis's spine like a razor.

"We only want one of you."

Reuben stepped forward. "Take me."

The Rakuuna hissed. "We need the royalty."

"You aren't taking the princess," Tal said flatly.

There was a commotion behind them, and then Grim came rushing through the garden door, an ax in each hand. "Your Highness, get behind me," he yelled.

"Grim, go back!" Tal snapped. "Get the staff to the stables. Get Charis out of here."

"We don't want the girl," the Rakuuna said, her eyes on Tal.

Charis glared at the creature. Was this the one who'd killed Father? Who'd torn Charis's world to pieces? She would find Charis to be every inch the princess her mother had trained her to be. There would be no sign of weakness. No quarter given. A predator only respected another predator.

Lifting her chin, Charis said with icy rage, "You want to speak to royalty. I'm the princess of Calera. Cease this invasion, and we can discuss your terms."

The Rakuuna ignored her and crept closer to Tal. He shifted his body to keep his sword between the creature and Charis.

"Your Highness, move!" Grim yelled, brandishing his axes.

"No, Grim," Tal said. "Do as I say. Get Charis and the others to safety."

Charis froze, looking from Tal to Grim. The groomsman's entire focus was Tal. He hadn't looked at her once. "Tal?"

"Percival Talin Penbyrn," the Rakuuna purred. "Your father has something we want. You're going to make sure he gives it to us."

"Percival?" Charis whispered as everything she thought she knew slid sideways and re-formed into something monstrous. Something agonizing.

He'd known the seven rathmas. He'd understood how Alaric thought. He'd made sure to spend time with Grim each week, and she'd never bothered trying to eavesdrop on their conversations. And Vahn . . . no wonder he'd known so much about her. No wonder he'd laughed when she'd said she'd hate to have any detail overlooked.

His brother had been the spy at her side for *months*.

"Charis," Tal said quietly. "This is what I wanted to tell you."

"No." How could her heart still beat rapidly in her chest when he'd just carved it out and left it for dead?

She stumbled back a step. Her bones felt like glass, brittle and frail. Her lungs ached, her breath scraping against the sudden tightness in her throat like a sword.

"It's complicated, but—"

"It's actually very simple." Her voice was as hollow as the abyss that had opened within her. "You betrayed me. You lied. All of it was a lie."

"No." He whipped his head toward her. "I came here under a lie, but my time with you was the truth."

Her eyes stung, but she refused to cry. He didn't **deserve** to see that weakness. He didn't deserve to see the absolute devastation that existed where once he'd lit a torch inside her heart. "How can it be the truth when I know nothing about you?"

"You know everything that really matters." Tal's voice was desperate. "You know me better than anyone."

The Rakuuna smiled, revealing two sets of bloody fangs. "Ambassador Shyrn recognized the boy from his time in Montevallo. Sent us a bird weeks ago with the news. The boy comes with us until the father pays what we need."

But Vahn had already sent a palloren to the Rakuuna offering to pay them whatever they required to leave Caleran ships alone. Hadn't he? Or was he, like his younger brother, nothing but a liar?

"He's not going anywhere," Grim said.

The Rakuuna hissed as Grim rushed forward with his axes. Reuben hefted his sword and moved toward the creature.

"Stop!" Tal shouted. "I'll go."

"What?" Grim skidded to a halt, his expression crushed. "No, Tal. We defend you. We get you out of here."

Tal turned to the Rakuuna. "I will go peacefully, but you must stop killing the Caleran people. You must let the survivors live in peace."

Charis tightened her grip on her sword until the hilt bruised her palms. She was a stranger in her own skin. A hollowed-out version of herself left with nothing but the ruins of the lies she'd believed and the mocking echo of the trust she'd placed in him.

"You don't negotiate with us," the Rakuuna hissed.

Tal whipped his sword around until the point was against his own neck. Charis's battered heart gave a pang, and she silenced it.

"Then I die, and you have no bargaining chip."

The Rakuuna flexed her fingers and cocked her head to consider the prince with the sword aimed at his throat. She clicked her mouth several times, and other clicks sounded from the hall. Finally, she said, "We have an agreement. We cease fighting, but we remain in control of Calera until the father gives us what we need. You come with us now. We will keep you in our kingdom so there is no treachery on the father's part that can save you. He can have you when the price is paid."

Slowly, Tal lowered his sword. Grim cried out, but Tal turned to Charis, his eyes burning, his expression haunted. "I love you. That's the truth. Now go. You know what to do. You know how to figure this out. *Go.*"

The Rakuuna lunged for him, wrapped her too-long fingers around his arms, and dragged him from the room. His sword clattered to the floor, and Grim rushed to pick it up.

Reuben turned to Charis. "Your Highness, the traitor is right. We must go. The stables first. Then what?"

She blinked at him as the torch Tal had lit in her heart flickered and died. Her entire world lay in pieces at her feet. She had nothing left.

Reuben's voice was uncharacteristically gentle. "The stables and then what, Your Highness?"

No, that wasn't right. She had something left. Her people. Her duty. And a bloody game of life or death to play against the monsters who'd murdered her parents and destroyed her city.

"The . . . armory," she whispered. "And then the fishing dock." She looked at Grim and spat the words at him. "You, spy, you're coming with us. We need horses for every survivor. As many weapons as we can carry."

She couldn't burn the Rakuuna's ships now. Not when a peace treaty had been established. Her people would pay the price for that treachery. But she could use her smuggler's boat. Sail out of the harbor and make a new plan once the ruined pieces of her life stopped carving their way into her as though they meant to leave nothing of her when they were done.

She hesitated for an instant, her gaze on the hallway where Tal had disappeared from sight. Long enough to remember the boy with the crooked smile who'd kissed her in the moonlight and told her he loved her. To remember the love in Father's voice when he called her his sweet Charis and the subtle light of approval in Mother's eyes when Charis proved to be the most ruthless person in the room.

Then she let the darkness within her swallow those memories like it had swallowed the grief for Milla. Turning, she ran for the door, followed her staff into the night, and began racing toward the stables.

FORTY-FOUR

As dawn traced a thin thread of gold across the horizon the morning after the invasion, Charis ordered the ship out to the open sea. Holland, Nalani, Orayn, Finn, Dec, and several others from their original crew had made it to the docks and onto the boat before she left. She also had the few staff members she'd been able to rescue from the palace, a merchant, Lady Delaire, and a few others Holland had managed to get to safety. Dec, it turned out, was another Montevallian spy sent to Arborlay to protect Tal, just like Grim. Charis could barely stand to look at them.

Her parents were dead, her kingdom was enslaved, and her heart was broken. How was she supposed to move forward from this?

"Charis?" Nalani's voice was hesitant as she climbed the stairs to stand beside the ship's wheel. "What are we going to do?"

What was she going to do? She couldn't bring back her parents. She couldn't unbreak her heart. All that was left was to save her people, but how?

When she remained silent, Nalani moved closer and squeezed

Charis's arm gently. "One of the maids told me about Tal. I'm sorry. He fooled us all."

"Do not speak that liar's name in my presence."

Nalani recoiled slightly and cast a quick glance over her shoulder at Holland, who was mounting the stairs to join them.

"I'd kill him if he was standing here," Holland said. "But he's gone, and wishing him dead won't do us any good. We need leverage against the Rakuuna. Where are we going to get that?"

Charis stared at the endless expanse of the sea as the rosy flush of dawn spread across the sky, reflecting on the water's surface like glittering fire.

They needed leverage.

Something to use against the Rakuuna.

Something that would shift the balance of power back in Calera's favor.

An idea formed, and dread sank into her as she saw the game, the players, and the one move that might give her the ability to save her kingdom.

Holland and Nalani were arguing as Charis turned to face them and said, "I know what to do."

They fell silent—the ship's creaking timbers and the slap of the waves the only sound between them. Charis ran through the facts one last time, checking for weaknesses, for something she'd overlooked.

There was only one course left to her.

"We're going to ask Solvang for asylum and use their libraries to learn all we can about the Rakuuna and the location of Te'ash."

Nalani shivered. "Why would we want the location of Te'ash? Aren't there enough Rakuuna in Calera without having to go looking for more?"

Holland slapped a hand against the railing. "They took over our kingdom, we can take over theirs. See how they like it."

"We can't take over theirs. You saw them, Holland." Nalani's voice shook. "We don't know how to fight them."

"Then we learn." He glared over Nalani's shoulder as if he could still see Calera on the distant horizon.

"We aren't going to take over their kingdom." Charis was grateful her voice didn't reveal the dark hole that had opened within her at Tal's betrayal. Forcing herself to sound as cold and dispassionate as Mother on her best day, she said, "We're going to rescue Tal."

"So we can kill him?" Holland reached for his sword as though imagining Tal stood before him.

"So we can use him." Charis lifted her chin and silenced the memory of Tal's lips on hers. "We need leverage. Apparently so do the Rakuuna, because they took Tal so they could force Alaric to give them the jewels they need. If we take Tal—"

"Then we have their leverage, and it's our turn to force Alaric to do what we want." Nalani reached for Charis's hand, her fingers cold as she squeezed the princess's fingers. "Maybe Tal will be able to explain himself. Maybe—"

Charis's laugh was steeped in bitterness. "I don't want to hear anything he has to say. He could die a traitor's death, and it still wouldn't be what he deserves. We'll learn all we can about the Rakuuna so that we know how to kill them. Then we'll find Tal, rescue him, and return him to Alaric so the Rakuuna have no leverage over Montevallo. Finally, I'll honor the treaty I signed and marry Vahn Penbyrn so we can use Montevallo's army to drive the Rakuuna back into the sea where they belong."

Putting words to her plan should have hurt. The idea of seeing Tal again and then marrying his older brother so she could use his army should have sliced into her, but the chasm that had opened within her swallowed the pain and fed her rage instead.

Tal had known what he was doing.

If he'd simply been caught impersonating a guard on his father's orders, she'd have been furious, but she would have understood the political gamesmanship at play.

But he hadn't stopped there. He'd gained her trust, her friendship, and then her heart. He'd kissed her and told her he loved her, all while knowing he wasn't worthy of the trust she'd placed in him.

Charis gripped the damp railing as Orayn finished tacking a sail and moved toward the ship's wheel.

Mother had been right all along.

A princess didn't get to be loved. Everyone either wanted to use her power or take it from her. It was the one lesson of Mother's that Charis hadn't been able to learn until now. Now, when it was too late. When all her soft edges had been consumed by the fire of her rage and turned to ash.

"Orders, Captain?" Orayn asked.

"Set a course for Solvang," she said, her voice as icy and fathomless as the sea beneath them.

She was a princess without a kingdom. Without an army. Without allies. But before she was done, she would burn the heart out of every last one of her enemies, and they would spend their dying breaths watching her rise to the throne they'd tried so hard to take from her.

ACKNOWLEDGMENTS

First and foremost, thank you to Jesus for loving me and for pursuing me when I need it.

This book took two years to get right. I started it during an incredibly traumatic time for our family when my daughter's life hung in the balance for months. Even after she recovered, I couldn't shake the lingering emotional paralysis. It's very hard to create when you feel emotionally paralyzed. And then the year of ye olde apocalypse 2020 happened and creating felt harder still. It took me three complete rewrites (changing major things about the plot and POV choices each time) to finally tell the story the way I wanted it told. I am so grateful to my editor, Kristin Rens, for believing in me through all of it, and for patiently giving me the time I needed to recover emotionally and produce my best work. Kristin, you are a true treasure, and I'm so blessed to be working with you.

I'm also thankful to my family. To Clint, for being my biggest fan and best sounding board. To Tyler, Jordan, Hannah, Zach, Johanna, Isabella, Sydney, Luc, and Emma for being all-around amazing people. To my parents for being so proud of me. To my sister Heather for helping unsnarl plots, beta reading, and for being always in my corner. To my BIL Dave for kid wrangling, computer fixing, and plenty of laughter. Keep your trailerous hams to yourself. To my DIL Hannah for beta reading *Princess* and loving it the way I do. And to Sydney for late-night chats and because here it is in writing that you are loved, you are valued, and your books will be on the shelf beside mine one day.

Thank you to my publishing team (who are low-key superheroes): my agent, Holly Root; the team at Root Literary (especially Alyssa!); my assistant, Hannah Cherie; and the team at Balzer + Bray, all of whom are simply the best. Thank you also to my sensitivity readers for their time and valuable input.

I'm blessed to be surrounded with friends who step in to encourage, to read, to listen to my heart, and to pick up the slack when I need help. Jodi Meadows, Mary Weber, Shannon Messenger, Melinda Doolittle, Lila Tuck, K. B. Wagers, Lauren DeStefano, Connie Reid, and Dave Connis, I love you all and am so fortunate you're in my life.

I have to thank Taylor Swift as well, whose *Reputation* album played on repeat while I was writing and was the key to truly understanding Charis. It's rare for an entire album to so encapsulate a character for me, and I'm grateful for Taylor's exceptional songwriting talent.

And finally, a huge heartfelt thanks to YOU, my readers. I treasure getting to know you on Instagram and our Facebook group (you can join Fans of C. J. Redwine if you want in on the shenanigans!). Talking with you is one of the highlights of every day. <3

Special mention to the following readers who preordered *The Blood Spell* and entered the contest (grand prize winner Meredith Giordan had her name mentioned in this book): Jamie Anderson, Kristi Housman, Cori Lynn Avila, Ester Salgado, Tami Sachse, France,

Melanie L. Schwanke, Shannon Dunaway, Kate Lemire, Ashley Powell, Olivia Farr, Caitlin Haines, Mercedes Veronica, Zachary Flye, Cindy Godsey, Chelsea R. Allen, Hannah Curtis, April Roodbeen, Kelda Sue, Chasidee Puckett, Shery Werbelo, Jennzah Cresswell, Marrill, Ani'a Dutton, Suzy Michael, Susan Burdorf, Michele Dwiggins, Maha J., Jessica Johnson, Andrea Loy, Carina Olsen, Annette van Geloof, Erin McWhirt, Jessica @ a GREAT read, Carley Julian (Pate), Allison Gross, Dakota Storie, Janna Boger, Ashley Silker, Kari Valdez, Michelle Rae Taylor, Shawna Wood, Erin Arkin, Sarah Mayhew, Ashleigh Hourihan, Larissa Soccoli, Ari Trujillo, Caitlin Gossett, Claire Ramsey, Mari, Veronica Mitchell, Dana Black, Charla Dailey, Yara TRV, RJ Metcalf, Ruth E. Anderson, Cait Jacobs, Emily Gray, Jess Dalton, Meghan Littrell, Ann Grime, Kristi Housman, Jessica Neagle, Makenna Fournier, Stephanie Harris aka Bookslovereaders, Teralyn Mitchell, Jessica Borg, Brandi Goss, Carine Verbeke, Kelly-Ann Kay, Jennifer Christensen, Ann Whisenhunt, Aimee Jenkins, (Princess) Linda, Isabelle Casparie, Candy Smith, Renee Dawn Smith, Rebekah Fuhrman, Katie Facey, Brenda Waworga, Franciska Jurendic, Amanda Anderson, Lacie Lester, Brenna Tormanen, Opal Lovitt, Bailey K. Orr, Ashley Mullins, Shannon Dalby Peebles, Classie Powell, Jebraun Clifford, Candice Blake, Jen Pirroni, Emily Sonderegger, Natali Marti, Ania Kubik, S. D. Grimm, Kelli Kielusiak, Meghan, Sonja Schrauwen, Patricia Keagan, Alexis Liner, Kayla Grey, Andi Tubbs, Jess Chillcott, Alyshia Coil, Aaliyah, Sarah E. LeVasseur, Jenna Romaine, Amy Sarfinchan, Danielle Gerardi, Erica Hoyt, Heidi Wilson, Emily Buxton, Brieann Fountain, Leah Lutheran, Sydney Smith, Alyx Koval, Bonnie Lynn Wagner, Rita Verdial, Gabriela Navarro, Lindsey, Tammy Manning @CrimsonRoseReads, Darlene Griffin, Eleanor Whitaker, Carmen W. from Canada, Charity Rau, Janette Garcia, Alea Hon, Dreamer

J, Destiny Rose Esparza, Clara Johnson, Jessica Santo, Hannah M., Ali Kiki, Mikayla ZM, LoriAnn Weldon, Holly Bryan, Jenny Hjort-lund Nielsen, Elizabeth Glover, Jordan Fleming, Alayna L. Olivarez, Emma Doran, and Aisha Farah.